TAKEN BY THE LORD OF THE NOCTURNE COURT

Dark Companions #1

K.A. Merikan

Acerbi & Villani Ltd.

This is a work of fiction. Any resemblance of characters to actual persons, living, dead, or undead, events, places or names is purely coincidental.

No part of this book may be reproduced or transferred in any form or by any means, without the written permission of the publisher. Uploading and distribution of this book via the Internet or via any other means without a permission of the publisher is illegal and punishable by law.

Text copyright © 2024 K.A. Merikan

All Rights Reserved

http://kamerikan.com

Editing by

No Stone Unturned – Editing Services

Cover by Trif Book Design

https://trifbookdesign.com/

Chapter 19	137
Chapter 20	143
Chapter 21	149
Chapter 22	157
Chapter 23	163
Chapter 24	179
Chapter 25	191
Chapter 26	199
Chapter 27	207
Chapter 28	217
Chapter 29	229
Chapter 30	237
Chapter 31	247
Chapter 32	253
Chapter 33	265
Chapter 34	271
Chapter 35	277
Chapter 36	283
Chapter 37	293
Chapter 38	301
Chapter 39	313
Chapter 40	319
Chapter 41	325
Chapter 42	333
Chapter 43	343
Chapter 44	349

This is a work of fiction. Any resemblance of characters to actual persons, living, dead, or undead, events, places or names is purely coincidental.

No part of this book may be reproduced or transferred in any form or by any means, without the written permission of the publisher. Uploading and distribution of this book via the Internet or via any other means without a permission of the publisher is illegal and punishable by law.

Text copyright © 2024 K.A. Merikan

All Rights Reserved

http://kamerikan.com

Editing by

No Stone Unturned – Editing Services

Cover by Trif Book Design

https://trifbookdesign.com/

CONTENTS

Chapter 1	1
Chapter 2	7
Chapter 3	15
Chapter 4	21
Chapter 5	27
Chapter 6	33
Chapter 7	43
Chapter 8	47
Chapter 9	59
Chapter 10	65
Chapter 11	77
Chapter 12	89
Chapter 13	99
Chapter 14	103
Chapter 15	109
Chapter 16	115
Chapter 17	121
Chapter 18	129

Chapter 19	137
Chapter 20	143
Chapter 21	149
Chapter 22	157
Chapter 23	163
Chapter 24	179
Chapter 25	191
Chapter 26	199
Chapter 27	207
Chapter 28	217
Chapter 29	229
Chapter 30	237
Chapter 31	247
Chapter 32	253
Chapter 33	265
Chapter 34	271
Chapter 35	277
Chapter 36	283
Chapter 37	293
Chapter 38	301
Chapter 39	313
Chapter 40	319
Chapter 41	325
Chapter 42	333
Chapter 43	343
Chapter 44	349

Chapter 45	357
Chapter 46	367
Epilogue	375
About the author	391

CHAPTER 1

Luke

"Would you like fries with that?" I ask, trying to not sound bored, but the man behind the counter doesn't seem to notice my disinterest anyway.

"Do they come with your number?"

This guy. This fucking *guy*. I may have accidentally swiped right on him on Grindr some time ago, and now he just won't go away. He is handsome enough, if not in the age range I tend to go for, and wears a studded leather jacket that screams midlife crisis. The red sports car waiting for him in the parking lot completes a picture of someone who would rather hit on a guy half his age at Best Burgers Bonanza than deal with his issues in therapy.

"No," I say, giving him a level glare, because I'm at work and hate it when people forget that I can't just tell them to get lost.

He raises his hands. "Jesus! I was just kidding. I know you're goth and all that, but it wouldn't hurt you to smile."

I don't even blink. "My mother died yesterday. Lung cancer," I add, because the yellowish tint on his fingers suggests he's a smoker.

I love seeing his face fall and eyes widen as flustered panic colors his cheeks. He glances at the tip jar. *Yes, fucker. Make it a big one, so I can actually afford a new car.*

A car in which I can leave this town one day and never look back.

No more flipping burgers.

No more mediocre hookups with locals.

And no more stupid bosses.

"Luke? Can we have a chat?" My boss's voice is like fingernails screeching over a blackboard. "Kurt, will you please finish serving this gentleman?" Marty asks my co-worker, who appears dead inside as he shuffles over to swap with me at the register. For Kurt's sake, I hope the customer's type is sad goth boys, not perky jocks.

"Sorry for your loss." The customer chokes out as I walk off.

Best Burgers Bonanza, otherwise known as BBB, isn't the worst fast food joint in town, but its years show in the peeling leather chairs and the paint that has long faded from a lively green to a washed-out mint.

Which unfortunately also happens to be the shade of my uniform consisting of a barfalicious polo shirt and shapeless black pants. I'm also obligated to wear a baseball cap with the BBB logo and that thing always makes my scalp itch. At least Marty lets me wear my combat boots and doesn't make me take out my nose ring.

He speaks once we pass the kitchen and reach the corridor leading to the staff room. His gray hair bristles, in a stark contrast to the flushed face.

"What was that? I know for a fact that your mother's alive, because I talked to her just this morning, to ask if she has any idea why you're running late."

I cross my arms on my chest and glance through the tiny window in the back door. The night outside seems especially appealing when the alternative is another hour here. "I told you why I was late. My neighbor found a bat in her attic and it needed to be taken to the vet. It was an emergency. She's an older lady, and her car doesn't work—"

Marty raises his hands. "I don't want your life story, Luke. What I want is for you to be nicer to customers. And yes, that does involve smiling, whether it's part of the *Lord of Darkness* agenda or not. Get a grip."

I roll my eyes, but what can I say, really? I might hate my job, but that doesn't change the fact that I *need* it if I'm to ever move out of my mother's house. I resent that I even got hired in the first place because Marty is some old friend of hers who may or may not be trying to get into her pants. I'd rather not think about that.

There aren't many jobs available for a guy with a chip on his shoulder, a neck tattoo, and no high school diploma, not in this small town at least. I could pretend I'm nice, and kind, and good, and agreeable, but most people know me around here, so I might as well live up to their expectations.

I did get one unsolicited job offer from this weirdo who said he'd employ me as a clown for children's parties, if I came to Montreal with him, but I'm pretty sure he wanted to harvest my organs.

I did sell him five feet pics though. Beggars can't be choosers.

So here I am. Working at BBB, living with my witch of a mother, and pipe-dreaming about a move to a big city that doesn't involve becoming someone's live-in sex slave. But unless my failing Etsy business suddenly becomes a viral hit, I'm stuck in small-town Maine, and considering that I sell a random assortment of skull-shaped bath bombs, bookmarks with my paintings of bats, and goth pet portraits, I don't see much commercial success in my future.

Guess I'm just a failure, a loser, and no amount of black eyeshadow can hide that.

"Sorry," I mumble, swallowed by my own darkness.

"Just... do better." Marty shakes his head before walking away, as defeated by this conversation as I am.

I return to the front of the restaurant with a heavy weight on my shoulders, but fortunately there are no customers, which frees me from the necessity of grinning like an idiot. It's not my fault I suffer from resting bitch face.

Kurt's busy texting, most likely with his new girlfriend, so I grab a mop and get to work. It's time for penance. At least the clock is ticking, which means I'm closer and closer to leaving this hell hole.

"Do you want to go on a double date with me and Daria?" Kurt asks with a smile. I don't know how, but on him, even the ugly uniform looks attractive. Maybe it's because his shoulders are broader than mine? Though I'm pretty sure his golden retriever smile and shiny blue eyes help elevate the outfit too. I would hook up with him if he wasn't so painfully heterosexual.

I lean against the mop. "How would that be a double date?"

"You and Larry?"

"Larry..." I drift off, confused until the disastrous date from a week ago pops into my head. Instead of fucking me, like a normal person, Larry spent three hours talking about himself and asked me a total of two questions. Yes, I did count. "Oh, Larry! God no, I've only been on one date with him, and that was definitely enough for me." It wasn't even supposed to be a date, but he roped me in by offering food and then I felt too awkward to refuse him conversation.

Kurt's smile turns into a pout. With a face like his though, it's no wonder he's never without a girlfriend despite barely making his rent every month and needing rides to work. "I'm so sorry, dude."

I raise my eyebrows. "Nothing to be sorry about, I'll be happy to never see him again. I don't know why I bother dating. I'm not looking to get married. I just want to have a good time every now and then. It's not like I'll be finding my Prince Charming in this dump anyway."

"Now that's just depressing, man. You gotta give people a chance, get to know them." Kurt says but doesn't seem too convinced himself as his blue eyes search mine for confirmation. At least he's aware he doesn't know the first thing about gay dating. "This one time, I met a girl who looked all preppy and shit, but then it turned out she did heroin every weekend."

I don't know what the conclusion is supposed to be, so I just stare at him. "That has literally no application to my situation."

Kurt shrugs. "Just sayin'. Don't judge a book by its cover."

Like he's ever read a book in his life.

I get on with the mopping, because I need to do something with the pent-up energy after such an agitating conversation. He doesn't get that not everyone is a serial monogamist. I don't want a relationship. I don't want to engage in any mushy feelings, buy Valentine's cards, or plan a future with some other guy while we both look at the stars. A dirty quickie in the back of a car has always been good enough for me.

"My relationship status isn't all that interesting and this county isn't exactly a bustling metropolis filled with eligible gay bachelors."

Kurt groans, leaning against the counter. "But I'm invested in my gay best friend!" We're work colleagues at best, but whatever. "You could be one half of the kind of adorable gay couple who get a dog together and make him little outfits. You could even have him be the ringbearer at your wedding. I could be your best man. I bet you'd make bank as an Instagram couple."

He doesn't specify how that would come about. I'm pretty sure he hasn't given much thought to the future he imagines for me, but I do kinda like Kurt, so I don't want to grill him about it. "I'm twenty-one. I'm not getting gay married just so you can say you were a best man at a gay wedding."

"That's homophobic, Luke. You get 'married', not *gay* married'."

I'm about to school him that *I'm* gay and therefore I can call it whatever I want, but I end up letting it go. It's too cute that he's such a big dopey ally.

Straight guys have it so easy. There's an endless supply of amazing women, and all they have to do is be a half-decent human being to attract one.

Then again... maybe that's my problem with guys? Maybe *I'm* not a half-decent human being. A quarter at best. But I don't want to date anyway so it doesn't matter. You don't have to be nice to get laid.

I mop the ugly tiles with more vigor as I ponder whether *I'm* the problem.

Kurt eyes me suspiciously. "Is it 'cause you want your guy to be goth, rocker, or whatever? You have to look beyond the superficial."

Do I? Do I 'have to'? I don't have to do shit. I need to pay my mother rent and afford my own groceries. Beyond that, I'm not *obligated* to anything, especially not dating. I was done being compliant when they kicked me out of boarding school in spectacular fashion.

I keep my thoughts to myself when Marty passes across the room, leaving dark footprints on the floor I've just cleaned.

"I'll be back in an hour or so. Don't burn the place down!" he says in a cheerful voice.

I give him the smile he wanted to see so badly, but as soon as he's out, I take off my cap to scratch my head. My hair used to be all green, but it's grown out a lot since the last time I had spare cash to dye it, so now it's dark brown on top, fading into green at the ends. Shorter at the front and with lots of layers, it is a shaggy mess that barely reaches my shoulders.

I hoped the earlier topic was forgotten, but the moment Marty leaves, Kurt is right back at it. "You should let me set you up. I know this one guy. He's a drummer in a band, and you know what they say about drummers..." Kurt wiggles his eyebrows.

"What do they say...?" I pretend not to know, just to mess with him.

He groans in exasperation. "That they're good with rhythm, so— Never mind! Want a blind date or not? I'll make sure he wears black."

My heartbeat picks up in panic. "What? No!"

Kurt stops typing on his phone and sighs. "You're hopeless. The Prince of Darkness himself could walk through the door right now and you'd give him the cold shoulder 'cause his horns are uneven."

Both of us turn our heads when the bell at the door rings and... speaking of the devil.

I can't help myself. I stare.

The man who steps into the restaurant drags the darkness in with him. He's well over six feet tall, clad from head to toe in black leather, with buckled boots reaching to his knees, and long hair falling down his chest in dark gray waves worthy of a hair conditioner ad. The width of his shoulders is amplified by pauldrons of black-tinted metal, and he's wearing a vest of hard leather adorned with a dark green crest with some kind of mer-horse in a seashell. I'd call it a breastplate if that wasn't ridiculous.

His face has androgynous qualities. A sharp jawline, but eyes with long dark lashes. Straight, thick eyebrows, but lips that could have been carved by Lucifer himself. His pallor borders on unnatural, but whether he's wearing powder and foundation or not, I swear there's a hint of kohl under his eyes.

Most strangely though, pointy ears peek from under his glorious hair. Hell, I didn't know my hometown attracted LARPers of this caliber. Maybe I should give role-playing a shot after all.

My heart skips a beat when his gray eyes pin me in place, and then it stops when he heads toward me. I expected to hear the squeak of leather or the jingling of buckles, but he is as silent as a cat.

I move the handle of the mop between us, but it's not enough to stop him from grabbing my shoulders. His eyes lock with mine, and those *have* to be contact lenses because the gray seems to shift from pale to dark, as if there's literal smoke in his irises.

His lips spread into a smile that looks positively predatory.

"Luke Moor. Finally. I am here to claim my Dark Companion."

CHAPTER 2

LUKE

I let out a nervous laugh that borders on hysterical. "...What?"

He cocks his head at me, and his hair moves over his shoulder like waves of dark gray silk. "Luke Moor. I have no doubt it is you, as I have pulled a thread from my shadow and tied it to yours. Surely, you remember?"

His eyes are like two whirls of smoke, and I meet them with a mixture of disbelief and nausea. I haven't told anyone about the terrifying dream from years ago, but this *must be* a prank.

Kurt holds back a snort. "Exactly, *Luke Moor*. He tied a thread to your shadow. Obviously, you *have* to date him now."

"Marry," the stranger corrects in a low voice that's like a purr going down my spine.

I try to compose myself and take a deep breath. I'm not about to lose my head and get pulled into some weird scheme just because a guy has nice hair, and his face looks as if he made a deal with the devil for his beauty. Like one weirdo asshole customer a day isn't enough...

Backing away and out of his grasp is step one. Then, I shove away the mop so that I can put the counter between me and this handsome, but also creeptastic, stranger.

I squint at him in the hope that my resting bitch face and demonic glare, as my mother likes to call it, chase him off. "I have no idea who you are."

He... bows. Actually, freaking *bows*. Hand on chest, wide gesture of the arm and everything. His long hair spills to the mopped floor. "I am Crown Prince Kyranis Nightweed. The future Lord of the Nocturne Court, Ruler of the Shadowild, Protector of the Nightmare Realm, and Knight of Grief Ocean, which you might know as the Sea of Sorrows."

Nope. I definitely don't know of a Sea of Sorrows.

I'm so stunned I'm not sure what to say, so I glance at Kurt, and that's it. When our eyes meet, we both burst out laughing. I don't know who's set me up, but I need a full-bellied laugh like this today. I'm wiping tears out of my eyes while the stranger stands there, lips in a tight line.

I'm still the slightest bit unsettled by the whole 'tied-thread-to-shadow' bit, because that same exact thing happened in my nightmare years ago, but it could be some weird coincidence.

"Listen, man, sorry, I'm not laughing *at* you. This whole thing," I point from his fine boots to his pointy ears, "is really top-notch. How about some fries and a shake on the house?"

Kurt's face is so red from all the laughing that his cheeks glisten like polished apples. "You really made our night."

Prince Kyranis frowns, and I have to admit it makes him somehow even more handsome. He's like a storm cloud so magnificent you look at it unafraid of the lightning about to strike. "I *am* taking you away tonight," he says sternly.

I roll my eyes when I turn to get the dude some fries. "Well, I don't finish work until nine, so I can't marry you until then."

He nods. "That is acceptable. I will wait for you to wrap up your affairs."

Or, you could go home, I think to myself.

When I hand him the tray with fries and a complimentary vanilla shake, his finger slides over mine and I notice he's wearing one of those metal claw rings. Way to commit to the role. A little cheesy, but I'm partial to a bit of tacky gothic indulgence. I can't usually afford the stuff I like, but I have some studded chokers and a bat-shaped belt buckle in my accessories drawer.

The handsome stranger gives me a once-over and walks off to a corner booth offering the perfect view of the counter. And me.

Creepy much?

But he's both odd and unnaturally attractive, so I can't help but look back at him every now and then as I pretend to clean.

He picks up one fry out of the packet with his long fingers, and glares at it as if he expected to find poison. Satisfied with whatever assessment he's made, he bites off half of the fry.

I hold back a smile when his perfect eyebrows rise.

"This is just the best," Kurt whispers as he sneaks a candid photo of Kyranis grabbing more fries.

"Do you think this show is for our benefit?" I ask while we watch the stranger try the milkshake next. I won't lie, it is pretty entertaining.

Kurt nods. "Probably, but I'm enjoying myself. You should give him a shot for all this effort. And you have to admit he's hot. In *your* kind of way."

I'd ask 'what is that supposed to mean?' if I didn't know the answer already.

As goofy as Kyranis looks while pretending he's not sure how to use a straw, he's tall, graceful but wide-shouldered. He has long dark hair, and the aura of a Byronic hero. He *is* my type on paper. And the fact that I've not seen him around town makes him mysterious.

Kurt's words finally hit me.

"What? Do you think he was actually asking me out?"

He rolls his eyes. "Well, *duh*. That whole talk about marriage, the 'dark companion' thing, and now he's waiting for you to finish work."

I swallow, and frost grows over my heart. It's all fun and games to thirst from afar, but would I actually date this guy? I'm not sure how I feel about that. The perfect goth prince is too real all of a sudden. He's not a hot dude on Instagram. He's *here*.

Would I fuck him? Sure. But he seems to want more, and it's all too much too fast.

And it's not just that I'm used to hookups and therefore getting cold feet about dating. I can't get it out of my head that he mentioned tying a thread to my shadow. It was so specific.

I'd pretty much erased that nightmare from memory, since I assumed it to be a figment of my overactive imagination. A fantasy my brain conjured at the worst moment of my life, when darkness almost swallowed me whole.

When I woke up from the dream, my wrists bore no trace of deep wounds, which convinced me that I must have hallucinated hurting myself after swallowing too many painkillers. But in the deep sleep I fell into, I drowned in a thick darkness, and its salty current pushed me toward nothingness. Eventually, I found the strength to reach above the violent waves, and someone grabbed my arm.

At that moment I felt I weighed as much as a thousand corpses, but the person who caught me didn't let go.

My memory of what happened next is fuzzy. After all, I was only fourteen at the time. But as I gasped for air on the bank of the imaginary river, a shadowy creature, who could have been the devil himself, asked if I wanted to live.

Faced with death's cold breath, hands grasping at air and blurry faces with purple mouths desperately trying to stay above the waves, I knew I didn't want to join them again. Crying my little heart out as my wrists continued to bleed, I told the cloaked demon I wanted to go back home.

The exact words we exchanged are a blur, but I agreed to trade my shadow for another shot at life. In the bright light of a giant full moon, both our shadows lay on the ground like two human-shaped blankets.

The living nightmare plucked a single strand of long hair from his head, threaded it through a needle, and then used it to attach his shadow to mine. All very surreal and therefore appropriate, since it *was* a dream. The pain in my wrists was strangely elusive when he poured something warm onto the wounds, but when I woke up, I was back in my room at the boarding school.

Which makes sense.

I had a nervous breakdown, I took too many painkillers, I thought I cut my wrists, but I guess I ended up not doing that, and then had the strangest, drug-fueled nightmare.

So why is this weirdo talking about tying one shadow to another, as if he knows my dreams?

He looks so out of place in the bright lights of Best Burgers Bonanza. The leather outfit he's wearing is so black it seems to suck the colors out of the seat, so much so that the mint upholstery appears to be a faded gray with only a hint of green. I can't help but think it resembles the skin of a dead body drained of blood. Especially with the old leather peeling and cracking.

It has to be some trick of the light, because what other explanation is there? I know from experience in painting that colors can seem different relative to what they are put next to.

When Kyranis spots me gawking at him, he raises his milkshake as if he's toasting our future marriage. "This is very tasty!" Fortunately, there are no other customers who could be bothered by this weird-ass display. "The food is salty, the drink sweet. I can see the appeal. We could recreate it for our wedding feast."

"Glad you like it!" I give him my customer service smile, but something about this whole situation gives me goosebumps and I can't ignore my gut feeling any longer. This guy knows my name, he mentioned the shadows, and is now casually waiting, as if I agreed to go out with him after my shift.

Kurt pulls me aside, behind the fridge with soda bottles. "Are you okay? You seem off. If you're unsure about this guy, I could lock the restaurant and walk you to the car. Or we could wait for Marty. Though I'm not getting any bad vibes from Mr. Prince Charming over there. Maybe he's just awkward."

I shake my head. "No, it's okay. I'm just not in the mood for entertaining him. I'll be fine. I'll leave through the back door." While I appreciate Kurt's concern, I'll be damned if I end up looking like a damsel in distress because of an overdressed cosplayer.

My need for independence borders on pathological, but that's what you get with an overbearing mother and years at a strict boarding school.

"Are you sure? He's a big guy, and you're... you know. You."

I frown at Kurt. "Thanks for that." I may be on the skinny side, but I know how to run. I've learned the hard way how important that can be.

Kurt drags his hands down his face. "You know what I mean. There's nothing wrong with asking for help if you're uncomfortable."

He's such a sweetheart. Only that there's *everything* wrong with that. I have to deal with this kind of shit myself, because there is no actual Prince Charming coming to save me. My life has been a string of failures, and it seems that Lord Creeper slurping a milkshake and threatening me with a wedding is the best date I can get.

"Nah, my car isn't far." I plaster on a fake smile and lower my voice. "But I'll go now, if you don't mind, since he's expecting to wait a little longer."

Kurt's brows pull into a perfectly angelic expression of concern. "Sure," he whispers back. "I'll let Marty know what happened if he comes back earlier than expected."

I shake my head. "No need to bother him with this. He'd tell my mother, and then I'd have to listen to a litany of reasons why I should clean up my act and date a 'nice girl'."

I steal one more glance at the Prince of Darkness in the corner booth and get my stuff from the locker. Kyranis isn't yet done with his meal, so I'm guessing this is a good time to dip out.

I wish I was more chill about this. Maybe I should have taken those kickboxing classes when the local gym offered a free trial. Then again, how much would I have learned in a month? Probably only how easy it is to kick my ass.

After a moment of hesitation, I grab a small knife from the kitchen, hoping the cook won't notice it's gone, and head for the back door. I need to be able to fend for myself.

Or maybe I'm freaking out over nothing. Could it not be a coincidence that a hot goth guy is trying to woo me by mentioning a romantic bond of shadows? Isn't that kind of thing a popular fixture in the dark fantasy genre?

You're on your own. No one cares. Your mother hates you, that's why she left you here. You're a burden to everyone.

I have to take a deep breath to chase away the shitty words of a man who called himself a counselor but was just a glorified bully.

I step out into the cool night air and scan my surroundings to work out the shortest route to my car. I parked it at the very far end of the lot, because I read online that it's a healthy habit. Well, I won't be too *healthy* if I get jumped, stabbed, robbed, or abducted so that point is moot.

The moon is hidden behind clouds tonight, so the only light is a yellow lamp above the back door and a streetlight that flickers ominously, as if someone wants to amplify my terror by pulling out all the horror tricks.

It's working. My heart speeds up for no reason, my palms are getting damp, but I face my fear and start walking.

When I move away from the lamp above the door, my shadow stretches, spilling over the asphalt. I make a point of staring at it, because I know I'm being unreasonable. It's just a shadow, and its size and color depends on the light source behind me, not on nightmarish deals with monsters.

It's vaguely formed into my shape, and when I move my arm, it moves with me.

Nothing out of the ordinary.

I roll my eyes at myself, wishing I was home already even though I'll likely start my evening by arguing with my mother about whatever she feels like blaming me for tonight.

A low horse whinny pulls me out of my thoughts, and I stop in my tracks, seeking the source of the sound in the dark parking lot.

For a moment, I'm sure I'm seeing things, but nope, it's there.

A motherfucking *carriage.*

It has a round shape reminiscent of Cinderella's vehicle of choice and is just as elaborately decorated, with wooden carvings covering every surface. But the comparison only works if Cinderella was going to a royal funeral not a ball. The carriage is black as if dipped in tar, so the thick red curtains are the only splashes of color. At the front stand four massive horses, black as ink blots, with massive plumes that quiver when the animals shake their heads.

I have no doubt this is the preferred mode of transportation for the *Lord of Shadows* munching on fries inside the restaurant.

Who he is and why he chose Best Burgers Bonanza as his new haunt will remain a mystery, because I'm sure as fuck not sticking around to find out.

A coachman, who had so far melted into the carriage with his own black attire, glances at me from afar. I won't be taking my time assessing him or trying to figure out whether he has no eyes or if that's just a trick of the light.

My car isn't all that far away anymore, and very soon, I will be home, doom-scrolling on my phone as I drink hibiscus tea until I forget all about this fuckery.

I walk faster with every step, painfully aware the stomping of my boots is loud in the empty expanse of the parking lot. Or I'm just overly sensitive to sounds because I'm terrified that I'm being tracked by a serial killer with a penchant for dramatic outfits.

I squeeze the knife, wondering if I would be able to protect myself with it if push comes to shove. And if Kyranis follows me or harasses me, should I attack before asking questions? Would that even be considered self-defense?

The squeak of the restaurant's door makes my blood cold, and I speed up, desperate to reach my vehicle before Kyranis can catch up to me.

"Luke! We made a deal!"

There it is. He won't give it a rest. His voice has lost its charm and has become demanding.

What deal is he talking about?

I don't know and I don't care.

I break into a run, not bothering to check how far away he is, because each step might make a difference. I'll be reporting this fucker as soon as I'm home. For now, I focus on reaching my car.

I'm panting out of fear, but a few steps later, my boots sink into mud—What mud? I'm on asphalt.

My eyes go wide, and I scream out when I notice that my shadow looks as if it's boiling. Bubbles of darkness form within its borders, and I can no longer pull my foot up. Oh, how I regret that my boots are tied above my ankle, and I can't just slip out of them.

I try anyway. Terrified, I scoot down to untie the laces, but the shadow is rising around me. Whenever the bubbles burst, they release little clouds of smoke, and I can only hold my breath for so long.

The scent overwhelms me with its dark sweetness. If there are flowers that only bloom at night, this must be how they smell—addictive and so rich it's making my eyelids heavy.

I lose balance, and my knees drop onto the asphalt, which somehow feels velvet-soft.

The lazy clop of hooves behind me is the last thing I hear before falling face first into my own shadow.

CHAPTER 3

Luke

When I wake up, the rattle of carriage wheels resonates in my brain. Even before opening my eyes I'm painfully aware that what I experienced in the parking lot wasn't a dream. But I'm still not sure what my new reality is as I look up to meet the eyes of the man who introduced himself as Prince but doesn't act like one.

They're a dark gray in the sparse light of the carriage. The red curtains are drawn, locking us in this casket, and the only illumination comes from an old-timey lamp. Or should I call it a candle, since that's what it seems to be. Locked behind glass, the green flame is both unnerving because of its strangeness, and soothing because it means I can see my surroundings.

Kyranis is wearing a dark cloak with a fur trim and watches me as if I'm a bug he needs to keep under glass, not his dark-companion-to-be.

"You know lots of people will be looking for me, right?" I ask even though deep in my gut I know this is no normal abduction. He hasn't bothered to tie my hands, as if he knows I'm not getting away so easily. "And there are several cameras in the restaurant and outside it, so costume or not, you *will* be tracked down. If you turn around now and let me go, I'll tell the cops it was all an elaborate prank on your part and we can go our separate ways."

Sadly, both the cameras and the people looking for me are a lie. I'll be lucky if my mother starts worrying in three days.

Kyranis shakes his head, and a strand of that silky-looking hair slips out from under the hood. "I don't think you understand your position. I was actually excited to come whisk you away tonight, but you had to spoil it by lying to me and attempting to escape. We're not off to a good start to our engagement, Luke."

Engagement.

I can't help it. I roll my eyes. "No shit. I don't even see a ring on my fing—" I lift my hand to make my point, only to get flustered because my ring finger is adorned with an exquisite piece of jewelry.

Made of some kind of black metal, it sparkles in the green light with several tiny gems on its band. They could as well be diamonds. At the heart of the ring rests a large blue stone that seems to shimmer with my every move.

"It belonged to my mother," Kyranis says in that smooth voice that is so infuriatingly beautiful. "The pattern on the band represents seaweed, and the jewel is a blue tear stone, a crystal found only at the bottom of the Sea of Sorrows."

I'm struggling to take it all in. I'd throw the ring in his face if it wasn't for the fact that I don't know where we are, and a piece of jewelry can always make for a handy asset during my escape.

Because I *will* be escaping.

"Is this a suggestion that our marriage will be a sea of sorrows?" I deadpan, glaring at him.

Kyranis frowns. "It doesn't have to be, but test my patience, and it just might."

I swallow the cold lump in my throat. My big mouth often gets me in trouble, but I don't want to prod this guy too much until I know more about my situation. He seems unhinged, but what happened in the parking lot with my shadow is still vivid in my mind. It wasn't a dream. I'm dealing with something beyond my understanding.

I'm taking the lack of shackles on my wrists as a suggestion that he's not afraid of anything I might do. Which either means he's underestimating me, or he's so confident in his own prowess he thinks he can subdue me with ease.

I'm about to ask more about this 'marriage' and what it means, why me, and a million other questions that could help me find my feet, but then we stop.

There's a *thud*, and after a short knock on the door, the coachman opens it.

To my relief, he does have eyes, they're just a strange milky blue with barely visible irises. He's wearing a tricorn hat, but his long black hair is soaking wet to the point of dripping onto his simple leather coat, and... is that seaweed tangled into it? I have to admit he's handsome even though he doesn't seem to have eyelashes. But where Prince Kyranis is the picture of deadly elegance, about to either stab someone or sniff a glass of wine, the coachman looks as if a witch dragged his pale body out of the ocean, then charmed beauty into him by force. There's just something... sinister about him.

"We're at the tollhouse, Your Highness."

Kyranis rises as much as the carriage allows his tall form and, to my shock, reaches out to pet my chin. "I will be right back, my sweet," he says and walks out with a swish of his cloak.

The coachman glances at me as if he can see through me. Like I don't deserve to be here. I didn't ask to be abducted, thank you very much. But I still feel a bit underdressed in my Best Burgers Bonanza uniform.

When he shuts the door on our staring contest, I give into childishness and stick my tongue out.

That's where my silliness stops though. I need to get out of here while I have the chance. My hand trembles when I reach for the handle of the door on the opposite side to the one through which Kyranis left, but it opens without issue. I leave as quietly as I can, my heart already rattling. I'm no super spy. I'm not used to any of this.

I swallow at the gust of cold wind and the thick scent of forest undergrowth.

The tollhouse is on the other side of the carriage. I can just about see its chimney, flanked by a moon that is a sliver away from being full. I stumble, shocked by how giant its glowing face is. I don't think I've ever seen it this large, this close to earth, or this bright. Even though it's the middle of the night, it bathes the forest in cool moonlight.

Looks like I have an ally after all, because otherwise I would have only my phone to guide—

I rush between the trees, already planning to alert as many people as possible to my situation. If I call the cops, will they be able to track me based on the GPS in my phone?

My heart sinks when I spot the exclamation mark signaling no connection. Not a single bar available. I send a message about the abduction and how it's not a joke, to several people, unsure who will get it first, or when it might reach the recipients.

For now, my fate is in my own hands.

The deeper I go into the trees, the damper the ground. I move low, to avoid being spotted, but my boots sink into moss so wet dirty water pools where I step. To make matters worse, there isn't a hint of a path as I try to find my way through thorn-riddled bushes.

I bite back a yelp when a particularly sharp one manages to rip not just my pants but the skin on my legs as well. What kind of razor thorn fuckery is this?

I push on in frustration. I will not be stopped by some *bushes*.

I can barely see the carriage from here, so I've made good progress, but I have to admit to myself that I don't know what to do once I'm out of Kyranis's clutches. I can probably survive a night out here—

The howl of a wolf leaves me stiff as a rock. It's so easy to forget how mortal you are when you live in a town, have enough food to survive, and a roof over your head. The threat of bodily harm hasn't happened all that often to me since I left school, but as I push deeper into the thorny bushes, I have to face the reality.

I'm frightened. I want to cry. I'm getting cold. I don't know where I am.

I hurt my legs in several places when trying to free myself from the bloodthirsty branches, but all it's done is get me more tangled. Wherever this strange place is, it doesn't seem... *natural*.

Just as I think that, a buzz of wings makes me yelp. I'm unable to hold it in this time and hope my abductor doesn't hear me.

I turn around to find the source of the noise, because it's always better to know what you're up against, but I'm not ready to face the beastie once its four beady eyes meet mine.

Its furry body is about the size of a kitten's, but not nearly as cute, since it's a giant-ass *moth*. The tree branch it's sitting on bends under its weight. Every now and then, it has to flap its wings so it doesn't fall off. This creature would be the stuff of nightmares in Australia, let alone in *Maine*.

The moth blinks as I get used to its presence all too close to my shoulder. That's even weirder, because moths don't have eyelids. Colors shimmer in its dark fur and wings as if it's been dipped in an oil spill. For just a moment, I forget the perilous predicament I'm in, and the rips in my pants, entranced by the creepy beauty of this... thing.

"What *are* you?" I whisper.

And then it flies at my face.

The hooks it has instead of feet are aimed my way, long red tongue rolls out, and I can't deny reality anymore. That thing's got a mouth, and needles for teeth.

I scream out and fall back to avoid it sinking its talons into my cheeks. It makes a nasty screech when I manage to slap it away, but thorns dig into my back before I can get away. I shift around, but no matter which way I turn, the branches of the bushes I've just passed through seem to tighten their grip on me as if they're snakes, not plants.

My heart stops for a split second, and I freeze altogether, to make sure I'm not imagining things, but no. The thorn covered vines *are* shifting. They trail over my skin, leaving deep scratches and pulling me deeper into their tangle.

"Help!" I cry out, because pride be damned at this point, and my abductor *is* the lesser evil. "Kyranis, please! I'm here!"

CHAPTER 4

Luke

"Luke!" Kyranis yells from afar.

I call him again, humiliated by the need for his help. I'm supposed to be running away from him, not begging him to save me. But faced with the reality of thorns biting into me ever harder, I choose the deal with the devil. Just like all those years ago when the dark river pulled me along its current, tangled with other dying bodies.

This is the first time I see him with a sword, and he no longer seems like a silly LARPer with fake ears. The weapon isn't *just* black. It's darkness in the form of metal, and when it swishes through the air, it leaves behind swirls of smoke that fall to the ground ever so slowly.

I see the prince in him when he approaches in fast strides, cutting through the bushes as if the sword and him are one. When his cloak catches on thorns, he leaves it behind, focused on one task only.

Saving me.

Call me a hypocrite, but right now my heart beats faster at the sight of him. I won't forget that he's why I'm in this predicament in the first place, but that's something for future me to ponder. The present me desperately reaches out to him with both hands.

"Please! They're cutting into me!" I feel so pathetic for having to say this, but when the thorny vines roll against my throat, tears spill from my eyes. I should be able to deal with everything myself, but I am utterly inadequate.

To make matters worse, I hear buzzing above me. Like that of the moth creature from before, but multiplied. Did that fuzzy fucker come back with reinforcements? Brought his whole family to gawk at the stupid human about to die due to his lack of foresight?

When one of the moths flies to a lower branch, staring at me with its beady black eyes, I writhe in panic. The bush is holding my arms, and if this thing tries to sit on my face like the last one, I won't be able to stop it.

"Stop moving! They're attracted to blood!" Kyranis yells, and I'm relieved that he's only a few feet away now.

When another moth flies by, the meaning behind his words sinks in. The scratches and punctures all over my skin might be shallow, but I'm *covered* in smears of blood.

"They will become voracious when they taste it," Kyranis says as my heart sinks.

He's basically telling me that those giant bugs will feed until I'm Swiss cheese. My morbid imagination suggests they'd then lay eggs in the holes they make. I get nauseated at the very thought, so I focus on the sound of Kyranis's sword ripping through the vines, and I can almost hear them whisper in protest.

"I'm almost there, hold on," Kyranis says when our eyes meet.

I'm stunned into silence by this reassurance.

He's just a few steps away, and while I hate him for taking me by force, it's good to have someone in my corner for once. Someone's willing to risk their own safety. For me.

I can yell at him later.

It calms me to see how proficiently he moves through the thickening bushes. The massive moon glows behind him, its light bouncing off the black leather he's wearing, and while he's lean, every time he brings the sword down, I see pure strength.

I no longer find his introduction as the Protector of the Nightmare Realm amusing.

Knowing he's coming for me, I manage to stay still, which does stop the vines from tightening. All I need to do is wait. I'll think about licking my wounds when I'm out of here and out of the range of flesh-eating moth monsters.

I look up at the toothed insect, imagining it falling from Kyranis's sword, but the moth rolls out its long tongue my way, as if it can hear my thoughts. It vibrates above my face, and I shiver in disgust as a thick drop of moth spittle lands on my cheek. I groan. At least it takes my mind off the pain of tiny cuts all over my body.

The little beast rises off the branch with a buzz that sends a shiver down my spine, and I freeze in dread as it's joined by its brethren. Six of them descend on me with no further warning, crowding on my shoulders and tangling in my hair.

I cry out again, no longer ashamed of my pathetic whining, because this is a nightmare. "Please hurry! Please!" I yell when one of the monsters licks a cut on my arm. Its saliva stings like a drop of sizzling oil on the skin. A pain I know intimately after making endless batches of French fries.

"Fuck! No!" Kyranis cuts down several more vines with more vigor, but then stops.

I catch his gaze, confused and terrified. Has he... given up?

His eyes meet mine and he takes the dark blade to his own palm. It cuts through skin with ease, and Kyranis slides his injured palm over the crest on his torso, leaving a red stain.

When the moths all raise their antennae to attention, I realize that he's trying to lure them away from me.

One after another, the ugly things shoot into the air and head his way like a flying army. He grips the sword with his bleeding hand, and as soon as the first of the swarm is within range, he cuts right through it. The two halves of its furry body drop to the ground with a squelch, but that's only the beginning.

Kyranis is a whirlwind even if his movements no longer seem effortless. He's panting as the little monsters land, attaching to him with their talons, but that doesn't mean the critters have any chance to win this fight.

When he manages to shove one of the moths off his vest, it's at the cost of it slashing through his leather armor, and only then does it strike me how sharp their claws are. Had Kyranis not lured the moths into this deadly dance, they would have scratched my flesh raw.

A strangled yelp escapes his lips when one of the critters crawls up his pale stomach and into the opening between two flopping pieces of hard leather. His face a picture of fury as he twirls to take down four of the monsters with one swing of his sword, and two with another. Only then, once they're all dead, does he reach beneath his ripped vest.

Kyranis grabs the creature, and I hear the crackle of tiny bones, followed by a hiss. Blood shines at the front of the damn pest's body as he pulls it out from under his clothes, only to twist its neck and throw it to the ground.

"Are you all right?" he asks even though he's covered with way more blood than me.

"Y-yes. I'm trying not to move," I whimper, failing at sounding any braver than I am. But can you blame me? I'm just a fast food worker with some painting skills and a love of bats. I'm not prepared to fight monstrous moths in a dark forest that is actively trying to rip me apart with thorny vines.

No longer worried about the moths, Kyranis makes his way toward me, mercilessly cutting through the bush and ignoring the branches trying to restrain him as if they had a mind of their own.

This is really happening. The ache in my flesh is too visceral for any of this to be a dream.

Kyranis doesn't seem annoyed with me yet, too busy slicing through the vines around my arms to free me. His porcelain pale face is spattered with blood, and he stains my uniform wherever he uses his bleeding hand to pull away the branches trapping me.

This reminds me of that time when I ran away from boarding school only to crawl back, begging for help after being stung by wasps in the forest. I'm ashamed of running off and causing Kyranis pain. I'm ashamed I didn't know what awaited me. But most of all, I'm ashamed that I feel sorry for him, when he *abducted* me in the first place. Is this how Stockholm Syndrome works?

"I'm sorry," I choke out, remembering Marty's words from hours ago.

Do better.

If only I knew what *"better"* is in the context of my sort-of-relationship with Kyranis. Prince Kyranis Nightweed. Lord of Sorrows. Or something along those lines. I have to admit that after seeing him come for me with so much ferocity, I have a new appreciation for him and his sword. From up close, the weapon is even more impressive. The carvings on it are barely visible in the dark, but they resemble some kind of plant, while the pommel is a black seashell.

"I hope this will be a lesson," Kyranis says through his teeth, back to his high and mighty attitude. "Just stay very still. I will cut the vine around your neck. My weapon is extremely sharp and I don't want to hurt you."

I don't know if I should hate or appreciate him, but I sigh first, then focus on not breathing as he leans over me, reaching behind my ear. He smells of blood. But also something darkly floral that messes with my head.

A streak of red making its way from between the flaps of leather on his chest catches my attention. I shudder at the memory of that moth crawling in there and I wonder how badly it hurt him, but he doesn't seem too worried and bends even lower, eventually kneeling in the bush, to reach for a branch behind my head. The slit in his vest opens right in front of my face, revealing pale skin covered in... tattoos? At least that's what I assume I'm looking at before I notice the patterns move. Shadowy snakes crawl all over him soundlessly. Twisting, overlapping in a slow dance of ink. If they're made of ink at all.

Not all of the tattoos are black. In the middle of his chest is a golden sun, and the dark creatures seem to avoid it at all cost. But as I take note of the smooth, hard lines of the symbol, it strikes me that it's not a tattoo at all, more like a deep scar that's been sealed with liquid gold. As if someone poured a medallion straight into his flesh.

I focus on his nipple for a little too long, but it's only because one of the creatures slithering over his skin makes its way across the stiff pink peak.

The pressure around my throat eases as Kyranis removes the last vine holding me captive, but then our eyes meet, and he knows what I saw, because now we're both looking down at his blood-stained abs.

For the first time since we met, his moon-white cheeks gain a splash of color.

CHAPTER 5

Kyran

My secret is out, and while Luke can't know what the symbol on my chest means, if he mentions it to anyone, it will be my end. I should have been more careful, but when he called for me, even if not by my *real* name, I dashed into the shadowed woodland like a stag ready to chase off a hunter chasing its partner. I should be angry at him for trying to once again break the terms of our agreement and run from me, but when I saw the distressed glint in his eyes and smelled fresh wounds, I lost all reason.

I don't need his face to stay pretty to use him as my Dark Companion, yet I ended up cutting myself just to get the bloodthirsty moths off him.

My thoughtlessness might jeopardize the plan I already sacrificed so much for, knowing that he saw the *real me* is a thrill. He doesn't need to know that. In fact, the less he understands, the more cards remain up my sleeve.

So I do what I know best. I resort to violence.

When his mouth opens to speak, I grab his throat. I would have put my blade to his neck if he didn't seem reckless enough to move against it.

"If you tell anyone about this golden tattoo, and I mean *anyone*, be it a cat or a sentient fucking *tree*, I will kill you. I will cut your tongue out, then drown you in the same river where I first found you. Do you understand, Luke? Nod if you do."

His pulse quickens against my palm, giving me a delicious surge of power. I know I'm being harsh, but my future is on the line, and I won't let this boy ruin it.

I've only been out of my prison for a few days, but I'm loving every second of this new life. No longer some feral secret locked in someone else's shadow, I am *royalty*.

When Luke nods, I let go and watch him, wondering if he will start screaming. Only my coachman and the toll mistress could possibly hear him, and they wouldn't care.

"Wh-what is that?" He points in the vague direction of my chest.

"All you need to know is that I am prince Kyranis—"

"Yeah, yeah, Lord of Darkness, Best Pirate of the Nocturne Sea, I get it." He rolls his eyes. He actually *dares* roll his eyes at me. Granted, they are big, green as the sea in the spring, and embedded in a pretty face with sharp, vulpine features, but that does not mean all will be forgiven.

"I just saved your life, you ungrateful boy!"

I'd have smacked him for insolence if he wasn't to be my future Dark Companion.

Luke grabs my arm, and I flinch, ready to fight off his attack, but he hangs his head in submission as tears gather in his eyes, reflecting the moonlight. "I'm just trying to understand what's happening! Where am I?"

I take a deep breath, reminding myself that humans are fragile creatures requiring lots of patience. Our interaction seven years ago had been brief and rather unpleasant, and were it not for the nearly full face of the moon above, I would have gladly given him more time to adjust. But there *is* no time, so I assess his ripped clothes and help him up.

"You're in the Nightmare Realm, or as we call it, the Realm. Stay by my side and do not attempt to run again. You will not succeed. Do you want to be ripped apart by wolves, Luke? Do you want tooth moths feasting on you until you're nothing but a dried husk? The wilderness hides a whole myriad of dangers. Remember that. If you venture out on your own, something *will* either try to eat you or trick you. Either way, you are safest under my protection." A slight exaggeration, but I don't want him out of my sight until our bond is made.

Luke holds on to my arm as I lead him back, cutting down thorny vines set on regrowing. To soften the blow, I pick up my cloak from the bushes and drape it over his shoulders. It can't heal him, but it will keep him warm until we reach the castle.

He stills with the furry hood drooping over his forehead, but when he looks up at me, his gaze is sharp like a precious gemstone cut to perfection.

"This is real, isn't it?" Luke asks, pulling the cloak around him more tightly.

"Very."

I rub some blood from his cheek, finding it hard to be mad now that he's back at my side and hurting. It would feel like yelling at a rose. It cannot be expected to understand its wrongdoing, nor is it responsible for being born with thorns. He's helpless without me, and that makes me want to keep him safe the same way my soft fur cloak is keeping him warm.

He is the first thing in my thirty-five years of life that is truly mine, and I don't want to spoil our relationship with unnecessary cruelty. I am not naive enough to expect this to be the end of his rebellion, though. Tears might glint like diamonds as they cling to his eyelashes, but he's still feral and will take time to tame.

But how hard can it be to woo such a pretty flower? The fact that I have never kissed anyone, let alone a human, might be a little hiccup in our grand love affair, but I've seen kissing often enough that it ought to be child's play. I can easily make up for lack of experience with the years of shadowing my rake of a brother. I guess he was useful for *something* in the end.

Other than dying.

The longer I watch Luke, the more ashamed I am of my violent reaction. This human has no reason to trust me, and since I know his kind lives in a different reality, how could he have predicted the consequences of his actions?

"Apologies," I tell him as we walk down the path I cut out with my sword. The vines retreat out of our way like bugs crawling from under a rock as my shadow darts ahead, burning them with its darkness. "I understand this is a shock. I should have taken you with me right after pulling you out of the river, and prepared you for your role, but that wasn't possible at the time."

Thanks to my idiot brother, who'd have gladly idled away his life, without ever needing to take on the responsibilities of the Protector of the Nightmare Realm. It is due to *his* negligence that I now need to scramble for time.

Luke glances my way, and I push a strand of hair off his face. At the roots, his mane is dark, but then it shifts into a beautiful dark green, making me wonder how many colors humans can grow. But I don't ask, since I don't want to seem unknowledgeable, like some peasant who's never left his village. He could use that against me.

Luke's eyes grow wider as we step out of the woodland, and he points at our vehicle. "What *are* those?"

The moonlight makes the skeletal faces of the four beasts harnessed to my carriage shine like ivory, and I realize that my coachman used his power of illusion to make them appear as horses back in Luke's realm. "Is this your first time seeing kelpies?" I ask as we pass the tollhouse.

He doesn't stray from me. In fact, he huddles ever closer as we approach the majestic creatures.

Luke's brows gather. "They're... monster horses from mythology. Of course I've never seen one. Are they not dangerous?"

Since he's so interested in them, I don't rush him to the carriage and indulge his curiosity.

"They are hardly a myth, if they brought us all the way here."

"Where is *here* exactly?" Luke asks, and my tongue stiffens as I watch him while fog thickens around the stone bridge ahead.

Right. Back when I made the deal with him, I didn't bother to take my time explaining what was going to happen in the future. I'm now paying for that mistake. "This is one of the few places where realms connect. One can pass through, provided the toll mistress allows it."

"I'm guessing the *prince* gets to go where he wants?" Luke asks with a deep sigh, taking another step closer to the kelpies. Their shiny black coats drip with water, and when they shake their heads, seaweed is clearly visible in their manes.

My mouth quirks as I take his hand and lead him to the front of the carriage, so he can have a better look at the draft team. "I am the beneficiary of the toll, so yes. I can come and go as I please, though there are rules to it that even I am obliged to follow. As for the kelpies, you don't need to be frightened. The males can be tamed, if one starts the training early enough. Besides, they're under Drustan's control," I nod to my coachman. "He is a kelpie himself, but lives in this vaguely elven form, serving my family."

Luke stares at Drustan's blank face. His heartbeat quickens, I can sense it in his hand. "So if they're tamed, can I... pet one?"

I grab the fingers of his other hand just as he's about to put them on the kelpie's mane, and I click my tongue. "Only with proper equipment. They're very sticky, you see, and if their skin touches yours, it might take a while for us to free you," I say and pull him against my chest. The fluffy top of his head tickles my chin, and my eyes close as I breathe in the earthy aroma clinging to his hair.

Seven years ago, I chose him at random, just one of many lost humans hoping to survive in the River of Souls, but he's grown into a fine man. I'm surprised how much I like looking at him.

And unlike everyone else in my life, he never knew the real Kyranis. He's the only one who knows me as *me*, even if under a false name.

It feels good to be seen.

He's tense in my arms but doesn't fight the embrace. Nodding, he looks back to Drustan, who watches us with his watery eyes. "If he's a kelpie, is his skin… sticky too?"

I never considered it myself, but now we are both staring. It's so interesting to see such mundane things through Luke's eyes. "I would… assume so."

Drustan's lip curls in annoyance. "Excuse me, Your Highness, but I must voice, that I am most definitely not *sticky*."

"Are you sure?" Luke asks, cocking his head. "Have you checked?"

I blink and squeeze his shoulder a bit harder when he leans forward, as if about to move. "You want to… *touch* my coachman?"

"Sorry! No. I—"

Drustan's expression couldn't be any sourer. "I am not a mindless beast to be petted and prodded!"

Luke pulls his hands back under the cape, and I already miss his touch. "I understand. I didn't mean any disrespect. I was just curious," he mumbles in a voice so velvety sweet I long to coax it back out with my tongue and kiss his warm lips.

How would they taste?

And his skin? Is it as sweet as the meringues it resembles in color?

"I'm sure he doesn't mind," I say and guide him to the steps leading into the carriage.

The green glow of the lantern inside gives half of his face an otherworldly sheen. "Is there really nothing I can do for you to take me back?" he asks with a tremble to his voice.

I steady myself, annoyed that for a moment I let myself believe he no longer hates my company. "No. I'm sorry. I need to wed my Dark Companion, and the full moon is tomorrow," I say, climbing inside.

Behind me, Drustan takes away the steps and closes the door, but I barely take note of his presence, focused on the small human sitting on the padded bench across from me.

Luke clenches his fists on his knees. "What kind of marriage is it if you force me into it? It's not fair. Why can't you find someone else? You're handsome enough."

I press my lips together, breathing slowly to keep my demeanor calm. I've never had to control my expressions, kept out of sight, if not out of mind, but the lack of training is now crawling back, like the thorny vines, about to tear apart my mask of politeness. "Because I cannot tether myself to another human's shadow for as long as you live. Do you want to die, Luke?"

He stills, and his Adam's apple bobs when he swallows.

Good. A little bit of fear never killed anyone.

"No," he mumbles as if my question wasn't rhetorical, and that somehow annoys me even more.

"If you wanted to keep your shadow, you should have stayed dead, not bargained with it."

He shakes his head, as if I'm the unreasonable one, and slouches against the door, not even sparing me a glance. Like a spoiled child. My brother would sometimes make that face, in the most egregious circumstances, and I hated him for it. "Are you going to sulk until we reach the castle?" I ask when the carriage moves.

He just shrugs.

Fine. I've got no doubt I can play the silence game much better than him.

CHAPTER 6

LUKE

I might be tired, but the aches and pains in my flesh prevent me from taking even the briefest nap. It doesn't help that the ride is bumpy, and I share a confined space with a man as infuriating as he is stunning. I'd like to deny his beauty, but I do have functioning eyes.

And I also have a nose, which means I'm enveloped in the luscious scent of his cloak. It's a mix of leather, some fruit, tied together by a mysterious flowery note. I wonder if that's how his hair smells too, and if it is as silky as it appears.

Kyranis catches me staring, and when he smirks, I look away, embarrassed. I shouldn't be lusting after a guy who's kidnapped me, but I've never had good taste in men. No reason to break that pattern now.

He did save me from those thorns in the forest, which further messes with my perception of him. Then again, he didn't do it because he's a knight in leather armor. He fought for me because he needs me, but if that's all there is to it, why did he hold my hand so eagerly, or put his arm over my shoulders? It couldn't have been only because he thinks me stupid enough to try running away again like some lemming headed for a cliff.

My resolve to stay silent dwindles as our time in the carriage stretches, but when the vehicle slows down, I direct my curiosity to the outside world. The big wheels of the carriage crawl onto a bumpier surface, and I push aside the blood red curtain.

The abyss beyond the edge of the wooden bridge we're crossing makes my stomach plummet, and as I move my gaze up, a castle takes shape against the backdrop of the massive white moon. Stretching up from a jagged cliff on the edge of dark, shimmering waters, it's all turrets and pointed arches woven into an intricate lattice of shapes straight out of a goth artist's fever dream.

"We're almost there," Kyranis informs me in a dry voice, adjusting his collar. He tied a belt around his breastplate so no one else can get a peek at the strange golden mark.

I realize my mouth is open, but I can't look away from the building. It's as if Snow White's castle had a baby with Dracula's and then this creepy bastard child got sent to perch on a cliff over the sea for all eternity as punishment for its eerie beauty.

The closer we get, the more details I take in. From the tall narrow windows far above, to the sturdy walls made of black stone that seem to keep the building captive instead of protecting it.

My heart jumps when we pass an elven woman casually holding a basket of fruit against her hip as she stands by the road, talking to a friend. They're both dressed in an amalgamation of classy peasant and renfaire, their long, puffy skirts hitched up with leather straps reveal black stockings and simple leather boots.

As soon as they spot us, their attention is on the carriage. I don't know what to do so I… wave?

I'm officially an embarrassment, but just as I'm about to retreat, so the rest of the village doesn't get a laugh at my expense, the two women lower their heads and bend their knees in curtsies.

The carriage rocks on the narrow, cobbled street filled with small houses covered in dark vines and murals depicting the depths of the sea. Large mushrooms and herbs I've never seen grow in pots hung under windows instead of flowers, and the scenery is reminiscent of a cursed mirror version of rococo France. Darker. Moodier. As strange as the medieval pictures of tigers painted by people who'd never seen one.

A part of me assumes this is all a strange dream. That one of my creepy admirers knocked me out, and I've hallucinated everything, including the warped version of my personal Prince Charming, which Kyranis embodies. But when I pinch myself, a big, warm hand squeezes my wrist as my abductor leans in.

"Stop that!"

I feel like a scolded puppy. Which is ridiculous. He has no right to tell me what to do. "I was just… checking if it's not a dream," I mutter, in no hurry to remove his fingers. I had expected them to be cold when he first touched me, but he's no vampire, that's for sure. Unless he feeds on emotion, and I'm yet to find out the extent of it.

Overwhelmed by the elves gawking at the carriage, I focus on Kyranis instead. If I am to ever escape this place, I need to pretend I'm more docile than I really am.

He swallows, staring at me as if he notices a particularly unsightly bit of my face, but as the silence stretches, he clears his throat and takes away his hand. "Everyone will want to meet my promised, my future Dark Companion. Folk are happy you're finally here. Don't be afraid."

My stomach clenches with nerves I don't recognize. I'm used to people overlooking me, mocking my eyeliner and painted nails. My presence being anticipated by someone? A bunch of royals *happy* to see me? That I can't comprehend. Only one answer comes to my mind.

"Will I be... sacrificed?" I whisper, because I still don't know what a Dark Companion is. From context, I'm guessing promised to be another word for *fiancé*. Maybe I should have spent my time in the carriage asking the important questions instead of sulking in silence, but I can't take back time.

Kyranis's forehead wrinkles. "You already made your sacrifice when we first met. Now you'll be fulfilling all your obligations to me and my people."

I rub my hands together as I glimpse guards in dark armor. How on earth will I escape a place like this? I'm not brave, or strong, or even fast. I can swim well, but it's not like that will come in handy.

"I don't remember that night very well. Did you actually explain what will be expected of me? What will you do with my shadow?"

Kyranis leans forward and rests his hands on my thighs. They're hot as tongues trailing ever higher up my legs. I barely stop a gasp from escaping my lips, and as he moves closer, I'm assaulted by the intensity of his scent. And while the perfume I can sense on the cape lingers on him too, underneath it all is salt. Wax. Smoke. Leather.

My lips open, tingling in response to the sudden change of atmosphere in the carriage, but then we come to a halt, and I hear the coachman's boots hit the cobbles outside.

Kyranis retreats, and in the glow of the green candle, I spot color on his cheeks.

The doors open, letting in the moonlight, and my abductor is gone. He goes down the steps provided by the coachman while I remain shadowed, intimidated by the flurry of voices outside.

He reaches his hand out to me with the grace of a... well, a prince. My damn heart won't stop rattling, because how often do you get so much attention from a person like him? An elf at that.

Never. The answer is never, because elves shouldn't exist outside fantasy novels and fairytales.

But he is here, touching me, and maybe I am seeking comfort in him, because I am still aching all over, especially where the thorns cut into my back.

The bratty thing to do would be to ignore him for all the elven nobility to see, but I'm far too frightened of what might happen if I do that. The kind of castle we've stopped in front of definitely has a dungeon.

I grab his hand, and he helps me out as I clutch the cloak, so it doesn't fall off me.

The smooth melody of several instruments starts the moment I emerge from behind the curtains. I blink, taking in a large courtyard filled by an innumerable amount of people in elaborate outfits, and it becomes clear that a quintet of musicians has been waiting for our arrival for God-knows how long.

I'm so startled my heel misses one of the steps, but just as I'm about to tumble forward, embarrassing myself in front of all those fancy people, Kyranis grabs me gently by the waist and places me on the cobblestones, as if he meant to do that from the start.

The crowd claps. Cheers. And then, I'm guided toward a grand arched entrance at the top of the stairs ahead. The open gates are decorated with a theme of mermaids and seashells, but the creatures all wield daggers, which is unsettling to say the least.

The elves part, all bowing their heads, as if I were their master's new queen, brought as spoils of war from abroad.

"Welcome to the Nocturne Court," Kyranis tells me in a breathless voice that makes me blink.

Maybe I'm not the only one intimidated by this after all? I don't know what his life is like, how old he is, or why he made the shadow pact with me in the first place. Gathering information will need to become my priority.

But I'm also a tiny bit shallow, so I'm glad that I have his cloak, because otherwise, I'd be showing off my Best Burger Bonanza uniform, with the name tag still on my chest. Changing wasn't my priority when I fled the restaurant, and now I feel severely underdressed.

These elven royals, with their pointy ears decorated by jewels, create a sea of beauty, and I'm dazzled by it despite my better judgment. I don't spot anyone in soft or pastel shades here. All the fabrics they wear are either dark, or in intense jewel colors like ruby-red and sapphire-blue. Lace and frills are everywhere I look, and some outfits shimmer in the moonlight, while others are so matte they seem dark as black holes.

Servants illuminate our way with bright lanterns on long carved poles.

I'm pretty sure I saw an elf with a massive raven on his shoulder, but he's gone in the crowd before I can do a double take.

"It's..." I don't have the words for it despite wanting to communicate how overwhelming this all is. I stay close to Kyranis and let him lead me, because what else can I do?

"They don't mind that I'm a man?"

Kyranis waves at his subjects, parading me down the well-lit passage between the courtiers, who all peek at us from under their bangs, hats, or from behind decorative fans.

"I don't understand. Why would they?" he asks as we start climbing stairs made of a stone in a dark blue shade with swirls of white. The low, wide steps remind me of cascading water, yet my feet remain dry as we walk.

His question means I really am in my own, personal la-la land.

"You can *marry* a man?"

"I intend to, yes," Kyranis confirms as he steps closer and lets go of my hand to place his arm over my shoulders in a gesture so protective I forget that my current goal is to find a way out of whatever's coming. If he has ulterior motives, of course he'd be lying.

But also... he smells so good.

I bark out a nervous laugh as we stroll along the marble floor of the corridor where the wallpaper depicts a pattern of bats hanging from leafless black trees.

"And out of all people, you chose *me* for that? You don't even know me. What if you hate me? What if you find out I have the personality of a rotten pomegranate?"

He pulls me closer, and as we move toward an arched vestibule with columns shimmering like silver, followed by a long train of courtiers, he flicks his thumb over my ear. "You're right. I don't know you. But your life is mine now, so you should be on your best behavior."

How can he flood me with so much terror while sounding so sweet? He even has a little smile on his lips as he says that. I should hate him for it, but didn't I bargain with my shadow? Maybe he *has* the right to me.

Or I'm just trying to absolve myself of all personal responsibility for my predicament.

"May we eat something? It's been a long evening." I also need to see more of this place and understand it better before he puts me in some room with no way out.

"It's midday. Do you not see how bright the moon is?" Kyranis stills, right in the middle of a floor covered by an elaborate mosaic pattern, and just as I'm about to apologize for my ignorance, a man as tall and slender as a reed stops next to us and bows so low his dark brown braid brushes the tiles.

"Your Highness. Welcome back. It's such a joy to see you with your promised at last," he says in a haughty voice before straightening his back to stare right at me. He has an angular face, big blue eyes, and lips that somehow look bold and soft at the same time.

"Thank you, Reiner," Kyranis mutters before clearing his throat as the crowd of fancily dressed elves fills the interior behind us. The musicians must have followed us as well, because the flowing melody they produce accompanies us even now. "Could you bring some food to the breakfast room?"

Reiner places his hand on his chest as his face scrunches.

"But Your Highness, it's no longer breakfast time," he says, as if this disruption of the daily schedule was a personal offense.

Next to me, Kyranis fills his chest with air before speaking in a low voice that echoes under the ceiling, no doubt reaching everyone's ears. "If I say it's breakfast time, it is breakfast time."

Reiner bows again, not missing a beat. "As you wish, Sire. I will get everything delivered with haste," he says and walks off, stomping as if he was marching to war, not ordering the cook to make eggs. Or whatever it is that they eat here.

"I'm guessing there won't be French fries?" I joke to lighten the mood. Or maybe to endear myself to my cruel captor. I don't know. I'm in survival mode.

Kyranis sighs and takes hold of both my hands as he faces me in front of dozens of people. "That is unfortunate, but I am sure the cooks will do everything in their power to accommodate your wishes," he says somberly, as if the absence of fries was a grave matter of the state. Before I can find my voice, he glances at the courtiers and speaks, "Dear friends, there's entertainment prepared for you in the ballroom. We shall join you shortly."

Several elves bow, some clap, but Kyranis wastes no more time on them and guides me farther down the corridor. Four guards in armor made of a material resembling flint create a wall between us and the others, to make sure no one follows. I kind of appreciate it, because I'm a fish out of water, and I don't want to be gawked at as I eat.

Kyranis squeezes my hand. "Your fingers are so cold. You must get a warm drink as well."

"I... um... thank you?" I'm stunned, because I don't recall anyone ever coddling me so much. I did get to pick and choose from the lunch buffet at boarding school, but once I left its walls I had to pay extra if I wanted food made for me.

No longer, it seems. Though I wish I already knew what price I'll be paying for such comforts.

Kyranis smiles and then pulls my hand to his lips, pressing a kiss to my tender skin. "Like ice. I'll have gloves made for you of the finest leather," he tells me before tugging me along the corridor, through a door so well-obscured by a massive tapestry featuring a sea monster that I would have missed it.

Behind it is a spiral staircase, and after climbing two stories, we're in a hallway with ceilings vastly lower than on the ground floor of the castle. The colors here are muted, the draperies hung on walls—heavier, but when Kyranis passes through one of the doors, we step into a bright space, with massive arched windows opening the small circular interior to the vast sea.

Two servants are lighting lanterns, but the moon itself illuminates the space in a way strangely reminiscent of sunshine, despite being noticeably dimmer. I drift to the window for a better view of the ocean.

This time it's Kyranis who follows me as the servants set the table behind us.

While the moon is pure serenity, the waves far below us are volatile as if they were trying to reach us with their green-black mouths made of seafoam. A large fish jumps into the air every now and then, teasing the dark birds flying above the water.

But then a massive shape catches my eye. A dark, snake-like shadow looms below the surface, cutting through the sea at an alarming speed.

"What is that?"

"A leviathan," Kyranis tells me as his chest presses to my back, and his hands settle on my hips. The monster pushes its head above the unruly waves before coiling its massive form around a jagged rock. I imagine this beast wrapping itself around a fishing boat and crushing it to pieces, but the prince is there to reassure me. "You're safe at my side."

"I'm guessing the beach isn't exactly a place to go for a swim?" I ask as one of the birds catches a fish. The moment it sits on a rock to swallow its catch, a tentacle bursts out of the water, grabs it, and pulls it under the waves.

Yep. I'm definitely not going swimming there.

Kyranis chuckles as his hand cups my chin. "Not without preparation. Those are treacherous seas, but my people have mastered them over millennia. Most of the things we eat here come from the ocean," he says and spins me around to face a lush spread of unfamiliar foods. Arranged on two tiered stands are small yet beautifully presented treats, but I can also see a selection of bottles and herbs, as well as a basket of fruit.

He's obviously trying to entice me, to make me drop my guard so I do what he wants. I keep that at the back of my mind, but the scent coming from a steaming bowl shaped like a seashell loosens my resolve to hate him. The smell reminds me of cherries and cream.

The rumble in my stomach is as embarrassing as it is telling. I haven't eaten since before work, hours and hours ago.

"Can I try some?" I ask awkwardly, because eating is the reason for our presence here, yet I still feel like I should be asking permission.

The same servant who approached us downstairs steps forward, ready to fulfill my every wish, but Kyranis chases him off with a wave of his hand. "Leave us."

"This is... unorthodox," Reiner mutters, but another glare from Kyranis sends him and a serving girl out of the door. As it shuts, we are on our own again, and my heart beats faster when Kyranis pulls away one of the carved chairs, offering it to me.

"Of course you can eat whatever you wish."

As enticing as his attention is, I can't help but feel not like a lover he is courting, a man he wants to marry, but like a pet, a feral cat he plucked out of the gutter and now wants to treat because it's entertaining to him.

Still, I will indulge the prince, because I need to play my own game if I am to get out of here.

"What is this... soup?" I ask, grabbing the ladle resting inside an elegant bowl, as having something warm is my priority. After a moment of hesitation, I pour some of the burgundy liquid into his cup first, because I'm not a tactless animal.

"Vanasme. Made with fruit from my orchard," Kyranis tells me, sitting right next to me, even though there's more than enough space around the table. He picks up a small jug shaped like a bird and pours thick black goo into my cup. He then picks up a silver spoon and fills it with the soup. I don't dare move when he brings it to my lips. "Taste it."

I hesitate for only a moment, because he wouldn't poison me after putting so much effort into bringing me here. Our eyes meet over the spoon as I take it into my mouth. There's something illicit about being fed by him, and I heat up.

The pudding-like soup is sweet, milky, and a bit tangy. In fact, its flavor does remind me of cherries, but I never had a warm compote like this, especially not with black... cream? Is it delicious? Hell yes. Now I can't wait to try more of the food like the greedy peasant I am.

My diet is usually comprised of chicken nuggets, sandwiches, with a tomato thrown in from time to time so I don't die of malnutrition, but that's because I'm not a good cook, and I can't afford much. One year, right after I left school and attempted to move out of Mom's place, I decided to save money by only eating rice with spices. The doctor who later diagnosed me with scurvy almost laughed me out of his office, but I've gotten better and learned my lesson. Too bad it involved moving back in with my mother.

Given half the chance, yeah, I'll gorge myself on fantastical foods even if I have to eat them from Kyranis's hand.

I purr in approval. "It's delicious!"

Kyranis laughs in a way that sounds almost honest and keeps serving me the food with the shell-shaped dainty spoon while his hand rubs my back in a way so suggestive I half-expect him to break protocol and marry me *today*.

That, or fuck me over this table.

I should feel offended if he intended for the latter to happen, but how am I to deny a man this attractive? A man who isn't embarrassed to express his interest in me in public, almost as if he's... proud to have me. That's definitely a new experience.

A large round fruit bursts with sweetness on my tongue as I bite into it. My eyes widen and I smile at him with my mouth full. My heart beats that bit faster, and I'm no longer cold. Only now I notice Kyranis hasn't eaten, focused on my needs. I can only hope he isn't trying to fatten me up so that he can feed me to a leviathan.

"I want to make sure you understand I mean you no harm. This might be sudden, but we are bound forever, and it will be a sweet duty," he tells me with a smile ghosting across his features. The fruit in my mouth feels almost tingly as the Prince of Darkness leans so close I can feel his breath.

Yep, he's gonna fuck me here, and I'm not even mad about it.

With my heart in my throat and my eyes on his, I reach out to stroke his hair. It's as silky as I envisioned. I already imagine it falling around my face and tickling my cheeks as he—

"Kyranis! At last! You're back!" says a female voice as the woman bursts through the door without as much as knocking.

"Forgive me, Your Highness. Your cousin insisted..." Reiner pleads with his eyes from the door, and the elongated, reddish mark on his cheek suggests she did more than just insist.

CHAPTER 7

LUKE

I watch the elven lady stuff a folded fan into an embroidered purse, and pull away from Kyranis with my cheeks on fire. Her hair looks like white gold poured over an eccentric wedding cake, with flowers and jewels adorning the various tiers of the updo as if she were cosplaying a gothic version of Marie Antoinette.

Her face is round, almost childlike, with a small, pouty mouth and big eyes the shade of violets in the spring, but her breasts, pushed up by her corset like two cupcakes, prove that she is indeed an adult woman.

"I hope I'm not interrupting," she says with a wide smile, and sits right next to us without waiting for an answer. Reiner appears exasperated that she didn't give him a chance to pull the chair out for her, but she pays him no mind.

"You are, Elodie," Kyranis says in a voice sharp as steel. "We didn't want to be disturbed."

"You shouldn't be shutting out family like this," Elodie quips and helps herself to a small piece of food reminiscent of a sandwich. "We all want to meet your promised before you two wed. I've heard rumors that you're being fast to avoid public courting. It's tradition for a reason."

"What is the reason?" I butt in, even though I haven't been introduced, but Elodie doesn't seem to care about rules, so I hope I'm not next in line for a slap.

She claps her hands, and the smile of her ruby red lips widens. "It speaks! It's been such a long time since I've seen a human."

I swallow this non-answer in frustration.

Kyranis sighs in defeat. "Luke, this is my first cousin, Princess Elodie Goldweed."

I would have to awkwardly lean over the table to shake her hand, so I settle on a polite nod as she scans me with her piercing violet eyes.

"What happened to his neck?" Elodie asks Kyranis as if I'm not there. "I hope you're not treating your future Companion poorly."

"It's fine," I answer because I've worked in customer service long enough to learn to not take people's shit. "Prince Kyranis actually saved me from deadly bushes and these moth thingies."

"Ah, always the hero," she says and spreads her fan, obscuring most of her face, so we only see her kohl-lined eyes. "Maybe with Luke's help, you will be able to find your father's Dark Companion? He's been stuck in the shadowild for what, seven years now?"

Kyranis tenses like a cobra before sinking its teeth into a victim. "There's no point in dwelling on the past."

But my fingers get cold again. "No, no, I'd like to know. What's shadowild? And why is a Dark Companion lost there?" At this point, I still don't know what my Dark Companion duties will be, but this feels much more pressing.

Elodie puts down the fan and makes the saddest little face as she picks up another sandwich bite. "It's where the Companion's body sinks to when his shadow is being used, but since Lord Nightweed has died while his Companion was in the shadowild, it's hard to say whether there's a chance to bring him back. Though to be honest, if he's lucky, he is dead. Imagine being stuck in an endless void of shadow forever, unable to get out, yet unable to die..." She shudders theatrically, but I'm not laughing.

I might have lost my appetite.

"Elodie!" Kyranis bangs his hands on the table, making the cutlery and plates roar, then walks off to look out at the sea. "This is unnecessary. I am twice the shadow wielder my father was. I shall not put Luke in danger."

He might not want to, but he could still do so accidentally. I'm guessing that's why he dotes on me so much. To lower my defenses.

Elodie gives me a remorseful glance as if she's sorry for me, which doesn't help my confidence in my position at this court of madness.

She waves her hand with a sigh. "Have it your way. No courting, a quick wedding with barely any time to invite guests, and an average full moon, when you could wait as little as one month for a blood moon. It's unreasonable, if you ask me, but I will work with what I'm given. Here, Luke. Please write down a few things you like so that I can make sure they're incorporated in the celebrations tomorrow."

She passes me a piece of textured paper and a pencil embedded in a long silver handle.

"We already waited too lon—" Kyranis starts when the floor and walls start trembling. Sweat dampens my back as one of the bottles falls over, spilling red liquid onto the floor, and Kyranis lets out a strange word, which I know from context is a curse. "We cannot risk it at this point."

Elodie meets my gaze, appearing almost bored with the earthquake while I hold onto the armchair for dear life. "Have it your way. Luke, if you please," she says and taps the piece of paper with an elongated nail.

I swallow and glance at Kyranis, who stares at the sea with a pensive expression. His profile is breathtaking, but I can't be this weak. With the wedding planned for *tomorrow*, I have to take any chance I can. Kyranis is holding back information for a reason, and I don't want to wait around to find out what his real agenda is.

And I'm sure as hell not promising to love and obey or whatever else, a man I've just met. Even if that *man* is an *elf*.

I take one more glance at Elodie's sweet face. She might be a bit all over the place, but I can only hope that as a woman, she will understand my peril.

'*PLEASE. Help me*', I write down and hand the note over while Kyranis is watching the waves. The paper whirrs as she folds it, giving me a conspiratorial glance, but Kyranis is back at the table, his long arm hanging over my shoulder as he wordlessly demands the message I've written.

"I should participate in this too."

My heart sinks in terror. When he threatened me about the tattoo on his chest, he sounded like he meant it. That he'd kill me. What would he do if he found out I'm trying to use his family members against him?

Elodie rolls her eyes and passes him a fresh sheet of paper. "Fine, feel free to write down any preferences, but I've known you long enough. I have a good understanding of what you like."

Silence settles over us as he doesn't respond, ignoring the empty paper. "Don't play games, Elodie."

She scoffs at her cousin. "Must you know everything? Is your future companion not allowed requests to surprise you tomorrow?"

I clear my throat, grateful for that excuse. "I'd rather keep it secret. It's a... human thing." I wish my voice wasn't a squeak, but alas, it can't be helped.

I stop breathing when a dark shape crawls from under the tabletop and moves toward Elodie, bubbling up the same way my shadow had moments before I was taken. She freezes, blinks, and then throws the folded piece of paper toward Kyranis.

"I should go. I can see you're keen for some alone time," she says, rising from her chair, and while her voice remains cheerful, there's tension in her movements, which betrays that whatever Kyranis threatened her with has shaken her.

Elodie moves away with so much fervor she pulls on a cup while picking up her fan, but she doesn't even turn around to look at it when it falls.

Reiner makes an acrobatic movement to save the cup, and while he succeeds, he does end up on his knees.

I'm too busy dreading Kyranis to care about the servant.

The prince opens the folded piece of paper and for a moment just stares at it. His eyelids lower, his long lashes make his eyes almost black, and he looks up at me with a face carved in ice.

I'm fucked.

So fucked.

CHAPTER 8

LUKE

Dread sinks its icy claws into my flesh as Kyranis's features freeze into a half-smiling mask. Not a muscle stirs in his handsome face, but his eyes darken from the soot of the anger burning inside him.

With a sharp gesture, Kyranis shoves a tiered stand with food off the table, sending the dainty canapes and nibbles to the floor.

"I think you've had enough food," he says in a voice made of steel.

"The soup was very nice..." I try, not daring to glance at Reiner who didn't even attempt to save the food. I'm feeling like that time BBB's regional manager came to visit our branch only to find out we'd broken the ice cream machine on purpose. Too bad it's my life on the line this time, not just my job.

Reiner takes half a step closer, his hands briefly rising, but he's smart enough not to utter a word and remains in the background, letting me bear the brunt of the Shadow Lord's anger.

"Oh, did you want to take it with you?" Kyranis asks, towering over me like a personification of fury.

"No, I—" *What to do?* I need to appease him, so I do the same thing I did when confronted by the regional manager. I lie. "Maybe I didn't choose the right words. I wanted her to help me prepare for the wedding, since all this is so new to me." It sounds fake even to my ears. Fuck.

Kyranis leans closer, and his hair becomes bushier, as if he were a bristling animal. I prepare myself for a punch, but he grabs my arm and drags me across the floor scattered with remains of food, and out into the hallway.

"I'm sorry!" My pitch rises, and I hold onto the cloak around me as if it can shield me from Kyranis's wrath. I acted too hastily. I was building a connection with him and should have gone down *that* route instead.

But is it really my fault that I panicked? It's not every day that you're abducted by an elven prince and taken to the Nightmare Realm. I'd say I'm freaking out less than the average person.

Kyranis's lips remain sealed as he leads me farther down the majestic corridor with golden and silver decoration, all the way to a tall, arched door at the very end. He makes an impatient gesture, and it opens before us, like the gates of hell.

"Didn't you promise the other... elves," I find it hard to say that out loud, "that we'll see them?" Not that I want to, but at least then I wouldn't be alone with Kyranis. Right now, he's as angry as he is beautiful, so I'd rather have company who might dissuade him from doing anything drastic.

It seems I won't be getting a choice, because he shoves me inside.

I can't help it, I yelp at the sudden pain in my back.

"Watch it!" I growl at him despite my better judgment. Sometimes, my rebellious side gets the better of me regardless of consequences, and he's pushing me to my limit.

Kyranis's tall form fills the door, so very dark against the illumination farther down the corridor, but then he flicks his hand against the wall, and the interior fills with a greenish light.

I spin around, looking for a way out, and when I spot a divider shaped like vines crawling up to the ceiling along poles made of a shimmering metal, I dash through the doorway in the latticed partition.

I know I've made a mistake when Kyranis chuckles and follows me without hurry. I don't have the time to take everything in, but there's a bed with a grand headboard, and red flower petals scattered over the silky black sheets.

I grab something off a dainty table nearby and hold it in front of me like a knife, but it turns out to be a hairbrush, which makes this ordeal all the more humiliating, but I stick to my guns.

"Stay back!" I yell, though I don't know what I'm threatening him with. That I'll brush his already perfect hair?

Kyranis enters through the door, and then... locks it, with a key, which he stuffs into his breast pocket.

My brain buzzes in alarm, and when I spot another door nearby, I dash for it, but instead of another corridor, it reveals a massive bathing suite.

I am locked up with a predator. And I've not only earned his wrath but also entered the cage on my own. No wonder he laughed.

I stand taller, even though I'm nowhere near his height.

"This isn't fair! You can't hold me to a promise I made when I was fourteen!" I try, feeling helpless and as trapped as the first time I tried to run away from boarding school, only to be caught crossing the fence.

But while I'm trying to reason with this man... this Prince of Darkness with magical shadow powers, I know it's a lost cause. He brought me here, and no one can save me anymore.

"I can and I will. It's best if you understand this now. It shall save you a lot of heartache," Kyranis tells me but doesn't come any closer and frowns, taking me in with a mysterious expression. Does he feel hate? Disgust? Self-satisfaction? I can't tell.

And I also don't know what becoming this Dark Companion entails other than handing over my shadow, which in theory doesn't sound frightening at all. But getting lost in 'shadowild' for all eternity? Well, I definitely have objections to *that*.

Am I expected to have sex with him? It's not like we can have shadow babies or whatever—or can we? My mind goes in directions I'd rather not explore, but it's too late. My panic reaches its crescendo.

I throw the brush at his face, grab one of the embroidered pillows, and then throw that for good measure, then follow that with throwing... myself at him. My cloak slides to the floor, but my only focus is the key he put in his pocket.

Just as I reach for my prize, weightless black tentacles climb my body and stiffen around my limbs, keeping me in place. With my heart in my throat, I look down to see a thick matte vine wrapped around my midsection and my legs. It emerges from the floor, where Kyranis's shadow touches the tips of my boots.

The Prince of Darkness is no longer smiling and instead watches me with a somber expression. "Why are you struggling? I don't intend to hurt you."

My breath becomes ragged, but I'm too afraid to move even if my hand could reach him. Against all my resolve, my lips tremble and my eyes itch. I don't blink, hoping to keep the tears at bay. My attempts are futile.

"You abducted me, you psycho!" I choke out, and a few tears streak down my cheeks when I lose my cool.

Who am I kidding? I never had any cool to begin with.

Kyranis's shoulders drop as he comes closer and slides the back of his hand against my damp cheek. His eyes are so deep, like two clouds of smoke looming at the bottom of a well, and I am suddenly so afraid of falling in.

"You wouldn't be alive if it wasn't for me. We made a bargain, and you no longer have a choice. You became mine when I threaded my shadow to yours. You are my crown."

I swallow and glance down to the thick shadow tentacle wrapped around my waist. I don't stand a chance. His face has a green sheen to it from the many lamps scattered both inside the cage and in the little space outside it.

If this place is real, and it is, then he's right. He did save my life. I didn't just swallow lots of pills. I cut my wrists, died, and he gave me my life back.

Yet now he's taking it.

"It hurts," I complain when the shadow slides higher up my back, ripping what's left of my uniform.

"You're struggling too much. Why is it that you want to escape me this badly? Is your life so enviable that you don't want all this and the attention of countless servants?" Kyranis asks, gesturing at the fine interior decorated with the opulence of a baroque palace. The columns holding up the canopy over a bed the size of the room I occupy at Mom's home are shaped like beautiful men and women in armor, the ceiling is covered with carved wooden panels, and the walls painted with an artistic depiction of sea creatures and mythological beasts, all in a lush gothic style I've only seen in fantasy illustrations.

I do love the stylistic choices here, but that's beside the point.

"This is, literally, a gilded cage," I say, fighting a sob rising in my chest, but Kyranis cups my face and wipes tears off my cheeks. His hands are big and pleasantly smooth. I can't help but see them as comfort, even though his gestures feel a little patronizing.

"My throne won't be secured until we're wed. The bars are for your safety."

I glance at the silver door of my prison with a frown. "Are... are you saying someone could try to kill me?" Suddenly, Kyranis's presence isn't so unwelcome anymore. Then again, this could be a lie meant to keep me in line.

He nods. "But don't be afraid. I'll make sure it doesn't happen. My future is tied to your life," he says as the shadow tentacles loosen their hold on me.

I'm left standing on my own, and now I kind of miss being held. Even if it hurt where they dug into my back, at least I felt... secured.

"And that happens tomorrow? Our bond?" I whisper, unable to look into his eyes. My dating life consists of hookups. And now I'm supposed to get *married*?

Kyranis opens his mouth, but then his gaze slides down to my chest, and he sighs. "How about I tell you more as I clean those cuts? It would be a shame for such beautiful skin to scar."

I glance at the few cuts at the front of my polo shirt with a sigh. Me? Beautiful? I'm a strong six in Maine, *if* you're into goths. And yet my toes curl in my boots where he can't see them, because Kyranis is most definitely next-level gorgeous and knows it. But I appreciate the flattery nevertheless.

"I'd like to know more, please." I take a deep breath and wipe away any remaining tears as he leads me to the bathroom.

What I didn't have the time to take in, is the sheer scale of this interior.

It's bigger than my mom's living room, with a massive stained glass window that fills the space with a blueish glow. The green carpet feels soft under my feet, and the tub is a massive spiral seashell tugged by a horse with the hindquarters of a fish. A merhorse? Just like the one in the prince's crest. Polished to perfection, the pale figure is frozen mid-stride, with its mouth wide.

"I have just the thing for those wounds," Kyranis tells me, approaching a black cabinet on dainty legs.

I wonder if I should be taking any drugs from him, but I've already eaten his food. It's not like he wants to poison me.

I take the opportunity to have a better look at him from the back. The leather he's wearing leaves little to the imagination, and I'm not complaining, because he's simply exquisite. Evil, yes, but that doesn't make his wide shoulders any less enticing.

But do I want to *marry* him? That's a step too far.

My polo shirt is ripped to shreds at the back, and I'll have to take it off if he's to apply any cream or magical lotion, so I get it over with and drop the uniform to the floor. The years in boarding school taught me that being self-conscious about nakedness is pointless, but Kyranis is not just any *guy*.

He's an elf, a prince, and the way he held my hand made it clear his intentions don't include a *platonic* wedding.

"Is that what you used for my wrists, years ago?"

Kyranis stills, but then faces me with a small box covered in mother of pearl. "Among other things. Since you're still here, I assume you changed your mind?"

I hug myself, self-conscious of my stiffening nipples. "We don't need to talk about it," I mumble. It's a memory I buried so deep that until tonight I really made myself believe it never happened. "I'd rather know why I'm so important to you. Can't you get any other human's shadow?"

Kyranis shakes his head and settles in a black throne in the corner with the box still in hand. He snaps his fingers, and I stiffen when water starts flowing in the bathtub behind me. "No, it cannot be just any human. The shadows of those drowning in the River of Souls are the most potent, soaked with dread or misery, so very close to death or dying already. It's a dangerous feat to pull a human out of there. Many of those who try end up dying."

I scoot to unlace my boots, but then realize I'm pretty much kneeling in front of his throne. Oh well, it's too late to take that back now, so I glance up as if all of this is perfectly normal.

"But what am I *for*? Why do you need my shadow in the first place?"

"It becomes mine. It's... like a resource I can use for shadowcraft, and it never runs out, for as long as you live. Shadows of humans like you are stronger than ours, because you are the children of the sun yet stood at the precipice of eternal darkness. When you are mine, I will be able to dip my ancestral sword in your shadow to give it sharpness no beast can withstand."

Why does it sound so dirty when he talks about dipping his *sword* in me?

Kyran continues, watching me as if he wants to flay me with his gaze alone. "When you drowned in the River because of your... condition, your shadow was untethered. That's when I was able to bargain with you for it. Most humans don't resist the bond when they are presented with the choice between life and death. It's getting you out of there that is the feat."

I shove my boots aside, trying to understand it all and soak up every word. But when I step on the carpet with my bare feet, I'm instantly distracted. "Is this some kind of... moss?" I ask, pressing on it with my foot.

"Indeed. Do you not like it? I can have it removed," Kyranis tells me, leaning forward until his elbows rest on his knees. As his dark gaze slides down my body, I wonder what he's so keen to see.

The moss is different than the one I know from my world. Softer, spongier, and warm. "No, I like it. But back to what's important." I approach him, because he did promise to put some of that healing cream on me. "You said I'm your crown. So until you take me as your Dark Companion, you're not... king? Or Lord? Or some other royal?"

"No, just the crown prince," he agrees before gesturing at me. "Remove your clothes."

I still, even though on some deeper level I was expecting this. Is it shady as fuck? Yes. Am I getting a little overheated in his presence? Also yes.

I slide my thumbs under my studded belt with a nervous chuckle. "Save something for after the wedding, Your Highness."

Kyranis cocks his head. "I've waited long enough," he tells me as a little smile emerges on his lips.

The room was slowly heating up from the hot water, but now there's more to it. Is it wrong that I'm excited to be the object of such intense interest? This night still feels like a strange dream.

I unbuckle my belt, trying to make it casual, but there's nothing *casual* about the way Kyranis watches me. Maybe he just wants to make sure I have no weapons on me? I've been subjected to a couple of strip searches in my life, and they were the farthest thing from pleasurable, but maybe he could make it fun?

"I mean, I guess I've got a few cuts on my legs too," I mutter, pushing off my pants.

"We should take care of all your injuries," Kyranis tells me, rolling the last word on his tongue, as if he were luxuriating in its sound. As he flicks his hand, the tub behind me stops filling. He pops open the first button of his leather top, then the second.

I want to see those moving tattoos again. It's a thought that overpowers the rational side of my brain, because at the end of the day, he might not be just a guy, but I am. So after a moment of hesitation, I sit on the edge of the bathtub in my boxer briefs and watch him.

At least I don't feel like he hates me anymore.

"If you can wield your shadow so well, why didn't you use it to fight the moths?"

Kyranis chuckles, opening his jacket. "Contrary to what you might believe, I'm not all-powerful. My shadow was busy protecting my own body from the thorns as I was trying to reach you." He rises from the chair, and the leather garments slide off him, I see a pit of snakes trailing over his skin in 2D. There's too many to count when they're constantly moving around, creating a strange animated image on the skin of his torso and arms. I can't take my eyes off one of the creatures as it dips into his pants, but when it disappears and I look up, the smirk on Kyranis's features tells me he's noticed me staring.

I can only hope that in the green light, my face appears a bit less red. He's... unbearably hot.

"What *are* they?" I catch myself reaching out, and quickly pull back my hand.

Maybe I should take off my underwear, so he can follow my example and show off the goo—No, Luke. Think with your *brain*.

"They're eels," Kyranis says as he approaches me in slow, elegant steps. "Each represents a shadow wielder's power. Each one stands for victory," he tells me with pride. "I can use them up if I need to, but they then disappear forever." He tips my chin up with his knuckles. "Unlike your shadow, which will be mine for as long as you live."

I swallow. At least that means it's in his interest to keep me alive. The proximity of his stomach, smooth and hard as if it's made of marble lovingly chiseled by a talented sculptor. The eels give me an excuse to stare. Though I try to not focus on the golden sun in the middle of Kyranis's chest, which even the eels seem to avoid as if it were some cursed mark. The tattoo I'm not supposed to ever mention to anyone... for *reasons*.

While I know I'm lithe like a Siamese cat, which some find attractive, I still feel painfully inadequate, because here he is, *Prince* Kyranis, Protector something-something, and I still live with my mother. A part of me wants to become useful to him. As if that would elevate me.

Dark Companion.

Doesn't it sound almost romantic?

I shake off the intrusive thought, then turn around, sliding my legs into the hot water and showing off my aching back.

I freeze when Kyranis appears right next to me. Did he move by magic? Or is he simply *this* fast?

"You're not yet naked," he tells me, and while I can sense sparks in the air, he doesn't touch me.

I swallow, torn between what I want to do (climb him like a tree) and what I should do (steal the key and run away).

I settle for a middle ground and slide my boxers off then chuck them onto the moss. "There. Since we know nakedness is required for medicinal reasons," I can't help the snark when cornered, but he doesn't seem to mind.

Kyranis pours some water over my chest. The drizzle slides down my stomach and into the water, making the atmosphere oddly intimate, even though we're not touching. A part of me wonders what it is that he wants, but asking him directly might just provoke him, so I stay quiet.

"Strictly medicinal," he says and then picks up a sponge before dipping it into the water, between my spread thighs. Only then it hits me that he followed up on my joke.

Next thing I know, I'm distracted by the feel of the unimaginably soft sponge against my cock. It lingers only for a moment, then slides up, but I still hold my breath. I *cannot* be getting a boner right now.

My sexual partners were either very to the point, or wanted me to make the move. I don't know what to do with this limbo of unresolved tension when I should be hating this fucking elf dude instead of considering pushing my face into his crotch and getting my hands on those hard abs.

But here we are. And as the damp sponge rides up my body, gently cleaning the cuts, I close my eyes and think of the spoiled burger meat I once discovered in a delivery. Because I definitely cannot reveal my cards yet.

"You'd be wise not to trust my relatives. They could also have a claim to the throne in the wrong circumstances," Kyranis says.

This sobers me up a little. Though it could, of course, be an attempt to stop me from seeking further help. And that damn sponge doesn't make thinking any easier. The bastard knows exactly what he's doing.

"But *you're* the prince. How would they have a claim? Surely only if you... weren't there," I mutter instead of 'if they murder you.'

The sponge makes wide swirls all over my chest, making me warm while he talks.

"I will have an undisputed claim to the throne only once we wed and I am crowned as Lord of the Nocturne Court. No one will be able to take that away. But if you die, I will have to find myself a new promised and that takes time and risk. I'm sure you would agree that isn't a pleasant prospect for either of us."

I swallow and nod. My death is definitely an unpleasant prospect.

He's so close it's impossible to not get enveloped by his smell, salt and a hint of leather with something vaguely flowery but so discreet I can't pinpoint it.

I'm glad there's foam on the water now, because when he puts his hands on my shoulders, my dick twitches, and I'd rather he didn't see that. I lean forward to give him better access to my ripped back while getting to hide my crotch at the same time.

Is he a top? He definitely has top energ—

Stop it, Luke. He's the enemy. He holds the key to your freedom.

I glance at the tattoo of an elegant key on my wrist, to remind myself that I didn't fight for my freedom just to get trapped in another prison.

"When you said the shadowy eels marked victory, did you mean that... you killed the other shadow wielders?" I end in a whisper. I want to gauge how afraid I need to be.

"I did. As you can see, I am perfectly capable of protecting you as long as you don't try to go behind my back," Kyranis says as he dries my skin with a towel as soft as goose down.

I'm confused, aroused, and frightened at the same time. No one's ever promised to *protect* me. Let alone someone capable of murder. I'm unable to count how many eels slither over his skin in some eternal dance of the dead, but it's *many*.

"I won't," I lie.

This might be the best bathtub I've ever used, and the fruit soup he fed me was exquisite, *but* he still abducted me.

I can do it. I can run.

I just need to be smarter about it.

Kyranis nods, and as he applies the cream to my wounds, the instant relief makes me shiver. "I hope we understand each other now."

He doesn't understand me at all. I'm not letting anyone entrap me. If I ever decide to date someone, it will be on *my* terms and because I chose to, not because a hot elf prince stole me away in a carriage.

"Thank you for the healing lotion. I'm feeling better already," I say in a docile voice I reserve for my manager when I'm late.

"I'm glad," Kyranis says, letting his hand linger on my chest, so close to my nipple I can feel it throbbing. I try occupying myself with something else, but as my gaze trails down the tattooed torso and descends lower, I'm assaulted by heat as I spot a stiff shape at the front of Kyranis's pants.

Oh fuck.

The outline... sure is something. I have to force myself to look away, but my dick is swelling between my legs like this is a regular Grindr hookup, not an abduction situation.

"Um... I'm really tired now, so..." Pathetic, but it's the best I can do. If anything, I should be applauded for my magnificent restraint, because if this was a bathhouse, or pretty much any other setting, I would be unpacking my surprise gift already.

Not today.

Kyranis can't fully conceal his disappointment, but he doesn't attempt to hide his arousal at all as he rises to his feet, showing me that magnificent bulge in its full glory. "Of course. You need to relax for the big day tomorrow."

I may have drooled a little when he bent over to pick up my clothes like he's my housekeeper, not a prince. Buns of fucking steel in that skintight leather.

Right before walking out, he turns my way and catches me staring. Again. I really need to work on my reflexes.

"If there's no sun... how will I know it's morning?" I ask because it's the first thing that comes to my mind.

Kyranis looks at me with a benign smile, as if I asked him what meat *chicken* nuggets are made from.

"Well, once the moon rises again, of course. Now rest. If you need anything, there's a bell on the wall right next to your bed," Kyranis says as he buttons himself back up, covering the tattoo I'm not allowed to mention to anyone.

"Sweet dreams, my promised," he says, and one wistful glance later, he's gone.

I sink deeper into the water, relieved that I'm not aching anymore, but that's just the tip of the iceberg when it comes to my problems.

Maybe I could fuck him first and only *then* run away? Would that really be so wrong? It could be considered a smart move. A distraction. Not at all a way to have my cake and eat it too.

"Fuck me..." I mumble into the water.

CHAPTER 9
KYRAN

I'm on fire as I wrap myself in the cloak, hiding the evidence of my arousal. He desires me too, I can smell it on him, but the proper thing is to wait until the wedding at least. He has every right to be scared and confused, and I ought to give him time to adjust, but it is so very difficult when for the first time in my life I am free to answer my needs. With the real Kyranis, my twin, gone, I am free to step out of the shadow and take any lover I want. No longer just a tool to strike from the darkness, I can live in the moonlight at last.

And what I want to do is climb into the bathtub with Luke and *take* him. Watch his pretty face twist as he rides my cock. Grab his hips, and legs, and arms so hard he's bruised under all the finery he will be wearing tomorrow. Leave a hickey that just about peeks out from under a high collar. I want—no, I *need* everyone to know he's mine in all ways.

He will wear my family crest.

He will eat my food.

He will live in my palace.

I need to be gentle when the situation calls for it and stern when he tests my patience. A perfect balance for a prince. One my spoiled brother never managed to maintain.

I'm walking out of the caged part of the room, locking my promised behind bars decorated with silver seaweed when someone opens the door as if it's their birthright.

I pull out my sword in an instant and force it to take the shape of a rapier, which will serve me better in close quarters than a massive sword. This might be an ambush, and I need to stand between whoever's coming and my promised.

Tristan stops in his tracks and lifts his hands palms up. "Let's not get too hasty!"

My brother's official bodyguard and all-around menace, Tristan Bloodweed. Another cousin who needed a position in court, so he got the job. A smart move on my father's part, because his title of Knight supersedes his princely origin and bars him from ever becoming a Lord, the only exception being if all the other princes and princesses die, but that's not happening any time soon. I have to reluctantly admit he has *some* skill in waving a sword around, and two eels around his forearms to prove it, but he lacks ambition. Which is a good trait in a royal cousin, but he would have been more useful if there was more than seafoam between his ears.

Like the rest of this branch of the family, his hair is dark red, standing out against his pale face like streaks of blood. He's dressed in a leather vest, and the red cape bearing his family crest is thrown over one shoulder.

He is also wearing a black cap with a wide visor on one side under an embroidered green BBB, the same one Luke had on when I came for him earlier.

"That's not yours," I say.

Tristan makes a face. The man is older than me by almost twenty years, but fools around like a kid. "I found it in the carriage. It's the human's, isn't it? Why didn't you take me with you? Drustan told me you had trouble on the way."

Drustan should have kept his mouth shut.

But I don't say that and offer him a polite smile. "I figured he would be even more nervous if there was two of us, and a couple of thorny vines can hardly be called *trouble*. Nothing I couldn't handle," I say and hand him the torn clothes I need to dispose of. If he's so eager to barge in here, he might as well make himself useful.

Tristan's golden eyes go wide. He might be the size of a bull, but when excited, he exudes the energy of a child. "Ooh! Are these human-made too? Can I take them? My sister will be so jealous."

"They're torn. We should have them burned," I say as his gaze lights up, making me consider what to do next. Tristan might be a fool, but he has his uses, like his physical strength or the unique skill of transforming his shadow into wings.

And he's loyal, I will give him that. My brother would sometimes treat him without any respect whatsoever, and whether it was because Tristan lacks the insight to understand he's being offended or just has an easy-going personality, he never once tried to seize any power, even when my brother wasted his time on pleasures and left the running of the principality to me.

Tristan hums over the dirty heap of fabric. "I'll ask Sabine if she wants them for something. She's having a baby in a month, so maybe she could use the bits that aren't torn... Either way, can I see him?" He steps forward as if I've already agreed.

Which I most certainly won't.

"No. He's resting now. Where were you when we arrived at the gates?" I ask, tightening my hold on the hilt of my sword. I've been watching Tristan from the shadowild since my childhood, and I do trust he doesn't want to harm me or my promised, but I itch to keep the pretty human to myself for a bit longer.

He sighs and clutches the clothes to his chest as his thick red brows form a groove above his large, shapely nose. Only now I notice he has a new piercing. A ring sits in his septum, and I should have taken note, because it's the same spot where Luke's nose is adorned with silver.

"Ah, it's a long story. I was at the Three Dead Mermaids and I met this woman who told me her cow had just given birth to a two-headed calf. You know me, Your Highness, I need to go investigate the unusual. It could be an accident of nature, but it could be a curse. Or some new kind of monstrosity altogether. What if a despair crawled out of the sea unnoticed by guards, and managed to infect this woman's cow? There has been more of them for a while after all.

"So I followed her home, and the calf really does have two heads. I checked the shadows of both animals, and they seem to be perfectly natural. I heard your carriage was approaching and was about to rush back, but then..." He sighs, shaking his head. "The bosom on that woman, Kyranis... And her dress was far too low-cut to be reasonable for working with animals. Let's say I got slightly distracted, she was more than obliging, and we ended up having a tumble in the barn. In a separate stall than the cows, just to be clear. I'm not a monster. I'm not about to take a newborn calf's innocence."

To my disbelief, he's still going.

"Oh, and then she pierced my nose. I like it."

"Are you now part of her cow herd?" I ask without thinking as my brain shrivels from this onslaught of dumb.

Tristan doesn't seem offended and laughs. "As long as she milks me often."

I smile, because Tristan and my twin shared an enthusiasm for milkmaids and other... maids, which is why I can't fully turn my attention to men, or it would be suspicious. But that is a price I'm willing to pay for power and freedom.

And for the boy who I wish to milk *me*. Maybe deep down I am no better than Tristan.

But then I look into the golden eyes, which hide very little thought behind them, and decide that's not the case after all.

"I heard you won't be courting him? That you're to be married tomorrow? Doesn't he deserve—"

"He deserves everything, but this cannot wait. You know the beast might crawl out of the sea any day now? You really think it's reasonable for me to parade my promised around, meet peasants, and have our portrait painted while we wait?"

I don't particularly enjoy company, as I spent most of my life in solitude, watching my brother from the shadowild. Nothing will be stopping me from getting to know Luke better *after* our wedding. Once our deal is sealed.

Tristan groans. "Well, I've been telling you to go pluck him for three years now."

Yes, I've heard those gentle nudges from him, but my hands were tied as the decisions belonged to my brother, and *he* wanted to delay any obligations for as long as possible. Now, it's up to me, and I don't care to wait. Unlike Kyranis, I'm ready to take on the responsibilities that come with my position at the Nocturne Court. The luxuries and privileges we have depend on us doing our duty to the rest of the Realm. Something I won't be shirking from.

And if I get a beautiful human of my own as a reward then… don't mind if I do.

"But I didn't *pluck* him. Nothing that can be done about that now, is there?" I ask, annoyed that the situation demands I explain myself.

Tristan takes a step back with a sour expression. "Tell me at least… You fished him out when he was so young… what's he like now? Is he pretty?" Tristan's eyes widen a little. I know all too well that he doesn't discriminate when it comes to the gender of his many lovers, and while jealousy wraps itself around my chest like a kraken's tentacle, I'm too proud of my companion not to boast about him a little.

The green strands in his fine hair are like seaweed. His long fingers are beautifully breakable, like the rarest corals, and his ears, so small and cute in their roundness, I wish to suck on them for hours. But most of all, he is only mine. My good-for-nothing twin might have been the one to order that I make an arrangement in his stead, but I was the one to pick Luke, the one to take him. He is mine in all the ways that matter.

"He is perfect. You will see."

Tristan bites his lip and shakes his head with a smile, making his long red hair move in sleek waves. If he wasn't holding Luke's clothes, he would probably shove my chest the way he sometimes did with Kyranis. A gesture I never really understood, but then again, I rarely got to interact with others.

"I will. I'll be in the first row at the wedding, and definitely not late. I bet Reiner and a team of seamstresses will be frantically working into the night." He nods at me with his chin, his long, elegant ears making a little twitch as he leaves.

I close the door behind him even though I should go too. But if I leave now, I'd have to walk with him along the corridor, and continue the interaction. It's better to wait it out a little.

Now that I talked about my promised to Tristan, all I can think of are Luke's pretty flushed cheeks and cutely round ears I want to run my thumbs over. Would one more peek at him hurt so much?

"Just for a few heartbeats," I promise myself as shadows whisper, enticing me into their depths. I stand in the corner and touch the wall, opening a small circular passage. The shadowild isn't tamed by the same rules as the material world, so I dip in my face and feel it emerge on the other side. The damp air smells of water and moss, and as my eyes open, I forget that the rest of me is standing in the hallway, separated from the bathroom with several walls.

My body stiffens when I see him from the darkness cast by one of the beams in the ceiling. And my cock reacts immediately.

My body moves on its own accord, face pressed to the translucent barrier reminiscent of silk so thin one can see through it. The flickering green lights make Luke's form appear fuzzy, but the closer I am, the better I can see him from the shadow on the ceiling.

My heart beats so fast it feels like it's about to jump out of my chest, because the vision below me is so erotic my whole body throbs with need.

Luke lies in the water with his eyes half-closed, cheeks flushed and mouth open as if he's already inviting me in. His pale chest turned pink in the middle, one long arm rests above his head, the other reaches between his obscenely spread legs.

He's pleasuring himself with lazy strokes and letting out the most enticing whimpers I want to lick out of his mouth. Strands of wet, green hair stick to his face and shoulders like seaweed, transforming him into a creature of the sea tailored to lead me to my downfall.

The moans are a siren's call, and I can't see the sharp rocks ahead, because I *need* to have him.

CHAPTER 10

LUKE

Kyranis is the most beautiful man I've ever seen. While I know he took me against my will and that his reasons are selfish, I can't help the way my body reacts to his presence. There's raw power in him, and not just in those firm muscles and wide shoulders. His eyes burn with the conviction of someone who knows what they want and how to get it. I've always fallen for the wrong guys, but this might be a new low. And still, as I curl my toes in the tub and work my cock, it's his face I envision above me. My imagination runs wild, reminding me of how his hands felt on my skin, how he led me to the carriage wrapped in his cloak, and as I slide lower into the water, I can feel the ghost of his cock against my hole.

He was *packing* under that leather and got *so* hard for me. As if I was the only guy that interested him in this court filled with beautiful elven royals.

What would he even be like in bed? Just as unyielding and demanding? I wouldn't mind that actually. I like when a guy knows what he wants.

I keep my eyes half open as I stroke my dick in the water without haste, enjoying the imagined touch. Shadows dance over the dark blue ceiling high above, flickering from the lights of the chandelier adorned with fish skeletons. This is the most luxurious place I've ever been in, and if it wasn't for the fact that I'm trapped here, I could imagine an alternative life in which I spend my days traversing the palace at an elven prince's side.

Dark Companion.

Such an odd title, yet it calls to me.

On the ceiling above, the shadows seem to... thicken? But this place is filled with strangeness, so I don't pay it too much attention, instead imagining Kyranis's face.

And then it appears for real, emerging out of a tar-black surface with eyes wide open and filled with lust.

I can't breathe, or think, or do anything at all, so I stare at him, with my cock pulsing rapidly in my fist as his large, elegant hands reach out to me from the ceiling.

"Luke." His voice has a raspy undertone that makes my dick stiffen, so I put my other hand over my crotch, but he's already climbing out of the shadow, closer by the second.

His cloak glides to the floor like a leaf off a tree, and I end up yelping in panic.

"What the fuck are you doing?" I screech, painfully aware that he must have been watching me from that void on the ceiling. He keeps smiling as he slides out of the black spot and then lowers himself on a tentacle of the same color, as if he were an exceptionally handsome spider.

He's right over me, still in the same leather set he wore when I saw him last, but by the time I snap to attention and try to flee the tub, his palm cups my cheek, and he slides into the water, caging me with his limbs.

"I think you need more of my attention."

I swallow, finding it hard to think when I'm naked, he's dressed, and one of his knees rests between my legs. I should be more scared than I am, I should be appalled that he spied on me in the bath, but it's difficult to focus with a raging erection and the man of my dreams so eager to touch me back.

He doesn't even care that his outfit is getting soaked.

"M-maybe..." I mumble against my better judgment. With him being my jailer, this is fuzzy on consent at best, but the touch of his fingers makes up for the creep factor because I'm too horny to care.

I want to see those eels again. I want to touch them. Touch *him* and forget that I never wanted to follow him here in the first place. Maybe this is only a dream, and I'm playing the role of a too-stupid-to-live romance heroine whisked away by the fae prince? What next? Will I get special powers and another competitor for my hand, who appears evil yet has been the good guy all along? Will *he* be blond?

My thoughts come to a rapid halt when Kyranis buries his face in the crook of my neck, smelling it and then tasting my skin. His tongue feels like it's made of fire, and I whimper when he rolls it over my ear before sucking the lobe into his mouth.

My hands drift to his shoulders, because trying to hide how hard I am is pointless. He knows. He was watching.

I smell his hair from up close, and there's more of that vaguely floral scent that is giving me a natural high. My heart beats like mad, and I languidly rub my foot over his leather-clad calf.

He grabs my thigh to pull my knee up and slides his free arm under my back, bringing me closer to his warm body, as if he didn't consider I might resist it.

"You're like the depths of the sea," Kyranis whispers, trailing needy kisses down my cheek. "So much to offer. So much beauty."

My heart skips a beat, surprising even me with just how much I like hearing that. Sure, I've gotten compliments over the years, but they were never this... romantic. A part of me wants to scoff, put up my walls and dismiss his words as empty, if charming, flattery. But the other part of me wants to drink it up and let him *in*.

This could be a trick to make me more compliant tomorrow, yet it's difficult to think logically with my leg wrapped over his hip and my cockhead rubbing against his leathers.

With a gasp, I let one of my hands slide down, and into the opening of his ripped vest. Jesus Christ. He's rock-solid muscle.

"You couldn't help yourself?" I whisper, daring to look into his eyes from up close, and as he cups my face with both hands, his smoky gaze darkens like the sky before a storm.

"I don't want to. Since I first saw you in that ugly hat, I knew I wanted to see you naked and make sure everyone knows you belong to me. Only me," Kyranis whispers, his gaze so intense I feel lightheaded.

And then, his mouth is on mine in an oddly chaste open-mouthed kiss.

I've been avoiding relationships like the plague, never willing to let my guard down, so it's not like I'm losing my mind for Kyranis, the Prince of the Nocturne Court. But whose heart wouldn't beat faster in the face of such declarations? I can imagine him fucking me in a back alley behind BBB, just so all my coworkers know who I belong to.

Toxic? Maybe.

Creepy vibes? Check.

Stalker? Definitely.

And yet I lean into the kiss of his soft lips. I run my fingertips over the smooth golden tattoo and squeeze Kyranis's meaty pec. The strap holding together his ripped vest got lost somewhere, and I'm glad for it, because he is a work of art. As I wrap my other arm around his nape, pulling him closer, I let my tongue dart out in invitation.

As I flick it across his lips, he lets out a soft grunt before lapping at my tongue. His body, which so far had felt so solid, trembles in my arms, and he squeezes me closer, as if he can't bear any space between our bodies.

"You're so perfect," Kyranis mumbles, and as his tongue dives between my lips, I taste the heat of his desire for me.

And I can definitely *feel* it too when he presses his stiff dick against mine through the leather. I can't sense the shadowy eels moving, but I'm sure they're there, each taken from a person he *killed*. I'm so in over my head, yet I kiss him back with eagerness.

I want to hear I'm perfect. No one's ever thought that way about me.

His tongue is shy, but no less eager than mine. I start rocking my hips against him, because there's no room for propriety between us, just the pure need to connect. Kyranis's mouth tastes sweet as he becomes more confident, the tip of his tongue playfully sliding over my palate and sending a shiver to my balls.

Restless as if this were the first time he was allowed to touch another person, he squeezes my flesh too roughly, no doubt leaving red marks on my back, sides, arms, and thighs. There's an urgency to it I've never experienced, and while most of his skin is covered by the fancy leather costume, I love that he can't be bothered to undress, too eager to touch me to waste time on such trivial things.

He gets more confident in his kisses, rolling his hips between my legs while our tongues join in a breathless dance. I have never felt so wanted.

I let my fingers explore the washboard abs and groan in pleasure when they tense under my touch. He drinks the sound right off my lips and makes the most adorable little whimper.

What. The. Hell.

I love it.

It makes me want to touch him all over, as if he were a puppy in need of cuddles. But also, like a man who I really want to fuck me. I can think about the consequences tomorrow.

The water makes me feel weightless, and I close my eyes, floating in this pleasure. I wrap my fingers in his silky hair and discover that some of the strands are already wet. Our moans and the splashing of water are the only sounds in the room.

I can't wait any longer and slide my hand down his perfect abs, cupping that prize of a dick with my hand. It feels even bigger than it looks.

Kyranis cocks his head, kissing my neck as he rubs himself against my hand with a soft moan. But his hands already trail lower, and when they squeeze my ass, I'm the one to arch and whimper, because—holy fuck—this man makes me *burn*.

"I want to be inside you. I want to fill you up with my essence and then feel it heat up your belly."

Weird.

And yet so fucking hot I hook my other leg on his thigh without question.

Straps and buckles still trap his erection, but with the water constantly shifting and caressing my flesh, I lose my patience. "Open it. I need to see you," my voice is raspy with lust, and I've lost all my cool. My cheeks are on fire, my hole throbs with the need to be filled just the way he said. Elves don't have STDs, do they? Probably not.

Kyranis rises to his knees between my spread legs, and any cool he so far displayed is gone. His skin is red like fresh sunburn, eyes glazed over, and as I squeeze my cock, watching him, he attempts to unbutton his fly with trembling fingers.

Right after he succeeds, his leather top flies to the moss carpet with a wet slap.

Do I really have such an effect on him? Little me from Blackwood, Maine, who's been a disposable one-night stand for so many guys?

I can't fucking believe it.

But I love it.

"Show me your hole," Kyranis demands, freeing his erection. It bobs out of the black leathers, long, and straight and with a girth that makes my head spin with excitement. A bead of pre-cum bejewels the tip, and I make myself a promise that I will taste it before the day is over. Or night. I think it's still daytime by elven standards.

But he wants my ass, and he wants it now, so I pull my knees to my chest without question, letting out a little moan when my hard dick rubs against my belly. Holding my legs up with one arm, I shamelessly reach down with my free hand and use it to expose my hole. His tool is so beautiful, so stiff it intimidates me, yet also makes me insanely horny.

The back of my head is submerged in this position, and I risk ending up with my face under the water once things get frisky, but I'm so excited I want to make it work. I already considered him handsome before, but now I see him for what he truly is——a flushed beast covered in scary moving tattoos and eager to satisfy his lust with me.

As he leans over me, pushing me under the surface, his form is a trembling shadow above the water, and while I shiver when his thumb traces my exposed entrance, there's only so long I can survive without coming up for air. He must understand that too and pulls me up by the hand, his eyes burning with frustration.

"Maybe... bed?" he whispers, rubbing my hip as if he can't bear letting go altogether. His beautiful hair now hangs down his torso in damp streaks, and it's as if every minute in his presence makes him more enticing in my eyes.

I glance at his exposed nipples and abs longingly, because I hoped to rub them while he fucks me, but also, no, I don't want to get out of this warm dream, dry myself and move this to another room. I want him *now*.

"No. Here," I beg, but when trying to shift position, I end up sliding lower and my whole face dunks under water. Again.

I hardly know what's happening when his big hands slide under me, pulling me up. I gasp for air when Kyranis turns me around, and my knees hit the smooth bottom of the tub.

I grab the edge of the bath and spread my thighs for him, glancing over my shoulder. When he pulls my buttocks apart, his face is the picture of wonder, but then he captures my gaze and grins like a wolf about to bite into the lamb's throat.

If I still had any defenses left, I've just lost them.

Without ever taking his eyes off me, he grabs a blue vial and scoops out some of the white cream inside before sliding the greased hand up and down his cock.

"You want it too, don't you?"

I nod, unable to avert my gaze, even though I'm getting a neck cramp. "I want you inside me. Your cock is... wow." My cheeks flush ever deeper as I watch the dick twitch between his fingers. It juts out of his leather pants so casually, and I need it in me. I shiver when he places his palm on the small of my back before trailing it up, to rest between my shoulder blades. Moments later, his slick cockhead parts my cheeks, and he bites his lip, staring down at my backside as if he's never seen anything more profound.

No one has ever looked at me like that, but as I suck in air to speak, he presses at my hole.

I might have experience, but he's *big*.

I let out a needy moan, pressing my forehead to the edge of the tub and arch my back as I try to relax. I'm not nervous. Just horny out of my mind. My own dick throbs like mad in the warm water, but I don't want to jerk off yet.

I wiggle my ass against him to give him a taste of what's to come when he prods at my opening a few times. The touch makes my gums pulse with arousal, and his hands going up and down my back remind me what an impressive man he is.

How strong. And decisive. And ruthless.

He is a royal after all.

It's only natural he can take whatever he wants.

Including me.

Or at least that's what I'm telling myself when he squeezes my hips and breaches me with a slow, careful thrust that makes us both moan.

At first, I hold my breath, but moments later, I'm panting as though I'm no longer human but rather an animal guided by base instincts. I even spread my legs to give him better access to my body, and he seizes the opportunity to slide closer, nudging my knees farther apart with his own.

The gesture is so hot I have to bite down on my hand to stifle a moan.

Kyranis's thick tool spreads me slowly, like he belongs there. As if it's his right to own me whether we're married or not. His breaths are shallower now, and he slides his fingers over my spine, making me shiver.

"You grip me so lovingly," Kyranis whispers, teasing my skin with his fingertips until his thick girth pushes past a sensitive place inside, and he's all in. His leathers are pressed against my skin, and as I get used to his presence inside my body, I'm weightless in the warm water scented like the sea.

I'm pretty sure he's the biggest I've ever had, and the lack of prep makes me feel even tighter around him. I'm far from complaining though. I love how he overwhelms me, how I'm turning into a puddle of goo with trembling knees.

All I can do is moan when he slides his hand across my stomach, then to my pec, rubbing the nipple. He's playing me now and knows it.

"Oh fuck... oh fuck..." I whimper, curling my toes.

"Give me a moment," he whispers, petting me as if I'm a scared animal in need of reassurance. His lips descend to the base of my neck, leaving so many kisses I'm losing count as the shaft lodged inside my body keeps being a distraction. "I can't help myself around you. My future Dark Companion. My crown."

He holds his hand over my chest, as if enjoying my heartbeat. I can definitely give him a *moment*, because I need to adjust too. Not even to his size, since that's pretty amazing, but to the unwanted feelings rattling inside me. I try to keep sex detached from my emotions, make it about two bodies getting sweaty, so both parties involved can get their rocks off and carry on with their lives without unnecessary baggage.

He's making it about more, but I'm so overwhelmed it cracks my emotional defenses. I want him to say nice things to me and compliment me between kisses.

I want to feel special.

If I become his Dark Companion, I want there to be no one else for him until I die.

I'm probably not thinking clearly, but it's hard to do that when his thick throbbing cock starts to move ever so slowly, and his thumb flicks my nipple.

"It feels so good. So intense. To fuck a prince." I chuckle between one ragged breath and another.

A fucking *prince*. Unable to control himself around *me*. As if *I'm* the catch.

His groan flips a switch inside me. He lowers himself, pressing his chest to my back, like a beast mounting its mate, and his tongue finds my ear again. I see stars when his dick shifts in my channel, pressing against my prostate. His arms settle around me, holding on as if I were a precious, breakable thing, but as he thrusts back in, I'm reminded that I'm not his pet. He wants to come inside me.

And I get off on getting fucked.

"And as soon as we're married, you'll be fucking a *Lord*," he mutters into my ear, rubbing his teeth over it.

But I don't have the brain capacity to answer when he moves his hips faster. Stars explode behind my eyelids, and I become shameless with my moans, because, fuck it. What do I care who knows or overhears?

I wiggle my ass against him impatiently and even clench a few times to give him the ride of his life too. Now that I've adjusted to his size, I revel in how full I feel, how overpowering it is. He's so big on top of me too. It's very obvious he could crush me yet treats me with so much tenderness. Only his thrusts speak of the power packed in all that muscle, and I moan every time his cock jabs in.

We rock together, with him holding me closer than any man before him, kissing and nipping at me as if he can't deny himself the taste of my skin. As if I was the best lover he ever had. And while he's quite rough in the way he squeezes me, by the time I need to hold on to the edge of the tub as Kyranis pounds my ass at full speed, splashing water everywhere, I want him to go faster, harder, and turn me inside out.

I want to forget reality, my shitty childhood, all the bad boyfriends of the past, and the never-ending grind in hope of one day earning enough to turn my life around.

In Kyranis's arms, all those things seem so distant they might as well be fake.

Each thrust makes me lose my mind a little, and as I feel him tremble against me, I brace myself, ready for his cum.

I've only ever gone bare a few times, back in my teens when I was young and dumb. I feel no hesitation about letting him breed me though. I should. I should probably hate him and spit in his face for spying on me, but there's no point in lying about just how hot I find him.

"Right there!" I whimper when he hits the right spot again and again, making me clench the rim of the bathtub. I might come before him if he keeps pounding into me like a machine made for satisfying hungry bottoms.

Water splashes out of the tub, but I guess that's what the moss is there to soak up so I don't care.

Kyranis's raspy panting teases my ear as he whispers, "You're all mine now. My precious Companion. Your tight hole, your pretty pink lips..." He slides his hand to my chin and slips his thumb between my lip and gums, leaving me breathless. "Who do you belong to?" He rasps, pushing into me with a hard thrust.

"P-prince Kyranis," I mumble around his fingers, losing touch with reality altogether.

He stiffens, briefly going out of rhythm, and for a moment I worry I've said something wrong, but then he presses a hard kiss to my neck and rasps, "Kyran. Call me Kyran. Say my name."

When he slides his other hand to my cock, all he needs to do is squeeze it and I go wild. I rut into his fist, impaling myself on his dick in the process, and I come so hard I might not know my name anymore, but I do know his.

"Kyran! Prince Kyran. Lord Kyran," I cry out, shattered with the spasms that make me clench my ass harder around his thick tool.

"Yess!" He sounds like a venomous snake, and moments later, as he braces himself against me, I sense him pulse inside.

Oh fuck, he's coming. He's coming inside me. And it's so perfect I can't even put it into words.

Trembling softly, he rests his face on my shoulder, then kisses it, and finally leans back, as if to sit on his heels. But when I expect him to slide out in the process, he instead grabs my hips and pulls me with him, until I'm sitting on his still-hard cock, my head on his shoulder as we both rest.

I'm way beyond fighting him. At least for a few more hours. At least until I can think straight again.

"That… I…" I close my eyes to gather my thoughts as he holds me instead of getting ready to leave like most of my lovers. "That might have been the best fuck of my life," I utter, weightless in his arms. My legs are spread without shame over his thighs, and I'm still catching my breath, not caring that the buttons and straps of his outfit dig into my ass.

"Really?" Kyranis—Kyran—asks before catching himself with a grunt of annoyance. "I mean… I loved it too. You feel so… so warm," he says, hugging me while we kneel in the water.

For once, my cynical mask slips, and I smile, sliding my hand over his. My heart is still racing from the mind-bending orgasm. "You shouldn't have been spying on me…" I mumble, so sleepy I have to fight my own eyelids to keep them open.

His laugh is raspy and so pleasant I could fall asleep to its sound. "You don't mean it," he says and lifts me until his softening shaft slips out of me.

My knees are marshmallows, and I'm ready to complain about having to stand up, but he holds me in his arms as if my weight is no issue for him. Kyran manages to step out of the bath while holding me without effort. I want to curl up against him and fall asleep. Is that needy? I'm so tired. He fucked my brains out, and all I want is a bit of comfort.

My eyes fly open when his finger slides between my ass cheeks. I should complain about him doing whatever he wants, but that would have been pointless. I let out a little moan, meeting his gaze as he teases a fingertip inside me.

Tomorrow, I'll have more of a backbone.

"Will I see you before the wedding?" I ask, because I don't want him to know that I plan to look for ways to sneak out.

The smoky shade of Kyran's eyes is somehow warmer now that we fucked, and as he carries me out of the bathroom and toward my bed, he offers me a wide, if tired, smile. "Oh, I will not leave you out of my sight until then."

With that, he rolls me onto the mattress, giving me a good view of the black eels moving all across his skin. They slide over his *GQ* abs, all the way down to the V-shaped muscles at his hips. If I were a shadow eel, I'd be slithering over there too.

He is an absolute *vision*. Asked to draw my perfect man, I'd draw him. And he knows it. The little smirk makes it obvious. I slide under the silky black sheet, watching him peel the wet pants down his hips.

He will be sleeping here.

Even if it's just because he needs to make sure I stay put, he's staying. This absolute elven hunk with beautiful long hair, the physique of an athlete, and the keen eyes of a predator will spend the night with me.

"You're beautiful," I give credit where it's due, as Kyran reveals his muscled thighs and sits on the edge of the bed, struggling to get the wet leather off. In the end, he lets it plop to the floor and utters a sigh of relief.

"So are you, my precious human. From now on, I shall take good care of you," he whispers and climbs onto the bed to join me under the covers. I should be scared, but I'm pumped out and full of cum. There's no energy left in me to worry.

Deep down, I do want that. For someone to take care of me. To shoulder half the weight of the world. When he slides his arms around me, and his thigh parts my legs, I can feel his strength. He'd probably be able to shoulder much more than half my troubles. I like the way he takes charge even though my brain knows I'm headed for disaster.

I close my eyes, without a single intrusive thought, thinking solely about his strong heartbeat against my back.

"Goodnight, my prince," I whisper.

Tomorrow.

I'll worry tomorrow.

CHAPTER 11

KYRAN

I'm exhausted, yet energy buzzes through me as if it's seeking a way out. I've barely slept, taken by the beautiful man resting next to me. The night was nothing short of transcendental, and while exhaustion would settle in every time we climaxed, I was too greedy to stop touching, kissing, stroking my future Companion.

I watched my brother have sex so many times, yet it did not compare to sharing this with another person. Luke was warm, and each time he invited me inside him, my senses erupted with sparks. For him, I wasn't a monstrous impostor but the man he desired. He saw more of me than anyone else ever, maybe with the exception of my long-gone mother.

I open my eyes, and in the first glow of the moonlight, see his angular face on the pillow. One of his cheeks is squashed, he's drooling a little, off to the dreamland only humans can enter, and he's so cute I just want to pinch his small nose and then trace the dark lines of the bat tattoo on his throat.

Despite the arguments we've had, despite the new position he's in, he still opened his legs and called me beautiful. That has to count for something. Everything else will fall into place with time. In a few hours, our shadows will be bound as tightly as a spidermoth in its cocoon, and no one will dare undermine my position at court.

But that will come later. For now, I kiss his naked shoulder and slide my hand over his hip, indulging in his closeness. Even now, when I rub my thigh between his legs, I sense he's half-hard already. Looks like he can't get enough of me either.

"My darling... are you up?" I ask with a smirk and roll him to his back as his eyes flicker behind lowered lashes. I roll on top of him, cradling his narrow face with my hands, and move the tip of my nose across his cheek. I love to feel the proof of his excitement pressing into my stomach.

He blinks, then his green eyes open wider. "Oh. Y-yeah. I'm waking up. Did I..." He glances at the window beyond the silver bars. "Sleep through the day? No. No sun, right? I guess I already got my vitamin D."

I don't understand the joke, but he chuckles, so I smile back anyway. My knee trails up the bed until it presses against his balls, and I lick the salt off his cheek. I'm baffled by the way his stubble feels on my tongue, but it's a good, ticklish sensation that soon makes me grin.

"I'll give you everything."

"But freedom?" he asks yet runs his fingers up my arms.

I still as dark clouds dim the fire inside me, but I remind myself that his reaction is understandable. As someone who's spent all his life in hiding, my individuality and personhood taken away, I ought to understand what Luke is afraid of. But I would never want him to hate me, so I press a kiss to his sweet lips and ask, "What kind of freedom do you want?"

Yesterday, he tried to attack me. Today, despite these silly grievances, he's docile as a bird drunk on fermented berries. Maybe he needed my body as much as I needed his.

"I want out of this pact. I want to go home," he whispers, yet instead of looking into my eyes as he pleads, he's focused on my chest, his fingertips following an eel off my bicep and down my collarbone.

Anger flares up within me, and he takes his hand away as the fish twist faster, reacting to my mood. I take a deep breath and grab his chin, making him face me. "Why? What's so special about your home?"

A family, friends, things you never had, so you can't understand, my self-loathing mind suggests, making me jealous of every single person in his life even though Luke hasn't mentioned a single soul. They have no claim on him, and I do.

Luke swallows, drawing my attention to his cute Adam's apple. "I just... I want to decide things for myself," he mutters with a little pout, which chokes some of my anger.

"I don't plan to keep you in a cage. When we're married, you will have your own security. You will have access to the whole palace, and I will make sure your every whim is fulfilled. It is an honor to spoil my Dark Companion."

Luke cocks his head. "Every whim? What if I want to sleep until…" He hesitates, glancing at the rising moon. "Midday, then eat cakes for breakfast, then read for the rest of the day without getting dressed?"

I chuckle and knead his small, warm ear with my fingers. "As long as we don't have any official engagements that day, you will be free to do that. So you like to read?"

He seems caught off guard by my question but never stops petting me. I'm already addicted to his touch and wish the wedding was over with so that I can spend another night putting my mark on him. *And* inside him.

"I do. Especially fantastical stories and horror," he says as he traces the golden symbol over my heart. "So this… I'm not supposed to tell anyone about it, I know, but what *is it*?"

I stall as shame burns the back of my throat, threatening to choke me. He doesn't know what the sun means, because he isn't from this realm, but if I tell him the truth, whatever sympathy he feels for me will fizzle out.

I pull away, placing my hand on the symbol, as it's making me feel stripped bare. "It's very complicated."

He sighs, and no matter how ridiculous that is, I'm upset over disappointing him, because I meant everything I said. I want to spoil him, I want to shower him with gifts and affection, I want to leave him a moaning mess. But this answer, I cannot give him yet. It's not safe for me.

"I'm not stupid, you know," he complains, but before I get to reassure him, there's a single knock on the door before someone strides in, heeled shoes clicking on the marble floor.

"Good mornin—" Behind the bars that keep us both safe from intruders, Reiner stops talking as I glare his way. But then Luke pulls me close with more force than I expect from him and twists us so my back is turned on my house master.

I want to chuckle at his modesty, but when he splays his palm over the golden sun on my chest I realize he's… shielding me. Despite my refusal to tell him the truth, he's chosen to protect me.

My heartbeat speeds up, and I kiss the top of his head, charmed by his kindness.

I scowl and look up at my servant. "You shouldn't stride in before you're invited."

Reiner purses his mouth, standing straight as he watches us through the bars. "Forgive me, Your Highness, I had no reason to expect you here."

Damn it. Of course.

It's in bad tone for me and my Dark Companion to spend a night together before the wedding, so I use my shadow to let Reiner in and meet his gaze once he comes a bit closer. "You did not see me here."

"No, Sire," he says and makes a little bow.

Reiner continues as he hauls a large wheeled chest to the bed. "The wedding day is upon us, and I wanted to personally make sure your promised is ready. I brought him a set of day clothes, and I will take it upon myself to make sure he is comfortable in his wedding ensemble."

I glance at Luke. "Make sure to tell him if you don't like something. There's still time to make adjustments," I say before Reiner manages to hide his sour expression. "Step outside. I will call you when we're ready."

"As you wish, Your Highness," he says and does as told, even though I know he's not happy about it. I can't get enough of my new position where it's me who gives the orders. I am finally where I belong.

I watched Reiner as I grew up in the shadows, and while he's been loyal to the Nightweeds for over two hundred years, he is a stickler for rules and routines. He plans meticulously and hates surprises.

But I can't fault him. He has been an amazing attendant to my slothful brother, and will make sure Luke is immaculate for the wedding as well as advise him on our customs at court.

Luke falls back with a deep sigh, offering me a good view of his pretty pink nipples. "Are we fucked? Was this, like… illegal?"

I chuckle, curling my hand around the one he used to shield me. "No. It's just… embarrassing, but don't worry, I'll keep our reputation pristine. Thank you for helping me, my promised," I say, kissing his knuckles while our eyes lock.

His pupils widen, his moonlight skin flushes pink, but he doesn't look away. He must feel our connection too. "I… I need to pee," he mumbles, sliding his hand out of mine.

When he gets up, I take my time assessing the little bruises and love bites I left all over him with such pleasure yesterday. He's like a cake I've taken a bite out of so everyone knows it's mine. But no one will know, because this is our secret.

I slide my legs off the bed and grab his hips, leaning in so I can kiss the wonderful curve of his spine, just above the round buttocks I'm now obsessed with. "This was the best of nights," I whisper, because I want him to feel appreciated.

He looks back at me with shyness in his eyes, even though he was very vocal about all his carnal needs last night. "I... I had fun," he says and slips out of my grasp to go to the bathroom.

I follow him and wash away the evidence of our coupling. Reiner is waiting outside, but I take my time to steal more of Luke's kisses. He is like putty in my hands, and he might not know it yet, but he *will* be a very happy Dark Companion. He just needs to give himself over to me instead of putting up walls.

And he will, because I adore him already.

By the time my manservant enters the room, I'm partially dressed and settle in an armchair in the corner while Luke stands in the middle of the room with a sheet wrapped around his hips for modesty. Little bruises and love bites are scattered over his pale skin, as if he was my very own canvas, but Reiner knows better than to acknowledge their presence as he opens the chest and pulls out a silky coat in midnight blue.

I love that Luke glances to me for guidance, silently asking if he should take the sheet off. Only once I nod at him does he let it fall to the floor. Reiner will probably be one of the very few elves who ever gets to see my Luke naked. Maybe the only one, if I get my way.

"So I'm getting new clothes?" Luke asks, eyeing the black shirt Reiner offers him.

"Yes. I have talked to Sir Tristan about your former attire, and we were forced to dispose of it."

Luke's eyes fill with disappointment. "Oh, but... I had this pin on my pants. With a lobster."

"You will have a hundred new pins."

I expect pushback about the trinket, but Luke shrugs. "Okay, I guess. I hated the uniform anyway."

Ah, so his life isn't all full moons and clear skies after all!

It should not make me happy, but if I can offer him more, he is likely to stop fighting the inevitable. Years ago, we made an arrangement, and we belong together like a man and his shadow. I will not let him leave, and not just because I need him to become Lord of the Nocturne Court.

I like him.

I claimed him.

And I *will* have him.

"What clothes do you not hate?" I ask as he puts on the shirt made of fabric so delicate his nipples peek through.

He's hesitant, but already glancing inside the chest. I'm glad to see him so curious. It bodes well for our future.

"I rarely get the chance to dress up, but I like to." Luke runs his fingers over the smooth fabric of the shirt with a little smile, and I already know I will lavish him with the finest wardrobe. "It's like armor against the world. A good outfit."

Reiner gives him an appreciative smile. "These will go underneath the breeches," he instructs, handing Luke a delicate pair of black stockings, which I'll be endlessly jealous of all day, until I get to remove the fine fabric on our wedding night.

"This is going to be interesting," I say, reaching for a decanter of morning wine, which would normally awaken my senses if they weren't already buzzing. Last night, I feasted on Luke for hours, but while there's a degree of satisfaction, I don't yet feel sated. In fact, I wonder if I ever get enough of a man as beautiful and charming as Luke.

Even his name is so very precious on my tongue. Smooth, delicate yet not porcelain-fragile, I want to keep saying it out loud.

Reiner clears his throat. "Your Highness, I'm sure you have other engagements on a morning this import—"

I wave my hand at him and smell the stimulating spice in the wine. "Oh no, I want to supervise every step."

Luke steals a glance my way, biting back a smile, his face flushed as he pulls the stockings up his legs, covering all that milky skin with a sheer black layer. I already want to take him to the capital, to the best dressmakers, and let him pick whatever he desires.

I definitely *desire* him in those stockings. Next up are the breeches, and, seeing Luke's enthusiasm, Reiner shares more about the outfit. "These breeches are made of a black shark's skin. The leather has to be treated in the caves under the castle. They lead all the way to the beach. When the bitter winds bring salt from the sea, it softens the hides so that they can be worked on. The only trouble is that sometimes opportunistic bats are attracted to the smell. But they can be reasoned with as long as they are given the shark's belly fat."

"You don't kill them?"

"It would be no use. More always come. It's better to make peace with some monsters." Reiner shakes his head and when he starts buttoning up the breeches at Luke's side from hip to his waist, I'm itching to growl at him like some primal beast. It's unreasonable. Reiner is just a servant doing his job.

Luke's attention strays to me again, giving me some peace of mind. "I really like bats."

"Oh. Why?" I ask, sipping the tart wine as I imagine myself standing between his thighs and squeezing those long, pretty legs, pulling down the stockings... He is such a prize. I couldn't have chosen better.

My brother asked me for a girl, since he always preferred them to boys, but, perhaps out of spite, when the time came for me to save a human from the River of Souls, I couldn't resist the pull of Luke's slender yet long and distinctly male hand.

I have no regrets.

"They're misunderstood animals. In my world, people can be superstitious about them, or fear them, or call them flying rats when really, they serve their place in nature. They eat lots of insects, pollinate plants, and... I guess I also just think it's cute how ugly some of them are. I've always been drawn to a dark kind of beauty."

As he says that, his eyes linger on me before Reiner turns him around to fasten the ties at the back of the breeches, cinching Luke's slender waist so that the outfit fits him like a glove.

And while I'm not sure about being compared to an ugly bat, that glance, somehow both shy and lusty, makes me smile.

"You will feel right at home at the Nocturne Court then," Reiner says, holding out a bejeweled vambrace for Luke's forearm.

"How so?" Luke asks, marveling at the pearls and sapphires. "Why is this place all darkness, skulls, and lace?"

The invigorating drink is already taking away the fatigue of staying up all night, and I shift in the armchair for more comfort as I meet Luke's gaze. "We elves in this part of the Realm know life is fragile. And nowhere is that truer than on the shores of the Sea of Sorrows," I say, starting to recite the words I've heard many times. "A vile beast lives in its waters, and for thousands of years it has consumed many lives until Larkin Nightweed, my ancestor, took the first Dark Companion, and together they fought the monster off.

"But while the lords of the Nocturne Court have since been successful at keeping Heartbreak from ravaging our lands, we need to always remain vigilant and remember that life can be cut short at any time. We dress in black and ornament our homes and even ourselves with symbols of death and decay, so we always remember the sacrifices made. Always remember that death might be around the corner and that it's better to accustom yourself with it than fear it."

Luke watches me with shining eyes, soaking up my every word. After years of barely speaking to anyone, it's exhilarating to be *seen*.

"Memento mori," he whispers and goes on when I cock my head in question. "It means remember that you will die. It's morbid, but also a reminder to live to your fullest, because you never know when death will come."

My heart skips a beat, and I lean forward in the chair, swirling the wine in my crystal glass. "That's so beautiful. Did you come up with it yourself?" I ask as Reiner picks out a silver necklace with numerous sword-shaped pendants and locks it on my Companion's neck. The many intertwined chains create a pretty lattice on Luke's chest, and I already can't wait to see them again as I undress him after our wedding.

"Yes," he says but I know he's lying by the way he smirks at me. "Is this beast, Heartbreak, just a legend? A metaphor?"

"Oh no, it's very real," Reiner says as he fastens the chains behind Luke's back. "Legend says Heartbreak used to be an elf who transformed into a monster through the grief of losing his child, but it's been so long nobody can tell how true that story is."

"You might have felt the walls shaking. That's a sign that Heartbreak will soon come to our shores," I add.

Luke's eyes widen. "What? Did you just say I'm supposed to fight some beast with you?" He points to himself. "Do I look like I can take on more than a cat in combat?"

Reiner shushes him as if Luke were a kitten. "It's just a metaphor. You won't be the one doing the actual fighting. But by letting His Highness use your shadow, you will contribute to pushing the monster back."

"That's how the Nightweeds became the protectors of the Realm," I add, finishing my wine. "This place used to be a penal colony. The prisoners were sacrificed to Heartbreak, to appease the beast. My ancestor was banished here and tasked with the position of warden, but fate had so much more in store for him. For our whole bloodline.

"On one of his walks, Larkin saw a beautiful human woman drowning in the River of Souls. He couldn't bring himself to let her die and risked his life to pull her out of the waters. Her shadow was magnificent. Fueled by the sun, it was more powerful than any Larkin had ever seen. When Heartbreak came, he used his Companion's shadow to pierce dozens of the beast's many hearts, and no lives were lost that time. He used the very same sword I now carry, the Gloomdancer. A millennium has passed, and the Lords of the Nocturne Court have been defending their people and the Realm from the monster. And now, I shall take my rightful place with you at my side," I finish, offering Luke a smile, because I'm so proud to have him here.

A part of me regrets that we won't get to court properly, but what could possibly stop me from introducing him to my people and showing him around once we're already bound? I bedded him before the wedding too, so tradition be damned.

Nothing is yet lost.

Luke smiles back shyly. If Reiner wasn't here, busy adorning Luke's fingers with more rings, I would gladly take him to bed again. I never knew just how much I needed someone of my own, but now that he's here, I'm angry I've waited so long.

"Is it dangerous when Heartbreak comes?" he asks, but a knock on the door interrupts us.

I exhale but pin my gaze to the entrance and invite in the pesky visitor. When Tristan strides in, still wearing Luke's ugly old cap, I open my mouth to dismiss him, but he speaks up before I can get a word in.

"I'm sorry, cousin, but you are needed. It's an urgent matter."

"What can be more important than the wellbeing of my promised on the day of our wedding?" I ask, souring, but Tristan steps closer.

"I must insist. There's been a sighting of despairs close to the shore. But there's also the matter of the Goldweeds—"

Which worries me way more than yet another sign of Heartbreak approaching our shores soon.

The main branch of my family, the one that so far has always held the title of the Lord, is called Nightweeds. The one Tristan belongs to are the Bloodweeds and then there's the bane of my existence, the Goldweeds.

They're all part of the royal family, and they support the fight against Heartbreak, but as long as I'm alive, they have no right to the throne.

Unless, of course, one of them finds out I'm not the prince but his secret twin. If that happens before I wed my Dark Companion, each of my cousins, princes and princesses could have a claim to the title of Lord or Lordess.

Hence, no time for courting when the balance of power hangs by a thread.

The Goldweeds have been meddlesome for as long as I can remember, always trying to influence my late father, always trying to outshine Kyranis in front of his people.

And now, even on my wedding day, Tristan brings me news I don't want to hear.

"What are they complaining about this time? The seating plan at the celebration?" I snap in frustration.

"Sylvan requests for you to be present during the testing of sea salt," Tristan shakes his head, but his gaze trails over my shoulder, to Luke. Suddenly, I want to scratch Tristan's golden eyes out, even though he is only doing his duty.

Maybe I should choke all the Goldweeds with my shadow instead and make it look like a despair attack? Heartbreak's spawn aren't that much of a challenge on their own, but being surprised by a herd can have deadly consequences. While my cousins are all gifted shadow wielders, their deaths wouldn't be out of the realm of possibility. I could deal with the gossip once I ascend my throne. Then again, their parents could always have more children—

"I'll take care of everything, Your Highness," Reiner says, as if he really thinks he's being helpful.

"My hat," Luke says, pointing Tristan's way.

Tristan's smile widens, and the kohl lining his eyes can't dim their glow. "May I keep it?"

"You don't need to give him anything," I say, because the last thing I want is to part my promised from his precious possessions. Even those as ugly as this hat.

Luke shakes his head. "You can keep it."

"Pretty *and* generous," Tristan says, and I can't push him out into the corridor fast enough. If he were any other knight, he'd be getting a slap, but as my cousin, he does have more privileges.

"His boots are clean. You don't need to lick them so early in the morning," I say, then face Luke, who watches me with the same soulful eyes that glazed over so many times last night.

Tristan has no idea just how pretty my promised can be in the throes of passion, and he will never know, because that will be for my eyes only.

"Will you be away for long?" Luke asks.

He's missing me already, be still my heart!

I step close and take both his hands to my lips to kiss each knuckle. "I will be back as soon as I can, my darling," I say, meeting his eyes, and while this is the thing to say on the day of our wedding, my words come straight from the heart. Moments later, as I'm about to step away like the gallant prince I'm supposed to be, I press my mouth to his lips for a second of absolute bliss.

I can already hear the wedding fanfare.

CHAPTER 12

LUKE

I thought the outfit I got in the morning was an elaborate gothic dream.

What I'm dressed in for my wedding (something I still can't fathom is happening) exceeds all expectations I may have had. It consists of fabrics that don't exist in my world, and a team of elves needed two hours to put it all on me as I played the role of their docile puppet.

I'm wearing at least fifty shades of gray (pun unintended). If I were to encapsulate what the designer was going for, I'd say, he attempted to transform me into a sexy moth who has more money than sense, and a flair for the dramatic.

Which actually captures my personality quite well if I consider my future husband's riches mine.

A long cape drags behind me as I walk, attached to both my nape and wrists, and embroidered with shimmering thread to resemble a moth's wings. My new breeches are like second skin, and over the flamboyant black lace shirt, I'm wearing something between jewelry and armor. The silver chest piece resembles a ribcage, it's decorated with pearls in several shades, and makes me feel like a minor god of death. If that wasn't elaborate enough, I've donned a matching tiara of silver seaweed.

My ears were not spared and are now both pierced and adorned with elongated black crystals. The servant responsible for the jewelry tut-tutted for the longest time over my nose ring but let me keep it in the end.

If the outfit itself wasn't insanity straight from a deranged haute couture catwalk, when I catch a glimpse of myself in the mirror, I don't even recognize my face.

The eyedrops they put in my eyes make my whites appear black, and the paint on my cheekbones swirls up and down, decorated with matte crystals. I wouldn't be out of place at a KISS concert.

Or at an Alexander McQueen show.

But while I'm stunned by the quality of clothes and accessories that would have made quite the wave if I posted myself wearing them on social media, my thoughts keep wandering to Kyran.

Obligations kept him away from me for most of the day but, as promised, he joined me around midday, so we could share a meal. He loved the term brunch and told me it was very clever. We spoke about my world a little, and he suggested we might go visit it once in a while, but our time together was over too soon, and I was once again stuck with Reiner, who alternates between complaining about stuff and complimenting both me and Kyran on the most random things.

At some point, he told me I would make a very pretty insect, and I'm still not sure whether it was praise or a dig at me.

"So, do you not have electricity because it wasn't invented, or because it doesn't work here?" I ask, wondering if there is the slightest chance of setting up Wi-Fi here in the future.

Reiner blinks at me, pulled out of thoughts that made him frown. "I'm not sure I follow. I've never been to the human world, so I wouldn't know."

He's leading me down a wide corridor and the heels of my new boots click against the marble floors with elaborate patterns of bones. Maybe it's not marble? I'm not sure, but I'm too busy stealing another glance at myself when we pass a mirror.

"There will be time for vanity in the coming months when your portrait is painted, Master Luke," Reiner says with the sternness of a Victorian governess, even though he's wearing breeches meant to accentuate his ass and thighs.

I look away, but at least my flush won't show under the pale makeup.

"What time is the wedding? Is there anything else we should do before that? And the reception? Will I be expected to dance? I can only do the tree dance, just saying," I say and laugh awkwardly when I imagine elven royalty watching me flap my arms about as I close my eyes and let the music lead me. But what works well in a dingy, dark nightclub on goth night might prove embarrassing in the light of the bright green lanterns.

Reiner spins on his heel and raises his hands in an exasperated gesture. "I wish! It's the custom to hold a ball before the wedding, but His Highness has rushed everything. We barely have an hour left. It's not making him any more popular," he says with a twist of his lips. "Maybe you can talk some sense into him. I think if the servants did their best, we could plan for the next full moon. It's going to be a blood moon too, so it's anyone's guess why our prince can't wait those few weeks."

He then turns away and mumbles something sounding suspiciously like 'it's not like he waited with *other* things'.

"You overestimate my influence," I say with a deep sigh as we walk into an even wider corridor.

On one side, the glow of the giant full moon floods in through floor to ceiling windows, illuminating a long wall of portraits.

Reiner smirks, gesturing at one of the paintings, which pictures a beautiful elven woman with a cascade of gray locks. Her long-clawed hands rest on the shoulders of a handsome man who's just as human as I. "No, it is you who is underestimating the power you can have. Many years ago, His Highness's great-great-grandmother had been too lenient with the peasants, and it was creating dissent at court. It was her Dark Companion, Anton, who told her about the way such things are handled where he was from, and the peasants have been bound to the land throughout her reign. A much more convenient solution than what we're dealing with now," Reiner adds with a satisfied smile.

I give him a bewildered glance. I can only imagine how that looked if the human in question was born three hundred years ago, or so. I choose not to open that can of worms and point out the next portrait, since it seems we have an hour to kill. I need a distraction from the itch under my vambrace.

"Do all the pictures here depict the rulers with their Dark Companions?"

I glance in amazement at the variety of paintings and wonder if it's possible that one day my portrait with Kyranis will be on this wall. Am I really about to leave behind all I know, vanish from my world and bind myself to a man I've known for a day?

I note that most of the couples are straight, but it seems that Kyran and I will be far from the first gays on the Nocturne Throne, which is rather reassuring. I can't say my town is the worst when it comes to homophobia, but there've been many situations when I've felt aggressively othered, and, well, I did get beaten up twice. In any case, it's comforting, even if surprising, to find out that this fantasy world doesn't share mores with medieval Europe.

I just never thought something like this could become my reality.

Reiner straightens. "All those who ascended to the throne after the Night of the Bloodknife."

I pause and raise my eyebrows. Okay. Looks like I'm up for yet more stories about murder.

"Lord Larkin Nightweed and his Companion are missing from this hallway," Reiner explains. "Sadly, the first Lord of the Nocturne Court has a troubled legacy. He ruled for almost five hundred years, creating a restless brood of children and grandchildren. After his Dark Companion died, he refused to take a new one for years, blocking everyone else from obtaining one, as per the laws he himself put in place.

"The Nightweed family, already splintered also into three bloodlines, and tensions eventually reached a boiling point, culminating in the Night of the Bloodknife. After killing the Lord, the royals turned on each other, and countless elves from noble families died. Those left decided on a trial, fighting a leviathan, to decide which royal line should ascend the throne. Princess Célestine Nightweed won.," he points out an elven woman dressed in black with long dark hair, which reminds me of Kyran's, "and the rest is history. It was also decided that no Lord or Lordess would rule for more than a century, which eased the tensions somewhat, but the Night of the Bloodknife is still remembered in these corridors as a time of absolute madness. My grandmother told me they were finding blood stains all over the palace for *weeks*."

I listen with my eyes wide. "Did Dark Companions die too?" The last thing I want is to get murdered just because I'm attached to the wrong royal.

Reiner sighs. "Well, Dark Companions are a precious commodity after the death of the elf they are attached to, but some were slain, yes. The match with a Dark Companion doesn't always result in strong romantic feelings, or even desire, though that is, of course, the perfect situation. That is the reason some Lords and Lordesses take additional wives or husbands. I'm happy the two of you don't seem to have such issues, even if you bent the rules to test your compatibility."

I soak it all in, desperate to know more about the union I'm about to enter. It doesn't sit right with me that Kyranis might take a wife while I remain his Companion, and my heart sinks a little.

"So it's mostly about my shadow being of use to him?" I ask, even though he showed me so much passion last night.

Reiner turns to me. "Oh dear. Please, do not make that face. It's unbecoming. His Highness is clearly smitten. In fact, I've never seen him this attentive to anyone, so I don't think this is something you should be concerned with."

When we hear the click of heels, Reiner gasps and steps in front of me as if he were a bodyguard, not the house master.

"Whoever you are, turn around this instant! The prince's promised cannot be seen before the ceremony!"

But two women turn the corner and reveal themselves anyway. Their elaborate dresses are a matching sapphire blue and their beautiful locks, golden.

"That is simply superstition, Reiner," Elodie says, approaching in a rush. "We have important matters to discuss."

Reiner's chest pushes forward, as if he were a peacock about to unfold his tail. "What could you possibly have to discuss with His Highness's promised? You should join the rest of the court and enjoy the refreshments."

"Is that him?" the other woman asks, tugging on her companion's puffy sleeve. "I am so honored," she adds, bowing in front of me. "Princess Vinia Goldweed."

Her features are very similar to Elodie's even though she's shorter and her eyes bigger.

"Luke. Luke Moor," I say, stepping out from behind an exasperated Reiner.

Vinia covers her mouth as she gasps. "Oh, you look so glorious! The perfect Companion."

Elodie turns to Reiner as I bite back a smile. "My matter is not with him, Reiner. Apparently, no one but you knows where the key to the Ancestral Sanctuary is kept. You must help us find it and time is of the essence. I brought Vinia with me, as I'm sure you wouldn't like to leave Luke unattended."

Reiner sucks in air, and his handsome face flushes. "His Highness told me to never leave him out of my sight, and, *as you know*, I can't have him seen. This is an impossible request," he says as Elodie pulls him away by the arm.

"Well, my cousin won't be happy if he's forced to desert his current duties so *he* can unlock the Sanctuary either. I wouldn't have bothered you if that wasn't of essence!"

I shrug to reassure him. "I will be fine."

Reiner frowns at me. "Do *not* leave this corridor."

I roll my eyes and nod. Like I'd know where to go anyway. I can only hope *this* isn't about to turn into a *Day* of the Bloodknife.

"I am so happy to finally meet you," Vinia tells me in a voice like candy in audible form. "My cousin, Prince Kyranis, rushed this wedding, and I didn't make it to the court in time for a first look at you yesterday," she says, eyeing the two elves walking away from us. But once we both hear the *click* of a door, her expression gets more serious. "My sister told me about the message you tried passing her."

I stiffen, instantly nervous. "It's... I was panicking. I think I understand my position better now."

She seems hesitant but leads me to a portrait farther down the corridor. "Are you sure? Prince Kyranis is not exactly known for his good temper. I imagine he takes after his great grandfather." She points out a picture of an elf surprisingly similar to Kyranis with his long dark gray hair and piercing eyes. Next to him stands a small ginger woman with sad green eyes. "Did he tell you about Bonnie?"

I swallow, unsure what she's getting at. "Not really, no. We didn't have much time."

Vinia sighs. "Of course he wouldn't. It's a rather melancholic story, and I'm sure he doesn't want to scare you. But one of my uncles is old enough to remember her, and he said Bonnie went mad from being kept in the shadowild whenever she wasn't of use. My great-grandmother tried to help her, but the Lord wouldn't change his mind, because he disliked her 'sullen face'."

"H-he could do that?" I ask as a cold pressure settles in my stomach, and the incredible silver ribs I'm decorated with start feeling like a cage. I still have nightmares sometimes about being locked up in detention at my boarding school and that would be way worse.

"She was a glorified slave to Silas Nightweed. A source of power he could take out of the box whenever he chose." Vinia points to Bonnie's neck. "He made her wear a collar and used to drag her by it. The painting was amended after his death to spare Bonnie's memory. She tried to end her life many times, but he always knew and saved her in time. He used to say that it's his choice if she lived, and one day, he did choose to end her. I'd call that mercy, but that was never his intention. What he wanted was a new Companion, and Bonnie needed to die for that purpose."

"And he could just do that? Without consequences?" I ask with growing dread.

"She belonged to him. Body, soul, and shadow. That's the point of the wedding. Do you know how shadow magic works for those with the talent to wield it?" When I shake my head, Vinia goes on. "It's very physical. As you use it, you become tired, even feel pain. You can faint, if the exhaustion is too much. With a Dark Companion and their shadow bound to you, one can push those consequences on the human. So any time Silas wanted to, he'd use Bonnie's shadow instead of his own, pushing her to the point of suffering."

I stand there, feeling like a fool in my finery. Am I really so dumb that a night of deliriously good sex made me forget that I value freedom? Kyranis told me none of these things, surely aware they'd push me away.

Vinia puts her hand over her mouth. "I think I have overstepped. Most Lords treat their Companions with respect and kindness. Forget I said anything!"

But dark clouds have already gathered around us, and I can barely breathe, as if the air was smoky. I look around the corridor, at the massive windows and the moon looming in the sky like an omen of future suffering. Of course Kyranis would promise me everything before the wedding. That's what lying is all about. It's also why he's been rushing it. He wants me in his grasp. And even though we have passion now, do I want my future happiness to hinge on whether he likes my company?

"No! I need to know these things. I... I'm frightened. He said I'd be able to visit my world sometimes, but will he have any obligation to keep his word?"

I freeze when Vinia's face falls. She locks her eyes with mine. "Well... that might prove difficult, especially if you have friends or family. Time passes differently here than it does in your world. He should have really mentioned that."

"What? What does that mean?"

"One day here is a year in the human world. It's happened to another Dark Companion. The Lord kept promising he'd let her visit her village but waited three months to fulfill the promise. By that time, the Companion's loved ones were all gone, and the world changed so drastically, she never wanted to go back again." Vinia shakes her head. "You cannot trust promises. They will always be twisted."

My heart beats faster, my hands are sweating, and I wish to rub the face paint off me in hope that my unsightliness would postpone the wedding.

"There must be something I can do. He wouldn't be this lovely to me at times if he could just force me, right?"

Vinia gives a little chuckle, but it sounds sad rather than joyful. "Kyranis can behave when he wants to, certainly. He's always been a charming man, but he gets bored easily. Still, he likes the decorum of courtship, so as long as you remain docile, your relationship should remain... acceptable. Yes, that's the word I was looking for," she tells me with a little sigh. "So don't worry too much. Just don't make him angry."

Well, *I'm* already angry. I clench my fists, wishing to rip off the stupid cape. "I'm *not* docile," I grit out through my teeth.

"Oh," she says and stares at me as if she was the one out of options in her pretty dress made of fabrics lighter than air. "Well, then you'll need to pretend."

As if that's an appropriate solution!

"I still have a little time. There must be a way out of here, right? Please. I know I'm nothing to you, but I don't want to end up on someone's leash." Metaphorically or literally.

She steps away from me, looking even younger than she likely is. "I... I can't do that."

But she is the only one I can ask for help, and if I can't convince her now, all will be lost.

"Please... aren't you a member of the royal family?"

Vinia lowers her gaze. "Yes, but I don't want him to think I'm not supportive. He's already suspicious about our branch of the family when all we're saying is that the Dark Companions shouldn't be the only weapon against Heartbreak."

I have to take a deep breath, but it does nothing to calm the rattle of my heart. "If you just show me the way, you could tell them I ran away. That you tried to fight me. You could be the one to alert them, if you just give me some guidance. I know the forest is dangerous."

She pales, frowns, licks her pink lips, and finally meets my eyes. "Maybe... I suppose if you went by sea... I don't think Kyranis would even think to look for you there," she says, and I can almost see the calculations in her eyes.

I grasp her hand, hoping that I can prove to her with touch that I'm a person made of flesh and bone, not just someone to be used for their shadow. "I would never forget your help." I don't know how to avoid Kyranis finding me again in the human world, but the imminent danger of our union is much more pressing.

I briefly think about a year of my absence passing, and while my mother is likely delighted that I'm no longer *"mooching"* off her, AKA living in her house and paying rent for the room I use, I imagine Kurt, and some of my other acquaintances are worried about my disappearance.

I did want to start a new life, in a new place, yes, but not like this!

Vinia swallows, then grabs me by the wrist and leads me to a large cabinet standing alongside the wall. I'm stunned when she reaches onto the top shelf, and the heavy piece of furniture moves, revealing that it's hiding a door.

"You will follow this corridor until you reach a crossing. Go left, and then through the caves. I'll make sure there's a boat waiting for you on the other side. Follow the shoreline until you reach the passage into your world."

I'm so grateful I want to kiss her dainty hands, but there's no time for such displays, nor do I know if they would be appreciated in the first place, so I pull on my long cape and wrap it around my forearm, so it's not a hindrance.

My heart is cold when I step into the dark passage, and she seems ready to shut the hidden door behind me when I clear my throat.

"W—where's the light?"

Her mouth opens into an O, and she reaches past me, pulling a lantern off a little hook. Moments later, it starts glowing with a bright golden flame, so different from the green ones I've become familiar with. "Here. Keep it close. It will make your shadow bond weaker, and you will be hard for Kyranis to find. It will give you more time. Take care of yourself. And remember, on the crossing, go left, and then straight ahead through the caves."

"I will never forget this," I say to her with my heart about to leap out of my chest, but there's no time to waste. Reiner could be coming back any second.

I take the first step down, then another, while Vinia pulls the cabinet into place with a metallic screech of finality.

I'm on my own. As always. And I *will* take care of myself.

CHAPTER 13

Kyran

I never thought the moment of my triumph would come, but here I am, standing in front of the whole court and about to ascend to a position I deserve despite it not being mine by right.

I'm almost surprised nobody has cast any doubts on who I am yet, because while I've been watching my twin all my life, I am not going out of my way to repeat his philandering ways. With a bit of luck, everyone might assume I've changed my ways out of love. Then again, sometimes I did take on the court duties he didn't want to deal with, so he might not have seemed as lazy as he was.

But as I stand at the top of the steps leading up to the onyx thrones meant for me and my Companion, the earlier silence transforms into a storm of whispers as the courtiers notice that Luke is late.

Wiser Gelert clears his throat and adjusts the Sunstag headdress worn as the symbol of his authority over magic. So far, he's been avoiding me with the same passion I avoid him. It's no secret the old mage does not think highly of his prince's conduct, but maybe he too will believe that even a wastrel like Kyranis Nightweed is capable of changing his ways.

But at the end of the day, his opinion doesn't matter. I am the one who can take on Heartbreak, and he shall do his duty and oversee the sacred rite that binds me to Luke for good.

I glance at the midnight blue rose resting on the altar between me and where my promised should be standing by now. It has a silvery sheen from the moonlight coming in through stained glass windows. During the ceremony, I will squeeze the razor-sharp thorns on the stem, and Luke will put his hand over mine as a symbol of me always taking the burden first before reaching for his help.

But I can't be his cushion if he's not here.

As my personal guard, Tristan stands at the bottom of the steps in steel armor with red decoration in the shape of seaweed. He's not wearing the human hat at least, but I don't like that he keeps shifting his weight from side to side and glancing at the door.

Something's wrong. I feel it in my bones.

And yet, nobody dares to question this situation, not until I address it myself, and I refuse to, so we're all locked in limbo until my Companion chooses to—

My heart leaps when the grand door on the other side of the throne room cracks open, but my relief turns to fear when Reiner's face flashes in the gap.

For a moment, everything around me blurs, but I catch myself in time as Tristan marches between the aisles of nobles, to find out what's going on. I barely restrain myself from rushing there too, because what if Luke was attacked, or became unwell, but abandoning my post now would be in bad taste, so I focus on my redheaded cousin as if he were my last hope.

Whatever light was left in my heart dims when Tristan faces me, shakes his head and mouths, *He's gone.*

For a moment I wonder how my arrogant brother would respond to this, and he would definitely not face this humiliation with apologies. That's something I won't be doing either.

Reiner whispers to the wiser while I turn around and walk off with a swish of my cape. I'm finding out what's going on right the fuck now, but without witnesses.

I don't even have to urge Tristan. He follows me through the side door, as does Reiner, and I hear Wiser Gelert apologizing for the delay.

Only once we reach a private room down the corridor, the one where I was preparing for what was supposed to be the most glorious day of my life, do I turn to my guard and servant.

My shadow buzzes, as if it were struck by lightning, and I lash it against Reiner's face. "Where. Is. He?" I roar, stepping toward him so fast he stumbles and falls on the floor, pale and sweaty like a man about to die.

"Elodie and Vinia Goldweed came and told me the spare Sanctuary key was lost, and I'm the only one who knew how to deal with the situation. I—"

"You left him on his own?" tears out of me as rage licks my insides, charring them to a crisp. My promised might be anywhere, even dead, and all because of a servant's incompetence!

"W-with Vinia," Reiner mumbles, and Tristan whistles, shaking his head in shock.

"You know the Goldweeds are your master's rivals."

"But she's so young. I didn't think—"

I push over a fine glass statue depicting a mermaid, and it crumbles into shards as it hits the floor.

"Let me guess," I say in an ice-cold voice. "She said Luke ran away on his own and there was nothing she could do?"

Reiner won't look into my eyes. He knows he had the right to refuse Elodie in a matter such as this.

Tristan rubs his chin with a frown. "If they did this, they're out of their minds. What do they think will happen if Heartbreak comes before you wed your Dark Companion? People will die. Their father served as a knight. He'd be called upon too."

But Anatole Goldweed doesn't care about his father's fate. What matters to him is my failure and the chance to contest my right to the crown.

"Luke couldn't have gotten far, Your Highness," Reiner mutters. "Unless magic we do not comprehend is involved, he must be reachable. Can you feel him through the bond, Sire?"

I know what he's really asking. *'Is he alive?'*

My hand shakes, and as Reiner crawls away from my shadow when it starts to bubble, I hiss, "Get out of my sight. Now!"

Reiner dashes to the door, not even trying to argue or apologize anymore, but once he's gone, I glare at Tristan and bare my teeth. "Get the knights. We need to find him. I want all the Goldweeds under watch."

"Do you want the knights aligned with them to participate in the search?" Tristan asks, for once without a hint of smile.

"No. Let them stand watch in the palace."

When I glance at the bright full moon, I'm all too aware that the chances of the wedding happening today are close to none. Time is ticking away all too fast. At this point, my focus needs to be on finding Luke.

But when I send a pulse of my heartbeat down our bond to locate him, I get the faintest reply. I can't pinpoint the direction, but he's alive. I want to throttle and kiss him all at once. How dare he run away from me? How dare he betray my trust when I'm offering him *everything*?

I almost hate myself for the intense pain in my chest, because I have only known him for a day and therefore shouldn't have this kind of weakness, but I already need him in my life, and not just because the future of my reign depends on it.

Tristan nods, and when he leaves, I face the big window, my mind racing for answers. There are numerous ways to protect oneself against shadow magic, and there is no way a human could know them. Someone helped him. And I know exactly who that someone is.

But until I can prove it, the most important thing is to find Luke.

To manage such a feat while our bond remains so weak and confused, I need more power than my own shadow has even on a full moon.

I roll up my sleeve in disbelief, because I never thought *this* would be the way for me to use one of the eels swimming over my skin. I've always held it as a point of pride that I've never had to use one, but I can now see how silly it was of me to think that.

Whether Luke ran away or was abducted, I need to find him all the same.

I call the eel all the way to my open palm, then pluck it out of my hand. It twists between my fingers, semi-translucent, with the details of its form barely discernible against the bright background. When I open my mouth and bring it close, its shadowy form gets sucked into my lungs, and my skin sparks with power I have never before experienced.

Closing my eyes, I go to my knees, press my forehead to the cold floor and reach into the shadow under my crouched form, calling out to my lost mate, because I already know I shall forgive him this transgression. Right now, I just want him safe.

As the eel amplifies my powers, a weak heartbeat calls out to mine, and my consciousness dives toward it, past floors, walls, and deep into rock.

And that's when I know that he's below the palace. In the caves.

But the sense of peace this discovery brings me is soon replaced by dread as I look out at the shimmering reflection of the moon's face in the endless waters.

It's high tide.

CHAPTER 14

LUKE

The stairs take me down to an abyss. They wind endlessly, making me dizzy, and I have to watch my feet on the narrow steps to avoid tumbling into the void below. Without the warm glow of the lantern, I would have probably slipped and broken my neck by now.

The farther I climb down, the colder it gets, and my wedding outfit isn't meant for any of this. I drape the cape over my other shoulder for warmth, but my focus is solely on getting out of here alive. At least the cardio I'm doing keeps my blood pumping as I sink further into the depths where silence is the loudest of all noises.

By the time I reach the bottom, I fear the soft padding of my own feet can be heard all the way in the castle, but no one's coming after me. As I leave the staircase behind and follow a narrow corridor deeper into the bowels of the rocky cliff underneath the court, I tell myself to stay calm and follow directions.

The walls around me are covered with salt deposits arranged into abstract patterns ranging from a pure black to white. But I don't know how long of a way I have ahead of me, so I focus on the path and walk on, guided by the glow of my lantern.

The passage narrows, following a labyrinthine path with too many bends to count. I worry that maybe I have taken the wrong turn, but moments later, I'm spat out into a cavern so huge the golden flame I'm carrying can't quite disperse its shadows. There were no doors on the way, not even curtains, yet now the noise coming from above overwhelms my senses. The intense scent of salt gets in my nose, my throat, my lungs, and burns them as I struggle not to let intimidation take hold of me. I narrow my eyes in an effort to see the creature twisting somewhere above.

It's too dark for me to see any details, but its form twitches near-constantly, as if it were a pit of snakes rather than a single being, and the buzz it makes sinks deep into my flesh.

The best weapon I have is the lantern and an impromptu knuckleduster made of bejeweled rings. Hardly a threat to something of *that* size.

I move at a slow pace, but at this point it must have spotted me, and I can't risk putting out the flame in my lantern. So instead, I lift it, in hope that the creature will fear the light.

Squinting, I'm trying to make out what it is, and I spot what could be the leathery wing of a bat as big as my bedroom. Or a… dragon? Not out of the realm of possibility in a fantasy world, right?

But as the monster remains docile, it hits me that it's likely not a living being at all but a multitude of shark skins. Reiner told me about them being treated in the caves under the castle.

My relief is short-lived, though, because something snakes over my shoe, all the way up to my ankle. I can't help it. I scream out and jump back, barely holding on to the lantern.

Only when I recover from the initial bout of panic do I notice that I wasn't attacked by some deadly sea snake. It was just a wave hitting my legs. Water covers my shoes for a moment before backing out.

But getting my boots wet can hardly be compared to a lifetime as a shadow slave to a malevolent elven prince.

The echo of my scream fades, replaced by several screeches.

I spin around to spot the creatures, but all I see is shallow water that's already making my feet colder. The cave is so vast it could probably accommodate a five-story apartment building, but while I don't have any idea about how wide it stretches around me, Vinia's instructions come back to me, and I look for the path disappearing under the shallow waves.

Maybe the squeaks belonged to mice startled by the noise I made? Surely, my savior would have warned me if there was anything insidious creeping in this cavern?

I exhale, roll my shoulders to loosen them up, and walk on, trying to muzzle my imagination as it attempts to poison me with ideas of monsters watching me from behind jagged rocks I can just about see in the dark.

The distinctive scent of the sea is overpowering but has a sweet undercurrent of rot that makes my lip curl. I'm trudging through ankle-deep water, but all I can think of is the beach I will soon reach. I don't have time for overthinking, and the warm light in my lantern keeps me grounded.

So maybe the life I'm running back to isn't all that great, but at least it's *mine*.

I'm twenty-one, for fuck's sake. I'm not about to get married because of a good dicking. And sweet words. And the promise of riches.

My body still aches in a few places after last night, and it's such a bittersweet reminder of just how into me he was. Literally. He couldn't get enough of me, and I ate it up. Talk about lovebombing—

The ground shakes, making the water sway from side to side as if I were standing in a pot held by an unhinged cook. I'm splashed all the way to my thighs, and only grabbing onto a nearby rock saves me from tripping. I freeze when the thump of small rocks falling echoes all around me, but moments later, the danger's over, and I straighten, damp with sweat.

What. The. Hell.

Then a screeching that almost deafens me echoes above. I know bat cries when I hear them, and there must be hundreds of them here. I crouch in terror when the calls get closer along with the thunderous flap of hundreds of wings.

Like a wave, they swish through the air above me. All I can do is wait, as a few fly close enough to push off my tiara. It lands in the rising water, and I desperately pat the ground under the surface, but just as I think I've found it, a strong wave takes it away. The pull of the cold water is so intense it forces me to my knees, but at least it seems all the bats are gone now, and I can continue my trek to the beach.

Maybe it is best that I don't linger. What could I possibly do with the tiara back in the real world? If I tried to sell it, surely I'd get reported for theft and get in all sorts of trouble, because it's not like regular people keep such items in the attic.

As I walk through the water now spilling into my boots and soaking my feet, my thoughts return to the way Kyranis smiled at me this morning and how excited he seemed about my presence. No guy ever gave me this much attention, but I don't know the culture of this place, and he's the literal ruler. No one can guarantee he wasn't being nice for the sake of winning me over. Once we married, I'd be tied to him, and how could I be sure of my safety then, especially in the light of what Vinia told me?

A desperate squeaking stops me in my tracks and forces my thoughts into the present. I want to trudge forward and out of the caves, but the pull on my heart is instant. That did not sound like an angry bat. It was a cry for help.

But how am I supposed to help any other creature if I drown? The first rule of helping others is to make sure you're secure first. So, with my heart in my throat, I rush forward. Once I know how far I am from the exit, I'll be able to decide—

The bat squeaks again, and I turn around without thinking. I can't just leave it there. It might have gotten injured by a falling rock. And I could save it if it's close.

A wave pushes at the sides of my knees, but I keep myself steady and raise the lantern, scanning the nearby rocks as I follow the distressed squeaks. With the light shaking in my hand, it's difficult to spot anything, but in the end, I find a little critter wriggling in the water in a pathetic attempt to climb out.

The animal is... vaguely similar to a bat, even though its purple fur is nothing short of extraordinary.

It's also much larger than any bat I've seen in person, and in truth looks more like a rabbit with demon wings. It has big yellow eyes, long ears and a bit of youthful chub. Can it still be a pup?

"It's okay, little guy. I've been helped tonight too. I'm not leaving you behind."

With my heart in my throat, I extend my hand, palm up, ready for a potential bite. But it whines, looks into my eyes and licks my finger with its warm tongue. I sigh in relief and try to assess what's wrong with it as quickly as possible. Its wing is bent out of shape, most likely broken.

The fuck can I do in this situation?

"Oh, baby..." I coo to it, bringing the lantern closer with a sinking feeling.

Should I... take it?

A wave hits my thighs, once more reminding me that I'm running out of time. I rip my cape off and take in the trembling creature. It's not trying to run or attack me, as if it understands I'm the only one who would hear its plea for help. For all I know, this baby could be venomous, but I couldn't look at my face in the mirror if I left it to die.

I open the silver rib cage, take it off, then cover my hands with the fine fabric of the cloak. I pick up the bat and wrap it, both for its comfort and to protect myself from its sharp claws. I'm still hesitant about my next move, but when the wave reaches my groin, I throw caution to the wind. I wrap the cape over my other arm and swaddle the bat against my side. Tucked inside the cocoon, it calms down rather fast.

I can't believe I'm doing this, that I've lost so much time, but when I feel the tiny body shiver against me, I know going back for it was the right thing to do, but I shouldn't waste a moment longer.

At times, I move against the wave as it tries to push me back, but right after, I'm sucked toward the beach. As the water keeps rising, I'm dreading what awaits me outside, because the currents feel more violent with every passing moment.

With no reference as to how far I still need to go, I decide to do the only sensible thing in this situation and hurry down the path. Focused completely on dealing with the rising water level, I trudge across the cave, my legs fighting the water with every step. I try not to think about all the monsters Kyranis pointed out to me in the sea yesterday, but they'd surely be too big to enter this cave system, wouldn't they?

I'm exhausted by the time I reach a wall on the other side of the cavern and see a passage ahead, but there's a chance the ground rises beyond this narrowing of the path, so I pet the bat when it squeaks with worry, and step into a corridor with smooth black walls and a naturally vaulted ceiling. The air here is warmer than in the vast space I've just left behind, and I feel like the meal of a monster passing from its stomach into the intestine, which, hopefully, means I'll soon emerge on the other side. Let's not go there with the digestive metaphor.

My arm aches from holding the lantern up, but there's a glimmer of moonlight in the distance. My heart leaps, and I speed up as much as the rising waves allow me.

I do wonder if I shouldn't have turned back and waited things out on the tall stairs, hidden from Kyranis, but it's too late to ponder that now. I have to finish what I started.

Something slides against my thigh in the water, and I yelp, chilled to the bone.

"Just seaweed, just seaweed," I tell the bat, but it's myself I'm trying to calm down, because that was definitely something capable of moving on its own.

The next wave reaches all the way to my chin, and I freeze when it pulls my feet off the ground, bringing my head dangerously close to the low ceiling.

The reality of my situation sinks in when I need to hold the bat up in order for it to still have access to air. I'm inside an unfamiliar cave system that's being flooded, and if I find no way out, I might just... drown.

Would Kyran even be sad over losing me or annoyed that I spoiled his big day? He did say he could get another Companion if I died.

I check on the bat when I get a second of reprieve, though the lowering tide means I'm getting pulled toward the exit. That's either good, or terrifying, depending on what's actually out there.

I don't have time to feel sorry for myself, but I can't help it. What did I do to deserve this? My mother hates me, but I didn't ask to be born. I'm just trying to do my best in life, keep my head above water, and now, what used to be a metaphor, is turning into my reality, because I'm about to drown, and there's no one here to help me. I'm on my own, as I've always been.

I suck in air when another wave shoves me against the wall. I raise my hand to protect my head.

"Luke!" Someone yells right before a wave covers my head.

CHAPTER 15

LUKE

I'm underwater by the time I recognize Kyranis's voice, but while I'm drowning, terror still penetrates my heart when I consider a future at his side. He might save me for his personal gain, but then keep me prisoner.

At least you'd be alive, a little voice whispers while another reminds me about Bonnie, who tried to kill herself so many times while stuck as Lord Nightweed's Dark Companion.

When I open my eyes, I'm stunned to realize that the water didn't extinguish my lantern. It casts an eerie glow under the surface, and in the murky green waves filled with bubbles I spot a creature the size of a massive pufferfish. At first glance, its pink color and irregular shape make me believe it's a floating chunk of flesh that used to be a part of something much larger, but then it emerges, revealing... a *human* mouth filled with crooked teeth. The jaws close on the lantern, glass shatters, and the last thing I see before water drowns the golden flame is blood spilling where the lantern's shards cut into the creature's mouth.

Water once again pulls me toward the mouth of the cave, and I see a glimmer of light from the full moon, but all I can think about is that insane-looking beast, which surely still drifts close by.

I cough, searching for Kyranis's towering form, because right now, he is my only hope, and I no longer care for dignity.

My boots weigh me down, but they feature so many buckles I can't consider trying to take them off now.

"Kyranis!" I call out, even though I left him at the altar and tried to run away. Again.

I thought I'd outsmart my captor this time, but now I see Vinia's help for what it was—an attempt to get me killed.

She sent me down here to my death. I fell for her sweet voice and big eyes like the biggest dumbass when I should have known a place called the Nocturne Court is like *Game of Thrones* on steroids.

I'm just a pawn in whatever game the Goldweeds are playing against Kyranis.

If I survive, I won't make that mistake again.

A green light appears in the form of a spinning ball above me, and in its glow I see him standing on a cliffside at the mouth of the corridor, where the cave opens into the sea.

"Luke! Don't move," he cries before leaping into the dark waters with the agility of a shark.

I see the next wave coming toward me against the backdrop of the night sky, and it makes my stomach shrivel. Carrying a huge amount of water, it covers most of the exit, and as it comes near me, I see it curling, turned green by the pulsing illumination above. I inhale, but this time I can't keep myself upright and tumble in the water, away from the surface. The little bat thrashes against me in panic, but we're both terrified as I hit the bottom and open my eyes to see the strange blob spreading its many arms as it nears me.

I thrash back with my last meal in my throat when I realize that what I thought were short arms are actually human fingers randomly growing out of the critter's body.

What.

The.

Fuck.

My fear is so primal, a screech tears out of my mouth, letting salty water choke me.

I kick the strange animal. It's pure instinct muddled by lack of air, but I just *know* I need it away from me.

In a flash, a black shape cuts between us, and the strange monster's appendages fall off, releasing clouds of blood into the ferocious water. I spin out of its reach, thrashing as if I were trapped in a giant washing machine. When the creature reaches for me again, Kyranis appears from the dark and pierces the monster with a sword, then cuts it in half, and as the now-dead body floats away in two pieces, his pale face turns toward me, with lush hair surrounding it like tentacles.

The way he zeroes in on me makes my heart stop. Even though terrible punishment might await me after this, I still hold my hand out and he grabs it.

His hold is like ground under my feet, and he must realize I'm struggling to swim in the boots because he pulls me close and lifts me so I can get some air.

I can sense his fingers on my legs, and I look back to spot a dagger in his hand, but moments later, the beautiful traps fall off my feet, cut open. He pulls me to my back until I float on the surface, my head in the cradle of his arm. I fear he might slap me for disobeying and embarrassing him in front of his court, but he says nothing and as soon as the next wave passes, he starts hauling me out of the cave.

To safety.

It's as if the push and pull of waves is nothing to him. He's like a titan made of stone. The elegant black and silver outfit he must have donned for the wedding doesn't affect his movements in the slightest. Shadowy tentacles, like the one with which he grabbed me last night, are stuck to his limbs and I wonder if they are what helps him move with such ease. I still remember the strength with which just one of them held me in place.

The green light ball follows us like a tiny star, and I check on the bat strapped to my chest. It coughs and whines, but it's alive.

I could cry. I feel so safe in Kyranis's hold. As if all responsibility has dropped from my shoulders because I know he will carry it for us both. He is that kind of man, and I already know I will beg for his forgiveness very, very soon. For now, I try to keep quiet even when tears of relief flood my eyes, even when regret chokes me. I've already made his life harder than it needs to be, so I swallow down the guilt and let him take me to safety, no matter how much I don't deserve saving.

The rocky vault of the cave soon becomes a bad memory, and I breathe a sigh of relief when the massive white face of the moon stares down at us.

Will he take me back to the altar like this? Soaking wet, with messed up makeup and a bat strapped to my chest? Do they even have an altar for the purpose of wedding a Dark Companion? I never found out because Reiner was far too busy to explain things he likely considered obvious.

But if the ceremony needs to happen during the full moon, Kyranis would have to marry me before the day is over.

I clutch his arm harder when something brushes my back under the surface. I'm filled with so much terror I don't know how much more I can take.

But he senses the hidden presence too and shoves me away before disappearing underwater. Chills travel down my spine as I watch the water bubble as if it were boiling, and then, a pink, gelatinous arm passes through the air, making it clear the creature that attacked us earlier was back for blood. Or wasn't the only one of its kind lurking in the water. I don't know what's worse.

The waves pull me deeper for a moment... then I find my feet just as Kyranis reappears. We're chest-deep, but with the moon so silver and bright, I can easily see our surroundings and we're not all that far from the shore.

"Get to the beach!" Kyranis says with determination painted over his face as he looks at the glistening surface of the sea.

Even now, with my life hanging by a thread, notice his beauty. His profile is so sharp against the moon it's as if it's been carved out with a scalpel. The high cheek bones scream noble, and the long, pointy elven ears are a reminder that he is indeed *otherworldly*.

"Luke! Faster!"

I back out, but keep him in my sight, in case he needs help. The water shimmers silver and green as I move my feet with care, trying to avoid falling over. Adrenaline pumps through my system, making every sensation more potent, and when Kyranis emerges from the waves, shoving back his damp hair, I want to shout in triumph.

His gaze meets mine in the bright glow of the moonlight, but the smile drops from my face when a dark shape pokes onto the surface right behind him. "What is *that*?"

He tries to spin back when he sees my expression, but the pink tentacles wrap around him so tightly he can't use his sword, and still, he screams, "To the shore! Now!"

Maybe it's stupid. Maybe I should just listen, but I can't leave him. For whatever reason, he came here to save me at the risk to his own life, and I owe this to him.

Nausea rises in my throat when I realize that this blob is much bigger and sports not one but two mouths, one of which is already biting into Kyranis's thigh.

I wade his way with the bat squeaking with every step I make, and Kyranis doesn't even fight me when I grab the sword out of his hand.

I don't know the first thing about using a weapon of this kind, but I have seen how sharp it is, so I whack it wherever I think the blob appears to be the thickest.

The wet *splat* makes my lips curl in disgust, but the creature loosens its hold on Kyranis while its other mouth makes a screech of protest. I slam the sword down again for good measure, and the monster lets go, taken away by the tide.

"Let's go!" I say, but Kyranis stumbles, resting some of his weight on me.

He glances at the place where the creature bit him, his gaze hazy. For a moment, he walks next to me, not asking for his sword back, but when we're ankle-deep, he falls to his knees so abruptly I don't get the chance to catch him.

I kneel next to him, worried that a stronger wave might still prove a challenge if it tries to pull us in.

"What's wrong? We're almost there."

Kyranis's breath quickens as if he was about to heave. "Take the sword. Find Tristan. Trust only him. Get him to take you back. If I die, you will be free game to anyone. You must go *now*."

My eyes widen in disbelief. Why would he say that? "I'm not leaving you!" I say even though not long ago I was so desperate to run away from him.

But he's no longer watching me. His gaze settles on the shimmering water, which looks as if it hasn't witnessed violence moments ago, and he lets out a choked shriek. "It's coming! Go! Go to Tristan!"

My head spins when I glance at the rip in his pants. Kyranis's skin has gone blue around the bite, so despite his pleas, I shove my arms under his and drag him out of the water. My back screams, threatening to punish me for this, but I cannot fathom leaving him now, so I ignore his commands and tug.

I didn't leave the bat behind, and I'm sure as fuck not leaving Kyranis.

I don't know what's going on with him, but if I leave him here, the sea will take him. He only stands a chance if I pull him out, so I continue my fight step by painful step.

My heart beats faster as I analyze Kyranis's last words before he slumped over me. Even though I ruined tonight's ceremony, tried to run away from him, and betrayed his trust, all he worried about was getting me to safety.

I bite my lip, trying not to cry, but I don't know how much higher the tide is going to get, so there's no time for self-pity.

Once we're far enough from the waves, I lay him down in a patch of grass and lean down to kiss his blue lips.

"I'll take care of you," I whisper.

My actions might not make a difference, but I will do my best to save him.

CHAPTER 16

Kyran

My body throbs with pain.

Nausea pulses in my throat.

But I'm alive.

As I slowly come to, it becomes clear I'm lying on smooth sheets, not sand, so whatever happened after I fainted, the elves loyal to me have found and taken care of me. Luke must have gotten to Tristan in time.

I open my eyes to see the shell-shaped canopy above my brother's—no, above *my* bed—and as the paintings covering the walls come into focus, I realize I'm not alone.

My cousins from both bloodlines, their parents, as well as all the other important courtiers stand watch over my ailing body, and I exhale with relief when Reiner approaches me with a cup.

"Drink, Sire."

The bite of a despair can often be fatal, as it was to my mother, but it seems my body was able to fight the poison well enough. I don't remember any of my nightmares, which is for the better. Elves aren't supposed to dream. It's always a terrible omen if we do.

"He is no 'Sire'," Anatole scoffs, his cold eyes like two shards of ice. His long, white blond hair lies on his shoulders, flowing all the way to his chest like a cascade, and he's wearing a blue doublet embroidered with gold thread.

He is the oldest in his generation of the Goldweeds and a thorn in my side, but it's still a shock to see him display such open hostility. I need to dampen my lips to chastise him, and the bitter taste of the antidote spreads on my tongue.

Which is strange, as it should taste sweet.

"Shut your mouth. You will never speak like this to me again, or I will have you strapped down in the caves at high tide," I say coldly, and while my voice rasps, I keep it steady as I meet his gaze.

Anatole's rat-like face twists into a smirk as he steps out from the whole group of courtiers who've been associated with the Goldweeds for as long as I can remember. "You better watch out, so I don't cut out your lying tongue, Sunspawn."

My stomach drops as if a huge rock appeared inside it out of nowhere. I look down, and my gaze settles on the golden mark revealed by the open front of my shirt.

The room starts spinning as the court erupts in whispers and moans of outrage. Only then I feel it, the silver collar around my neck, forged in sunlight to inhibit my shadowcraft.

"Impostor!"

"Where is the real prince? What has he done to him?"

"It's always the twin. Rotten."

"Dregs of a prince."

"They should be put down at birth," someone whispers from the other side of the bed as my heart sinks.

I can't hide the truth anymore, but as I scramble to find a sensible answer, something that would protect me when I'm so painfully vulnerable, my gaze lands on Reiner.

"Where's Luke?" I ask.

All the hair on my body bristles when Vinia giggles behind her sister, hiding her face with a fan.

Reiner swallows and won't meet my eyes. "He drowned."

It's like a punch to the chest. I hold my ribcage and shove off the covers, scrambling out of bed, but as I step onto the floor, my leg gives up, and I tumble like a marionette with a torn string. Laughter echoes in my ears, and I blink, staring at feet in pretty blue shoes coming ever closer. The collar around my neck tightens like a noose.

"You have no right to the throne," Elodie says.

I can't think. How long have I been asleep? I glance at Tristan, but even he turns away from me as if my presence offends him.

"I swore to protect Prince Kyranis. Not whoever *you* are."

"Luke..." I whisper, because that's the only thing my mind clutches on to.

How... How did he drown when I told him to leave me?

"I'm here," he whispers and squeezes my hand.

But... how? Didn't I get up?

No. I'm in bed.

I open my eyes, and while my body still throbs with the pain of despair venom, my relief is so great I squeeze the long, warm fingers and seek out his face. It's blurry at first, but as I blink, the handsome features of my promised come into focus, and I choke up, so very relieved I have trouble finding the right words.

"You... you're alive," I mutter with sawdust-dry lips, patting my neck with my other hand just to make sure I'm not wearing the collar that haunted my dream.

"Yes. You saved me." Luke gives me a weak smile, pulling his chair closer. His eyes are bloodshot and the skin under them——dark, but to me, he couldn't be any more beautiful than he is now, tired out from watching over me. "How are you feeling? A medic said that many don't recover from that monster's bite. He told me this creature poisons the mind with terror and nightmares, that the antidote doesn't always work. So I..." He licks his lips. "Stayed up and always held your hand, hoping your body would understand it's not in danger."

My heart thumps, as if it's sinking deeper into my chest, and I squeeze Luke's hand. I see all of him. Bags under the eyes, seaweed hair, and the worried frown. "Then it was you who pulled me to the surface," I whisper, overwhelmed by the waves of emotion clashing over me and sinking deep into my flesh.

I realize the nightmare I just had, the one I've woken up from, was one of many iterations of it. I must have been trapped in it over and over again. It's what elves who have recovered from a despair bite are said to experience.

Luke's face scrunches, and tears drop from his pretty green eyes. "I'm sorry. I got scared. Vinia told me about Silas Nightweed and Bonnie, and how time passes differently here than in my world, and I just—I took her lantern and ran. I should have... I don't even know."

My pain dulls as anger overwhelms my senses. If I wasn't so very exhausted, I would have gone after my cousin immediately. "You know she was trying to get you killed, right?" I mutter but hold on to Luke's sweaty hands. It's comforting to know he cares whether I live or die. He could have left me on that beach. With a bit of luck, Tristan could have gotten him to safety, back home, yet he stayed.

Luke nods. "I think so. She must have known the caves would flood. But you came for me. Even though I betrayed you."

I exhale. "I told you not to trust my family. Well, Tristan is all right. Do you believe me now?" I mutter before coughing as my dry throat protests.

He gets up to bring me a drink, and while I appreciate it, I'm already missing his warm fingers. "I do. Is it true that a day here is like a year in my world?" As soon as he hands me the glass, he grabs my hand and the gesture is even sweeter than the antidote-infused water.

I squeeze it, and while my fingers ache, the discomfort the motion causes me is almost welcome. "No. It is not true. Time isn't relative. She lied to you. I'll have her—"

I freeze, and as the memory of the nightmare poisons my thoughts, I touch the middle of my chest, realizing that I am wearing a clean nightshirt, tightly laced to hide my sun mark. "I... did anyone see...?" I mumble, seeking the answer in Luke's eyes.

"No. I don't know what it is, and I'm sure you have your reasons not to tell me, but I understand it's important, so I made sure no one saw it. Hope you don't mind I changed your shirt. You were wet." Luke snorts and rubs his face. "Keeping your secret is the least I could do."

I swallow, overcome by a wave of tenderness. It was that feeling that pushed me so hard to save him. My pride had been hurt, yes, and I did want to keep him alive so my rights to the crown remain uncontested, but at the very end, when I fought the despairs at the shore, those weren't my reasons to continue the fight.

I wanted to keep him safe.

Because I couldn't let him get hurt after holding him in my arms all night.

No one before him has made me feel so complete, body, soul, and shadow. While he might not reciprocate my sentiment yet, I am now positive that he's fond enough of me to keep me safe when it counts.

"I—this means a lot, Luke. It really does," I whisper and bring his hand to my lips.

"May... May I?" He gestures to the bed, and I move to the side, making room for him. I can't wait to hold him in my arms again.

"I know I ruined the whole wedding, but you must understand it's all scary to me. I'm completely out of my depth. I'm used to doing everything on my own and trusting a man enough to *marry* him isn't something I can just jump into." Though as he says that, he climbs into bed and under the covers. All he's wearing is a simple long black nightshirt and it's a struggle for me to focus on his words instead of imagining how easy it would be to slide my hand under the flimsy garment.

Not that I have any energy for bedroom activities this soon after surviving a despair bite, but his arms feel so nice around me I lean into the hug, eager for more of the tenderness he showed me last night. It hurts that he's scared I might betray him, but I can't demand trust without offering it myself.

There's things he should know about me, and since he already proved that he can keep his lips locked, I exhale, swallow, and meet his gaze.

"I'm not who you think I am."

CHAPTER 17

Kyran

I feel as though I've just stepped off a cliff on a night so dark even the most powerful shadow magic can't save me. My guts coil, like eels hiding between rocks, but when Luke's pretty vulpine face relaxes, I know there's no way back from this. A potion can explode in an alchemist's face if they hesitate too long before adding the final ingredient. It is a huge risk, but he's already proven his readiness to keep my secrets, and after a lifetime in hiding, there's a part of me that longs to be seen for the man I am, not the illusion of my brother.

"Wh-what do you mean?" Luke asks, cocking his head. His attentive eyes don't appear so bloodshot anymore, and the way his fingers skirt over my chest makes my heart beat faster.

I hate that he feared me enough to run away from our wedding. Maybe if he gets to know me, we won't have to overcome so much by the next full moon? Maybe he will understand where I'm coming from and see that I have no reason to put him in danger.

Still, even though I volunteered the truth about myself, now that he's asking for more information, chills throb under my skin as I clear my throat. "This is related to the sun mark, and you have to promise to never tell anyone, no matter how trustworthy they seem," I say, playing with his beautiful, rosy fingers.

He nods, and the look in his green eyes is so sincere I'm ready to tell him everything. I know he'd break under torture, but it will never happen under my watch. I'd be dead if it ever came to that, and then, my secrets wouldn't matter anyway.

For a moment, I struggle to decide how to start, but it all comes down to the fact that he's an alien to my world and has no point of reference for what the symbol I've been carrying since birth stands for. I clear my throat, slide my arm around him, so we're closer, and whisper, "I know the sun is something normal in your world. Legend says we used to have it too, so long ago even the oldest of elves don't remember that time anymore. But when it was still around, it was so very jealous of its twin, the moon," I say, looking at the dark sky beyond the windows of my bedchamber.

"Before it was chased away forever, it tried to consume the moon to take its place in the sky and, well, it is believed that is always the story with twins, so it is a cursed thing to have two children out of one birth. It is very rare, but when it happens, the second child to come out is marked as the sunspawn," I say, and while I often forget the mark on my chest, now it seems to burn with raw fire. "Some parents banish the child to your world or leave it out in the wild, for nature to take its course, others make sure it knows its subservient role to its sibling. The mark cannot be taken off, and no illusion can hide it. It's for everyone to see, because the sun child is expected to be cruel and jealous."

Understanding spills across Luke's face like ink in water, and his eyes widen. "B-but... Why? Just because you're the younger twin? The prince's twin..."

I lower my gaze and tighten my hold on his fingers, worried he might pull away at this revelation. "One thing is definitely true. I was jealous. All my life, I've seen my brother's existence as a slight to me, because if he hadn't been born first, I would have been the one to live in comfort and splendor. Instead, I was a creature of the shadows," I say, meeting Luke's gaze again as fire sparks deep inside me. "Replacing him when it was convenient, and nobody but my parents and him even knew of my existence."

He swallows, but instead of backing out, he pulls the comforter higher, giving us more warmth. "How could your parents do that?" Luke asks, but then his expression sobers. "I guess some parents just don't care."

I don't know what reaction I was expecting, but it wasn't... this, and I find myself leaning closer, until his arms lock around me and my cheek rests on his arm in the warm cocoon of bedding. "It was the best they could have done for me, though not without benefit to the royal line," I add with a scowl. "I was a spare prince, and they expected me to always watch over Kyranis. The eels on my skin? I got them killing assassins sent after my brother or shadow wielders he provoked into fights for sport and glory. I don't know if he ever won a single battle without me helping him from the shadows," I add, not even trying to hide my disgust and bitterness.

"My parents thought I'd be an asset and great support. They even named me Kyran, as if I were only a part of my brother. But my very existence made Kyranis lazy and spoiled. He never had to learn as much as a prince would have otherwise. I stepped in during his fencing lessons as he slept off his nights of revelry, and even after our father's death, he left most decisions and council meetings to me. He never cared for the crown the way I did. Maybe because it was served to him on a silver platter. But he always made sure I understood my place. In his shadow."

I didn't even notice when Luke's fingers tangled into my hair, but he's now stroking it, soaking up every word I say. I've never felt so *seen*. Even to my father, I was only ever an extension of Kyranis, like a useful appendage which could nevertheless be cut off if necessary. Luke? He's ready to see me for who I am, not who I am in relation to Kyranis.

"So you were never able to live... as *you*?" Luke asks with a growing frown.

I nod, hugging him a bit more tightly. While he hasn't grown up with the same prejudice as elves, a part of me feared he might reject me, but Luke is still here, offering me his undivided attention.

"No. Most of the time, I was alone, hidden away in the shadowild and watching over him. I would only ever be out when he required something from me. Look through boring papers. Fight a dangerous beast. He never hesitated to put me in my place. One time, I felt drawn to another boy and made the mistake of telling him about it. He went after him and fucked him just to mock me while I watched. And he didn't even like boys that much."

My heart stops when I see tears glisten in Luke's eyes. "That's horrible. Kyran—" He stops himself from saying the 'is', and my heart beats faster. I feel like I'm emerging from a shell in front of him. "Kyran, you couldn't have deserved that as a child. Are you saying they kept you there? In this shadowild place? What does it even look like?"

I sigh, and while I am still recovering from the despair encounter, sinking into the shadow realm is like second nature. This time, I'm taking my promised with me. To my sanctum. To the place where both of us can be utterly free. Instead of veiling us with my powers, I go in deep, to the very place where I'm most at home.

The gray walls surrounding the shadow palace vibrate and bubble up in protest, as if they're not ready to accommodate another person, but I calm them down with ease. The bond we have makes it child's play.

Luke gasps, looking to what used to be a window but is now an opening into the void.

"Is this safe?" he asks, his voice a pitch higher than usual as he clutches my shirt.

"As long as you're with me," I say and stroke his hair.

"Your... eyes," Luke mutters and reaches for my cheek as if he were chasing off a fly. Only then do I remember how needy the shadows can be and voicelessly order them off me. My eyes tickle as they retreat with a rumble of annoyance. They're not sentient, but I still feel loss, because it's like chasing away a part of me. When I'm here on my own, I let the shadows envelop me and it's as natural as breathing, but Luke is not ready to see the monster I become when that happens.

He takes another deep breath and takes in the space. It's not merely a copy of a real-life bedroom, but my own iteration of it, which features a flamboyant canopy woven out of shadow tendrils.

"So it's a... palace? In some form? We could go explore?" Luke points to the door. "Or are there monsters here too?"

"I could take you around. I crafted it all out of nothing. When I was a child, this place was a cave surrounded by darkness insisting on pushing closer every time I looked away. My mother spent a lot of time teaching me how to keep the shadows at bay. But creating this room alone took many years and skill."

Luke reaches out to touch the bedpost. "It's... velvety."

"Yes, it's not real wood. I made it out of shadow."

"Like a sculptor?"

"It's a mix of shadowcraft and my imagination."

Luke is amazed as he strokes the pillow by my face. "But it's so dark here. I can hardly see."

I'm reminded that Luke doesn't have my elven sight and isn't used to darkness the way we are in the Nightmare Realm. So I snap my fingers to evoke a swamplight that bathes the room in a green glow.

"After my mother died, I didn't have anyone to accompany me here. Sometimes, my brother would throw me a book. At that point, I'd read the boring documents just to have something to do. I'd spent countless hours practicing my shadowcraft skills or fighting techniques. Our father always took Kyranis's side, so I tried to make the best of what I had here. Which was nothing, until I actually built it myself."

The jade glow reflects in Luke's eyes as he takes in everything around us. I have shelves filled with books, a large table, and several armchairs in different shapes and sizes as if I envisioned entertaining guests here a long time ago.

"I'm so sorry about your mother. What happened to her?"

I sigh and stroke Luke's head, elated about sharing my secret chambers with someone after all this time. It's been long years since anyone visited this place. Since her passing. "She tried to befriend Heartbreak's spawn, and they gored her. The medics couldn't do anything for her. She was gone forever. My father and brother didn't want to engage with me unless it was necessary, so I've been very lonely since. What I do know about social interaction, I know from watching others, but it can be a tricky thing to follow so many rules, when my own life and feelings are suddenly at stake.

"But being on my own pushed me to pursue excellence in my craft. Every single thing you see in this realm is my own creation, and I am yet to meet a fellow shadow wielder capable of besting me in a fight. I might not have the social polish my brother learned to put on like a mask when it was convenient, but I will be twice the ruler he could ever be," I add in a firm voice.

I want Luke to know I am the best of the best. I want him to value my skill and trust it.

He gasps and pushes into my arms when several shadows press on the canopy above.

"They just want to get to know you," I say, "but maybe it's time to go back and save that for when you're more comfortable here."

I let the shadows around us fall and moments later we're back in the bedroom.

Luke's heart pounds so hard I know it was a good decision to come back. "That is better," he admits with a nervous smile. "Thank you for taking me there though. I'm a little overwhelmed, but I'd like to see it again one day."

"Of course," I tell him and press a kiss to his forehead. I don't know if it's his presence that fuels my strength, or if enough time has passed since the bite, but my flesh is warmer and feels revived. "You will be my Dark Companion, and I want to make sure you feel safe in my shadowild," I tell him before gently kissing his lips.

There's hesitation in him that makes me wither, but after a prolonged silence, he speaks. "Um... I have to ask. What happened to your brother?"

I still, worried he's found out the truth somehow and resents me for it, but Luke's eyes remain kind and receptive. I exhale and rest my head on the pillow as I watch him. "Hunting accident. I chose to... hide his body and take his place instead of letting my relatives fight for the throne. You might think it makes me dishonest, but after being stuck in the shadowild for so long and only used as a tool since birth, don't I deserve a life and recognition of my own?"

Luke's gentle fingers trail over my neck as he nods. "You do. Why would you give up on that? Because of superstition? You can carve out your own destiny. That's what I believe."

Relief washes through me, purging all the dark thoughts as I kiss my promised. I had no idea how much I longed to hear that from his lips. "It's such a comfort to be here and not have my existence questioned. To finally touch people, not just watch them."

Luke nods, locking his eyes with mine. "So you must understand the value of freedom better than most..." He kisses my lips, as if trying to sweeten the bitter fruit he's just handed me.

I know what he means. I just... I hoped he might have changed his mind after his escape attempt.

Still, I'm no coward so I meet his gaze and stroke his cheek. "Just say it."

I hate that he seems frightened to do so. "I'm lost here. I don't want to live in a place where my whole existence and safety depend on another person. No matter how amazing this person seems. It's not fair for you to kidnap me and force me to stay here in a role you decided. I know I made a deal, but I was fourteen, and in... a really bad place."

I'm at a loss, even though this is pretty much what I've expected to hear. Maybe it stings that the time we've shared does not mean to him as much as it does for me. But how could it? I'm hardly the first person he ever touched. There are likely people in his life he misses way more than he could ever miss me.

Does it make me weak that I want to be special to him?

"I understand. It must be scary, but I would never hurt you in any way. I want to give you everything. Fulfill your every whim." I lift his hand to my lips and kiss his palm. "But you have to meet me halfway, sweet thing. You may have been young, but by that age, I already killed someone."

Luke's breath becomes shallow. "Are you suggesting I spend the summers here or something? I can't—"

I shush him. "I don't want you to feel trapped, Luke. But I need you to become my Dark Companion. There is no other way. But if you do this for me, if you wed me next full moon, I will let you go and only ever call upon you when it's absolutely necessary. I will compensate you for that time, and you will otherwise be able to live your life in the human world." He can never understand how much it pains me to present him with this offer. After last night, I was sure my Dark Companion would also be my lover, friend, and confidante. I thought I could keep him if I only tried hard enough. But entrapping him with brute force wouldn't give me what I want. I would never want to inflict the imprisonment my family thrust upon me on someone else. Especially not the one person who knows the real me.

"Really? You'd take me back?"

"If that's your wish," I say, trying to make my voice stronger, so I don't sound like a pet whining for love. "You're also welcome to stay with me, of course. The door's always open. Though you will need to remain at my side during courting and show your enthusiasm for it. No one needs to know of our plans."

"So for a month." Luke nods, as if calculating, and all I can think of is that I have one moon cycle to make him love me. "You saved my life three times by now. This sounds like a fair deal. *Courting*," he says with emphasis and a little smile on his lips. "How will the prince court me?"

Oh, he likes that part. Of course.

"I'll take you around my lands, introduce you to people, we might go dance at the annual Ardournalia celebrations, get our portrait painted, and engage in many courtly games meant to show how compatible we are," I say and push my nose into his hair, to smell him. Ah, the salty scent of the sea still clings to his flesh. "It's tradition. When the first Lord of the Nocturne Court took his Dark Companion, she was resistant to being in this new place, away from everything she knew, so he went out of his way to convince her that a life with him would be much sweeter than the one she had to leave behind. They spent many happy years together."

"I've never really dated anyone, but I imagine it will be easy to pretend I fell head over heels for a prince." He smiles, unaware that he's driving a knife through my heart already.

I don't want him to *pretend*.

But I will take what I can get for now, and maybe courting will fulfill its purpose and by the end of it, he will see that his place is at my side.

"Really? Never?" I ask, curious about the extent of his experience.

"I'm... not good with feelings, relationships and all that stuff." He stalls as if he's remembered something. "What about you though? Did you say you only got to *touch* people after your brother died? When was that?"

I freeze, and even in his arms I feel a little bit cold. "A week ago," I mutter, embarrassed of all the things Luke is no doubt reading from that statement.

His eyebrows rise. "Oh. *Oh*. And did you... have a *busy* week?" He bites his lip as his eyes drill into me inquisitively. The way he circles his fingertip around my nipple is not helping my focus.

I clear my throat, looking everywhere but at his eyes. "Well, I did need to acquaint myself with many things so that nobody notices I replaced Kyranis."

"Did that include any of his lovers?" he asks, but his smirk tells me he knows the answer.

My voice dies before it can leave my mouth, and I shake my head, embarrassed to confess my inexperience. When Luke hums, my nerves fly through the rooftops.

"And even if our courting will be for show, can it still include—"

"Yes," I hate how needy I sound, but he kisses my jaw, and it makes me groan in relief.

"So you're telling me a man like you, with a dick like *that*, never got a blowjob?"

I stall, staring at him. "A what?"

He laughs, but it's not like my brother's cruel mockery. He's being playful, and I love it. Luke slides his hand down my stomach and I'm already hard. "Given you pleasure with their mouth."

Just thinking about Luke's face hovering above my cock has me stiffening so rapidly it's giving me vertigo. I shake my head, breathless as he grins at me, beautifully confident. "I've seen it done."

His eyes meet mine and he's no longer a trembling flower. "How about you experience it for real?" He gives my lips a teasing lick, and I sink into the sheets, ready to take *everything* he has to offer.

CHAPTER 18

Kyran

Just a month ago, if anyone had told me I'd be in bed with the prettiest human boy in the Realm, I'd have laughed in their face. A hypothetical situation, of course, since my brother was the only one to know of my existence, and he'd have never suggested I could be independent or happy for my own sake. But now I'm here, in the soft bed, with Luke grinning at me like a sly fox as he rises to all fours.

"I'm so glad we found an agreement. That makes me so relaxed." Luke says and leans in to kiss me. "Like I can enjoy this with a light heart."

His lips are so soft against mine, and I can't wait to nip on them.

My heart beats fast, and the fatigue I've been feeling doesn't seem so burdensome anymore as I cup his face and stroke the prominent cheekbones. Such a lovely feature. It makes me happy that humans can also have them, and I tease the smooth skin in the middle of his cheek with the tip of my tongue. It's sad that he can't relax knowing I want to keep him at my side, but I'll take what I can get and see if I can convince him to offer me more. Learning how to duel includes a component of understanding the opponent's psyche, so while Luke isn't my enemy, the same principle applies. I have to learn more about him. And that will be my pleasure.

His hands drift over my chest, and the fabric between us is so delicate I feel every touch. He knows who I am, and he's still so eager to kiss me. I can already imagine his hot mouth on my cock, but I'm sure my imagination can't live up to the reality of his wonderful tongue.

When we kiss, lightning sparks between our lips and shoots down my torso, scorching every bit of flesh in its way. My cock twitches, and even the weight of my shirt feels like an intense touch.

I've never desired anything more. Not being seen. Not my brother's position. Not the crown itself. They all pale in comparison to the possibility of owning Luke, and as I roll us over, pushing my knee between his thighs, my head resonates with hymns of triumph.

I'm addicted to the way he gasps as his pupils widen. He's so slender and easy to handle, but instead of finding it weak, I enjoy the ease with which he becomes putty in my hands. Will I learn to master him with the same proficiency I mold shadow?

He puts his hands on my shoulders and squeezes. "Are you sure you're well enough?" he asks, but bites back a smile. The little green fox is teasing me, but if I truly am to only have a month with him, there's no way I'm wasting a single opportunity to take him in my arms.

"Perhaps not, but I'm not letting that stop me," I whisper against his tattooed neck before marking him with a swirl of my tongue. I adore the way he arches under me, spreading his thighs as if he can't help his need for me either.

His fingertips slide over my neck, then all the way to my cheeks. "So many years of pent-up need, coiled in such a magnificent body," he whispers, looking into my eyes. "I want to taste you, Kyran."

A shiver of pride goes through me. He *does* see me for who I am. He calls me by my name.

He is mine, not Kyranis's.

"I pulled you out of the river for him, but he wasn't worthy of you. I'm glad you never met him," I rasp as my mouth touches his. I drag my fingers up his ribcage, intent on learning his body by heart. He is perfect.

Mine.

Mine.

Mine.

If I was obligated to hand him over to Kyranis now, I'd sooner rip my brother apart than let him put his hands on Luke.

"I'm not much. I'm just a human," Luke tells me with a soft expression.

His breath hitches under my touch, and he rocks his hips to let me know how excited he is to be mine again. He doesn't understand the power he already has over me, and maybe that's for the better, because he could have made me do terrible things with a flick of his bony wrist.

I want to worship his pale skin, seaweed hair, those long fingers with rosy knuckles, and tiny ears.

"No. You're more. You're my Dark Companion. You're my power. You're my pride," I rasp, lowering my body on top of his as our breaths synchronize. The proof of my lover's excitement pokes at my hip, and I grin, placing my hand over it, just touching it through the nightshirt.

He can be so moody at times, so seeing his mask melt away makes my heart beat faster. I want to be as close to him as possible. Body, soul, and shadow.

His touch gets firmer when he slides his hands down my sides, all the way to my hips. He's pulling up my night shirt. So needy for me.

"Then give me what *I* want. Let. Me. Taste. You." He underlines the demand with a lick to my lips.

I got so wrapped up in taking him again, I almost forgot his earlier request. It's so hard for me to comprehend that someone, my promised at that, wants to please *me*.

Me. The impostor. The younger twin. The spare.

But deep down I know he wouldn't have wanted Kyranis the way he wants me, and I would have never let my brother use him for his shadow.

"Greedy," I mutter, and when my lover pushes at my chest, I roll back, spread out under the covers as Luke moves between my legs with a grin that tells me he knows exactly what he's doing. I have to fight the urge to ask for the names of every human he's ever been with. I can't wipe them from existence just because Luke fooled around with them once. It would have been unreasonable. Then again, do I always need to be reasonable?

He pushes up my shirt all the way to my pecs, and I flex my abs because I've seen his eyes spark at the sight of my muscles. His gaze follows one of the eels sliding over my hip, but then all of his attention is on my dick, and he wastes no time.

Luke kisses my cockhead with a happy groan, then licks all the way down to my balls, making my prick twitch in excitement. It's like being teased with a hundred feathers at once, and my eyes shut at the shock of this sensation. "This... oh... this feels good."

Luke's eyes shine with glee, as if I've given him precisely what he wants, and he wraps his arm around one of my thighs, holding it still as he lowers his face again. His pale features look so sweet and delicate as he nuzzles my engorged erection, and I long to see him lose some of this calm, like he did when I fucked him last night.

But it seems it's my turn to fall apart, because when he opens his soft mouth and sucks in my cockhead, the heavens open, and the bright glow of the moon shines upon me despite it being the middle of the night.

I moan and slide my fingers into his hair, afraid it might be too much and that I'll come too soon. He glances at me, lowering his head over my cock and taking more of it into his hot mouth as he toys with the underside.

He's a demon under that pretty mask.

A very pretty demon who wants to leave me within a month.

That cannot happen.

Surely, I can make him see reason by that point. Can he really do better than an elven Lord?

With a raspy moan, I spread my thighs wider, to give him all the access he wants, and he gently squeezes my balls while teasing my cock with his lips.

I wish I could reach his tight little hole at the same time. It gave me so much delight last night. But I can barely think straight when his tongue makes those teasing little swirls and he bobs his head over my cock with increasing speed. I clench my fingers in his hair when my cockhead hits the tight channel of his throat.

With one hand on my balls, he slides the other up my stomach, greedy for me.

I'm half-lucid with desire, but I drift off entirely when he arches his hips higher, so focused on taking my dick he doesn't pay attention when his nightshirt rolls up his back, exposing his pale ass.

I zero in on it as electricity jolts over my body, and while I can't reach his delicious buttocks with my hands, my shadow climbs Luke's milky thighs and solidifies as it dives between the cheeks. It's not the same as touching him with my own skin, since the shadows feel neither pleasure nor pain, but I *sense* him. The delicate, wrinkled skin, and the lovely, lovely dip of his opening.

"Oh, my treasure," I whisper, stroking Luke's cheeks as he freezes with my flushed dick halfway down his mouth.

Luke makes a little whimper that vibrates down my shaft so gloriously I bite my lip to swallow a moan. He glances at the shadows wrapping around his thighs, so to make my point clear, I pull and spread his legs wider.

He whines again, but never lets my cock out of his mouth, as if it were his lifeline. And when I push on his hole with my shadow, he sucks harder, wiggling his hips insistently.

I send a few more vines of shadow under his nightshirt to pull it up. Even they are trembling now, since my mind is vibrating with arousal.

Luke is flushed and panting when I pull him off my throbbing hot dick by the hair so the shadows can undress him completely. "Is-is this safe?" he asks while I slide the tentacle into him, past the tight muscle of his sphincter, then let it swell and harden inside him.

I love the color of his skin right now. It's such a pretty dark pink that if I didn't want his lips back on my dick, I'd be pulling him up for a hundred kisses. "You are always safe with me," I tell him as the tentacle withdraws, only to drill back into him in shallow, gentle thrusts. But he's trembling, overheating, he can barely speak as he lowers his face and rests his cheek on my groin.

This excites him.

"Do you like being held like this?" I rasp and spread his legs farther with my shadow before wrapping a twine of it around his midsection and holding him firmly in place.

He pants hot air on my saliva-slicked cock, making me want to come on his pretty soft lips right the fuck now.

"This is so hot. It's fucking me at the right angle," Luke whimpers, pushing his needy ass against the shadow as much as I allow him. His mouth then finds my cock again, and he sucks it with new fervor, but I need control over his frantic body.

My shadow grabs his wrists and pulls them behind his back. With his head so beautifully trapped and his hole getting the fucking it needs, I piston in and out of his tight mouth, holding his head with both hands. Our eyes meet. He *twitches* with raw need, and seeing him so wonderfully undone breaks the floodgates of my desire.

I come with a moan, and as I empty my balls down his throat, his eyes roll back, so my tentacle pushes into him with more force. I make it throb so he can feel the intensity of my desire. "*This* you can only get from me," I whisper, clutching at his messy hair.

He's panting, swallowing all I have to give him, but his glossy eyes are on mine. Raw and unguarded. He wants this. Just needs a nudge.

Luke's mouth is still full of my cum when he thrashes in the hold of shadows, releasing hot spurts of seed on my thighs and bedding. I hold him tightly, because his frantic rocking has nothing to do with a desire to escape. I sit up, gather him in my arms, and grab his cock, pumping it until he's done and embraces me back.

"I'm here," I tell him, in case he needs reassurance, and kiss the top of his head as we slide back into a horizontal position, with him shivering on top.

He's struggling to catch his breath and I smirk, knowing it's my doing. Luke let me take charge, and I'm glad that despite my inexperience I was able to give him something no one before me could offer.

I love how he melts into me now, so vulnerable and sweet. Maybe I have been too hasty trying to grab him out of his world and thrust him into a marriage within the span of a day.

"That was... I've never..." But Luke can't put together a coherent sentence, so I let him rest in the cradle of my arms, gently rocking him back and forth.

"You're so beautiful," I tell him, stroking his cheek with the back of my hand. And I'm not lying. Even the texture of his skin is so lovely I long to cover it with kisses.

"Right now, I'm filthy and I need a bath," Luke chuckles as his heart regains its normal rhythm. To think that I could have lost him in the sea... I will have Vinia's head for that.

Despite still feeling dizzy, I need to show off my strength. I push my arm under his knees before gathering all my power and lifting him from the bed. For a moment, the room sways around me, but once the furniture stops moving, I walk toward the bathroom with my heart in the clouds.

"Nothing a long soak can't help with."

Luke is quick to wrap his arms around my neck, and it feels so natural I just know we're meant to be. He's not yet convinced, but I have a month to show him a life at my side will be one beyond his wildest dreams.

"I did get to wash quickly when I came back, but I didn't wash my hair, so I'm sorry if it still smells of sea and a despair guts." He looks into my eyes as I push on the door of the bathroom with my foot. "You, on the other hand, were *delicious*."

I chuckle as I carry him to the tub, enjoying the mossy floor. "If it wasn't clear enough yet, never *ever* let a despair touch you. It's best to avoid them altogether."

"What are they anyway?" Luke asks as I gather all the strength left in me to put him down. Moments later, I join him in the tub filling with warm water.

I clear my throat, not sure where to start. It's like attempting to explain reasons why folk need to eat and sleep to survive. "They're spawn of the dangerous beast haunting our shores for millennia. Heartbreak. He returns from time to time, and a greater number of despairs usually means that time is near."

"So he's material, like the despairs?"

"Yes, he feeds on both bodies and souls of sentient beings. If I hadn't pulled you out of the river all those years ago, he would have eventually found and consumed you."

Luke shivers despite the flush still so clear on his cheeks. I can see his eyelids are heavy, but he's trying to understand my world. He leans against me, happy to snuggle under my arm.

"That thing, the despair, it had human teeth and fingers. Do those souls... still live within Heartbreak? Are they going through eternal suffering?"

I exhale and rest my chin on the top of his head, eager to float in the warm, fragrant water. He left me oh-so-pumped-out and satisfied. "I never... thought about it."

Luke's eyes shut and I'm ready for him to doze off against me. After all, he watched me as I slept fighting the despair's poison.

But a few little screeches sober him up and he sits, shaking his head. "Flap?" he asks the empty room. I'm confused, but then a purple bat jumps up to the edge of the tub and perches on there, watching us with beady yellow eyes. One of its wings is carefully wrapped with a bandage, and while the critter seems young, it has sharp claws and teeth nevertheless.

Before I can slap it as far away from Luke's bare skin as possible, Luke speaks.

"Please don't be mad. Tristan warned me they can be dangerous, but this one's just a baby, and its wing was broken. It would have drowned in the cave if I didn't take it."

I stall. "Tristan let you bring it home?"

The bat watches me like a hawk, and I wouldn't put murderous intent past it, but I can always make use of my shadow if it decides to show its true colors.

"I kinda... smuggled him in, since everyone was absorbed with trying to help you. Sir Tristan gave me a lecture when I finally showed Flap to a doctor, but he let me keep him in the bathroom for now. Apparently, they always go for the eyes first, but look at him. Does Count Flapula look like he could hurt anyone?" Luke coos and, to my horror, extends his fingers to the tiny beast.

I have to admit, it does not look threatening at this time, even though I would have twisted off the beast's head if it as much as left a scratch on Luke's perfect skin. "'Count Flapula'?"

"You know, like Count Dracula? But he flaps around because of the injury..." Luke continues when I stare at him blankly. "Dracula is from a book about a powerful vampire in my world, and vampires can turn into bats so— Are there vampires in the Nightmare Realm?"

Chills go down my spine. "They don't dare come anywhere near the Nocturne Court, but I can assure you that I can protect everyone from bloodsuckers. You're safe."

"I've got a lot to learn..." he says absentmindedly, and the bat opens its mouth. My heart stops, but the critter just licks Luke's finger.

"And looks like I have a book to read." Because I want to understand where Luke is coming from too.

"I have a special edition at home. I'll give it to you on your birthday. I like... all things dark and dangerous." Luke smiles at me when he says that, and I'm pretty sure it's because he means to suggest he likes *me*.

"Well, it's your lucky day, because there's plenty of dark and mysterious things I can show you during our courting," I say and follow the bat with my gaze as it attempts to fly off toward the window, only to float to the floor. Pathetically.

Luke slides back under my arm, puts his cheek on my pec, and closes his eyes. In this moment, I understand why he wanted to save that baby bat. "Now that we're in agreement about what things will be like between us, I'm looking forward to this upcoming month. This is all so... magical. I want to find out more about this world. And you. Thank you for sharing so much with me."

My heart throbs as if it's been touched by the moon itself, but maybe there's no greater power anyone can ever have over me than this small human who doesn't yet know he will *want* to be mine.

Tomorrow, I will start courting him in ways he cannot even fathom.

I wonder if he's ever witnessed an execution before.

CHAPTER 19

LUKE

I can't believe I'm thinking about it, but I miss Kyran. He's only been gone for a few hours, yet I'm already itching for his company. And to feel his lips against mine.

We slept in the same bed, something I barely ever do with a lover, yet it felt like the most natural thing in the world. I miss him even more than I miss my phone, and that's *something* for a terminally online guy like me. I wish I could put a photo of Count Flapula on Instagram, or check if there's any new drama in the world of indie bath bomb crafters, but most of all, I wish I could text Kyran.

A needy part of me wants to ask where he is, what he's up to, whether he's feeling okay after the despair's bite. He still has a bruise where the creature bit him. If I had my phone, I would *WebMD* the shit out of that.

But I don't.

So I'm stuck in my digital detox, living in the present, and being 'mindful'.

It is kinda nice, actually. I spent some time brushing Flap's fur and just enjoying my time with him instead of also listening to a podcast or watching TV at the same time. It made me notice little things about my new pet, like how he really does look like a bunny, but that his feet have longer fingers and claws. I'm guessing he uses them to hang from branches or rocks.

I wish Kyran was here, so I could ask him about it.

A knock on the door makes me shut the elaborate cage my dark prince had his servants bring in from some far-off corner of the castle. I leave Flap inside as I rise to my feet, ready to see him.

A part of me wants to rush to the bathroom and make sure I'm presentable, but I also don't want to make him wait.

Seeing Reiner enter with the same wooden chest as yesterday makes me go limp as if I were a balloon with a hole.

"Master Luke, are you well?" Reiner asks, opening the door in the silver bars and passing through it.

"Y-yes," I mutter. "I just thought Kyran... might have come back. The last day and night were so turbulent..." Understatement of the fucking year. I almost got married *and* murdered on the same day, then had sex with shadow tentacles. I don't think even the heroes of the most popular soap operas could rival me in terms of unexpected twists to their lives.

Reiner's face scrunches, and he drops the handle of the chest, letting it fall to the floor. He collapses in front of me and grabs the edge of my robe. "It is all my fault. Please, forgive me, Master Luke. I swear I had nothing to do with that vile woman's plan! I was only trying to make sure the wedding goes as planned. It has not, and it's due to my actions. I don't even know what would have happened if you died! I would have never forgiven myself."

I freeze, out of my depth. Most of my life, I couldn't even afford restaurants with table service, so I don't have much experience with waiters let alone *servants*.

It's awkward *as fuck*.

And I believe him. He's so into his job, but he's not a bodyguard.

"It's... um... I understand you meant well." But I did almost get killed. "Maybe next time be more wary?"

Reiner hides his face, cowering in front of me as if he's playing some lowly wretch in a high school play. "I've worked here for over two hundred years, and I have never failed so completely. From now on, I shall be a paragon of good service and obedience!" he declares in a shaky voice.

What? Two hundred years? He doesn't look a day over thirty. But everything falls into place as soon as I take my time to consider it. Those people are *elves* after all.

"Just... do better," I say, remembering what Marty told me after my latest fuck up at work. Am I, like, the manager now?

I'm mortified when Reiner kisses the tip of my silk slipper, but he's back up before I can say anything. "I will. The service I shall provide will be unrivaled by anything you've ever experienced."

Clearly, he has no concept of what kind of life I led before Kyran swept me off my feet in the parking lot of Best Burger Bonanza.

I wonder if anyone is searching for me yet.

"I've got no doubt. You have two hundred years of experience after all, am I right?" I give a nervous laugh, because he's about to undress me, and that's weird. I might have to assert myself once I know how to handle the clothes he brought for me.

"Indeed, Master Luke. Yesterday's mistake is a stain on my whole career in the service of this royal family, but I hope to stay here and make up for my crime."

I struggle to keep my face straight. Did I almost die yesterday? Yes. But is the way he speaks hilarious? Also yes.

"So how old are you? Or is that rude to ask?"

Reiner clears his throat. "I'm an experienced two hundred forty-eight years old. The oldest of all the servants at this court," he says, straightening his reed-thin form. "Every single year in service has been a joy."

I ponder that as I take off my robe and nightshirt and he hands me a garment reminiscent of... cycling shorts of soft black cotton. I'm assuming it's their version of underwear.

Every day working in customer service was a pain in the ass for me, so I struggle to understand Reiner's desire to please.

"You didn't want to do anything else? For two centuries?"

Reiner shakes his head and turns, opening the chest to reveal a sea of shimmery black fabric. I take this opportunity to quickly put on the boxer shorts-like garment.

"No, this is the perfect place to live and work. Safe. *I* don't have anyone making sure I'm fed and well," he says, reminding me of the heroic way Kyran saved me yesterday. "There's always something going on, I get to dress the members of a noble family in the most glamorous outfits, and there are plenty of handsome men to pick from in my time off. What's not to like?"

I snort, surprised at how candid he's being. "You have time for men?"

Reiner smirks without meeting my eyes. "I make the time when I deem it worth my while. Though mastery in any kind of work takes effort. I'm proud to be in the position

I am, attending the Lord and his Dark Companion. It allows me to be part of something truly special."

"What was the last Lord like?" I ask as he assists me in putting on a shirt made of black fabric that shimmers in the moonlight. Red thorns are embroidered on sleeves that have the most flamboyant volume.

"Stern," Reiner tells me without hesitation. "Much sterner than His Highness Kyranis. He didn't like to gamble nor go to the theater, nor take many lovers. Do you want me to be frank, Master Luke?" he asks, closing a long row of buttons at the front of my top.

"Yes."

"He was a bit of a bore."

I snort and shake my head. "Was a boring master better, or one who needs his sheets changed every night?"

The same shark skin, high-waisted breeches are given to me as soon as I put on a pair of stockings. They're red this time, and I don't even feel self-conscious about them, because it's the fashion here. I don't have to worry about someone teasing me because of my style, despite this outfit being way more flamboyant than anything I could afford with my meager earnings.

Reiner scoffs. "I do not judge my betters for their choices."

He absolutely is, but I let him get away with this lie and grin as he continues talking.

"I can hardly blame His Highness. Your beauty is way beyond that of all the other Dark Companions at present."

When he hands me a thick vest that needs tying at the back, I feel encased. Safe. It's like armor I can face the world in.

My mind takes a moment to circle back to what Reiner just said. "*Other* Dark Companions? The prince told me no other royal is allowed to marry one until he has."

Reiner clears his throat and kneels in front of me, holding a pair of boots made with soft leather in a shade that matches my stockings and adorned with silver buttons.

"Other shadow-wielders can *have* Dark Companions, but no one is allowed to take one when the heir apparent remains unwed to one of his own. So all of His Highness's cousins have been waiting for almost a decade, but their seniors, those who obtained their Companions during the reign of the previous Lord, they just aren't allowed to be at court until His Highness marries you. It's tradition."

"How many are there?"

TAKEN BY THE LORD OF THE NOCTURNE COURT

"Only two," Reiner says, and he gestures for me to sit down on a dainty chair in front of a mirror. "There were eight, not counting the Lord's Companion, but they all died along with their wives and husbands, attempting to fight off Heartbreak. It was an incredible sacrifice on their part, and while the Lord didn't survive his wounds, no civilians were hurt. Heartbreak didn't even reach the shore."

My stomach drops. My arrangement with Kyran is that he will only call on me when he deems it necessary. I'm guessing that Heartbreak's attack will be one of such situations. As much as that gives me a chill, I do still feel it's a fair agreement.

"How often does this beast come?"

"Not that often. Perhaps once every ten to fifteen years? There was one time when it returned after just three, but another time, we lived in lazy peace for over forty," Reiner says as he sprays something onto my hair. The mist smells of the sea, and I close my eyes, not wanting to get any salt in them.

I'm still getting to grips with him being almost two hundred and fifty years old. He has more energy than I do some mornings.

He must notice I'm tense, because he strokes my shoulder before getting back to coiffuring my hair. "We have alchemists and scholars working on the secrets of when and why Heartbreak arrives. You shouldn't worry about things that cannot be helped, and focus on your role at court. When a storm comes, all we can do is open our umbrellas."

"How old is Prince Kyranis?"

"He will be thirty-five years young later this year," Reiner says with a fond smile. "Don't tell him I said that, but you seem to be a good influence on him. He's... different now. In a good way," he adds, unaware it's not the behavior that's changed, but the whole man. The original prince really sounds like a piece of work.

"May I?" Reiner asks, leaning over me with a tiny brush loaded with red paint. I'm guessing the question was only a formality, because he then goes on to grab my chin and applies the color under my eyes.

"Is there a reason for all the red, or am I just your personal fashion doll?"

Reiner purses his lips. "It's a special occasion, for the prince to disclose."

I smirk. "Does it have to do with our courting?"

"My lips are sealed."

As if Kyran knows he's being discussed, he walks in, dressed in a coat with wide, pleated skirts and a tight-fitting outfit of black shark leather with many buckles. My heart leaps when he smiles and places his hand on his torso. "Oh, you are perfection," he states as Reiner drops the brush, lowers his head, and steps away from me as if he wants to turn invisible. I just hope he isn't about to beg for Kyran's forgiveness too, because it was awkward enough to witness that once.

I get up so he can get a better look at me, and yeah, I do a slow twirl, showing him how the breeches hug my ass. "I do kinda love it."

"If I may, Master Luke, the finishing touch," Reiner says and approaches me with a red silk scarf. He then ties it under the collar of my shirt into an intricate bow. "All as you wished, Sire," he says and once more backs away.

But my... fiancé——or should I say *"promised"?*——doesn't seem unsettled by Reiner's actions and pulls me into a kiss that makes me fall into him as my knees weaken. "I've been missing you."

I smile, rubbing my hands up his leather-clad chest. "Big same."

For a moment, he seems unsure of my wording, so I add, "as in, I missed you too. A lot."

I know he won't get the reference, but his smile is like sunshine in the middle of summer. Nobody has ever been this happy about my presence, and I can't help enjoying it.

"I wanted to be with you sooner, but I was busy preparing your gift."

"My gift?"

"Yes, it's a surprise," he says and kisses my hand before entwining our fingers and leading me out of the room.

I smile at him. "I love surprises."

CHAPTER 20

Luke

Guards in armor that's been polished to perfection stand watch along the corridor as Kyran leads me forward like a book boyfriend come to life. I half expect him to carry me to a Rolls-Royce in front of a jealous ex and frenemies, but the people I dislike aren't here, and his kelpie-drawn carriage is so much better than even the fanciest car.

Not that it matters, since I'm staying here temporarily.

The boots on my feet are so light and comfortable, it's like wearing clouds, the pants make me feel like a movie star walking the red carpet, and Kyran is easily the best-looking man I've ever seen. *And* attentive in bed on top of that. What is there not to like? Why not enjoy myself for a month in this gothic wonderland?

I slow down to take in a tapestry depicting knights in black armor holding their swords up. They stand knee deep in water as lighting strikes the moon above them. To the right, a massive shape floats closer. It has no mouth, no eyes, and it's made of hundreds of naked bodies, their arms reaching out helplessly, fingers like claws. Sparkling jewels in pink, red, and orange adorn the artwork where the creature's bulk emerges from the waves. Under the surface, the monster becomes a shimmering cacophony of dark green, then black, yet it's decorated with the same artistry.

"Is this Heartbreak? It can't be this big, right?"

Kyran sighs, giving the tapestry a reluctant glance. "It can, but I can assure you, it is much more hideous than any artist can imagine."

"Everything is so darkly beautiful here. My world is so mundane in comparison."

"Ah, but you are not," my personal knight says and kisses my knuckles as we walk the lengthy corridor toward a doorway guarded by two elves.

"Then it's only fitting that I get a man who looks like a Prince of Darkness." I smile at him appreciatively.

"I *am* the Prince of Darkness." Kyran winks at me, and I chuckle, because it's true.

He's taller than me, broad-shouldered, and the leather outfit showcases his form so magnificently I could just about pull him into a broom closet and jump his bones.

But we're pretending to date while staying chaste... the exact opposite of what is actually happening, so no can do. Not with so many guards watching at least.

Kyran smiles and strokes my hand with his thumb as we approach the ornate doors. Two female knights open them for us, revealing a huge space with ceilings higher than the roof of my mother's house. The walls are covered with gold, silver, and copper paint arranged into scenes featuring heroic deeds. The room is also full of courtiers, who disperse to stand by the walls the moment music starts playing on a balcony above.

Tristan doesn't have my hat on when he approaches. In fact, he's wearing a metal breast plate. I knew I could trust him last night, but I didn't even need to look for him. He found me as I was dragging Kyran off the beach, and organized help within minutes.

His long red hair is tied back into a braid, but from behind him emerges a small elven lady with the same hair and golden eyes as him. At first glance, I assume her high-waisted dress is a fashion choice, but then I realize she's displaying a pregnancy bump.

As soon as all the polite greetings with Kyran are exchanged, I am introduced to Sabine Bloodweed, Tristan's sister.

"I am so excited to meet you, Luke, and I cannot wait to hear all about what's new in your world. I'm a scholar you see, and I'm beyond fascinated with where you come from. I have something for you."

I perk up while Kyran watches at my side. Sabine hands me something small swaddled in a silk handkerchief. I smile as soon as I open the parcel and spot my enamel pin. It's not big, maybe two inches long, and features a red cartoony lobster with the words *Lobster n' Roll* wrapped around it.

"I thought it got burned with my clothes!"

Sabine shakes her head. "Tristan kept it. Maybe for the wrong reasons," she says, side-eyeing him, "but I figured it might be an heirloom, so I insisted that we return it."

I pin it to my chest. "It's not, but it's important to me. Thank you so much."

She beams and places her hands on her rounded stomach. "I am so joyful. Perhaps you will be so kind as to come up with a name for my child. I was considering Biff, but my husband dislikes it. What do you think? Is that a good human name?" she asks, taking her time while all the other courtiers stand by the walls and stare at us, whispering.

For a moment, I imagine an elven royal called like an 80s movie bully. "M-maybe this isn't the right moment for it. But I'd be happy to help."

Sabine nods with understanding. "I'm in charge of the library. Please come and see me if you have any questions about our Realm. It's been a while since we've had a human at court."

And yet not everyone is happy to have me here, as I found out yesterday. I've learned my lesson, and until Kyran gives me the green light, I'm not going anywhere on my own.

I'm still talking to Sabine when commotion erupts behind my back.

"Oh no, there he is. The shortest elf in the Realm," Tristan mutters, and when I turn around to find out what this is about, Tristan stands in the way of a much shorter, baby-faced elf. His white hair barely reaches his nape and has a faint golden sheen. He's wearing a dark blue coat designed to lengthen his silhouette, likely for the same purpose as the inch-high heels of his boots. But he still appears tiny when standing next to someone as tall as Tristan.

"Kyranis, please, talk to me," the stranger whispers loudly enough for me to hear him despite the music.

My Prince of Darkness meets his gaze. "I appreciate your sentiment, Sylvan, but you must know I can't let this go."

Sylvan shakes his head, so exasperated his cheeks flush. "She's just a child—"

"She's twenty. She made her choices, as we all do." Kyranis squeezes my hand, and the tension between the two elves makes my heart beat faster.

"Then banish her. To the human world even. Wouldn't that be a fate worse than—"

"Enough," Kyran says in a voice so dull it feels like a punch to the heart, and even I feel uneasy, despite not being the object of his anger.

Sylvan's blue gaze darkens. He lowers his head, purses his lips, and stills.

"The best you can do is keep the others from repeating her mistakes," Kyranis says before facing me with a smile. "I may need something for good luck."

"Good luck for... what?" I frown, but I get my answer before he can speak.

A large door on the other side of the room opens and Vinia is led in. Flanked by two guards she seems shorter than I remember, and while she's wearing the same fine dress as yesterday, her makeup and hair are a mess.

I remember the sweet smile she offered me as she locked me in the hidden passage, like a spider sending me right into the middle of a sticky web. And when I realize her lips bear a striking resemblance to Sylvan's, as does the color of her hair, it strikes me that he must be a Goldweed too.

Vinia looks at several elves in midnight blue. Elodie's mouth quivers, and she sends her sister a kiss in the air, while an elf I haven't met yet, with long straight hair like milk with honey and a cold expression in his blue eyes steps forward.

"You've shamed us, Vinia," he says.

Her face falls. "H-how can you say that? Sylvan?" she cries, turning her gaze to the short man, who just approached us, but he shows her his empty hands in a gesture that has tears falling down her cheeks.

"Luke? Luke, please tell them! I beg you!"

As her blue gaze settles on me, along with every single pair of eyes in the huge room, my feet freeze to the floor.

My heart hardens when I recall the way she used my fears against me and lied to further her own schemes. It reminds me of that terrible night when I ran away from boarding school and begged a bus driver for help, only for him to nod and agree... then take me right back to that hellhole.

I straighten, more confident with Kyran at my side. "You told me to go into the caves at high tide. You knew they would flood and that I stood no chance."

My voice is like a crystal glass shattering on marble floor.

Vinia shakes her head. "He's lying! He's trying to cover his tracks!"

The crowd of courtiers gasps and whispers, and the space around the Goldweeds empties, as if even touching them might leave stains of blame on one's fine clothes.

Close to us, Sylvan rubs his eyes, motionless, but doesn't protest anymore despite his sister still shouting in her defense.

"You all heard my treacherous cousin. She doesn't have a drop of regret in her heart." Raising his voice, Kyran leads me up the steps at the very end of the room, where two identical thrones of black obsidian wait for us, as if I was the consort of a king and deserved a place at his side. Ferocious wolves and sea snakes are carved into the two armchairs, and the thinnest silver thread hangs between them like a reminder of the unbreakable bond between the master of the Nocturne Court and their Dark Companion.

"Traitor!" Some overeager courtier yells from the crowd.

Vinia stomps her heels like a frustrated child throwing a tantrum and lets out an angry scream. "Mother, do something! Those are all lies!"

A woman as tall as Vinia's long-haired brother steps forward in all her midnight-blue glory. Her pale blue eyes are like twin stars surrounded by nebulas of sparkly eyeshadow. "You are no daughter of mine. You put all of us in grave danger." She then turns to Kyran and bows. "Do what you need to, my Prince."

Vinia stills, as if the frost of the woman's voice has made her bones brittle. She opens her mouth, but no words come out. The reality of her position seems to dawn on her at last.

No help is coming.

Kyran stops next to one of the thrones and nods when the backs of my thighs touch the edge of the seat. He holds both my hands as I settle, then presses kisses to my knuckles, and no amount of cynicism can stop the flow of warmth in my veins.

I don't yet know what punishment Vinia will receive, but no one has ever avenged any suffering I've been through, so I can't help the bloodlust throbbing in my gums.

"So how about that lucky charm?" Kyran whispers with a smile ghosting over his lips.

The decision only takes me a second. I'm dressed in extravagant finery, but just one thing I'm wearing matters. I take off the little lobster pin and attach it over Kyran's heart like a Lady giving her beloved knight a handkerchief before battle.

I can't take my eyes off his as I do so, searching for answers. I don't know what he will need luck for, but he's my protector in the Nightmare Realm. Whatever it is, he needs to stay safe.

His expression softens, and it almost seems like he wants to speak to me again, but then his gaze strays to the courtiers gathered to witness whatever ceremony is coming.

Kyran rises and speaks up. "Vinia Octavia Nightweed. For the crime of betraying the Nocturne Court and the attempted murder of a future Dark Companion, you shall die," he says, facing the room.

Kyran takes two steps down from the throne, giving me a good view of Vinia's pale face, but my mind is empty.

Die.

He did say 'die'.

Maybe he means it metaphorically. Like, taking away her shadow power, or stripping her of her title? Maybe she will be dressed in rags and made to work in a pigsty? I'd appreciate *that*.

I have most definitely often fantasized of cruel punishments for those who've hurt me. But not about their death. Not even for the teachers at my boarding school. I'm too stunned to find my voice again as Kyran descends the steps toward her.

"But I shall be merciful, since we share blood. I'm going to give you a chance to fight for your life. A duel. May the best win."

In one of the mirrors on the walls, I see Kyran's smile widen, and even his teeth seem sharper than usual in that predatory expression.

He will kill her and enjoy it.

But will I?

I don't know, but while my heart thuds with each step he takes, I don't try to stop him or beg him to forgive Vinia. Maybe that tells me more about myself than I'd like to know.

CHAPTER 21

LUKE

I can't believe this.

This man, whom I spent last night with, and who saved me from certain death is about to choke the life out of someone, and not even in a moment of desperation. Cold and calculated, he will make an example of Vinia in front of everyone. She might have the slightest chance of fighting back, but the grave expression on Sylvan's face as he approaches a spot on the edge of the impromptu arena tells me she's doomed. For all intents and purposes, this will be an execution.

I might have an interest in all things dark and morbid, but I've never *seen* someone die. I also usually run *from* violence, not toward it.

Under the watchful eyes of the guards, Sylvan pulls out a narrow rapier from a sheath at his side and hands it to Vinia. He whispers something to his sister, but he's pushed back into the crowd soon enough.

The guards standing between the courtiers and the empty arena in the middle present their swords. It seems like an empty ceremony at first, but moments later, a bright blue glow emerges from each hilt, creating a domed shape around Vinia and Kyran. With my gaze focused on the broad back of my prince, I'm startled when I sense a presence close by, but the moment of worry is gone when I realize Tristan and Sabine flank me on both sides.

I get self-conscious sitting while a pregnant woman stands, but when I offer Sabine my seat, her eyes go so wide it's like I've grown a second head.

"It's the Companion's throne, Luke. I couldn't. Besides, I see better like this," she whispers, leaning against my seat. "Did you know Vinia folds book corners and returns them to the library that way?"

I don't know what to say, because... did Sabine just suggest Vinia deserves to die for dog-earing books? I sink deeper into my seat, glancing at the bloodthirsty gloss over Sabine's golden eyes. I'm definitely not in fucking Kansas anymore, and now I know why my outfit for today features so many red elements.

The crowd of onlookers in fine clothes simmers with not-too-discreet bloodlust, which makes Sylvan's slouched form stand out all the more in the far off corner. He alone is mourning what is to happen here, and while his sister did try to kill me, I can't help but feel responsible for her impending death.

A part of me feels she's already gone, and seeing her step back and bristle as she watches Kyran like a cornered mouse might a cat seeps guilt into my heart. If I stood up and asked my prince to stop all this and grant her mercy, would he do it?

If he did, would he resent me for embarrassing him in front of the court? Or would he simply ignore me, proving once and for all that the respect and adoration I'm being given are smoke and mirrors.

Decorum.

Pageantry.

Meant for the bedroom at best and taken away at his whim.

But I sit in silence, because deep down, maybe I'm not that good a human being. I remember the water rising around me, Kyran almost drowning to save me, his pale lips turning blue after the despair attack. Back then, I hated Vinia with all my heart and wanted her to suffer for what she did.

I watch her tear-streaked cheeks now and find myself not caring that she's small, or a woman. She knew what she was doing and even manipulated me into thinking I was talking *her* into sending me down there.

But will I still think that when I see her blood?

Tristan leans a little lower and whispers, "The prince will be fine. He always lands on his feet."

Yes. In the past. Because the prince Tristan is thinking of, had a capable twin brother always watching over him. This Kyranis is all alone against adversity.

"If something goes wrong... will someone intervene?" I find myself asking as the languid music quickens, adjusting to the way the two opponents size each other up. Kyran makes his first move, circling Vinia like a wolf would a lamb.

Tristan frowns. "Oh. No. Once the duel is announced, there's no going back. But don't worry. Vinia doesn't have much skill with shadows."

I swallow, more distressed than I expected to be. My stomach clenches, bile rises in my throat, yet I can't look away from the man wearing my good luck charm. I'm not excited about this spectacle the way the courtiers are, but I stare all the same, squeezing the armrests of the throne.

"Will it be quick?" I ask, but before Tristan can answer, a light erupts in what has become an arena. The same warm yellow brightness that emanated from the lantern Vinia gave me as she urged me down those treacherous stairs, is now filling the dome and dispersing every shadow inside it.

Sabine covers her mouth, and the atmosphere sobers, as if everyone has realized their punch has been poisoned. A chill crawls up my spine when Tristan takes a step forward, visibly tense.

"Did you know she can do that?" he whispers. Sabine shakes her head as Kyran stands straighter, almost as if he only got serious about this fight now.

The warm light rakes over the faces of onlookers with its brightness, changing the pretty elven faces into Halloween masks.

"What is it?" I ask with my heart beating faster.

"It's Sunlight," Sabine says through clenched teeth. "It weakens shadow magic, and since she knows her life is at stake, she's using all she has."

"Where the fuck did she get it?" Tristan huffs, clutching the back of my throne.

"She might have been born with it if her parents planned it well in advance. It would explain why she's unable to wield shadow," says his sister.

I listen to those musings, desperate to soak in as much knowledge as I can, but all I can think of is my prince's safety.

"Is this dangerous to Kyran—is?" I choke out.

Tristan grunts. "If you were his Dark Companion, he could just use your shadow."

Guilt seeps even into my bones, because it's my fault I'm not bound to him yet. And while I feel I had the right to fear the rushed marriage, my actions put Kyran in danger.

"How so?"

"Your human shadow was forged under the sun. It can't be dispersed. Not by the guards' wall, not by Vinia's Sunlight, not even by Heartbreak."

I watch Kyran pull out his sword but initially it appears he's grabbed at air. It's only when he changes his stance a bit that I spot the very outline of the blade, which is transparent now, as if made of glass. Not a wisp of shadow in sight.

"I hope Gloomdancer doesn't shatter," Sabine mumbles, adding to the weight mounting on my shoulders, because all this is my fault. Sure, no one forced Vinia to deceive me, but none of this would have happened in the first place if I didn't try to run away.

Kyran wouldn't be in danger, and I... I would be a married man, in this world at least, as unbelievable as that is.

But there's no room for what-would-have-beens when Kyran charges at Vinia. She steps back, wide-eyed, but just as he's about to stab her, a bright light bursts from her hands. Its power stings my eyes, but the elves cover their faces and turn away, as if the voiceless explosion is sending shockwaves through the room.

Kyran recoils, shielding himself with one arm, and as everyone looks away, Vinia lunges forward, the edge of her weapon glinting like platinum. I rise to my feet with a cry, and Kyran jerks back right on time. The tip of her blade misses his stomach by a fraction of an inch, but he's blinded along with everyone else, and there's only so long he can rely on other senses and good luck.

Tristan swears behind me, squinting to watch on. "This can't be happening. But I've seen the prince fight," he adds grimly. "Some days he's a master, and at other times, barely relies on his luck. At least he's not fighting the older brother, Anatole. That bastard is a demon when it comes to fencing."

"Is she allowed to *kill* him?" I ask.

"Yes," Sabine says, her voice like a guillotine.

But Kyran never stops moving in the arena. Now I know why he's wearing the long cape, which could be a hindrance in any normal fight. In his violent dance, the fabric swishes and billows, creating shadows. As soon as he shields his sword behind it, black tendrils grow around the blade, but when he tries to strike or reveals his weapon to push back Vinia's rapier, the shadow on Gloomdancer withers.

I don't know how long she can keep the blinding light alive, but it glows even in her eyes, making her pupils invisible. She fights as though her life is at stake, because it is.

Kyran is frantic too, but his shadow can't reach his opponent. I know how much power those dark tentacles have when he's able to use them. He just needs—

"Shadow..." I whisper to myself as my heart stops.

Vinia swishes her rapier forward, and Kyran manages to avoid spilling his insides onto the floor by taking a step back and pulling in his stomach, but his cape betrays him. He slips on it and falls to the floor.

I turn to Tristan with all the authority I can muster as Kyran's promised.

I point to a lantern glowing green on the wall. "Hold it behind me!"

He's not used to taking orders from the likes of me, but to his credit, he does exactly what I ask, and moments later, my shadow spills down the steps and passes through the blueish barrier, into the dome. I move so it can reach Kyran, who rolls away from Vinia's attack and strikes her with his hand, landing a blow for the first time since the fight started.

She cries out, spinning away as if this is a dance, not a fight to the death, and Kyran drags himself up with a scowl. He's avoiding my gaze, as if he's ashamed of how long the duel is taking, but once he spots my shadow, our eyes meet, and he offers me a smile that has my heart thrumming with an excitement I haven't felt in... forever.

That predatory smile now gives me a thrill. He knows he's won. Maybe that makes me an accomplice to the impending murder, but Vinia had no issue with throwing me under the bus or trying to stab Kyran, so she can reap what she sowed.

I rise to my toes and even though Vinia huddles in the farthest corner of the arena, my shadow reaches her shoe. It feels like I'm towering over the room, as tall as the ceiling. No one's stopping me either, so I feel more vindicated in my actions. Of course I'd do anything to save Kyran.

My prince.

My... promised.

Kyran sinks into the stark black strip I cast on the fine floor, disappearing from sight, and as Vinia gasps, her blue eyes darting in every direction, I can almost sense Kyran's satisfaction within me. It... tickles. I don't know how, but I *feel* him in my shadow. The contentment only lasts a moment, because Vinia collapses to the floor with a sharp cry, her foot bent at an unnatural angle. The sight of Kyran's hand around her ankle shakes my confidence.

But I don't get to think through my choices as he pulls her into my shadow and slices through her throat.

The Sunlight flickers in her eyes, only to fade as she gurgles, no longer fighting his hold.

I shouldn't admire him now. I should consider him a brute and murderer... but he's a magnificent beast, crouched over her, panting and with the blade still in his hand. When Tristan lowers the lamp, my shadow slides off Kyran, revealing his leather-clad form. He's like a renaissance painting come to life with his long dark hair dipped in the blood pooled on the floor and the cape thrown over one shoulder.

Leaning over Vinia's still form, he touches her torn neck, and while I am disturbed by the strange gesture, everything falls into place when a black, elongated silhouette slides onto his finger. The shadow eel is cautious at first, but when Kyran gives its side a tentative stroke, it darts forward and disappears under his sleeve.

My thoughts return to the uncountable creatures slithering over Kyran's naked body as he fucked me silly. He told me each one stands for a shadow wielder he's killed, but seeing is believing and now the truth about my fiancé's nature is impossible to ignore.

I know it's wrong, but my whole being throbs with yearning for him. I take a step down without thinking, as if he's pulling me closer by the thread tied between our shadows.

Now that the light is gone, the elves are able to see the result of the duel, and all erupt in cheers, clapping their hands as if this is a competition at sucking up to the future Lord. I feel the bitterness of bile in my throat when I notice how loud the Goldweeds are in their applause. Only Sylvan stays quiet, huddled in the corner of the room and short enough that I can barely see him in the crowd.

I almost feel sorry for him, despite having no warm feelings for my own mother, but my attention is soon diverted when my prince approaches, reaching out for my hand.

I hesitate. There's blood on his fingers. Red and fresh.

But when I see the uncertainty in his gray eyes, all I want is to disperse it, so I take one more step down and grab his hand. I've been part of this execution. There's no use in pretending otherwise. I chose between him and Vinia, and I don't regret my decision. Maybe that makes me a monster too.

I can almost physically feel the relief my gesture brings him. And while I now see that blood stains my pin too, I close my eyes when Kyran leans down to kiss my forehead, at peace and safe with him as my protector. The coppery aroma of death is thick in the air, but it's too late to overthink this, so I smile down at all the courtiers when Kyran holds my hand and addresses his flock.

"Justice prevails."

He waits a moment for the initial applause to subside, and as disgusting as the Goldweeds are, cheering while their own blood lies dead on the floor, maybe this is a lesson I need to learn if I am to survive this next month.

Even family can't be trusted.

Only Kyran.

No. Even that isn't certain, but he at least has vested interest in keeping me alive.

Vinia's blood is sticky between our fingers as Kyran kisses my knuckles before speaking again.

"This human will be my Dark Companion, and anyone who even *thinks* about hurting him in any way will suffer the full extent of my wrath. He is the blood pumping through my heart, my promised, and I *will* burn the Realm for him if I have to."

It shouldn't thrill me to hear it, but a shiver still runs down my spine. When I look up at Kyran, it's as if he took some of Vinia's light. He's beautiful, he's deadly, and set on winning me over.

I swallow and sense myself smiling despite my better judgment. My fingers itch to tremble, but he holds them steady. Kyran has declared his feelings for me in front of the whole court, and even though he's made it clear to others before that I am to be his Dark Companion, the truth only hits me now, as everyone's eyes are on me.

To him, *I* am the prize. The one worth fighting for, the one worth avenging.

My trust issues are a thousand sirens blaring in warning, but I want to feel safe for a moment longer and indulge in the false belief that he might really care about me so deeply.

When Kyran reaches for the pin on his heart, I stop him, putting my hand over his.

"Keep it. Looks like you might need the luck," I say, trying to be cool and cocky, but my voice still comes out shaky.

Kyran's brows lower, and he rubs my cheek with the back of his bloodstained hand. Maybe I should be disgusted, but all I feel when he leans over and kisses one of my hands like some old-timey gentleman is bliss.

I know that to him my worth lies in my human shadow, with the novelty of sex adding a bit of spice to our relationship, but a toxic part of me doesn't care that everything we share is only surface-level. I just want to be adored. This once. Even if it's not meant to last.

"Are you certain? You said it's important to you."

I hesitate, unsure if I'm ready to open up this much, but I'm already so deep into my... entanglement with him. "When I got to leave school, my mother didn't come to pick me up, so I hitchhiked with this trucker. I mean that he gave me a ride. On the way, we stopped at this local diner famous for its lobster rolls. He bought me lunch, and got me this pin with the name of the place. I... really needed kindness at that point, and he wanted nothing in return. I kept it to remind myself that the world isn't always out to get me. Maybe you need that too," I finish in a whisper, feeling sillier than ever.

My chest feels heavy with emotion when Kyranis meets my gaze. "I will forever cherish this gift. Thank you for your help," he whispers, seemingly unaware of all the attention we're getting from our audience.

"All I did was stand up." I shrug, not used to praise. I can't even hold his gaze. What I'm used to is 'do better, Luke', and 'you ruined my life, Luke', and 'I spent all that money, and you didn't even finish school'.

But Kyran only has smiles for me. "I already think of you as my Dark Companion, Luke," he says and sits me on the throne.

The sight of Vinia sprawled on the bloodstained floor makes me stiffen. Sylvan approaches her, pale as a ghost, but his own brother, the one with lush long hair, stands in the way. While their standoff is silent, I can almost see the sparks flying off their bodies.

That's what this court is. Death is an integral part of the Nightmare Realm, and the courtiers all embrace the dark and morbid.

Kyran spreads his arms and raises his hands as if he's a preacher. "I am officially announcing the beginning of my courtship with Luke Moor, a human from Blackwood in the state of Maine. We will marry on the day of the Blood Moon. I invite all of you to hunt the Stag of Sunrise alongside us in two weeks' time. May the moonlight shine brightly upon this court for a thousand more years!"

CHAPTER 22

Kyran

Sunlight is a challenge for even the most experienced shadow-wielders. I've never encountered it, and its glow was as shocking as it was painful. It made my eyes ache, my ears buzz, and by the time nausea took over, I could barely keep track of Vinia's movements.

The Goldweed sharks have been preparing for this since the day her powers first appeared and, in my pride, I walked right into their trap. My head is still throbbing, and my vision hasn't yet returned to normal, so how was I to defend myself against a foe so treacherous?

An icy eel coils in my guts when I think about what could have happened if my promised, my Luke, didn't have the clarity of mind to step in and aid me.

I could have died today.

It could have been my blood staining the floor.

Luke abandoned to the harpies greedy for his shadow.

Just the thought of it makes my blood boil all over again. Whoever poached Luke after my death might have treated him with unjust cruelty just because of the connection to me.

The last face I want to see right now slinks toward me with fake worry in his eyes. Anatole Goldweed. His handsome features are filled with so much concern I almost believe that his intentions are sincere.

Tristan stands close but I gesture with my fingers, allowing Anatole to approach. I resent that instead of spending my time with Luke, I'm stuck fulfilling my princely duties, and those involve mingling with the courtiers after the execution. Even courtiers who've kept Vinia's skills a secret and may or may not have set me up for this duel.

"Anatole," I say coolly, entwining my hands at the back to keep them farther from the bastard's pale neck. The treacherous swine has no business being this handsome.

"My Prince. I thought it especially important to approach after what happened. I need you to know I didn't realize she was cursed with the Sunlight power, and neither did anyone else in our family. I don't know how she hid that from us, but I will make all the necessary inquiries and punish anyone who kept that secret."

When he bows, my instinct tells me to punch him down and then place my foot on his cheek, but I am the future Lord of the Nocturne Court, and a degree of decorum cannot be avoided. So instead of lashing out, I punish him with silence until he understands what I require and bows deeper. I only speak once his locks touch the floor.

"It must have been quite the shock," I lie, meeting his gaze. "I do expect you to deal with this matter promptly," I say as my gaze drifts above the crowd, to Luke, who stands in Sabine's company, assaulted by a crowd of his own.

A greedy part of me doesn't want Luke talking to anyone else. I want to hoard his attention and lock it away, no matter how unreasonable that is. But I only have so much time to make sure he wants to stay with me, so every second spent with the likes of Anatole feels wasted.

"I will. As the current head of the family," because of course he needs to underline his parents have opted out of the line of succession, "I promise to manage any threats to the crown."

I don't know how he is supposed to manage *himself*. His brother, Sylvan, might be a thorn in my side, but he wouldn't challenge my rule. As for their remaining sister, well, she seems intent on supporting her oldest brother's ambition and reaping the potential benefits of his ascension. Either way, I'm not letting him off the hook so easily.

"What is your plan? How will you find the culprit? How will they be punished?"

He hesitates with the answer, which tells me his words were empty promises. He must have known about Vinia's skill. I spent years hidden in the shadows and watching people, so I'm pretty good at telling when they lie.

"I've already spoken to my mother, and she recalls a foreign merchant whom Vinia met a few years ago. She bought a Sunlight lantern from him, but we will find him and establish whether he helped her awaken that power."

As Anatole speaks, I can't help but glance over his shoulder, and Luke's eyes meet mine. He must miss my presence too. My heart skips a beat when I think back to the way he moaned my name and clutched my shoulders. How my presence made his eyes soften and how he thought on his feet to save my life.

I smile. So does he, but then I realize Anatole has gone quiet, so I meet his gaze and nod at whatever gibberish he said when I wasn't paying attention.

"Thank you. I grant you and your whole family leave to make arrangements regarding... all that happened."

It seems Anatole wanted to say more but understands he's being dismissed and doesn't push his luck. One bow later, he walks off, but light bounces off a large silver star on his shoulder straight into my eye, as if to spite me.

I glance at Luke again to cleanse my palate, but this time I find him staring at a servant cleaning blood off the floor, and he's no longer smiling.

"Can't look away, can you?" Tristan muses, tapping my shoulder before he steps forward so we face the room together. The music flows softly now, suggesting to the courtiers that this part of the day is over.

But as much as I want to join my promised, his somber expression freezes my feet to the floor. "Does he seem... happy to you?"

Tristan shrugs. "Who doesn't appreciate a righteous execution? She sure did," he says and discreetly points out Marquise Coralis.

Dressed in a black gown that hugs her curves as if it's tar dripped straight onto her body, she stands out among the women who wear the more fashionable full skirts. She's holding a crystal chalice with a sparkling red drink and watches me intently. But she's not seeing me. Not really. She thinks I'm Kyranis, the man she's been bedding quite often in the past year.

I exhale. A part of me was hoping I could ignore her attention until the whole matter is forgotten, but the affair was fairly public. I can't count on everyone suffering from amnesia at the same time.

"Well... but what about Luke?" I ask, once again trying to capture my companion's gaze, but he seems busy talking to Sabine. I pray for her to start giving birth so she can no longer distract him.

Tristan raises his eyebrows. "Luke can't really satisfy *all* your needs, can he? Did you have a falling out with the Marquise? Did she not say she was ready to become the mother of your children?"

I clear my throat, remembering the last time I got a glimpse of my brother and the Marquise in bed. It would be an understatement if I said I didn't plan on continuing that arrangement. Not because there was anything wrong with the beautiful lady herself. The only thing I could fault her for was falling for someone as vapid and self-centered as my twin.

That, and being of the female persuasion.

"I'm perfectly content in his presence," I say and adjust my cravat to avoid Tristan's gaze.

"Is it the novelty of the connection? He is pretty, but you've always focused on women..." Tristan cocks his head, and his golden eyes glow with the need for gossip.

I've stepped in as my brother many times, but rarely in situations requiring social skills. At least the practice I did get means I'm not completely out of my depth.

I lick my lips as memories of last night flood back, showing me the plains of Luke's back arching and stretching as I mounted him. Sweat glistening on flesh like diamond dust. Moans like the softest music.

I cover myself with my cape as I take a deep breath, trying to control myself. The hold Luke has over me is unmatched by anything I ever experienced.

"He is... magnificent in every way."

Tristan turns to look at my future Companion. I want to blindfold him, just in case, but I know Tristan is my most loyal guard. He wouldn't risk my wrath. "Is it different with a human? Or is it the betrothal bond between shadows that makes a difference?"

Does it make a difference? How can I know when I have never as much as kissed anyone before Luke?

Does it even matter?"

"He enchants me like no one else. Maybe once you take a Dark Companion of your own, you will understand."

I expect some silly dig from Tristan, as that was often his dynamic with Kyranis, but he smiles, watching Luke become more animated. "He really has changed you. I don't know if that's possible for me, but if there's anyone who could keep me loyal and interested, it would probably be a human. They're so... different."

"So fragile," I agree. "I'll need your help to keep him safe, cousin," I say to make sure he understands I consider him my family. But my attention is again on Luke's smiling lips, on long arms I want to feel around me.

I have wanted men before, but never the way I desire him.

"With my life," Tristan says. "It's been so many years since we've had Companions at court. Some of the courtiers might have forgotten what the addition of his shadow means."

But the truth is, I'm not thinking of Luke's potent shadow right now. I'm far too busy considering the way he looks at me when I touch him, or how he offers me his body.

Me. Not Kyranis, who wasn't worthy of my Luke.

He knows who I am and kisses me with so much passion I could drown in the waters of his tenderness.

I know his soul isn't mine yet. But it will be. I have time to make him trust me and forget the world he needs to leave behind.

When Marquise Coralis starts walking my way, I pretend not to see her and head for Luke instead. I will talk to her another time, but right now I need to make sure Luke isn't conflicted about the execution. Some humans can be gentle like that.

One gesture sends a couple of courtiers still left in the room aside, and I stride for the figure in red stockings. I've picked out every piece of clothing he's wearing, and right now I wish to undress him, just so I can have something that already carries his scent.

Will he notice my presence behind him? Will he look my way?

No. His senses are so painfully human I could slit his throat and he wouldn't even realize what happened before he died. Of course, I would never as much as scratch his pretty neck, but it only reminds me how protective I need to be of him.

"...and then when you throw them into the bathtub, they fizz, making the water colorful and bubbly. I prefer painting to making bath bombs, but those are harder to sell."

I am at a loss for words.

"You... paint?" I ask, staring at the top of Luke's head until he spins around and meets my gaze.

Ah, his mouth is like the softest of pillows, and I would have tasted it now if it wasn't bad manners.

He swallows when our eyes meet, and the red liner under his eyes makes his appearance much more demonic than his nature truly is. Can't say I don't like it.

"Y-yes, but it's not very good," he says, raising his hands. "I don't have so much time out of work to practice."

"Nonsense! You are my promised. You'll have as much time for your art as you require."

"Perhaps you could gift him a set of paints, cousin," Sabine suggests, and in that moment I want to bless her future baby and put it in a golden cradle.

"Oh yes! Would you like that, darling?"

The smile growing on Luke's lips is all the answer I need. "I'd love to find out what types of paint you have here."

I give him a chaste kiss on the cheek that only makes me desire him more. I need to be alone with him and I have just the excuse.

"I know what you need to see as an artist," I say and pull on his hand, thrilled when his fingers slide between mine.

"Where are we going?"

"It cannot be described, it must be experienced."

CHAPTER 23

Kyran

The orangery is the size of a beached Leviathan, and the steel frame supporting the glass walls and ceilings casts beautiful shadows on the marble floor. The ribs of the roof are covered with filigree patterns, and while the skeleton encapsulating a richness of trees, flowers, and other plants is stark black, the moonlight touches us with its silvery gaze.

Tristan gave me a knowing look when I asked him to stay back and make sure no one else enters this indoor garden, but he's already aware of me breaching protocol when it comes to intimacy with my future Dark Companion.

And I can't help myself.

Luke's face is sweet as honey when he takes everything in, mouth open in awe. But as impressive as my palace is, he is the most beautiful flower here, all ruby-red and black as night. Even the pattern of thorns on the sleeves of his shirt makes me liken him to a rose. I would have locked the doors and kept him here if I didn't know any better by now. I need to pace myself to avoid spooking him. I'm an experienced hunter, and a slow, cautious approach makes for a favorable outcome. Last time I got ahead of myself, he ran away before our wedding.

"Is there a reason you brought me here?" Luke asks, glancing my way as we stroll through the orangery.

Heat steams up the inside of my shirt when my gaze drifts down his back, counting all the spots where the lacing at the back of his vest is crisscrossed. I picked it because it pulls in his waist, in turn making my lover's buttocks appear fuller. The red looks so good on his legs, and I wish to get my hands on his calves already. But the last thing I want is for him to think I only want his body.

My brother was notorious for his womanizing ways and, despite having the personality of a clown, broke many hearts. I would hate for Luke to feel used when he is *everything* to me. So I take his hand, stroke his jaw with my finger, and then gesture toward the orange trees growing out of pots shaped like dragon eggs. "I thought you might feel less homesick surrounded by plants from your world. But that's not the whole story. The truth is that I wanted for us to have some peace and quiet."

Reiner arranged Luke's hair into fluffy waves. Some of the strands fall over his forehead in a way so picturesque I have to forgive my house master for the transgression before the wedding.

"I've... never seen someone die. I wasn't expecting it. Was that supposed to be a positive surprise for me?"

My smile drops. "You... hated it."

He frowns, running his fingers over the petals of an intensely purple orchid. "A good person would. I'm shocked, but... I don't know. Maybe she did deserve it."

Worry is smudged across Luke's features, and I fall to one knee, hoping to wipe it away with a kiss to his delicate hands. Oh, how I adore their shape, their frailty, even the little scar on the side of one finger where a knife must have cut in not that long ago. He's wearing the ring I put on him when we met, and it reminds me just how much I wish to keep him forever.

"She did deserve it. Had I been slower, you would have been taken from me. I cannot fathom a greater crime."

I sense his pulse quicken in his palm. Luke's gaze is so intense when he meets mine I wouldn't be able to look away even if a pack of wolves was approaching us. "I was conflicted when you fought her, but when I remembered how I dragged you out of the ocean, saw how she almost stabbed you, I didn't have mercy for her left in me."

And that's why he's such a perfect Companion for me. He might still have a lot to learn about my world, but he picks up on everything so fast.

Moved, I lean in, pushing my nose between the buttons of his vest, to get a whiff of his natural scent. Fresh yet warm, it makes my head spin, so I hold on to his legs and close my eyes as a sense of contentment spreads through me.

I have lived without touch for so long that the gentle way he's stroking my head pulls right at my heart. But now he's here. Mine to touch. To cherish. To adore.

I have a month to convince him that he ought to stay, and I intend to use every trick in my arsenal.

Well, with the exception of love potions. I want real affection, not some stunted lust puppet.

"I'm sorry you were scared. I thought you would appreciate the revenge. But how come you've never seen death? Were you... sheltered?" I ask, watching him. The shrub of opulent blue flowers behind him creates such a great background for his beauty I wonder if this is where we should get our portrait painted.

"Not really. It's just not so common to see in my world. And maybe that's wrong. We're very removed from death until it comes. It's strange to consider. We live much shorter lives than you, so you'd think we'd be more at ease with the concept of dying. A lot of things are different where I'm from."

I latch on to every word from his mouth and rise to my feet before pulling him down one of the paths winding through the artificial landscape. "In what way?" I ask as I step over a stream leading to another part of the garden. I then turn and offer him my hand. I am certain he can cross on his own, but I enjoy offering him my services too much to resist this opportunity.

He doesn't hesitate for long, and I love how he puts more trust in me with every passing hour. Making him understand I mean no harm will be a journey, but I'm willing to take it if my prize is his love.

"Even the way you treat me in front of others. You tell everyone how much I mean to you, you intend to *marry* me, and you touch me in public. In my world, this kind of thing is often forbidden between two men. In some countries by law, in others it's just frowned upon. And sure, there's also places where such things are acceptable, but my experience, in my stupid little town, is being disliked for being openly into men. And sometimes 'disliked' is a euphemism for 'hated'."

I'm stunned and pull him close, kissing the side of his head as he stiffens, only to melt into my arms as if he were made of butter. "What? Why? That makes no sense. Why only between two men?" I want to unfasten his thick vest just so I can offer him more comfort and feel his skin.

"Between women as well. It's hard to explain without all the context of my world. There's religion, there's the matter of sexism, but I think the fact that only male-female couples can produce children is one of the major reasons for the prejudice against people like us. What you need to know is that a lot of people find it shameful, unnatural, or even disgusting. But I feel what I feel. I can't change that about myself. I don't want to." Luke's arms slide under my cape, and I'm at a loss. Why would he want to return to such a hateful world?

The question comes out of my mouth on its own. Maybe I should have bitten my tongue, but the truth is that I do want to know.

"It's where I belong," Luke tells me. But when he rests his head on my shoulder, it's as if he's trying to let me know he'd like to stay at my side. "Your realm is... a beautiful, if dangerous, fantasy, but I do have to face reality. I'm strong and stubborn. I can handle whatever life throws at me," he says as if he needs to convince me. He's not going to. In fact, I am now confident I can make him change his mind about our future. He just needs to understand that the life I can offer him is a far cry from all the difficulties of his world.

I can take away the pain causing the strain in his voice and make him mine. "Do you want children?"

Luke pulls away enough to look into my eyes. His face pales. "Huh? Please don't tell me I can get pregnant here."

I chuckle and give his cheek a playful pinch. "Don't be silly. You don't have the right organs to sustain a child inside your body. But we could... use a potion so someone can carry *our* baby instead," I say, and while I have not thought this far into the future, or even about my own legacy, right now my head is full of vague images featuring a baby with eyes as green as Luke's.

I could teach them to be the best shadow wielder to ever carry the Nightweed name, but they'd be as sweet as Luke.

His eyes widen, and he seems to be considering what I've said. I hope the outcome is in my favor and gives him another reason to stay when he has to make the choice. "Oh. *Oh...* I haven't really considered that. Most men I've been with weren't exactly family material. A lot of them wouldn't even acknowledge me in the street. And I'd need to have enough money. I'm guessing a prince definitely wants children?" he asks with a little smile and strokes my cheek in a tender gesture that has me leaning into his touch like a pet. But no one will see us here.

I can't wait to get my hands on his naked body again, but I also want *this*. He sees me. He wants to know me. And with every new fact he shares about himself, I want to learn more. Just today, I found out that he paints and that he likes the clothes I offer him.

"I do. In the future," I add, because there is no reason to hurry. We can have all the time we want. "But I want *you* more. And I want my people to share my happiness. I cannot fathom why your past lovers would ignore you," I add and pull him along the path, past statues imitating a group of beasts roaming my garden.

I can see in the way he lowers his head that it bothers him, but he shrugs. "Some were married, some just didn't want people to know they slept with men. It's fine. I didn't want to date them anyway. We both got some pleasure out of it, and that's that."

Anger buzzes deep in my chest. Luke isn't some dirty secret to hide. He is beautiful, kind, and saved my life less than an hour ago. He deserves *everything*. "They didn't know what a gem they were holding in their dirty hands."

But instead of smiling, Luke rolls his eyes which is… more hurtful than I could have expected. "You're saying that because you want something from me, but maybe they were the honest ones. At least there was no need to sugarcoat things."

Now I want to travel to his world to end every single man who's ever hurt him. I want them torn apart by beasts, and maybe I would even make it happen in an arena, for my own and Luke's enjoyment.

But I already know he doesn't always feel the way I do about brutal revenge, so I swallow the flood of murderous promises and consider my next move. "That was uncalled for," I mutter, painfully aware of the hollow space between us.

And to make things worse, he not only pulls his fingers away, but even crosses his arms over his chest. I don't have to read minds to see he's getting increasingly agitated. He pretends to study a rose bush, but his eyes glisten, and his lips are twisted into a scowl. "Well, I'm sorry if the truth is ugly. When I was a teenager, my mother sent me to a boarding school where I learned how cruel and untrustworthy people can be, so yeah, maybe my world is shit, but at least I know where I stand there."

Looks like my rose has more thorns than I was aware of.

My chest sinks, as if he's punched it, but I've endured much too, also at the hands of those who should have cared for me, and I will not let him push me away. If anything, learning this side of him makes me want to take care of him more. "I'm sorry. I wish I could do something to make it hurt less."

Luke stays quiet for a long moment, but then sniffs. If I could soak up whatever pain he's going through, I would. I might not be used to dealing with other people's emotions, but for him, I want to keep my cool.

"Just... don't say things you don't mean," he whispers with sadness painted all over his face. It's so clear in the glow of the moonlight I want to kiss it off him. "I can handle the situation between us. You don't need to lie to me so I follow through."

Lightning shocks my back and crawls all the way to the tips of my toes as I hold his shoulders. "You think I'm lying? Right now, I am stopping myself from finding out the names of every single person who hurt you in the past and going on a bloody rampage," I say, nudging him back, toward a plush-covered swing hanging from a tree surrounded by midnight blue roses. "You might not see it yet, but I am yours, and I can be your prince as well as your beast. Just say the word," I rasp as we reach the elevated seat and Luke falls into it. He gasps, but his eyes are on me again, wide and filled with intense emotion. No longer glistening with tears. "You'd avenge me?" He smirks and pulls on my cravat, but I'm dead serious.

"Tenfold. Just to make your eyes spark and your lips praise me," I whisper, leaning in as my balls throb in response to his touch. So far, I have been the one to take the initiative, but the way he is holding me now, as if I'm his pet, awakens a new kind of desire.

The scent of roses is intoxicating, but not as much as the kisses I need from him. "You did do well with Vinia," he whispers. "No one's ever... stood up for me," Luke admits, and I appreciate him opening to me like this. I want him to feel safe at my side.

A shiver runs down my spine, like a droplet of warm oil, and my breath catches as he tightens his hold on my cravat, as if it was a leash. I'm stronger. A royal. And yet, when he looks at me this intensely, I feel that it is he who has all the power. I have never tasted anything as sweet as this praise, and I blink away the rush of emotion that makes my eyes sting and my throat tighten.

I want him to be mine. To only crave me.

"Whatever you wish, I will provide," I whisper almost soundlessly, only an inch away from his tempting lips. I long to sink into them as if they were wild strawberries, but I wait, captivated by his green eyes.

His breath quickens right before he pushes himself up to kiss me. His hurtful words caused so much turmoil in my heart, but the touch of his lips is so soothing I can breathe deeply once more.

I gasp with my whole body and pull on a chain that lifts the swing a bit higher. As soon as it rises, I push between his legs and wrap my arms around him as our tongues clash in a sweet, if hurried, dance. It couldn't be any clearer that I am his too.

I might not have much experience with love, or even people, but nothing has ever felt more right than his touch, and I wouldn't dream of letting him go. Dragging my hand down his thigh, I roll my hips, and we both whimper when our erections meet through layers of fabric.

"I want to see you naked," I say, forcing my eyes open.

He bites his lip, looking around the orangery filled with plants and stone statues of gargoyles poached from his world by my great grandfather. "Here? No one will come in? It does take a while to put these clothes on…" But he's already pulling on the red bow around his neck and opening the silky scarf.

He wants this.

He wants *me*.

Just needs time and reassurance.

"Tristan won't let anyone through. We're alone, this is my palace," I whisper, my lips pressing to his temple as I tug on the front of his vest. "And you look so beautiful in the moonlight."

"What do you like so much about me?" he asks as if he wasn't a *vision* in the clothes celebrating the death of his enemy. He sighs, and while I unbutton his vest from the top, he joins me starting from the bottom, and our fingers meet in the middle. "Sorry, that's so needy of me."

I shake my head and reassure him with a quick kiss. "No. I want you to know that you are the best thing that ever happened to me," I say as my chest fills with sweetness. My life used to be so lonely, but now that I have him, every single minute has gained intense color. "You don't judge me for being my brother's shadow. You *see* me. You have the sweetest little ears, and soft lips, and a smile that makes my stomach feel ticklish. Your tongue can be sharp and cut deep but also give me so much pleasure. Your eyes hide depths I've never seen despite living on the shores of the Nocturne Ocean. And you saved my life today. Again. I don't think I could ever thank you enough."

Even when my immediate family was alive, I always knew I was on my own. Luke is giving me a glimpse of a life where I can bask in his attention. Make love to him, and kill for him if need be. Seen and recognized. Connected.

"You have such a way with words..." Luke sighs with a smile as I absentmindedly unfasten his breeches at the sides of his hips. I might not be privy to all his secrets yet, but at least his body can be mine.

"It's not hard to speak the truth," I say and slide to my knees, pulling my fingers down his calves, all the way to the boots made of the softest leather in the Realm. His eyes cloud as he watches me descend, but I can't wait any longer and cradle his foot in both hands. I kiss the tip of his fine red footwear, then rub my cheekbone against it while my fingers pop open each button.

Luke licks his lips, and some of the wavy hair falls on his face when he looks down. His cheeks are flushed as I reveal his stocking-clad foot. Now that I've lifted the swing, his toes barely reach the ground.

"Is that a place for a crown prince? At my feet?"

He's being playful, but all I can think is that he could as well be *my* prince. Tender and carnal feelings rise inside me, creating an intoxicating concoction.

"Where any man's place is in the presence of the one he adores," I say, putting away the boot as I massage his foot, which is clad in a thick blood-red stocking. My lips graze his knee, and I repeat the same with his other boot, steaming up under my coat.

"You're just horny," Luke sniggers, nudging me with his other foot. His chest rises and falls fast, and his nipples are stiff against the sheer fabric of his shirt.

"I'm what?" I ask, pulling my hands up his legs. He gasps when I push apart his knees and slide between them, burying my fingers in the lush shirt.

"Hot for me. Aroused. You're hard, and all you can think of is my body giving you release. Nothing wrong with that," he whispers. "I can barely control myself around you myself."

The scent of roses intensifies as I brush my nose against his, seeking the intimacy only he can offer. "How do I make you feel?" I ask and crook my neck, licking his stiff nipple through the shirt.

His gasp makes me want to pinch and bite him. I love to see him so responsive. It makes me feel as though he really is in my grasp.

"Like I *want* to trust you. Like I want to forget the circumstances we're in, because all I can think of is how you take charge of me, make me sweaty and brainless. I want to be *open* to you. It's why I like your cum in me so much."

Such dirty words come from those pretty lips.

I can't get enough.

I want to lick every inch of his skin. Consume him whole and never again feel alone.

"Oh, I can make you as sweaty as you like. I love to see you squirming, flushed, and dripping with my cum. That little hole of yours is meant for me."

I grab the folds of his shirt and tug, ripping it open. Buttons fly and scatter, but they're forgotten by the time I kiss Luke's pec, nipping and sucking on flesh more intoxicating than the finest wine.

His moans are music to my ears, and the nightbirds seem to agree as they start their pretty song in the tallest trees of the orangery. Luke slides his hand into my hair, but he doesn't tug in any way, just pets me. He might enjoy some force from me but is so gentle himself that I want to make sure no one else ever lays a finger on him.

Lying back on the large plush swing, he holds his legs open for me, and I doubt he has any idea how frantic with lust that makes me. I want to map every inch of his pale form, know the location of every beauty mark and scar, but even then, I will not be satisfied. He is already an addiction, and I will need more each day.

Rubbing my face against his fragrant chest, I pull down his breeches and underwear, but don't bother removing the stockings. "You smell so good. It's making me... horny, was it?"

"Yes," Luke rasps, and his cock twitches between his legs, begging for attention. "I've never been in such a frenzy with anyone."

The admission only makes pride swell in my chest, and I pull on his legs, resting his calves on my shoulders. The stockings are buttery soft, smooth, yet as warm as his flesh, and I turn my face to kiss the side of Luke's knee as my gaze drifts up his bare thighs, to where his hard cock juts from a bed of dark hair.

Pleasure dances over my skin as I lean forward, enticed by the musky aroma of sex.

"Me neither. And now I can't look away."

I've not had the chance to please him with my mouth yet, and I can't wait. His cockhead has a dark pink shade and I teasingly lick the slit at the top. He moans and pulls me closer with his legs. This is how I want him. No barriers, no emotional walls, and his attention on me only.

"Oh, fuck..." he whimpers, arching his hips off the plush bench of the swing.

I had no idea how much I'd like sucking him, but I already love how much control I have while he's losing it. It's as if the leash is in my hand, and the collar—on his neck.

And we both love it.

I close my eyes, wrapping my arm around his thigh to explore his body, and as I tickle his shaft with my tongue, getting used to his fresh yet musky flavor, my fingers comb through his pubes, rub the base of his stiff rod, and explore the shape of his balls.

It's as if I've been offered a whole dessert table, and I drop the cock out of my mouth to push my tongue against the soft skin of Luke's sac, my mind blown by the tingling all over my skin.

"Fuck... what are you doing to me...?" Luke whines, tightening his fingers in my hair.

I have him right where I want him.

When I suck one of his balls, he gets so restless he clenches his ass and wiggles his hips, but there's nowhere for him to run. I've got his thighs in a tight grip and will take as much time gorging on him as I want to.

"Anything I want," I whisper, my mouth wet against his flesh, and while I'm overheating, touching him takes precedence before shedding my own clothes. In the pocket of my coat, I find a small bottle of the oil that makes sex smoother, and as I lick my way up Luke's dick, I pour some on my hand and tickle his crack with one finger.

I'm torn between keeping my eyes on his face, and the pink pucker between his legs. The way his pupils widen and his mouth turns into an *O* is everything I need to know about Luke wanting me inside him. I love how needy he is. His feelings might be guarded, they might need to develop, or be captured, but this? He leaves no doubt as to how much he loves the intimacy between us.

"You sure you haven't sucked off some shadow demons in preparation for this?" He laughs nervously, but he's breathless, his pink nipples stiff, and his cock leaking delicious pre-cum.

"You like it," I whisper against his cock and move my finger up and down his crack before pushing at his entrance, which initially tightens, only to let me in a moment later. It's smooth, and snug, and just as hot as his mouth.

He nods before he can find his voice. "Yes. And that you're so fucking hot. And dangerous."

Maybe I should fuck the truth out of him more often, because his uninhibited self is irresistible.

We both gasp when my digit pushes in up to the knuckle and I start twisting it inside him, searching for his pleasure spot. Luke's cock is in my mouth again, and I suck around it, not even trying to take it in deep. I know I'm not ready, but I love the saltiness of his juices and want to build up his excitement until he can't cope with it any longer.

His feet slide over my back, as if to push me closer, but he's not using much force. He's just showing me how needy he is for me.

My own cock is trapped under leather, but releasing it from its confines would mean having to let go of Luke and I'm not ready for that. I glance at his flushed chest, and all the way to his parted lips. Every moan escaping his mouth makes me lust for him more intensely. I don't know how I would have survived courting without tasting him.

My lips tighten and move up and down his shaft as I suck on his flesh, but my mind is torn between the beautiful dick on my tongue and the tightness of his body as I go into a rhythm that soon has Luke rubbing his thighs against my face and arching on the swing.

Hypnotizing, enchanting, our physical connection consumes me from the inside, replacing emptiness with the joy of companionship and pleasure.

I only pull away when the lacing of my pants makes my own cock throb.

"I need you," I rasp and fuck him with my finger as I stare at the wet cock resting on his stomach.

"Yours," he mutters between one moan and another.

He might not mean it in the way I want him to yet, but he will one day. For now, my physical cravings take over and I relish his words for what they are.

'Fuck me'.

'Come inside me'.

'Be one with me'.

We are connected by the thinnest strand of shadow, but I can still sense the pulsing heat of his desire down that thread.

I shoot up and pull my hand away before shoving off my fine coat. I'm cooking in my own juices at this point, so my leather top goes next, forcefully dragged over my head. I get trapped inside the garment but I'm speechless when I free myself to the most luscious of views.

Luke rests on the swing bench with both his legs up. His feet are braced against the chains, his hole is beautifully presented as he strokes his cock, watching me with tempting eyes.

I can barely breathe.

This is everything I've ever wanted.

"So. Beautiful," I whisper, stroking his stocking-clad legs all the way to the leather straps keeping the red fabric above the knees.

He bites his lips as he glances at my open pants. "Show me." And as he says that, he slides his other hand to his pink hole, to toy with the slick pucker awaiting me. His eyes are glossy, his hair in disarray, and one sleeve slides farther off his shoulder.

He is the full moon.

The calm waves at midnight.

He is spider silk and feasts lasting deep into the night.

I will not let go of him. Not ever.

In one way or another, I will convince him to stay.

My mind feels as though it's going feral from this wait, and I give a soft gasp as the front of my pants opens to release my cock. It throbs with discomfort but points straight at Luke's entrance, and I follow its lead, rubbing the head against the slickened pucker.

"I *will* make you mine."

And I'll stop at nothing. If my dick is what ends up keeping him at my side, that's good enough for me.

Luke's hands roam up my arms. "Christ... it looks so good," he mutters, glancing between our bodies.

I grin and look down, at the eels swirling over my torso, all the way to the heart-shaped valley between his buttocks.

I push in.

I grunt as bliss spreads through my body. He's so tight for me. Snug, hot, eager. He whimpers when I pull him even closer, gripping his thighs. I lean over him as his fingers slide up my chest. He's as greedy for me as I am for him. I can see that in his lowered eyelids and smell it on him.

"Is that how you like it?" I tease, lowering my lips to his. I stop half an inch away, so he has to reach for me.

"Fuck yes," Luke murmurs and closes the distance between us.

As I fall forward, burying my elbows in the plush upholstery, the swing moves with us, and I sink deeper, until my cock is fully inside him. Joy burns in my chest as I watch his eyes turn forest-green, almost luminous where they reflect the moonlight.

I kiss him again, not yet moving, but the pressure in my balls tells me I'm not going to last long. This is too good. Too perfect for me to keep myself from filling him up soon.

"My precious human."

Luke is so quick to grab me, wrap his arms around me. Without words, there's no room for complication. It's just him and me, and he wants to connect, wants me inside him.

"My prince," he whispers against my shoulder as if he doesn't actually want me to hear it.

But it's hard to focus on speaking when his body squeezes my cock in such a lustful way and his stiff dick rubs against my stomach. He awakens the beast in me. Whether it's to protect him, or to ravish him doesn't matter right now. My thinking is animalistic either way.

I brace myself over him, my hands planted on his arms as I thrust in, rocking the swing with the power of my need. A few drops of my sweat drip onto him as I shiver, rolling my hips when the pressure is almost too much. Each stroke of his palms over my chest and stomach is like a lick of fire, but I want to step closer to the flames and watch him as each jab with my cock moves him in the air.

I love to see him trembling and out-of-control, but I'm beyond desperate for release as well. My balls feel so tight, and I want to cream his hole as soon as possible. My movements are jerky, my breathing raspy, but he's still the first to grunt in pleasure.

His cum jets out of his cock and between us, some splashing my stomach, some landing on his heaving chest. Luke arches his head back and a few droplets even land on his throat. As he fights for air, the bat tattooed there seems to flap its wings, as if it was trying to fly into my arms.

The sight of him, combined with the heat of the orangery, the intoxicating scent of roses, and the delicious way his ass tightens around me, push me over the edge, and I stand tall, watching his sprawled form take my dick a few final times.

My knees go weak when I finally come, but I squeeze the chains and stare down at him as I empty my balls.

"Can you feel it? All warm inside you."

His face is flushed, eyes dazed, but he still stares back at me from under a strand of hair stuck to his cheek. "So hot…" he whispers. "Still throbbing inside me…"

I let him experience that for a few more seconds, but eventually, my cock slides out of his pliant body. I rest my knee on the edge of the swing, then climb in alongside him. The structure creaks, swings farther away, but manages to hold our combined weight as I kiss his sweet neck, and then nuzzle the adorable round ear.

"You're my treasure."

Luke laughs and holds on to me as he looks up at the hook holding the swing. When he's sure we're not about to crash, he settles into my embrace and even entwines our legs.

I must have fucked all the nerves out of him, because he's so relaxed against me now. I can just see us like this years from now, on a restful summer's day.

"Nah, this is the treasure," he grins and runs his fingers over my chest, enjoying every ridge of hard muscle.

"Both can be true." I smirk. The swinging keeps bringing us close to the rose bushes, but it will only last so long, so I reach toward one of the flowers, swallow down the discomfort caused by its thorns, and break it off.

Luke blinks as I smell the flower before tapping it against his cheekbone. "As beautiful as you."

He shakes his head with a smile. "Cheesefest." Whatever that means, he still runs his fingers over the petals, and I can't wait for one of these midnight roses to seal our bond at our wedding. "These are actually beautiful too, with their creepy faces, teeth, and wisps of shadow in their tails," he says and traces one of the shadowy eels making its way over my pec.

I stretch, resting in the afterglow of pleasure. "This? This is the skin of a killer, Luke" I boast, proud of every single duel I've won.

I expect him to gasp or become thoughtful, but instead, he laughs so loudly, the sound must be heard even outside. He turns to his back and won't stop giggling. He's laughed with me before but this time he has tears in his eyes, and appears so at ease all I want to do is snuggle him and pinch his cheek. I don't know why he's this amused, but it's so adorable I can't take my eyes off him.

Pure, unadulterated joy beams from him, brighter than the moon above us, and I realize I'm going to do anything to make him laugh like this more often.

"What's so funny?" I ask and swirl my fingertip through the cum drying on his chest.

He tries to speak, but half of what he's saying is gibberish because he keeps laughing. "It's just—from a movie—I don't know how—" He takes a few deep breaths to calm down and looks into my eyes, happy like a frog in a bog. "What you said... it features in a story in my world. It's hard to explain. I'm sorry. I'll show you one day." He leans in to kiss me, stroking my chin, but he doesn't need to apologize. I'm not offended.

"I'll make you laugh like this every day. That's a promise," I say, stroking the rose as the swing slows its rocking. "You know, during the wedding we will hold a rose like this together. And I want that to happen, but I'd rather the full moon was far, far away."

"Why? Don't you want to finally possess my shadow?" Luke asks, piercing me with his eyes as if he wants to unearth all my thoughts.

My heart speeds up, and for a moment I consider coming up with a dismissive answer, but I want him to know the truth of my thoughts, so I kiss his shoulder and place my arm across his body. "Yes. But I want you more, and after the wedding, you might leave."

Luke cuddles up to me, unafraid of the fact that I could overpower him with ease. Maybe deep down he knows he's the one who pulls the strings. "Maybe... you could visit me? You know, after." He yawns and closes his eyes, resting his cheek against my arm.

Joy pulls at my heart, and I rub my nose through his fragrant hair. "No distance will be too far, my darling," I whisper, and as he presses closer, I promise myself that I will always make sure he feels important.

I will anticipate his needs and let him come to me slowly, if that's what he needs.

If he believes people are untrustworthy and cruel, I will prove him wrong.

He will be my Dark Companion.

I will be the lord of his heart.

CHAPTER 24

Luke

It's been over a week since Kyran plucked me out of my life and brought me to the Nightmare Realm, but it feels like at least a month.

He gifts me so many bouquets of midnight blue roses my room overflows with them, and while it felt weird at first to get flowers, I have to admit it's a lovely gesture. I like flowers, and the roses are exceptionally beautiful, so why would I deny myself the pleasure because of human gender roles?

Every day Kyran treats me to foods I've never tasted before, and servants cater to my every whim, as if I'm already a member of the royal family. A painter from another elven realm has been called upon, and we pose for our portrait every morning, so that it's finished by our wedding day. Kyran decided he wanted our likenesses to be captured in the orangery, with me sitting in the swing where he fucked me silly. It's a nice little inside joke, but I like that our portrait will feature roses.

But most of the time, I get to do whatever the fuck I want in my opulent room, like reading in an armchair soft as clouds, taking two-hour baths while staring at the moon, or creating art with the new set of paints Kyran provided me with. It features colors in shades that differ from the ones in my world, and I already visited the library to find out more about how they're made.

Downsides of no internet. I can't just google this stuff, but it's not like I'd find information on pigments in the Nightmare Realm online anyway.

At first, when I approached Kyran about leaving my room without him, I worried he'd not allow it, but he's more than obliging and happy that I want to acquaint myself with the palace. As long as Tristan is with me, I can spend as much time as I want in the library.

It only hit me when I first went there that we speak the same language as the elves. I was so frantic about everything else going on that the topic of linguistics didn't even occur to me until Sabine pointed it out and then gave me a quick rundown of the history behind it.

There are countless worlds. For hundreds of years, one could easily pass between the one occupied by humans and the Nightmare Realm, but that changed after some drama, or war (or something) two hundred years ago. Since then, magic has become much rarer in my world, but we still share our language due to all the intermingling in the past. Which would explain why the elves sometimes sound so old-timey to me.

At least it also means I can read most of their books unless they're from some faraway place or were written thousands of years ago.

After I mentioned that I find reading in the dim green light difficult, and that I'm not sure the colors in my painting look right, Kyran brought me glasses made of moonshard. They make everything brighter and pretty much eliminated the strain I've been feeling in my eyes. The first thing I was reminded of when I put them on my nose? How handsome Kyran is.

He looks exactly how a prince of elves from a place called the Nightmare Realm should. His eyes have that piercing darkness that takes my breath away, his lips are pale, with the faintest shade of pink, and his cheekbones are the stuff of gothic fantasies.

And yet when he's with me, I'm starting to see him as a man of flesh and bone. When he laughs at my jokes, he never fails to meet my eyes, as if wishing to connect on a level I'm not ready for. When we fuck, his icy facade is replaced by a flush and lust so raw I don't feel worthy of it.

But I embrace it and gorge on his attention anyway, because the man fucks like a demon, and the many bites and hickeys on my skin are proof of his need. Who am I to tell him that I'm nothing special if he wants me this much?

To him, I seem to be some sexual sensation, a creature made for pleasure and capable of fulfilling Kyran's every carnal fantasy. But once he's gone, busy attending to matters bigger than either of us, uncertainty creeps back in, reminding me of my mother's scornful gaze, the fact that my father didn't bother to meet me, and all the lovers who wouldn't give me the time of day once they got their rocks off.

I wasn't a good enough artist to attract thousands of followers. My business sense is so lacking I overinvested in seasonal bath bombs and needed to get an additional credit card to pay off the debt when they didn't sell. The only people who want me are those I don't want back.

Well, there's Kyran, but sex is still a novelty to him. Once he gets his bearings and realizes how much better he could do, I'll end up being moved around the palace, like an item that is still very much necessary but embarrassing to have around.

Do I even know what he does when he leaves me to my own devices? He could already have other lovers and only act so sweet toward me so I go through with the wedding.

I feel shitty as soon as I think that, but I can't help it. Suspicion is ingrained in my DNA.

So I decided to take matters into my own hands. The truth is, my life here has been luxurious. I don't have to go to work, I wear the finest clothes, sleep as long as I want to, soak in a massive bathtub, eat delicious food made for me and served on silver platters.

I feel... pampered.

If I can trust Kyran won't break his promise after the wedding, maybe I could stay here after all. Would it really be such a strange choice? People move to, like... New Zealand or Japan. People move to places with different foods and social norms, languages they don't know, and they're able to make a new home for themselves. Why not me?

But to do that, I need information, so I'm at the library, perusing corridors towering over me like a medieval cathedral. As in the orangery, the roof is made of an arched frame and glass, and the blueish light of the shrinking moon and stars bathes the vast interior in a cool glow. Books are stored on shelves even someone as tall as Kyran couldn't reach without a ladder, and taxidermied heads of massive animals that are unfamiliar to me yet reminiscent of creatures found in my reality take up the space under the ceiling. I smelled flowers placed on some of the desks from the moment I entered, and as I close my eyes, I can almost imagine I'm walking through a park, with Tristan trailing behind me in complete silence.

He's not often this quiet. On the contrary, most of the time, he has questions about my world, and since I have them about his, we've resorted to trading information instead of a war in which each of us is trying to get more of theirs answered.

I'm also pretty sure he's been flirty a few times when he got a bit too comfortable, but he respects his crown prince, and I never respond to the compliments. Once, I did tell him his hair looks like waterfalls of fresh blood, and things got so awkward after that, I now make sure to keep such comments at bay.

I believe he's tired today, since he did mention staying up all night with someone. I still count on his reflexes in case an assassin decided to pounce at me from a top shelf, but the library is his favorite place for naps, so I'm guessing that's what he'll do as soon as I choose a book.

I've already noticed there are times during the day when the aisles between shelves and reading nooks crowd with courtiers, but since lavish parties, gambling, and nights of debauchery are an integral part of life at the palace, most of those who have time to read don't bother getting up before lunch. To Tristan's dismay, that makes mornings my favorite time to be here, but to his credit, he never complains about my habits. Not directly at least.

"Do you not enjoy the dark?" he asks out of nowhere as I walk past a set of daybeds meant for reading. "You go to sleep so awfully early."

"Unlike you, I don't see well in the dark. I'm lucky to have these." I tap the silvery glasses. "Though there's other reasons to go to bed early," I add with a smirk.

A squeak turns my attention to the leather satchel Reiner customized for Count Flapula's needs and comfort. I asked for it to be studded with silver spikes for my own pleasure. I want it to look cool, not like I'm wearing a baby carrier.

Though I do baby-talk to my bat when we're alone. His wing is healing so well, and even though Kyran is skeptical of my attempts to befriend the little creature, I try to spend lots of time with Flap, so we can bond.

I should prioritize finding out more about the Nightweeds, to work out any hidden truths about Kyran, but today I plan to read up more on these bats to make sure I'm feeding him right and giving our tiny 'count' all he needs.

"Right, you're prey," Tristan says matter-of-factly and yawns, leaning against a tree-shaped column. I have to admit he looks damn good in the outfit of snug shark leather, with a looser jacket that barely reaches his waist, and a sword attached at the hip. Were Kyran not in the picture, I might have made a move, but one beautiful elven prince is more than enough for me.

Plus, Tristan's a manwhore, and I've already dealt with my share of them.

I frown at him. "Excuse me? I'm guessing you fancy yourself a predator then?"

Even Flap is offended, because he peeks out of the satchel with another squeak. I'm so happy to see his long bunny ears perk up, because when I first took care of him, they laid flat as if he were terrified to lift them. I rub my fingertip between them as Tristan plays with his fiery hair.

"Kyranis did hunt you down. And I have a feeling he keeps hunting you day *and* night," he adds with a smirk, and while I feel that I should be offended, nothing about his smile is malicious.

I shake my head. "I don't kiss and tell. You wouldn't know where the section on creatures, monsters, or animals is, would you?" I ask to change the subject.

Tristan's lip curls in distaste, as if a suggestion that he might know anything about the library is a personal affront. "No idea. You're better off asking my sister." He points down the corridor of bookshelves.

Under a collection of blue lights, illuminating the portrait of the previous Lord of the Nocturne Court with his family, stands a large desk. Even from afar, I spot Sabine's mane of red hair as she's browsing through some papers.

"You can take a nap if you want," I say to Tristan. "I will be a while."

For a moment, Tristan's gaze drifts to the day beds, but when a tall, slender figure emerges from the shadows and approaches Sabine, he steps forward, leading the way toward her. "I wanted to ask how she's been anyway."

I glare at him, then at the dark-haired beauty whom I haven't yet seen at court. The man has an elongated silhouette and dense locks styled into a knot at the back of his head. The clothes he's wearing feature more color than I've seen since arriving at the Nocturne Court, and lots of layers, which makes them distinct from the tailored finery I'm gradually getting used to.

After my initial excitement about the exquisite fashions of the court, I had to admit to myself that constricting corset vests and high-collared shirts aren't what I always feel like wearing. I managed to work out a compromise with Reiner, so I now have three distinct sets of outfits. During daytime, I get to wear comfortable shirts and pants with a gothic flair. For evening and event wear he gets to dress me as if I'm his personal fashion puppet, and then there's loungewear—a concept I had to introduce him to—soft, comfy fabrics and not too many buttons for when I'm out of my nightshirt but staying in my rooms.

Kyran appreciates them all. In fact, he rather enjoys the ease with which he can remove a dressing gown or pull up a nightshirt and have me undressed yet, somehow, still clothed.

I lead the way along the rows of shelves, and Sabine smiles up at me as soon as she spots us. Her lips are painted black today, and her golden eyes shine like two coins.

"Magnus, you've got to meet the future Dark—"

"I'm her older brother, Prince Tristan Bloodweed," Tristan says, stepping in front of me to capture the entirety of the visitor's attention. He takes the man's elegant hand and bows to give it the gentlest peck before getting to his toes, because Magnus is taller than him.

Sabine fills her lungs with air, but whatever she wants to say ends up stuck in her throat as she rests one of her hands on her protruding belly. Her deep sigh tells me everything. She's going to let her brother flirt.

Magnus seems a little confused and tries to glance my way, but his expression changes when the floor under our feet shakes with a violent tremor. It lasts longer than ever before, and I have to grab the desk. Fortunately, Sabine can do the same, but as the shaking doesn't stop, the inevitable happens. Books start falling off nearby shelves as if catapulted our way.

I put my arm over my head, holding Flap close to my chest, but as a massive tome is about to smack me in the face, a dark shadow emerges out of Tristan's back, fast as a whip. I don't yet comprehend what's going on, but the solid darkness becomes a wall between all of us and the books.

Only when the trembling subsides I manage to inhale and assess what I'm seeing.

Wings. Massive black wings reminiscent of a bat's (or a demon's) have sprouted out of Tristan's back. By now, I have seen enough to recognize them as a product of shadowcraft rather than physical parts of Tristan's body. He winks when he catches me staring, all self-satisfied. He knows that's an impressive wingspan.

Magnus's lips are parted, and he reaches out to touch them. "That's... magnificent. And those are also made of shadow?"

"Yes, they are," Tristan says, sheltering us all with his creation. "I can show you what else they can do if you meet me at moondown."

That's when Kyranis and I start our evenings together, freeing Tristan to do his thing... which today might involve getting a thank-you-for-saving-me blowjob.

Magnus's dark skin doesn't flush, but he lowers his gaze, frazzled by the attention, as if he isn't drop-dead gorgeous himself.

I swear I am yet to meet an elf who doesn't look like a snack in one way or another. Even Sylvan, who Tristan mocks for his height, has the appearance of a cherubic twink, big blue eyes and flushed cheeks included. Though I don't trust the angelic exterior one bit as he is most likely as prone to backstabbing as his pretty (and dead) sister.

"Oh... well, I suppose I could come."

Sabine rolls her eyes and sits on a bench to wait out the remaining shocks. "You chose an interesting time to visit the Nocturne Court. Heartbreak might emerge at any moment."

Magnus smiles, as if she didn't just tell him about a beast whose proximity can make people's hearts stop out of sheer terror. "Oh yes, that's what I'm here to study. The tremors are a signal of impending approach, aren't they? Do you think it will be possible to observe it from the towers? I heard it's filled with the blackened hearts of those it devoured."

Thinking about it makes me a bit ill, because as far as I know Heartbreak looks like his spawn, the despairs, but on steroids. I wouldn't travel to see a mountain of elf and human parts encased in body juice jelly if you paid me.

Tristan nods as his wings close behind his back. He's probably keeping them visible to impress Magnus. "I can show you where the book section on Heartbreak is," he says and ushers Magnus his way with a gesture.

And there I was, thinking Tristan doesn't read.

He likely knows the elven realm's equivalent of the *Kama Sutra* by heart.

Briefly wondering how long it will take Tristan to move on to another pretty flower once he has his way with Magnus, I grab a lidded cup that fell during the tremor and hand it to Sabine, who rises back to her feet. She's almost due, and I don't envy her current state, especially with the encroaching danger.

"Wouldn't it be safer for you to stay someplace farther from the ocean?"

She blinks, sipping some herbal tincture from the cup. "And miss the sight of Kyranis chasing Heartbreak back where it came from? I wouldn't do that for the world."

We both fall silent as we watch Tristan leading Magnus away by putting his hand on the small of the other elf's back.

"So... I was hoping you could help me find some books about the kind of bats that live under the castle?" I ask, studying the massive (and now crooked) portrait of Kyran's parents with his brother. I don't know what it is about the young elf's expression, but even though he's Kyran's twin, I can tell it's not him. The Kyran I know is determined and doesn't hesitate to give people orders, but I'd never seen him with the smug half-smile crooking the handsome features of the boy in the portrait.

Sadness floods my heart as I stare at the image, realizing that Kyran's family didn't bother to even hint at his existence with some clever metaphor, like perhaps the young prince holding a mirror. It's as if they forgot about him altogether.

Sabine nods. "Yes, I can think of a few resources, but nothing in life comes free. I have a question first," she says but winks at me to soften the blow. She pulls out a notebook and reads from it. "Chad. How about that for my baby's name? Is that a good one? I've found out that it's the name of a saint in one of the human religions, so I presume it's considered dignified?"

I try to not make a face. "It's... okay."

But she clocks my reaction and huffs with exasperation. "Oh, no. You don't like it. What's wrong with it?"

"Not *wrong*, but just... nowadays it can be considered a bit funny. Like... you know how sometimes a name fits a certain type of person? If Tristan was human, living in my world now, he'd be a Chad."

She squints, giving that some thought. "I think I understand. Okay," she adds and makes a little note next to the name. She loves to pick up my slang. "So what would make a strong name for a boy? I feel that each name I pick is not good enough, and my husband told me it's my choice this time, so I need to get it right," she mumbles, hugging the cup to her chest.

"I'll think about it and get you some options, but I only have so much time here today, so..."

Sabine rolls her eyes. "Fine, fine, let's go find out more about this little critter," she says and pets Flap's head in passing when she walks out from behind the desk. He makes a happy squeak that convinces me he *can* be domesticated. Or I'm delusional and he was simply excited about the proximity of very biteable fingers.

She leads the way among fallen books. When I offer to help pick them up, she dismisses me, saying library assistants will put them back where they belong.

"I'm not being pushy, I hope. It's just been so long since we've had a human at court. Over seven years now. Only two Dark Companions survived the battle with Heartbreak." She glances back at me. "It's not typical, just a lot of bad luck. Baron Glassdrop and his

Companion have been away in the capital for three years now, and only Lady Guinevere and Carol are staying close by. They're allowed to live on the outskirts of the nearby village but can't enter the court until you and Kyranis marry, so I can only see the human so often. But she's been here for years, so her information about your world might be outdated."

Sabine is always very chatty, so I'm happy to soak up all she has to share, but this bit of information makes my brain whir with excitement. I worried the surviving Companions were out of reach, but there was one nearby this whole time? Wouldn't talking to her be the best way to find out the truth about the Companion's role without the rose-tinted glasses Kyran keeps putting on my nose? If another human reassured me that living in this Realm is not actually a nightmare, maybe I could... stay?

My thoughts race as Sabine chatters, bringing me to a small shelf.

"Our late Lordess was actually a keen observer of the natural world. Several of the books here were penned by her, and I'm sure she also researched the bats. I might even have..." Sabine rummages through a stack of smaller books, only to pull out a leather-bound folder. "Her notes. These must stay in the library and cannot be taken to your rooms. While I'm sure the prince could probably force a different decision on me, I insist that you don't pull those strings."

I stall, tracing the fine embossing on the cover. The depth of the grooves is somewhat uneven under my fingers, as if the decoration had been added by hand rather than by utilizing a machine. "You mean... those are by Kyran's mother?" I ask before I can catch myself, but Sabine likely assumes I'm shortening the prince's name because of our familiarity.

"Yes, she loved to spend time around beasts. Found them fascinating, you see. It was her downfall," Sabine adds with a brief glance at Count Flapula's satchel.

"Oh, but not by... bats, right?" I ask, giving Flap's massive, innocent eyes a nervous glance.

"No. She tried to capture a despair to study it. Sadly, she ended up bitten by several of them and there was no saving her. But what is life without striving for knowledge, hm?"

I think about Reiner, who has been living a long and happy life avoiding danger at all cost, and I can't make up my mind on which option is better, so I just nod.

"Make sure your hands are clean as you handle the notes, and absolutely no drinks at the desks."

"Of course. I'll be very careful, thank you."

We chat some more about electricity, which is a concept that seems especially interesting to both Sabine and her brother, but I'm eventually alone with the handwritten tome and hurry to the nearby desk. I sit in a clam-shaped armchair and stuff my left hand into the satchel, then smile when Flap nuzzles it before resting his head in my palm.

I open the notes without ceremony, but the sight of the even, precise handwriting makes me stall on the title page signed by the Lordess Isabeu Nightweed. I don't know what I expected from the tome, but as I browse through the pages, I find everything from descriptions of the bats' habitat, their full scientific name being *Verspersal Lepus*, to diagrams of dissections, and the setup of a typical colony. There's drawings of the bats at various stages of their development. The young are fluffier and grow up to look more like hares with bat wings, elongated feet, and long claws with which they hold on to rocks.

It reads almost like poetry, and I find myself sinking deeper into a world full of personal anecdotes, sketches featuring favorite bats, playful names the Lordess gave them, and details about their favorite foods. But as interesting as the notes are, my mind halts when I find the mention of a familiar name.

It's small, scribbled on the margin next to a drawing of a bat not much younger than the one in my satchel.

Should I bring one to Kyran? He'd be less alone. More research needed to see if it's safe.

I stare at the note and read it several times, but it definitely discusses *Kyran*, not *Kyranis*.

My heart beats faster when I think of his childhood self stuck alone in that shadow palace and only allowed out when it was convenient for the rest of the family. Was he able to make any friends at all? Would he be let out to play instead of his brother, or would his parents be too worried that their embarrassing secret might come out?

Did he have no one to talk to? My mother was a terrible parent, but she was around at least, and I could always count on other people for company. The nice neighbor living two houses down the street would even make me lunch sometimes, when I grew a bit too thin, but who did Kyran have?

I grow determined to learn more. This here is definite proof of the truth behind what he's told me so far. It would be nice to believe people at face value, but in my experience, sincerity is hard to come by. I was burned too many times. As long as I can confirm this though, maybe I could... trust him.

Just the thought of it makes me nervous, but I don't have time to self-psychoanalyze, because a long red nail taps the very top of the folder in my hands.

I look up to spot a stunning elven woman reminiscent of Morticia Adams in her tight-fitting black dress with a low neckline. She smiles at me with blood-red lips.

"Luke Moor? The future Dark Companion of our prince? His promised? I am Marquise Coralis."

CHAPTER 25

LUKE

She's almost too beautiful to be real, and while I've never had any interest in women, her grace and confidence are intimidating.

"Good... day," I mutter as my gaze darts to the waning moon outside. I wonder if I could ever get used to the constant darkness in this realm, if I choose to stay, but I then remind myself there are more important things to focus on right now. Like the fact that she speaks to me as if I'm expected to know who she is.

Her brows furrow ever so slightly, as if I'm an object of pity. "Has Prince Kyranis not mentioned me?"

When she sits on the table by the notes, I can already imagine Sabine's expression of fury, but the Marquise seems as at ease here, as if this is her own space.

"Should he have?" I ask, trying to hide my nerves. Has a game of word chess already started, and this is yet another opponent sent by the Goldweeds?

After nearly losing my life in the caves, I decided to heed Kyran's warning and trust no one but those he authorizes. This woman is unfamiliar, though I have a vague sense I saw her at the execution.

Her hair is the blackest black I've seen and so smooth it appears wet, but there's no water dripping from it onto her exposed bosom as she takes a deep breath.

"I know him fairly well, and he's been quite distant since he fetched you from the other world," she says.

Oh.

Oooooh.

My senses go on high alert. Could it be that she was Kyranis's lover? Irrational jealousy flares up inside me even though the twin she was with has died. Is it strange to feel that way about my own lover's brother? Just because they looked the same?

Does she hate me?

I would have hated anyone who started hoarding Kyran's attention.

But that might be a matter of my rotten personality.

I choose to tread lightly. "It's been quite the whirlwind," I say, knowing it means exactly nothing. And that's the point. I'm gonna stay neutral and say noncommittal things, so I'm not again drawn into some intrigue at court.

"They say he lavishes you with attention even when there's nobody to see," she says and wags her finger in mock-disapproval. "And you aren't even married yet."

I smile, avoiding her penetrating black gaze. "If no one can see, how would they know? I assume the prince is charming toward anyone." Unless he's about to kill them.

"He definitely can be. He's a man who likes to spread his charm around," she tells me, and as she leans back, the tightly laced dress wraps itself even closer around her waist.

If I were anywhere near bisexuality, I'd probably be whimpering '*mommy*?' by now.

The idea of Kyran *"spreading"* his charm takes me aback for half a second. Not because I'm a stranger to slutting around, but because he seems so focused on me. I don't think he'd have the time for anyone else. Of course, Kyran is not the same person as *Kyranis*. My Kyran was a very horny virgin, but definitely not the rake this lady is acquainted with.

"I don't think it would be appropriate while he courts his promised," I say, even though I have no idea what the rules around that are. What if the elf courting their future Dark Companion was already married? After all, it was made clear to me that not all Companions have romantic or sexual relationships with the people to whom they traded their shadow.

She hides her mouth, but I still spot her initial, uninhibited reaction, a surprised smile, as if she sees me as painfully naive. "I'm just... surprised that you're a man. That's not his usual repertoire. Is he... *enthusiastic* in his courting?" she asks, no doubt wanting to find out if she's been dumped without a word. Can't fault a lady for wanting to know where she stands.

How can I milk the conversation for the information I want? She's been around Kyranis and his family before. While she doesn't look a day over twenty-five, for all I know, she could have been born earlier than Kyran's parents.

I glance up at her, pretending I have no idea what she's talking about. I can only hope no bites are visible on my neck from under the high collar of my shirt. "*Very* enthusiastic. He brings me flowers, we eat together every day, and he indulges my new pet." I point to Flap when he decides to peek out of the bag I put on the table, pushing aside the book. He yawns, showing off his needle-sharp teeth. "Didn't his father have a male Dark Companion as well?"

She sighs, glancing past me, perhaps to study at the portrait I was admiring earlier. "Indeed. He was already married when he chose his companion, which became a... source of tension. Not everyone can cope with other people in the relationship. It was probably Her Majesty who didn't want him in this painting."

I dread to think of Kyran ever wanting an elven spouse. Which is silly because I've told Kyran that I'm leaving him after the wedding, so why wouldn't he consider marrying someone else once his shadow bond was secured? He would need companionship and an heir, among other things, but I hope he'd only choose another partner after my death. It's selfish of me, but no one needs to know my intimate thoughts.

"That must have been complicated. But at least the late Lord had someone to support him after his wife passed."

The Marquise's long eyelashes lower as she watches me. "The shadow bond is forever, but it's not always based on love. In their case, the late Lord's companion couldn't offer him what he lost with his wife's passing."

I sense my cheeks warming with a flush as soon as I think about sharing a love bond with Kyran. It's silly, since I know our relationship is one of convenience. We have great sexual chemistry, and we're developing a friendship, but Kyran will one day find someone who can give him *everything*. Which shouldn't sting as much as it does. Will he eventually call upon me for a reason of 'grave importance' only to introduce me to his beautiful elven husband on the day of their wedding?

Just imagining that hypothetical situation makes me sick.

Since I've fallen silent, the Marquise picks up the conversation. "I've heard that in the years before the Lord's tragic passing, he argued a lot with his Companion. I don't know the reason. Maybe there was too much affection between them, or too little? Now he's lost in the shadowild. Whatever happened, his fate wasn't as grave as that of those fallen in the battle against Heartbreak. They became part of the beast's flesh, you see. We just don't know if it devours their souls, or if they are somehow forever trapped with the other unfortunate victims..." She reaches out to Flap with a long nail, blood-red as her lips.

"Is it possible that the former Lord's Dark Companion is still alive?" I whisper.

She exhales and pulls away her hand the moment Flap leans in to smell her skin. "Oh, no. It's been seven years. Even if he had access to water and non-perishable food in our former Lord's shadowild, he would have gone mad being there all alone. I suppose that's why many Dark Companions always carry poison, or something else that can quickly end their lives."

Something cold drips down my throat and into my stomach, tainting all the trust I've built with Kyran so far. He's not mentioned this.

"Has anyone... looked for him?" I say in a voice lower than I intended. My throat tickles, and I have to clear it.

She shrugs. "There's been a few divers over the years, but—"

The Marquise keeps talking, but the moment my ears pick up a familiar gait, it's all I can hear. Even, confident, yet somehow almost too studied, as if Kyran is worried that if he were to make one wrong move, his secret identity would be revealed to all.

He walks out from behind a bookshelf as tall as a house, but the smile he's carrying drops the moment he spots me sitting with the Marquise.

She follows my gaze. "Looking dashing today, Sire," she says with the kind of familiarity I imagine she must have had with Kyranis.

I hate it.

I also hate that she's stirred up some very reasonable doubts in me. Can I not live on Cloud Nine a while longer?

I don't think Kyran is a devilish mastermind fucking me just to make me more compliant, but despite our growing bond, there are things he's not telling me. Things I need to find out if I am to consider staying at the Nocturne Court.

"Like every day," I say, and wink at him, because fuck it, we are courting after all.

I am surprised to spot Reiner trailing behind Kyran. He's still in groveling mode around the prince, eyes cast down, face somber, but I ignore him for now, focused on Kyran, who stares at us as if he's walked in on his wife and mistress having a friendly chat. I'm just not sure which one of the two I am.

He squeezes a small blue box topped with two roses in lieu of a ribbon and clears his throat. "You both look excellent too," he says, and I can almost see the beginnings of a grimace, which he skillfully masks.

Is this a new kind of situation for him? He seems more than capable of wooing me or giving orders, but the courtly pleasantries seem to be as calming to him as a Mentos thrown into a glass of Diet Coke.

The Marquise slides off the table with grace, as if she's made of liquid. "I thought I should acquaint myself with your promised," she says with a courteous nod. "He is most charming. I cannot wait until he is introduced to more elves at the hunt. No need to keep him to yourself. I know I would always be happy to spend time with him," she says, clearly making a point about being fine with some sort of polyamorous arrangement, unlike Kyran's late mother.

I give a nervous laugh. "I'm still adjusting, but maybe it's time to see more of your Realm, my prince. I haven't even set foot in the village close to the castle yet." And I'm dying to find out where the Dark Companion, Carol, lives. Until I talk to her, making any binding decisions feels impossible. Kyran won't deny me in front of the Marquise, will he?

He clears his throat, catching my gaze. Is it a trick of the light, or is he blushing? "No, of course, it's a wonderful, clear day."

"I hear there is a festival. Shall I accompany you two, Sire?" The Marquise asks, and I cannot miss the tension in Kyran's shoulders. Is he annoyed that I got to talk with her?

She takes a deep breath, ready to offer her reasons, but Kyran cuts her off. "Maybe another time. I have something to discuss with my promised."

"As you wish," she says with a stiff curtsy, but living with a mother who could have been a subject in a study on passive aggression taught me all the signs. The Marquise is raging. She doesn't even say goodbye as she struts away with a swish of her long sleeves.

Only now I realize that the confrontation has left my heart pounding, and I still don't know what her real intentions are. Unfortunately, as long as Reiner is here, we can't discuss what Kyran's twin brother was up to with her.

We both remain stiff until we can no longer hear the tap of her heels, and Kyran approaches me, reaching for my hand with a deep exhale, as if her departure offered him a bit of relief. "Where is Tristan?"

"Here!" Tristan says from afar, already taking quick steps our way. His pale face is almost as red as his hair. "Luke is always within my sight, cousin!"

I don't know how long I managed to read the notes before the Marquise accosted me, but it seems to me that Magnus and Tristan didn't waste any time. Still, I'm not a snitch, so I grin at him before meeting Kyran's gaze. "He leaves me plenty of space but is always watching."

Kyran squeezes my fingers, satisfied by my lie. "Did you have a good morning?"

As soon as we touch, the tension in my body recedes even though I'm now plotting to go behind his back in the village. His presence is overwhelming in so many ways. Kyran makes me feel safe, but also horny, but also like I wanna cuddle, but also like he could kill me with ease if he wanted to. The fact I like it all is disconcerting.

I squeeze his fingers when I look up into his dark eyes. Maybe I'm just this shallow and his beauty has me dick-whipped. "Very much so. Reiner got me this new shirt," I stand back to show off the translucent garment. "And I had bread with a paste made out of sea flowers. I was told they take root in floating islands of moss. It was pink. And delicious."

Kyran smiles, stroking the chipped polish on my nails with his thumb. "I wish my day so far had been this pleasant. But I wanted to spend the afternoon with you. We could even go to the village, if that's what you wish for. It's festival day after all," he says and kisses my knuckles. I struggle not to fist pump.

It's still weird to be treated this way as a man, but romance doesn't seem to have gender in this world of elves and dark beauty. And in this pairing, I am *the pursued*. He's wearing the lobster pin he got from me as if it's a precious jewel, which tickles my heart every time I spot it.

Kyran smiles and offers me the box he's been holding all this time. "For you. I figured you might have need for this."

I'm so greedy for all and any tokens of appreciation I don't waste time, and snap the box open.

"It's nail polish." Black, midnight blue, and a green as deep as my hair.

That seems to wake up Reiner who takes a step closer. "What a magnificent present, Sire, I will immediately learn to master the art of applying this product!"

But I'm baffled as I pick up the rectangular bottle. "This is... *Dior*."

Kyran's lips tighten enough to go a bit pale. "Is that not to your liking? I was reassured it was in good taste. I requested the best kind your world has to offer." Darkness passes over his face. "I will have those smugglers flayed alive—"

"No, no!" I step in, eyes wide, and put my hand on his chest. "It's *so* nice! And the colors... It's just very expensive. I never used anything like this. Thank you."

This calms him down, and he smiles, putting his hands on mine. I'm not tiny, or girly, but Kyran is much taller than me, more muscular, broader in the shoulders. Even his hands are larger, and seeing them over mine is weirdly arousing.

"Good. I told them to get something of quality. I want you to always have the best, my sweet," he declares, watching me with eyes full of happy sparks.

I glance at my chipped nails and can't get over how thoughtful it was for him to surprise me this way. I get to my toes and kiss him chastely, because people are watching us, but I secretly hope gossip about this reaches the Marquise. I'm sorry she lost Kyranis, but I'm not sharing *my* prince.

"Even a prince needs to use smugglers?"

"The rules around travel between realms are far too complicated for such a short-notice dash."

"I love those. The perfect selection of colors too."

Kyran pulls me close, his nose against my neck. "Do you want to use them now or—"

"No, let's go out. Reiner can paint my nails when we come back," I say, grinning at the servant, who bows so deeply I can see the hair at the top of his head. "But..." I bite my lip, leaning in to be closer to Kyran. "Can we lose Tristan and spend some time alone?" I'm being manipulative, since I want less eyes on me when we're in the village, but that doesn't negate the fact that being alone with Kyran makes my blood sizzle. We fucked in the morning, right before he had to leave, and I'm already missing his touch.

I know he feels the same way about me.

Or do I?

I cannot be sure what he's up to when we're not together, and while he was a virgin when we first met, the novelty of sex might soon not be enough for me to keep his interest in a castle full of elves way more gorgeous and interesting than I could ever be.

Kyran glances toward Tristan, who's talking to his sister by the main desk, but he's already decided. I can see it in his eyes.

"Excellent idea, my darling. Reiner, prepare our riding outfits."

Reiner bows again. "Horse or kelpie, Your Highness?"
Kyran smirks when our eyes meet. "Kelpie."

CHAPTER 26

Kyran

My morning was filled with difficult conversations. The alchemists can't quite tell when Heartbreak might come ashore, and if so, what is their purpose? Between the despairs attacking fishermen and frequent tremors, I don't need an elf of science to tell me that the beast is readying itself for another attack. It's obvious to anyone with half a brain!

So much time wasted, and none of the solutions meant to protect the inhabitants of the area proposed to me are even remotely useful. Barriers? Waste of resources, since Heartbreak can crush them with ease. Potions? None have ever been proven to work, and no amount of *"encouraging"* experiments on the monster's spawn have given promising results.

The only person who could aid me in the fight against Heartbreak spent the early hours apart from me, browsing dusty tomes in the library and playing with a little beast that might gauge his eyes out. I'm not comfortable with him spending so much time with the critter, not after finding out my own mother died because she had grand ideas about befriending monsters. But he seems so happy I can't bring myself to spoil it for him. After all, the bat's still young, too small to hurt my promised.

It is a shame we haven't yet married, but if Heartbreak comes ashore before that happens, I will have to come up with something. For now, the best course of action is to ignore my worries and make sure Luke understands the life I can offer him is superior to whatever existence he led in the human world.

As he emerges from the dressing chamber attached to the stable, ready for our little trip, all my noble goals disperse, replaced by raw lust.

I'm very aware how good I look in the riding outfit made of sleek black leather, but seeing it on Luke is a whole different story. It hugs his lean, angular body in ways I want to with my hands. In fact, it encases him so tightly I'm almost jealous of the leather. Several buckles jingle when he struts my way in riding boots that reach his thighs. The black octopus skin is polished to perfection, and green light bounces off every shiny crease in the outfit.

Luke rubs his gloved hand over his chest, as if unaware of what he's doing to me with that gesture. "Wow, this is... tight," he says with a healthy flush.

My gaze trails down his form. I always liked watching men in these outfits, but Luke is incomparable to anyone else. The leather somehow showcases his figure in even more detail than his naked skin would have.

I nod, staring at his graceful legs.

He laughs and shoves my shoulder. "Don't look at me like that in front of the kelpies!"

And yet I notice him stealing a glance at my hips as well.

"I bet they don't mind," I say, stepping closer, until Luke's cheek is against my chest, and I enfold him in my arms.

There's a sense of peace in holding him. His hair carries the distinct scent of sea salt and rose oil, which takes turns exciting and calming me. The aroma of hay and wood hanging in the crisp air compliments it so well I slide my hand into his black-green mane, relaxing under the vault of the ceiling high above.

Skulls of kelpies who are no longer with us hang high up on the walls, each marked with a name and dates of their service to my family. My father also had the huge antlers of a Stag of Sunrise put up, a testament to his love of hunting. The interior itself is rather dark, with swamplight burning in only a couple of spots. I like to think it's because this reminds the kelpies of their underwater home, but right now it creates an intimate atmosphere for me and my promised.

We're alone in the stables, and as my hands start their slow descent toward the backside I've become so utterly obsessed with, Luke gets to his toes and gasps into my ear.

"I never got why some people like to wear latex, but..." he slides his hand up my arm and the leather squeaks, "I think I get it now." Luke gives my earlobe a teasing lick that tells me he's just as excited to see me after the few hours apart as I am.

At times I get so jealous of all the men he's been with I want to choke each of them with my shadow, but then he looks at me with fondness, and I let myself dream that maybe I am special to him too.

I will do whatever it takes so he forgets any other arms that ever held him.

"I like looking at you no matter what you're wearing," I say, grinning.

He slips out of my grasp and stands at arms' length. "Just looking?" he asks with a smirk. The expression makes his sharp features even more fox-like.

He is delectable.

"No, not just looking," I say and grab his hips, pulling him back to me. Oh, I can already sense a rush of heat down my body.

"I missed you," Luke whispers, and it feels like being fed the sweetest little cake when he adds a kiss to his words.

I shiver at the throb of excitement in my balls.

"Yes," I rasp and make a fast dip to grab his thighs and wrap them around my hips.

I live for the sweet, surprised gasp I get in response, and for the weight of his slender arms around my neck. That's the one collar I'm willing to wear for as long as I breathe.

"Fuck. I keep forgetting how strong you are. You carry me like I weigh nothing," he says, smiling, and I would gladly freeze this moment in time.

After being stuck in my brother's shadow my whole life, I'm not only seen, but also touched, hugged, kissed. Luke plays with my hair as if I mean more to him than a way to pass the time as he waits to go home. But my thoughts also turn much darker when I sense his cock harden against my stomach.

I wonder if he'd have liked my twin as much as he likes me. He was just as handsome, and a part of me worries that maybe Luke would have preferred a real prince, not the impostor, but as my lover leans in, kissing me, the gloom is chased away. I stumble toward the nearest empty stall and place him on top of a tall wooden box so that he sits at the height of my hips. "I like having you close and despise every hour we're apart."

He stills, silent for a moment as I run my hands up and down his thighs, unable to stop touching him. The way his legs open for me drives me mad.

"Same. I'm glad you can take time out of your busy day filled with princely duties to *court* me." His fingers slide up my stomach in a teasing motion, and the thin layer of leather separating us somehow enhances the sensation instead of being an uncomfortable barrier.

"No day is too busy for my promised," I rasp, supporting his back with one hand while I rub my face into his fragrant neck, then leave kisses on his shoulders before finding respite in the warmth of his chest.

Sometimes, I wish our flesh would merge so he wouldn't even consider leaving me behind after we're wed, but I still have time left to show him that he will only gain by staying at my side. I can't wait to feel his shadow easily within reach of mine.

"You're just saying that 'cause you're horny," Luke whispers with a grin and slides his hand over my trapped cock. He almost purrs, looking into my eyes. I never imagined being so lucky with my choice of Dark Companion, but it seems destiny does know better than any elf can.

Kyranis wouldn't have valued Luke for what he is. He would have used and discarded him, and thinking about it makes my latent hate for him burn hot again. Because Luke is sweet and deserves more than being a convenient weapon. I would have never committed him to a life of containment in the shadowild, and not just because I know painfully well how lonely an existence that is.

"I only have one horn, but I see you've already found it," I rasp, rolling my hips against his hand while my own fingers wander over his flesh.

"Maybe just one, but the size of it..." Luke laughs and bites his lip, rubbing his open palm over my stiff dick.

He's the perfect match for me. I knew it from the moment he let me inside for the first time. Back then, he was afraid of me but couldn't deny himself the pleasure of my touch. Beautiful, with his slender fingers and round ears, he's a willing vessel for my lust. Whenever I worry that I might be suffocating him with my greed for his flesh after years of unsated need, he proves he wants me just as much. It's a revelation I sometimes question even though I am handsome, attentive, and powerful.

My gaze drops to where his cock is trapped under the thin layer of octopus skin, and I kneel, opening my mouth to lick the cockhead. The clean aroma of leather spreads on my tongue, but the heat of his arousal is impossible to miss even through the barrier. "I want you to smell of me."

His breath quickens. "Mark me then."

A rush of emotion drives me to suck where his balls are trapped under the suit, and as he stiffens, letting out a choked moan, I come back up, kissing and squeezing his lean torso on my way.

I'm a bull in a rut, and I will shatter anything standing between me and my mate. "That's what you want? To walk among our subjects knowing I've had you so recently?"

His eyes gloss over, and a flush reaches the tips of his ears. "Is that *proper*, Your Highness?" Luke teases as if he's not encouraging my love bites every day. He loves his neck sucked so much I might have to turn into a vampire to satiate his need for it. I'd do that for him.

It scares me how much I'd do for him, but he brings me so much joy, consequences cease to matter.

I shake my head and spread his legs wide before thrusting between them to make our groins rub. The squeak of leather never aroused me before, but I suppose there's a first time for anything.

"Not proper at all. But you have a way of getting under my skin, little human."

He rocks against me, and an unruly lock of hair falls over his face, but he doesn't seem to care, moving his gaze between our cocks and my face. Every bit of him is hidden under the skintight outfit, and I'm torn between wanting to hide him away, and showing him off so everyone can see his beautiful shape and know they'll never taste him.

I need to see his ass. I just do. So I step back and pull him off the box. A yelp escapes his lips as his feet land on the floor, but I don't give him any time to think and spin him around. With elbows resting where he'd just been sitting, he pushes his hips back, and I'm enchanted by the curve of his spine and the tempting line of his backside.

Maybe a man like me doesn't deserve all this beauty, but he knows who I am and he's never tried pushing me away for it.

"Excellent," I say, sliding my hand over his taint, and then down his inner thigh. He whimpers and spreads his legs wider for me as I glide my thumb between his buttocks. "You should have a fastening here, so I have easy access to you when we go out riding..."

"Oh, fuck..." he whispers and pulls one of his gloves off as I unbuckle the clasps holding up the flap of leather at my crotch so I can rub against him and leave my mark, as promised. Plucking my hard dick out, I slide to my knees and kiss his buttock, nipping on it as I pump myself.

It's the best piece of meat I've ever tasted, and as Luke stirs, pushing back against my face, I imagine there being an opening I can access at any time, even just to tease him with my fingers.

"I'm sure this could be arranged, my sweet darling. I could come inside you right now," I utter, stroking my cock as I kiss his rump, but when I rise to my feet and tap my cock against the small of his back, Luke's shoulders hunch in sweet submission. He knows taking off the whole outfit would take too much time and opens the front flap to touch himself.

He rocks against me, uncaring that someone could walk in on us, or that one of the kelpies in a far stall did in fact turn its head our way. I won't spoil the mood by telling him they're more intelligent than your average beast.

I can't focus on anything but rubbing my cock against the leather that is like a second skin. He can feel my touch, and it gives me a thrill to see him needing it so much.

I spit in my hand and use it to add some moisture to our delicious rutting, but as I lean over him and my mouth finds his cute little ears, I lavish them with attention.

Neither of us is going to last long.

Luke whimpers, wordlessly begging me for more, and I deliver, sliding my cock against his pert ass while I squeeze him with both arms, eager to be close.

His moans and the slapping sounds of him jerking off tip me over the edge. He craves me so much even this is enough for him. I hold him, sucking on his ear as I release spunk all over his buttocks.

"I'll be coming inside you later tonight," I whisper.

"Yes, I wanna be full of cum," he whines, jerking off fast. The motion spreads my cum over his outfit, making me wonder if elves with exceedingly sensitive smell will be able to tell we've fucked.

Luke stiffens under me, and he must have forgotten where we are, because I have to stifle his moan with my hand.

"That's it," I whisper, squeezing his pec as he pleasures himself. "Finish so I can lick it off your fingers."

His body twitches in my embrace as he comes, and I love feeling his orgasm so viscerally. It's like melting into him. For those precious seconds, there is no dubious past in which I abducted him, and no murky future in which he leaves. Just his beautiful scent, the heat of his body, and his strong heartbeat.

I grab his right hand and bring it to my lips, kissing off his seed as he's recovering, so warm and sweet against me. There isn't a single part of him I don't like, and I hope that one day he might feel the same about me.

I've heard it said to my brother that no human can resist an elven prince or princess. Luke might be coy about staying by my side, but his actions speak louder than words.

He loves the Nightmare Realm. He's excited to wear our fashions, taste our food, and explore the palace. He seems happy curled up in my embrace at night or lounging in the bath as we both read. I selfishly even want him to bond with the damn bat, just to give him another reason to stay. Or maybe he will fall in love with riding a kelpie and that will be the final push he needs to understand he's better off here. At my side.

Luke turns, looking dazed when our eyes meet. "So good. Anything with you is *so* good," he whispers, breathless, and kisses me with eagerness that makes my heart beat faster.

With him, I'm not a tool of death hidden away to be wielded when needed. With him, I get to be a whole person with many facets, emotions, preferences, and a voice. He wants me, not my brother.

"I will make sure you never want for anything, my darling," I whisper and grab a clean towel from a rack nearby. I drop it to the floor once I'm done using it to wipe my mate clean, but then we're facing one another again, and I kiss his lips, drunk on this connection I've never shared with anyone.

"We're never getting to that village at this pace," Luke says with a smile and pulls me out of the stall. "Tell me how to act around the kelpies. Do they bite?"

I put my arm around him and lead him to my favorite mount, Crab. The tall, skinny beast is somehow always dripping with water, as if it were its sweat, and as it watches me with cold, milky eyes sitting deep in its skull-like head, I have the sense it understands what's transpired.

I push away that thought and pet it with my gloved hand. "You're right. Time to go."

Encouraged by my gesture, Luke reaches for the kelpie's neck. I notice his bare skin just as he presses his palm to the beast.

The wide smile dies on his lips, and his eyes go wide in terror. He can't stroke the kelpie's neck. He's stuck to it.

Luke turns to me in panic. "I forgot! I took the glove off in the... stall," he says with his face flushing as Crab snickers, stomping his hoof. "We can unglue it, right? I'm not losing my hand because I wanted to jerk off!"

Damn it.

I pull him close in an effort to calm him and then shout, "Drustan! We need immediate assistance!"

CHAPTER 27

Luke

Thank fuck getting my hand off Crab only took half an hour and a generous application of seawater, not ripping skin off my palm. Drustan was nearby as soon as I needed help, which makes me suspect he was snooping on us, but I try not to think about that. He remained as silent as possible during my ordeal, not even berating me about the glove.

Despite the kelpie's skin being a trap, the beast is otherwise obliging, and didn't flinch when I scrambled onto its massive back, then promptly slid off the other side. Kyran's shadow was there to break my fall.

I was surprised by the two-person saddle at first, but then realized I don't have horse-riding experience, so it's for the better that I have Kyran behind me.

I wonder if we'll get some sort of escort after all, but there are no guards at our side as we ride through the main gate and onto the bridge, heading away from the sea. I don't know if that means we're safe here, or if Kyran is just that confident in his shadowcraft.

The moon looks like a cookie someone's nibbled on already, but it still provides enough light to guide us on the empty road. The sky is dotted with bright stars, but I also spot a pale cloud resembling a distant galaxy, or nebula.

I wonder if this world and mine share the same planet, or if stepping past the veil transported me to another place in the universe. But unless the elves have a space program that doesn't depend on electricity and fossil fuels, Kyran can't possibly answer that question.

The castle is imposing with the moon creating a backdrop for its tallest tower. Kyran told me it's (very creatively) called the Moon Tower, and it serves as the place for detaining important prisoners, particularly those proficient at shadowcraft, as the tower is warded against that kind of magic. Kyran claims being kept there is a kindness in comparison to spending weeks in the dungeon, but a prison is a prison. I was relieved to hear no one resides there at the moment.

To our right is a forest, which we must have passed on the way from my world, but as Kyran nudges our mount with his heels, Crab moves uphill, climbing a path marked with green lanterns mounted on wooden poles.

I feel like a dainty princess with Kyran's arms around me and holding the reins. If a princess wore black latex that is. I've always been somewhere between slutty and self-conscious when it comes to my body, but after almost two weeks with Kyran, I feel like maybe I am as hot as he says. I don't know if it's the shadow bond muddling his perception, or if I'm just exactly his type, but does it matter? Why not take the compliments at face value? Especially from a hunk like him.

So yeah, I'll be wearing skin-tight leather when we get to the village, and since Kyran has no objections, then it must be socially acceptable.

I'm wearing my glasses to see everything, as elves have much better vision in the dark than humans. I'm glad I've brought them with me, because what they consider daylight here is just a bright night in my book. The glasses have a frame made of what Kyran called 'moonshard' and no lenses, but the glow of the stone rims affects everything I see. He couldn't explain how that works but offered to take me to the craftsman who made them so I can ask all the questions I might have.

I'm glad he's not tired of my constant questions, because I've got *so* much to learn.

"So only the royals have access to kelpies?" I ask, stroking Crab's slippery mane. I've got no idea how seaweed can grow out of his body, but it's clear the Nightmare Realm doesn't operate the same way my world does.

"Only the royals, yes. And servants who have permission to train them," Kyran answers, resting his chin on my shoulder as we reach the top of the hill.

The first thing I see is a flood of lights in the valley at our feet, but then my gaze meets a grouping of bright red dots glowing at us from a nearby pasture. I initially take them for lightning bugs, but then notice the sharp contours surrounding the dots, and realize they are in fact eyes.

Big red eyes belonging to creatures the size of elephants that stand on the way to the village.

I lean into Kyran with my whole back, frozen in fear even though he's acting as if we aren't about to confront a dozen massive beasts.

"Wh-what the hell are those?" I ask, pointing to the horned creatures. As if I could offend them by staring. If they wanted to, they could probably trample us, but Kyran continues to ride toward them as I push deeper into his chest.

What. The actual. Fuck.

"Oh, you don't have cows in your world?" Kyran asks just as one of the monsters gives a moo so low it hurts my ears. Were they to make this sound at once, the walls of the castle might crack!

I shudder, unable to tear my eyes away from the absolute unit of a cow walking down the slope alongside us.

"Yes, we do have *cows*, not whatever *this horror* is."

They're black, and their fur is so matte it sucks in any moonlight that falls on them, and their horns are bigger than those of a massive Texas longhorn.

Kyran laughs. "They're mostly harmless."

This doesn't put me at ease at all. "'Mostly'?"

"Well, it is calfing season…"

I take a deep breath and push forward in the saddle when I realize how silly I'm being. "Their size is unreasonable. And what's with the glowing red eyes? Are they not creepy enough? When we get back home, I will draw you a cow. And a human next to it to show you how big it should be." I shake my head, never taking my eyes off the monstrous bovines.

Kyran laughs, an easy, sweet sound that wanders down my back as if he's just covered me with a plush blanket. "Please, do. Next you'll tell me their milk *should be* white."

I shake my head, but his relaxed attitude puts me at ease. "Well, it should, but now that I've seen these 'cows', I'm no longer surprised about the milk being black." I'm ranting, but the truth is, all of this is so exciting to me. Creatures I couldn't even dream up, a handsome Prince of Darkness, we're riding a kelpie with a skull for a head, and the strange massive moon shines above us. All of this is so removed from the reality in which I'm flipping burgers, saving a few bucks a month, and sucking mediocre Grindr dick.

Why would I ever go back to my cramped attic room in the house of a mother who never wanted me?

Kyran's amused and kisses my neck as we pass the cows, descending toward the bright lights of the settlement. "That being said, you should never approach a beast you don't recognize. Even a little bat could pose a threat, and you wouldn't know."

"Like the tooth moths." I nod and sigh, remembering my near-death experience in the forest. "It seemed so interesting and friendly. I wanted to give it the benefit of the doubt. Not everything that frightens you is actually a threat..." I arch back enough to give his jaw a kiss. Okay, so I may have a little crush on him. Sue me.

He drops the reins and wraps his arms around me, as if he had a sudden need to hold me close. "This worries me. My mother would tell me the same thing. And now she's gone," he says in a dull voice.

My heart sinks. "What happened to her?" I ask quietly, unsure if it's even appropriate to ask. I heard she was killed by despairs, but without any details. I don't really have many friends, and I learned to be guarded to survive so it's unnerving to step into such painful territory with someone. It's intimate in ways I never experienced.

Kyran cocks his head until his cheek rests on my shoulder, and he strokes my forearm, as if seeking my touch. I entwine our fingers, but my heart quickens to a nervous rhythm.

"First, I have to explain to you more about her. My mother felt beasts could be tamed. She was the one to bring the kelpies to court. When someone found a kelpie baby on the beach, she took him in. Kelpies can shape-shift, but it becomes harder as they grow, so she had a collar fashioned, to let him remain in elf form. That's how Drustan became part of our household, and over time, he lured in more young kelpies from the sea. But I think my mother grew too bold."

"What do you mean? Did she not have guards with her?" I ask, stroking Kyran's hand with my thumb. Crab seems to know where he's going without being urged with reins, so we're free to just hug as we watch the world pass by.

"She was extremely capable at shadowcraft, and confident about it too. At some point, she started theorizing that there might be a different, more permanent way of dealing with Heartbreak. For some reason, she decided that it might be tamed. She wanted to start with the despairs but ended up attacked by a large group she couldn't fend off. By the time she was found, there was nothing anyone could do to save her. I didn't even get to be at the funeral. It was too big of a risk."

My heart breaks for him, and I squeeze his hand. "I'm so sorry. You deserved so much better. How old were you when that happened?"

I feel Kyran's chest expand, and he holds me more firmly, as if he's worried the despairs could get me next. "I was ten. Nobody ever visited me in the shadowild after that."

It's like a stab in *my* chest, even though it's him who went through years of entrapment, pulled out only for training as if he were some beast. I can't imagine how that must have affected him, yet I'm also not surprised that his palace in the shadowild is so intricate, because he must have had more time to craft it than he knew what to do with.

I can't take it. I pull my leg up over the saddle and sit sideways with my legs over his thigh so I can hug him. "Not even your father?" I ask. I want him to know he can talk to me about it. He seems so strong, so put-together, but I'm noticing the cracks now, and all I want to do is mold myself into them and be the soothing balm he needs.

Kyran's quiet, and he plays with my fingers as Crab continues down the path. When he speaks, his voice sounds as if it's coming out of a hollow log. "My father never spoke to me. He was always of the belief that a twin shouldn't be left alive. He never said my name, only called me *the Sunspawn*. Mother was the one to set me up in the shadowild. And my brother? He enjoyed having me do all his dirty work. But he'd never thank me. He felt it was *I* who owed him my very existence. That I should be grateful he gave me the opportunity to leave the shadowild at all."

I know what Kyran thinks about that by the way he clenches his jaw. I rest my cheek against his chest, and even the strange, rubbery feel of the leather can't dissuade me. When we made our agreement, I had the hots for him and a lot of mixed feelings, but within just a week, we've become so… close. Maybe that's bound to happen when two people with gaping holes in their hearts attract each other.

"I'm sorry you only had so much time with your mom. I read some of her notes on bats today, and she seemed to be a very passionate person."

"'Notes'?" Kyran's head jerks up. "What notes?"

"In the library. She wrote several books about different creatures, but she never finished the one on bats, so Sabine let me look at her notes." I clear my throat because it's about to clench with sadness. "She wrote your name on the margin. She wanted to try taming one of the bats for you. So you wouldn't be alone. *Kyran*. Not Kyranis. She must have loved you."

A strange noise leaves Kyran's throat, and he lowers his gaze, his hand tense in mine. "She should have taken me with her. I would have protected her from the despairs. I might have been ten, but... I was already excelling, and I could have—"

I rise to kiss him. The shadowy eels on his body are proof of what he can do, but I now see the vulnerable parts of him, and I'll do anything to protect them. I have to remember that it hasn't even been a month since his brother died, and all of a sudden he has to deal with the world in a whole new way. He'd never admit it, but I imagine he must be overwhelmed with the freedom and afraid it might be taken away at the snap of someone's fingers.

"You were put in an impossible position as a child," I say and stroke his cheek, fighting my own demons. Maybe I see a bit of him in me because of my own miserable upbringing. I wish someone could have been kind to me too.

"Do you really not mind?" Kyran asks. "My brother was an awful person. But also the real prince."

I smile at him and give him another kiss. "I've heard quite a few things about him, and he sounds absolutely terrible, so no, I not only 'don't mind' *prefer* my dark prince. Let's be honest," I cup his cheek, trying to lighten the mood. "With a face like this, I would have probably fucked him, but I wouldn't stick around for a rotten personality."

Kyran stiffens and takes hold of my arm. "I wouldn't have let you. He never liked men. Not really. You deserve better."

I don't know if he's just worried about me, or jealous, but I kinda like it regardless.

"Is that why you waited seven years? Did you dissuade him from taking me? Or do you have laws on abductions needing to be age-appropriate?" I wink at him.

There's miles of countryside around us and a dense forest to one side of the road, yet I feel so safe with him even the stupid cows can't distract me. I need to know what he truly feels, yet I'm so afraid of ending up as a gullible dumbass who sold his soul to the devil.

Kyran laughs. "It's risky to fish for souls, and he didn't want to endanger his princely life, so after our father died, he told me to pick a human for him. Since we are identical, the bond would have worked for us both. But he wanted a girl, and I found a boy to spite him. I'm sorry," he adds in a soft voice as the glow of the green lantern deepens the shadows on his features. "I think he didn't want to deal with that for as long as possible, too busy finding new lovers and pleasures to indulge in. I think deep down he might have known I'd be the one making the bond, because he wouldn't be the one fighting Heartbreak once it came back. But he didn't want me to have anyone. As if that could make me more real. If anyone knew he wasn't half the shadow wielder he claimed to be, his world would have crumbled."

I now hate Kyran's brother even more. "You have nothing to be sorry for. You may have put me in a tough position, but I would have died without your help that night. I'm glad I never met him," I say, meeting Kyran's eyes so he understands how much I mean that.

He holds my gaze, then looks away, as if my declaration embarrasses him. "Sorry about unleashing all this on you. Nobody ever knew me the way you do, and I barely know anything about your life."

A lump gets stuck in my throat, and I'm a deer in the headlights, because while I let him pour his heart out, encouraged him even, sharing any of my reality feels so painful I recoil on the inside.

I want to push away his questions with cynical jokes about being fine as long as I have coffee and French fries. I want to tell him I have a black soul so nothing can hurt me, but I settle on, "My life is terribly boring, so there's not much to know. I'm not a prince. I work at Best Burgers Bonanza, and I'm not even employee of the month."

"I don't believe you," Kyran says, playing with my fingers as I hear a rhythm in the distance, as if someone is playing music. "You risked your life to save a little beast, you make tinctures that make water smell divine, and you can draw things from your imagination. That's quite incredible. Oh, and you make amazing fries," he adds, as if he believes the fast food I served him at Best Burger Bonanza was my own culinary creation.

I smile at the memory of him sitting in the mint-colored booth at the back of the restaurant, slurping a milkshake. I guess white milk must have been a novelty.

I turn around so I'm resting my back against him again, because I'm afraid I might cry if I keep facing him. I'm *not* a crybaby. I'm strong, I depend on myself, and I buried my traumas so deep I don't need to dig them up anymore.

"I live with my mother, I have to pay her rent, but at least the house is nice. Though *she's* awful, so I hope to move out in the future." *Maybe to the Nightmare Realm.* "Sadly, she's also right about many things. I'm nothing special, my art is just about average, and I can't actually cook, I just put together ingredients. I know this might sound like I'm fishing for compliments, but I'm not. I'm just facing reality."

I don't want pity, but when he hugs me, my eyes sting and my chest aches as if it's about to start bleeding all the infected pus I've gathered there over the years. "You can't believe that. You are smart, and graceful, beautiful, and a real artist."

I shrug, but my insides still flutter at the compliments. Best I ever got back home was *"nice hair"*, or *"you really know how to suck dick"*. "Smart? I never even finished high school."

"High school, low school, doesn't matter! You fit in so easily, and understand people, and... you say such funny things, like that comment about cows. Others want my favor, but you are always truthful. You listen. You're bright like a flame in the middle of a dark forest full of bloodthirsty beasts."

My little goth heart beats faster at the fuzzy feeling thrumming through it. He really likes me. Not just because he wants to secure my shadow. All I need to do is trust him.

"That is... very sweet." I put my hand over his. I can sense his warmth through the glove, and it puts me at ease.

"Maybe I feel tainted because my mother never wanted me in the first place."

"What do you mean?"

I have to take a deep breath and fight the instinct to avoid burdening others with my personal issues. Kyran has shared so much about his parents. He deserves the same trust in return. "She got married young because she got pregnant with me. Her husband convinced her to keep me, even though she didn't want to. I know, because she told me many times. He left us a few months after I was born. I never even met my dad, but no regrets about that. He must have been an awful person." I rub my eyes, frustrated that talking about this causes me so much pain. I shouldn't care about it anymore. "I don't know if it's because she had to take care of me on her own, or because I'm the son of a man she hates, but she never failed to make sure I knew just how painfully lacking I am. When I got to my teens and started acting out, things went even more downhill. But at least I'm no longer trying to please her. Nothing I'll ever do will be good enough."

Kyran tightens his hold around me. "You are not lacking in any way, and I will make sure you understand that even if it takes me a lifetime. Your value isn't tied to your mother's opinion."

We ride in comfortable silence as I mull over his words.

"Maybe I can be special to *you*. I'd like to feel special," I whisper, because it's such an embarrassing thing to admit. '*Luke wants to be a special little snowflake*' I can almost hear my mother's mocking voice. And still, it's what my heart yearns for. To do something different, to excel at something. To prove to my mother I wasn't a waste of womb space.

"Of course you're special to me," Kyran whispers as the music gets louder upon our approach to the village. It's vibrant, full of wind instruments and tambourines, like something one might hear at a renfaire, but right now all I can focus on is the soft whisper of Kyran's breath in my ear. "Destiny brought us together. I let it guide me and pulled you out of the depths of death. And since I've been getting to know you, it's been almost uncanny how well we fit together. Like a shadow and the man who casts it."

No one's ever been so tender with me, and I can't help but lean into it with a smile. Kyran might be a murderous elf prince on a ruthless quest to steal the crown of the Nocturne Court, but I can't deny the way he makes me feel. He is a whirlwind, untamed as the Sea of Sorrows when we're in bed, yet tender as if I were made of porcelain when he handles my silly feelings.

When I'm with him, I don't care whether I come off as corny. I'm not self-conscious about expressing my joy. Instead of criticizing my style, he gets me new nail polish, just because he noticed it chipped. He might not like Count Flapula, but he still let me keep him, because it makes me happy.

Maybe he's right, and some kind of invisible hand of destiny did bring us together.

I want to believe that.

I squeeze his hand where he holds it on my chest, but I don't have fine words, so I resort to jokes. "And now we'll need to pretend I wasn't easy, and didn't put out on the night we met. We're still *courting* after all."

I will do my best to locate Carol in the village and talk to her so I can put my heart at ease once and for all.

Kyran laughs as we approach two columns marking the entrance into the village. Green flames illuminate homes beyond the symbolic border, and I watch them as he kisses my cheek.

"Nothing feels easier than being with you. It's as if it's in my nature."

I tell my heart to stop beating so fast, because I can't be falling for him so soon.

CHAPTER 28

LUKE

My skin itches as we approach the village. The trees on either side of the road reach for us like the claws of a giant. Back in my world, I'd be convincing myself there's nothing to be afraid of, nothing malevolent hiding in the dark, but as Kyran strokes my forearm and invites me to lean against his strong chest, I fear nothing.

I've learned not to trust anyone, even less so the men I've been sleeping with, but in the two weeks since he snatched me from Best Burger Bonanza's parking lot, Kyran entangled me in a web of charm, and I can only wish it's not being held together by a bunch of lies.

Because right now, as I sense his warmth against my back and the strength of his thighs pressed to mine, I feel more connected to him than to anyone else in my life.

Two figures loom at the gate, and the pink glow of the torches in their hands turns their faces into grotesque masks. Kyran remains as confident as ever, so I allow myself to remain calm as well even when one of the men walks toward us with a pike. "Who's there?"

"Do you not recognize the kelpie under me, guard? Maybe you shouldn't have any liquor on duty after all?" Kyran shouts back, unperturbed.

"It's the Lord—I mean Prince, Prince Kyranis" one whispers to the other, then quickly steps to the side. "Excuse me, Your Highness."

The other guard smiles, watching me with the curiosity of a puppy meeting a cat for the first time. "If I may say so, the cherin is both potent and delicious this year. It must be tried."

The guard who didn't initially recognize Kyran pulls the torch close to his chest, so close in fact that for a moment I worry he might set himself on fire, but he's focused on me now, his big, round eyes widening with a sense of wonder. "Then is this... your promised, Your Highness?"

Kyran's murmur, low and dark, trails down my spine like a caress. "Indeed. I figured it's time he meets his future subjects. And there's no better day for that than the Ardournalia."

The elf sucks in air, stares toward the other guard, and when he's given a nod, he bows so low the cap he's wearing almost falls off. "Welcome. I'll... let them know."

And with that, he's gone, running past the bushes, toward the dark silhouettes outlined in pink.

We ride along the road without hurry. "What are they protecting the village from? The cows?" I'm joking, but I do want to know more about every aspect of this place.

"You would not want to meet any of the beasts roaming our lands, my dear," Kyran says and tickles the underside of my chin, as if I was his pet cat. "This is a dangerous Realm."

I shudder. At least the sea creatures stay in the water for the most part. Even the despairs can only roam on land for so long before they die.

"I guess you're right. I'm just a human. I can't bend shadows to my will or produce Sunlight. Hell, I don't even see well in the dark," I say as Kyran nudges Crab forward, toward buildings that could have been produced by the mind of Tim Burton. Narrow, with sharp edges and tall windows featuring stained glass, they look like a stylized movie set, yet people live here. Kyran's people. As we come close enough to see details revealed by pink flames, I'm enchanted by the strange beauty around me.

"Commoners aren't usually born into magic either and they learn to survive," Kyran says and strokes my hand as we approach the source of the insistent music playing far ahead. It's full of discordant sounds which somehow create a harmony that makes my feet itch for a feverish dance. It sounds pagan, wild, yet also sweet with longing, as if the instruments were made out of strings stolen from someone's soul.

I glance back at Kyran even though every detail of the houses around us scream for my attention, from the candles burning with pink flame in the windows, to the colorful mushrooms planted by doors in massive dark seashells.

"They can't just... learn it? I thought it was inherent to elves to see shadows the way you do."

"Elves have the chance to be born with certain aptitudes, but no one can truly tell who will manifest talent in, say, shadowcraft. It's most prevalent in certain noble bloodlines, yet Sylvan Goldweed can barely pick up a saucer with the strength of his shadow, while his sister was born with Sunlight burning inside her. It's why we test all children, even those born to the simplest folk. Those who manifest special talents are invited to hone their shadowcraft on the Nocturne Court's coin. With the forest always encroaching, we need all the skilled individuals we can get."

My heart beats faster. "Could... I be tested? Is there any chance a human could secretly have a dormant power like that?"

Kyran strokes my hair. I sense the answer in his sigh, and my shoulders droop. "I can put you through the test, but it's unlikely, my sweet. Unless a human has elven blood hiding within their ancestral line, it's impossible for them to be born with a natural talent for any elven magic. Is that something you would like to possess?"

I glance ahead, where the pink light is much brighter, the music louder, and I'm already getting a glimpse of dark silhouettes dancing at the end of the street. Of course I'd love to be part of this world for real.

"I just... I wish I was special for once. I know it's petty coming from someone who is your promised, and the future Dark Companion to the Lord of the Nocturne Court, but you have access to this whole world of shadows I can't even really understand any of it. And I wish I could."

Kyran goes quiet, his gaze becoming smokier when he presses a little kiss to my shoulder, as if he wants to tell me that *to him* I am special. I know I'm unusual to all the elves by the virtue of my species, but he is still the one who can manipulate shadows. He is still the prince, the one with all the power, and no matter what he claims now, sooner or later he will get bored of me.

I'm not used to being pursued, but the thought of losing his affection makes my throat close and my chest tighten around my heart.

"I'm sorry I didn't give you everything you need," Kyran whispers.

I laugh it off. "It's okay, I'm used to disappointment. One time, I thought I'd treat myself to this special set of wax crayons, but on the day they were delivered, I had to stay late at work. They were left on the doorstep in the sunshine, and by the time I got back home, they all melted together. Sunshine is very hot," I add, unsure if Kyran would understand.

"So you... couldn't use them," he mumbles before putting his arms around me in the most comforting of hugs. It would be so easy to believe that he truly has feelings for me, but I don't want to set myself up for disappointment in the future any more than I already have.

I will only be able to take it if I don't let myself hope for things someone like me isn't meant to have. But I'm afraid of how tempting it is to fall for everything he's promising. His sturdy presence is like nothing I've ever experienced. Not just because he's the hottest stud I've ever been with, it goes well beyond any of that. His support for me never falters, and his interest in me seems etched in his skin like that golden sun on his chest—impossible to be removed.

I don't want to dwell on any of that, too afraid it will lead me down a path of no return, so I focus on our surroundings instead. On the hearts drawn in chalk on each door, and the—

"Are those human skulls?" I ask, pointing out several skulls hanging under the eaves of the thatched roof of a house we pass.

Kyran pulls my hair back behind my ear. As if he needs an excuse to touch me. "Oh no, they're elven."

I spin my head back, and my frown must have communicated my utter shock, because he grins and indicates similar displays on nearby homes. "It's their ancestors. The older the skull is, the more prestige a family has. There's been feuds about skulls being stolen by rivals and secretly disposed of."

It's so morbid, but I can't help a laugh. "Oh, my God! What? If they're so precious, why not hide them in a chest or something?"

"They need to be proudly exposed to moonlight. The skulls of all my prominent forebearers are displayed in the Ancestral Sanctuary, the second highest place in the castle. The roof there is glass, like in the orangery, so they are always looking at the stars. We even have the skull of Lord Larkin Nightweed and his Dark Companion. I will show you on our wedding day, when you become a part of my family, and we make our sacrifice," Kyran says as Crab stands still, keeping us away from the crowd ahead for that bit longer.

I stiffen and laugh nervously. "I hope it's not *human* sacrifice?"

Kyran smiles and brings my hand to his lips. "Don't be silly, sweetheart. We will cut open the cocoon of a matra spider and feed her some of our hair, then release her into the Sanctuary. That way, her children will weave cobwebs with a piece of us all over the castle."

I stare at him. "That's messed up."

"It's tradition." He shrugs as we ride through a narrow passage between two houses. A flash of movement draws my attention there, but I look away as I spot two elves so engaged in... *relations* they don't even notice us. A lush skirt is hitched up to uncover pale thighs, but I don't let my eyes linger and stare ahead, where the shadowed street opens into a richness of pink light.

Would it be improper for a prince to fuck his promised in a dark alley? Probably, but a boy can dream.

The glow originates from a massive bonfire, and while I have no idea how they tinted the flames such an unnatural shade, the figures dancing around it feel familiar despite their clothes. Like a dark and gothic renfaire night on Valentine's Day. The mix makes me smile and look around in awe even though we're being gawked at as soon as Crab emerges from the alleyway.

Sitting so high up gives me a chance to take everything in. The town square a the bonfire in the middle, but tall trees at the edges. Around each thick trunk, elves sit on wooden benches, busy eating, chatting, and laughing. Stands with foods, drinks, and trinkets are to one side of the square, and sellers loudly advertise their products, but I'm still too far away to hear any details. Everyone is bathed in the pink glow that reflects off their clothes and faces despite fashion dictating that most attendees wear black.

I want to feast my eyes and ask so many questions, but a woman approaches us with two elves in simple black tunics. Her gown is long, with lots of draping, and a massive headdress featuring antlers and a veil that seems to be made out of spiderwebs. Tiny jewels are woven into it, reflecting the light like dew drops.

She looks like a witch. Or a goth elder, who's been in the community since its inception but who has, miraculously, not aged beyond thirty. I freeze when she bows, followed by her two companions.

"Our prince and his promised! It's a shame you didn't notify us about your arrival, we could have prepared better." Her voice has a rasp to it as if she's smoked one cigarette too many.

"That's all right, it was a spontaneous trip," Kyran says, sliding off the kelpie with the kind of grace I can only dream of. But he's there to hold my hands and catch me when I make my attempt at not falling face first. Miraculously, my boots make it to the cobblestones as if I was made for riding kelpies.

On the other hand, I'm not sure now if I should bow to the witch lady.

Before I can work out my social standing, Kyran introduces me. "Luke Moor, my promised. Luke, this is Ana d'Luna, the wiser of the village. She oversees the Ardournalia celebrations and provides us all with insight into the tides of shadows even our alchemists can't provide."

I'm pretty sure he's working his flattery magic here, but just knowing this is someone he cares to flatter is worthwhile information. I open my mouth and remain mute, because what should I say to someone who's this important? Is she the equivalent of a mayor? A religious figure? The next Sailor Moon villain (going by the black crescent moon tattooed on her forehead)?

I cook under my clothes while she gestures to one of her assistants, who produces a shallow basket. The wiser reaches inside and pulls out a wreath made of vines, tiny flowers, and crisp white fishbone. As I lean in to see it in more detail, she places it on my head like a crown.

"Welcome. Your presence brings joy to our unbroken hearts."

The square resonates with whooping, as if every single elf present has been waiting for this moment, and I seek Kyran's hand, intimidated by all this attention.

I smile, hoping I'm not some fishbone prince now, marked as an offering to the kraken.

"Thank you," is all I can muster, but then I remember my customer service experience, and go on. "It's my pleasure to be here, and a privilege to be part of the Nocturne Court."

I must have done something right because the wiser's moon-white lips spread into a smile. "My Prince, may we speak in private?"

Kyran's gaze darts to mine, but I don't want to be a burden, so I offer him a smile and nod. He gives me a little kiss on the cheek and steps away, led by Wiser Ana, who touches his back as if they're friends, not a prince and his subject.

I immediately sense the weight of too many glances, but as I turn to Crab, eager to busy myself stroking his flank with my gloved palms, someone leads him away. It leaves me deserted in the middle of the empty space between the stalls and the bonfire. I'm not usually shy, but here I'm a curiosity everyone wants to ogle, and without Kyran to lead me through situations I don't understand, I'm a sitting duck. My gaze darts to the dancing couples, and it looks as though the renfaire has organized a bisexual party, because I spot women with men, women with women, men with men, some passing into different arms between sets of figures.

For a moment, I imagine myself and Kyran among them, him lifting me up until I feel weightless in his strong arms, and—

"Is that really him?" comes a hushed voice from under one of the trees. At first, I'm annoyed with myself for assuming that every single thing said would be about me, but then the whisper continues, drilling into my ear despite the music. "The former Lord's companion was so handsome. I thought Prince Kyranis would have picked someone prettier."

The fuck? Right in the fucking insecurities, huh? Why not comment on my skincare routine while they're at it?

Torn between throwing back a snarky comment and inadequacy, I just stand there, taking my time to look everywhere but at the gossiping elves. I wanted to visit the village to find Carol, the Dark Companion, or at least work out where she lives, and I won't be distracted by—

"The prince can always find himself a lovely spouse later," one of the hushed voices says, yet I pick it up as if my ears are elven. "He's so handsome, so pale, and his hair is like shadow itself. Do you think he will invite any elves from the Realm for courtship?"

"You're so dumb. You're a hairdresser who does mushroom brewing on the side. You don't stand a chance with the prince."

Maybe it's the years spent at a boarding school from hell that make me so good at eavesdropping, but I wish I hadn't heard that. No matter how many times Kyran tells me I'm perfect, one stupid comment is enough to send my mind spinning. I'm not ugly, but there's many men, human or elven, prettier than me. Beauty might be in the eye of the beholder and all that, yet how long can Kyran's enchantment with me last?

People usually date within the same level of the attractiveness scale for a reason, and Kyran is not only as handsome as a classical statue but also holds the title of prince and is literally the most eligible bachelor in this Realm. How could I ever hold his attention for more than a couple of months?

With a rock growing in my throat, I leave the gossiping elves behind and approach the stalls, drawn closer by the savory scent coming from pastries placed on a metal rack. Each is stamped right out of the oven with a heart-shaped stencil, and as I see a girl buying one, I wonder how they taste. Instead of biting right in, the pretty elf spins around so fast her two braids wrap themselves around her shoulders. She runs to a cute brunette with biceps bigger than mine and presents her with the treat, offering it with both hands.

The other girl yelps, touches her chest then leans in for a kiss, which is applauded by the people gathered close by.

An arm snakes over my shoulder, and I flinch, but Kyran's scent instantly calms me down. "Elves buy them for their sweetheart at the Ardournalia. It's supposed to keep the heart strong if Heartbreak does approach, but really it's just an expression of affection."

I swallow, glancing up at him. "I... don't have money." It's pretty pathetic that I only realize it now. I've been pampered like a sugar baby since the moment I stepped into the Nightmare Realm. I kinda love it, in a vain sort of way, but in moments like this, I'm lacking agency.

I wish I could gift Kyran this stupid heart pie. It might be only a gesture, but I want it. I want to do something special for him, but how can I when everything I have comes from him?

His fingers twitch before tightening around my hand, and as the crowd of dancing shadows moves behind Kyran's back, he leans in and gives me a coin. "You do. As my promised, you are entitled to a stipend. I will have someone discuss this with you tomorrow, if you'd like that."

I nod and, with a shy smile, ask the salesman for a pie, parting with the one coin I possess. When I hand the food to Kyran, I'm very aware of all the people watching us And I hope the elves gossiping about my looks are seeing us now.

"So your heart is strong," I whisper, going breathless when a lock of Kyran's hair slides down and cuddles up to my cheek. He's so tall. So handsome. Yet when he looks at me the way he does now, with adoration I don't feel worthy of, I can believe this isn't an act. He accepts the pie and presses our foreheads together, for everyone to see.

"You make it stronger every day, my darling," he rasps, and when our lips meet, I can feel pink flames licking me from the tip of the head to the toes.

The music swells around us, and I deepen the kiss for a little too long, pulled back to reality by a whistle from the crowd. Kyran winks at me and bites into the pie.

My cheeks are on fire, but I'm so... *happy*. I've never felt a connection like this with anyone. My first crush on a boy when I was a teenager now feels like just that—a crush. I thought I was in love, but my feelings were only the butterflies of first attraction, not the wide-winged moths fluttering in my chest whenever Kyran as much as looks my way.

"What's that?" I ask and pull him to the next stall, eager to distract myself from the overwhelming emotions.

He offers me half of the pastry, and I take a bite, leaning into the cozy space under his arm as we take in...

"Stuffed birds. There's nuts and dried fruit inside, and the bones add a lot of crunch," Kyran tells me while the seller beams at me and offers us one of the roasted morsels on a stick.

"On the house, Your Highness."

The birds are no bigger than a child's fist, but seeing their little charred bodies doesn't spike my appetite. But it would be rude to outright refuse food when it's offered, so I awkwardly take the stick from the proud salesman and thank him, already wondering how to dispose of this dubious treat.

"I don't want it. It's freaky that it's a whole bird. What do I do?" I whisper to Kyran right before he feeds me the last piece of the pie. Unperturbed, he takes the stick from me and puts the whole morsel in his mouth. He bites down with a crunch so loud I can't help but laugh.

His brows go up, and he mumbles something that sounds like "Amused?"

It makes me laugh harder, and I gently punch his chest when he leans in to kiss my forehead with his mouth full.

"Thank you for bringing me here," I say. I may have ulterior motives, but I love spending time with him all the same. "Ooh, that smells good!"

I turn my head and a tall elven lady is already reaching out to me from behind a massive cauldron. The cup she hands me is filled with black goo that smells of milk, honey, and something fruity. "This year's cherin. Spiced with ground cherry nuts."

The guard called this beverage 'potent', and it certainly smells that way. The boozy aroma tickles my nose even before I take my first sip. With the consistency of gooey pudding and a milky smoothness, it's a drinkable dessert.

I turn to Kyran with wide eyes. "Delicious!"

He hands the seller some money and gets a cup of his own, pulling me away, to where two young ladies are decorating heart-shaped cookies with icing. I've seen some people wearing those on their necks, like amulets.

Kyran chooses this moment to press his cup to mine with a grin. "Your teeth are black!"

I cover my mouth in panic. "What? No! Will it come off?" I ask and lick my teeth. Who am I kidding though? I *will* be having more of it.

He takes a gulp of his own and stirs as if he never had anything like it. "Oh, that's strong," he says, revealing his own tinted teeth in a smile. He's beautiful regardless, but I still laugh at him and get to my toes so we can kiss.

I should be using this opportunity to find Carol and speak to her, but as Kyran shows me around, I keep delaying my secret mission. We participate in a game of pouring wax onto water through a heart-shaped stencil. It's meant to predict whether a couple stays together or grows apart, and while I don't believe in superstition, when our wax heart breaks, I'm a little sad. But then Kyran dutifully uses a candle to glue it back together, and all is good again. We throw balls at towers of little wooden cups (and win nothing), and then get more cherin, which maybe we shouldn't, because its alcohol content is clearly a bit too much for Kyran.

He acts as if every single thing I say is hilarious, but fortunately, the booze doesn't affect his balance, so we end up dancing too, and he spins me in the air, just like I imagined. I wouldn't have recognized the elves who gossiped about me, but I hope they're watching.

"Is that Anatole?" I whisper with my head still spinning and point out the oldest Goldweed sibling by the bonfire.

He isn't looking our way but must be aware of our presence, as we've been here for at least an hour or two now. Anatole is putting something into the massive effigy by the fire. It's supposed to represent Heartbreak and will be burned by moondown. Maybe I'm prejudiced, but I trust Anatole as much as I trust a drunk driver, and his sheer presence here feels sinister. The Goldweeds have been busy groveling, but I didn't buy any of it. Not after Kyran and I almost died because of Vinia's actions.

A low growl comes from Kyran's throat, and he hugs me so tightly I need to pull back for air. "Always in the way. What is he doing here?"

"He slid something into the effigy."

Kyran sighs, stroking my back. "That's tradition. Anyone can place something of their beloved's between the dried branches. Then you check the ashes the next day. If it's not burned, it's a bad omen for your relationship."

"Does he have a lover?"

"I never cared enough to find out," Kyran says with an odd smirk.

He stirs when a lady with smudged makeup around the eyes grabs his shoulder, as if she's forgotten propriety and decorum. Her lips are stained black too, which explains her conduct, but when she whines about being scared of the monster hiding in the ocean, I step away, leaving Kyran to deal with this one. I whisper to him that I will be around, and head for Crab, who awaits us on the edge of the square.

"Not just yet, boy," I whisper to him, careful not to touch him as I pull out one of Kyran's gloves from under the saddle.

Okay, maybe I'm a little lightheaded from all the cherin, but I *will* be putting something of Kyran's into the effigy. Can the hand of destiny tell me the future of our relationship?

Though as I make my way toward the Heartbreak made of driftwood and filled with dry seaweed, I do take in my surroundings. This might be the perfect moment to search for Carol, so why am I wasting time on superstition that isn't even my own? Isn't that what I came here for? I could at least ask someone about her. I'd just need to go about it smartly. I'm about to go through with that plan, but my feet first lead me close to the pink bonfire that's sending golden sparks into the air. After all, it won't take much time. With a smile, I slide Kyran's glove into the dry seaweed and only step away once I'm certain it's secure.

But as I step away, heading for the stall with cherin, where I hope to get the information I need, someone steps right in my path. The hope in me dies at the sight of Anatole's face.

"Your shadow is exquisite in this light," he says.

CHAPTER 29

LUKE

I didn't expect Anatole to approach me, and I certainly didn't anticipate any compliments either. But my guard is up, because Vinia was sweet as a bag of Twizzlers too, and she literally sent me to my death. I am not falling for that kind of shit again. I now trust Kyran's opinion about that snake pit of a family, and I'm determined to keep Anatole at arm's length.

That might prove difficult, because he's hiding behind lies and the facade of a smile, which I can't openly dismiss for the same reasons you can't tell the passive-aggressive head cheerleader you're seeing right through her frenemy act. If high school taught me anything, it was to keep my cards close, and I intend to take full advantage of those lessons.

As much as I want to hate Anatole though, I can't deny his beauty. For all I know, it's part of his predator camouflage. His pale face looks as if he's doing that Korean skin care routine with seven steps and has never missed a day in his life. His long, silvery blond hair could give Legolas a run for his money and land Anatole a L'Oréal commercial. He's wearing his usual midnight blue, and his velvet jacket has skulls embroidered on it with silvery thread. The pattern would have been a sinister giveaway for a villain if the aesthetic of every royal at the Nocturne Court wasn't flamboyantly gothic with a touch of marine life.

I've never paid much attention to my shadow, but when Anatole points it out, I glance to the ground, and seeing it next to his sends a shiver down my back. I don't have to be a shadow wielder to see that the darkness behind me is like black coffee, when everyone else's appears milky in comparison.

I guess physics doesn't work here the same way it does in my world. Which reminds me I was supposed to ask Kyran why the moon waxes and wanes if there's no sun here, but that can wait.

"Um... thank you?" I finally say to Anatole. "Yours is... nice too?" Okay, I'm a little drunk and unsure what the protocol is here. Is this like teens comparing each other's dick sizes? Thumbs? The denseness of that first mustache?

Anatole's mouth quirks as he meets my eyes with an intensely blue gaze. It's like being pinpointed by two sapphire lenses, and I can't help the tingle at the back of my neck. Am I flattered? Intimidated by a threat my brain doesn't yet comprehend?

"You're not at all what I expected," Anatole says before I can wrap my mind around the way I feel. "When I go looking for a Companion of my own, they will have a lot to live up to."

He's lying, of course he is, but I still feel my cheeks flush. It's most likely the cherin. I don't think Anatole's stupid enough to be making a move on me when Kyran is right across the square, but maybe my shadow really is such a catch and he can't help himself? Or maybe he's just the god of chaos trying to sow discord in the Realm.

"What did you expect?" I ask, curious about the other Companions. Which again reminds me I should be looking for Carol, but maybe Anatole can provide information about her whereabouts.

"Someone... more frightened maybe? Humans tend to be skittish for a while after being taken. I was impressed by your quick thinking at my sister's execution."

My heart stops. He wants to kill me.

"I... Kyranis needed the—"

Anatole shakes his head. "Please, Luke, don't misunderstand me. It is a true compliment. Our prince was in mortal danger, and my sister was a traitor. She kept secrets right under our noses and served some wicked agenda of her own. I don't want any bad blood between us because of the way her schemes ended."

"Oh... okay," I say awkwardly, but he's right there to save the conversation.

"Are you excited for the hunt next week? I, for one, cannot wait. It's not often all us royals have equal chances to get our hands on the Stag of Sunrise. Even Lady Guinevere is allowed to come, since the event is held in the royal forest, not at the court. The prize is so exciting, and yet a mystery."

I frown. "You mean... the venison?" Has he never had deer meat? To be fair, I only tried it when Mom's hunter friend brought us some. We ate it for every meal for weeks until I vowed to never have it again.

Then again, Kyran could persuade me if he sat me in his lap and fed it to me with his fingers—

I stop daydreaming when I realize I'm salivating, but Anatole doesn't seem to notice.

"Oh, Luke! You're so funny!" He stills, realizing my question was genuine. "Has Prince Kyranis not explained what's at stake?" He makes a pause, so I get to question why my promised might be keeping something from me, but then speaks up before his victim can gather their thoughts. "The Stag of Sunrise is a magical beast, rare and precious. They're drawn to human blood and tend to appear in the area when someone takes a new Dark Companion. Their meat is flavorful and tender, but the real prize is the power burning deep inside. The one who hunts the stag down is granted a mysterious gift of shadowcraft.

"The last man to fall a Stag of Sunrise gained the ability to travel great distances through the shadowild, and even visit other realms that way. I don't want to get my hopes up, but I lie restless at night wondering what could awaken in me if I were to take the beast's heart."

He seems so genuinely excited, some of my resolve to hate him dwindles.

"That sounds incredible. And none of the hunters know what power the stag can give them?"

Anatole nods. "That's part of the draw. The unknown. You must agree mystery can be endlessly enticing?"

I think of this Realm and the mystery of the future it might hold for me. Great love? Riches? The best sex of my life? Or a dungeon in the shadowild? Would that be worse than going back home? At least *that* would be familiar misery. Am I ready to jump into the unknown, hoping for a great prize?

I smile at him, lost in my own thoughts. "It is. The chance for something *more*, even if you don't know what that might be."

I stiffen when Anatole reaches for my face and picks something out of my hair. It's a leaf, and he drops it to the ground with a smile. "I would very much like to get to know you better. Would you grant me a dance?" he asks, nodding toward the crowd spinning on the other side of the bonfire.

I don't *want* to dance with him, but what if refusing to is a terrible social blunder? It's pointless to antagonize anyone here, but Kyran warned me about the Goldweeds. Anatole might be setting me up to break protocol and embarrass myself, and while Kyran and I didn't discuss dancing with other people, *I* would be pretty pissed off if he were to take another boy for a spin.

As my gaze settles on the dancers, my body hair bristles, because I spot a face that does not belong. There's a variety of features among the elves, but they all look more chiseled than the average human, a bit like postmodern sculptures that retain a degree of realism yet are somewhat strange.

But the features beyond the veil of pink smoke are round, soft, and so human it brings my heart to a frantic rhythm.

Is that her?

Is that... Carol?

"I..." My brain is frying in its own juices, because she's watching me. Shorter than most elves (other than Sylvan) and a little plump, she has bright blonde curls framing her face. "Maybe, but... would you mind getting me a drink first? It's just that all the smoke and dancing..." I drift off, hoping that my request doesn't carry meaning I don't intend. Gender roles here are pretty vague and varied, but romance is still based on there being a pursuer and a pursued. Anatole is acting like the former, though I'm not sure what he's trying to gain. If not a night with me, then my favor. Maybe he even hopes to gain Kyran's favor *through* me. Not that it matters.

I know my ruse has been successful when Anatole offers me a curt nod and says, "Don't go anywhere," before walking off toward the cherin stall.

That is my cue to go, and I dash past the effigy of wood and dried seaweed, skirting the edge of the dance area with my eyes pinned to the person I presume to be Carol. I can't see her ears under lush blonde waves of hair, but I'm recognizing my own kind the same way I knew something was off about Kyran the moment he stepped into my life. She retreats into the shadows surrounding the illuminated square, and my feet itch to start running.

I *need* to talk to her without Kyran influencing what she says to me. How else will I ever confirm if I should stay?

I glance back to check if Kyran isn't following me before I dip into the alleyway, but I stall mid-step as I single him out.

He's drowning. Surrounded by the villagers who have somehow backed him against a wall, he looks around the crowd as if he can't cope with this many talking mouths at once.

The Kyran I've gotten to know is confident, decisive, and powerful, but when a pregnant lady holds onto his arm and sobs, he stiffens as if she were a landmine about to explode.

When he and I are together, it's so easy to forget that he's spent most of his life in the shadows and isn't used to dealing with large groups of people. It must be so much easier at court, where everyone follows protocol. As I watch him swallow and wipe the skin above his lips, it's clear to me that he must be overwhelmed.

Kyranis lived his whole life dealing with people and getting used to handling elves both in the palace and the villages. My Kyran? He barely spoke to anyone, trapped in the shadowild like a sheathed weapon. But no matter how sharp a sword may be, it can't soothe a crying woman, or slide out of a conflict without bloodshed. Kyran proved many times that he's good at fighting with his words, cutting with them if need be, but I know he doesn't want to antagonize the elves of the village. He might be ruthless when he has to be but wants the best for his Realm. If he didn't care, he could have left the royals to fight over succession after Kyranis's death.

I glance to the alleyway where Carol disappeared, but I already know I'll be joining Kyran and helping him deal with whatever's going on.

I do have customer service experience after all.

Or I'm too drunk for my own good and don't recognize my own limitations.

We will find out very soon, because I'm feeling weirdly protective of this man who could crush someone's skull with his shadow tentacles.

As I approach, I start hearing what the commotion is about.

"...and what if the beast comes sooner? If the prince doesn't get to make him his Dark Companion, their bond will not be strong enough to fight off Heartbreak. My daughter was bitten by a despair last week, and she barely survived. And she wasn't even at the beach. The spawn crawled into our garden!"

It's my fault we aren't yet married, though I don't think I can hold it against myself that I didn't want to marry a stranger.

Kyran captures my gaze as I come closer. When he reaches for me between two bodies, I grab his hand and slide right into the middle of the gathering, putting myself between my prince and his subjects.

"There you are," I say before facing the crying woman and stroking her arm. "Is everything all right?"

She sobs once more. "I'm so sorry. I just worry I'll be in labor when the beast attacks. What will happen then? Should we come to the palace? Or is it safer to travel farther from the shore?"

"And what about the palace guards? My son serves there," a man says, clenching his jaw. "It's been seven years, and no one has been able to take a Dark Companion. I understand the grief for your family, Your Highness, but every month of waiting is a month too long!"

I take a deep breath and force myself to recall every corporate apology I've ever heard. "We sincerely apologize and take full responsibility for the mistakes made during the first attempt at the shadow bond." I squeeze Kyran's hand tighter. "Due to unforeseen circumstances, we failed to deliver on our promise to all of you, and as a member of the Nocturne Court, I will do everything in my power to amend that. The safety of those living in the Nightmare Realm is our priority, and we are dedicated to upholding the trust you have placed in us. I don't know if Prince Kyranis has mentioned that already, but we have established an office ready to receive letters with both your worries and ideas, to ensure you are heard." I smile up at Kyran. "We are here to listen. But the written form will be much easier to process, and lets us make sure no issue is forgotten. Every letter will be formally acknowledged and given the attention it deserves."

When I glance at the stunned faces, I know I've succeeded. What an amazing way to say so much yet commit to so little. As I pull Kyran out of the gridlock, the first person I spot is Anatole, who stares at me with two cups of cherin. I offer him an apologetic smile, but Kyran spins me around, and his lips press to my ear.

"Thank you. I... didn't know what to do," he mumbles as if his tongue was a bit too big for his mouth. I pull away to do a double-take at his flushed features and drooping eyes.

"Are you drunk?" I whisper.

Kyran's lips twist. "I... think so. It was so sweet. Like a dessert. I might have had too much after never having it ever..."

I pull him farther away from the disgruntled elves and back into the merry crowd. "You never had alcohol?" I stand on my toes to give him a kiss. "Who will drive the kelpie home?" I tease, even though he probably won't understand the allusion to DUI.

"I'm still standing," he argues. Were this a comedy, he would have tripped right after saying that, but reality is kinder.

Though only for so long.

"Your Highness, would you do us the honor and set the effigy on fire?" Wiser Ana asks, emerging out of nowhere with a pink torch in hand. Salty wind pulls her veil dangerously close to the flames, and I'm already imagining her turning into a bonfire in her own right.

"Yes," Kyran says right away and swings his hand toward the torch she's holding. I grab it before he can. I don't want him handling fire right now.

"Wiser Ana, may we do it together?"

She stalls, giving us both a prolonged look, then nods.

As we approach the effigy, the rhythm of drums quickens in tandem with my heart. Could this be my future at his side? Yearly trips to the Ardournalia, helping him handle matters of the Court while also embracing these pockets of pure joy just for us, like when he saved me from having to eat that bird on a stick?

I frown at the massive drop of wetness hitting my forehead. I am mortified that in this pompous moment, with hundreds watching us, a bird has shat straight on my head.

But no, another drop of cold wetness spills onto my cheek, and a second later Kyran lifts his hand, palm up, as if the very existence of rain was shocking to him. The villagers, who all gathered closer to see the effigy burn, whisper among themselves, and I quickly move the pink flames of the torch to the wooden Heartbreak. The bits of seaweed catch fire, but the rain grows heavier, and Wiser Ana lifts her face toward the sky as the moonlight dims.

"A sign," she mutters as people retreat under stalls, and trees.

Within moments, the rain extinguishes our torch and attacks the bonfire with ferocity. Kyran must have sobered up a little because of the cold, and he ushers me away from the effigy and toward Crab. Water streams down my face, and I frown when I taste it.

"It's... salty," I say to him.

"Saltwater. A warning from Heartbreak," Kyran mumbles and reaches into the saddle. He stares at the single glove left there in confused silence.

I rub my face as my gaze drifts to the effigy. It won't burn. Nor will Kyran's glove. Is that an omen for my relationship with him?

"I... put it in there. Sorry," I mumble, embarrassed.

Kyran opens his mouth, staring at me as the falling water transforms his wavy hair into a sleek mane similar to Crab's. He's only missing the seaweed. "That's adorable," he says, grinning, and pulls me close, as if the perspective of it not burning means nothing to him.

Maybe he's too drunk to realize what that would imply? Maybe he believes it to be just a superstition?

I never thought of myself as *"adorable"*, but I don't even fight him on it, because what the hell. We're kissing in the rain, drunk on cherin, and he's a prince. I won't be denying myself this moment.

CHAPTER 30

Kyran

Following my first-ever hangover, I promised myself to never *ever* have more than one cup of cherin at a time. The second half of the Ardournalia are brief flashes of memory, and I spent the greater part of the following day ailing in bed. I don't even remember riding back home, and while it was embarrassing to have Luke see me in such a pathetic state, he insisted on nursing me back to health.

I rested my head in his lap, and he stroked it while reading my mother's notes on bats and despairs. He insisted he had experience dealing with the state I was in, and there must have been something to it, because I let him decide when and what I should eat and drink, and he managed to get me back on my feet sooner than it would usually have taken for my brother after a night of hard drinking.

Another week has passed since, and while we've known one another for such a short time, I can no longer imagine spending the rest of my life without him. Despite our union being essential to the safety of my people, a part of me is grateful we did not end up marrying after only a day together, because it will feel different now. I have such a fondness for him that the marriage no longer feels like an obligation, something for me to thrust upon him. I cannot wait to wrap my fingers around the midnight rose and call him truly mine. But he's still uncertain, and I'm prepared for anything to show him that this realm is where he belongs.

With me.

I can give him what he needs—peace, care, safety, passion. He only needs to let me. Now that I've known him for almost a month, I realize he wears armor around his heart, but I've managed to crack it here and there. Like when he told me about his mother, or when he laughs with me, or when he moans my name.

I want everything. I want to know his every interest, find out where his pleasure lies, and learn about any sorrow he might have experienced. I will be like shadow and sneak in through the cracks in his pride, so by our wedding, he won't even know how it happened, yet will realize I'm in his heart.

And during today's hunt, I will take one step closer to making him mine when I give him what he craves.

I need to make sure I'm not too distracted by the way his ass rides up and down in his saddle, or I will have no chance of hunting down the Stag of Sunrise. He looks as good in regal riding clothes and a light breastplate as he does in a nightshirt, but with his hair braided back and my crest on his torso, it's obvious to me that he belongs here.

Belongs with me.

Today, I will bond him to my realm in a way he won't be able to resist.

Kelpies are too large for this dense forest, so we're both riding our own horses, especially since I need to be as swift and mobile as possible for this challenge. I made sure Luke's mare was sufficiently docile after being fed some boiled calmshrooms, so his lack of experience with riding shouldn't result in falling off and breaking his neck. In fact, they seemed to have become friends, and he's petting her mane and smiling blissfully unaware of what's at stake today.

But I am, and I will be the one to hunt down the stag, even though it's invulnerable to my signature weapon—the shadow. A crossbow with silver bolts will have to suffice. At least unlike in the ocean, I'm able to dip in and out of the shadowild in the royal forest, which might come in handy.

I'm not the only one to feel like this event has their future hanging in the balance. All the Goldweeds are here, as well as all the Bloodweeds, and a flurry of other nobles bearing their sharpest blades and swiftest arrows. Those who cannot participate are to wait for the hunting party in the camp made up of large tents, where we might spend the night if the beast remains unslain until moondown. Refreshments are being served by dozens of servants, and musicians play a merry tune for the highborn children who run around without a care in the world.

Those are all trifles, distractions, and no battle has ever been won in a comfortable chair.

The moon is rising, and its glow will guide us through the forest, but when I look up, all I can think of is just how close I am to marrying Luke. And on the night of the Blood Moon at that! Maybe the thwarted wedding was destiny at work after all?

When I see Luke glancing up, I wonder if he's thinking about the same thing, imagining us holding that rose together as I vow to protect him, and he shares his shadow with me for eternity.

The weather's perfect for riding through the forest, with a cloudless sky and barely any wind to disturb the ancient trees reaching for the moon with their leafy claws. Several hunting parties are forming, each meant to penetrate a different part of the woods. Most consist of those who believe they might get lucky and hunt down the stag and elves who accompany them to help, entertain, or secretly thwart the others' efforts.

I tried to keep my own party small for that very reason. Elven longevity can breed plans so long in scope I can't be certain of anyone's true intentions. Though Tristan has proven himself loyal, and I am relatively sure he will not try to rip the prize out of my grasp for an elusive promise of more power. He's coming with us. To aid me and to protect Luke, who will be my priority today, regardless of how the event goes.

I'm lost in my thoughts when Luke rides up to me and nudges me with his foot. "Maybe we could go with them?" he suggests, pointing out a group of four, consisting of Lady Guinevere, her Dark Companion, Carol, Marquise Coralis, and Prince Sylvan Goldweed.

It's only natural that Luke wants to chat with the only other human present, but he can do that later, when we gather to celebrate a successful hunt. I don't want to be anywhere near Sylvan after the hunting horn blows. He might carry the bored expression of someone who is only attending the hunt as part of his royal duties, but his future is at stake too. Born without much talent for shadowcraft, he resorted to studying alchemy in order to compensate for his meager skill. If he manages to capture the stag's heart today, the power gained from the beast might pull him out from under his older brother's heel and make him a player in his own right.

Even his presence in the same party as Carol is strategic, because the Stag of Sunrise is always drawn to the scent of a human. Having one around in the woods improves the chance of setting one's eyes on the beast.

When Sylvan's cold, sapphire gaze cuts into Luke, I ride up to my promised from the side, to shield him from the cursed eye. I open my mouth, but when Marquise Coralis rides up to us with long hair pulled into a tight bundle at the back of her head, and in a sharp suit meant for comfortable riding, I speak to her instead. "I'd rather not join them, but the Marquise would surely want to ride with her dear brother?"

The glare she sends me feels like a shard of ice stuck in my chest. "He and I are not on speaking terms, Your Highness. I would think you of all people should remember why," she says in a voice made of razors.

I stall, and in the brief time it takes for us to make this exchange, Sylvan's group rides off, with Anatole as its final member. His remaining sister, Elodie, is arguing about something with her father, Baron Gabriel, who is a skilled hunter. A man who often traverses the forest for days on end, he might be one of my biggest competitors. My guess has always been that he does it to avoid his wife, but it's a habit that resulted in him knowing the area better than any other noble.

"Oh... my apologies," I mumble. I don't feel it necessary to appease my twin's former lover, but I don't hate her either. The last thing I want is for this uncomfortable situation to continue. She should know by now where my interests lie.

Luke stares after the group longingly, which makes me want to hide him in the palace and never let him as much as gaze upon another man. I know it is unreasonable. He's not interested in the Goldweeds. If anything, he's wary of them because their sister almost killed us, but I can't help myself.

It's the Marquise's presence that makes me so scattered, which is doubly frustrating because I should be focused on the stag only.

I look back at Tristan who's busy chatting to a very drunk bard instead of mounting his horse. Couldn't he focus on the Marquise instead so that his rakish ways are actually useful for once?

I wanted our group to stay small, with Tristan being the only additional member, but when the Marquise joined us without asking, I found myself unable to refuse her after so clearly offending her. But when I catch a glimpse of Elodie Goldweed trying to follow us, I glare straight at the baron and say, "Good luck at the hunt, Uncle. I hear the western flank of the forest might bear fruit."

Or, as Luke would have said it, *'Fuck off, I don't want you here'*.

Baron Gabriel stalls, surprised by my rudeness, but quickly catches himself and offers me a stiff smile. At least he rides off and takes his liar of a daughter with him.

"Are we ready?" I call out to Tristan, who glances my way with his hand on the flute in the bard's hand.

He nods, winks at the beautiful musician and jogs back to his mount. Free from his charming presence, the bard combs back his auburn locks and struts to a large boulder marking the spot where one of my ancestors was once gored by a boar. I say nothing when the bard slides off the mossy surface and waves at his assistant, who rushes over as if she's about to perform surgery.

"No dogs for the hunt?" Luke asks, sitting alongside me on the pliant brown mare.

"What are those?" I ask, eager to find out about any way to earn an advantage.

He stares at me with his lips parted, which must mean he thought the object of his question was obvious.

"Are they a weapon?" I urge him.

"N-no. They're animals. Kind of like... wolves, but tamed to be pets."

It's my turn to stare at him wide-eyed. "Are you telling me humans domesticated *wolves*? Beasts with more teeth than they know what to do with and claws like knives?"

Luke rolls his eyes. "Hm. Maybe the wolves in our world are more friendly. Since everything here seems that bit more homicidal."

"Now I see why you think you can have a pet bat." When he makes a face, I lean over for a quick kiss. "You're human, so maybe anything is possible for you. But no, we don't have pet wolves to help us hunt."

We both stiffen when the bard manages to stand on top of the boulder with the aid of his assistant, only to lean forward, as if the surface under his feet were rocking. The poor bastard must have drunk enough cherin to believe himself to be on a boat, but when he shows everyone the bejeweled horn, I dig my feet deeper into stirrups. We sit through a convoluted, if brief speech about sportsmanship, but when the bard blows the horn, it's the stag, not fairness that's on everyone's mind.

I look back, to make sure Luke is doing well, but his eyes shine back at me with glee as he rides his mare behind me, and our party heads between the trees, urged by the insistent call of the horn.

The woods are especially beautiful today, with the silvery glow of the moon painting big, meaty leaves. I love the scent of nature, something I've been denied for most of my life, yet which I find so soothing. The damp, earthy aroma of herbs, worms, and mist reassures me with each inhale. As we go deeper into the woods, led by the colorful glow of wild fungi, each stride of my mount feels easier, smoother.

"How will we know what to look for?" Luke asks.

Tristan butts in before I can answer. "Easy, you're the bait, the stag will come for you. The best we can do is to ride deep into the forest, far from the other parties."

"What?" Luke chokes out, stiffening.

It's not how I would have answered, because there's no point in scaring Luke, but Tristan is correct.

"You're in no danger around us, my darling," I say and stroke his back through the velvet cape. "The Stag of Sunrise is drawn to you, but we will catch it when it approaches. You will recognize its golden fur from afar. It carries the same glow Vinia fought with. We think it doesn't actually want to kill humans, but because it can sense sunlight still lingering on you, it wants to be... *one* with you. Sadly, that usually means getting gored by its antlers and eaten. Something that will *not* happen to you," I repeat so it's clear to him that he's safe.

Luke seems lost in thought as he assesses the dense woods around us. "Should I have... a weapon?"

"Not unless you're proficient with it," I tell him as we ride down the path and into a narrow gully shaped as if a giant struck the rock with a massive axe.

"If it has the power of Sunlight, is it also invulnerable to your shadow? Will I need to lend you mine?"

"That's why we have regular weapons," I say and reach back to tap the ornamental crossbow on my back. "This is the one my father killed a Stag of Sunrise with." It's odd to talk that way about a man who barely acknowledged my existence. As if I took a step too far into impersonating my brother.

"My Prince, may I have a word in private?" the Marquise asks, riding up to me from the other side as soon as we are out of the gully.

Really? *Now*?

I make myself glance at her, but all I can think of is that the other hunting parties are close, and that I would rather leave them all far behind, so the stag doesn't end up killed by Sylvan, or some other upstart, as it's on the way to Luke. "Can't it wait?"

"Must it?" she asks, "I have been trying to speak to you for *weeks*."

I hate that Luke is hearing this, but he reaches out to pat my thigh.

"Maybe this is a good opportunity?" Luke suggests, already slowing his horse, as if to make the choice for me.

He's right. It's childish of me to avoid an unpleasant interaction. I've killed, I've spent weeks alone, and I pored over books on taxation and Court policy. I can talk to one woman, who thinks I used to be her lover.

"All right," I say, pretending that my stomach isn't cramping as I nod at Tristan, to let him know it won't be long.

I invite the Marquise along with a broad gesture and ride into a thatch of dragonweeds growing a bit farther to the right. The thick, purple leaves slap my face the way the Marquise surely wants to, but I use those last moments of silence to gather my thoughts. Maybe I shouldn't have stalled. Maybe I should have been clear with her early on instead of waiting for her to get the hint and maybe focus on some other man? Just a few moments later, we reach a moonlit clearing and I pull on the lead to turn my horse and face her.

With black paint outlining her eyes and mouth, she appears intimidatingly somber, as if she's about to attend an audience with the emperor, not end a relationship. Then again, maybe she still refuses to acknowledge that whatever flame she believed used to burn between her and my twin has long been extinguished.

"Marquise," I say, nodding at her with stiff politeness.

She takes a deep breath and one more look around before our eyes meet. "I understand that you have brought your future Dark Companion into the fold, that you need to court him and pander to him, but is there really a need to toss me aside like some old plaything? We never made promises, but it's not right. I deserve an explanation."

Whatever words I believed I had for her are gone, as if her gaze has poured acid into my skull. "I— that's not—" I clear my throat and comb through my horse's mane, hoping that avoiding her face might make this easier on me. "You know what kind of man I am," I say, and while this is exactly how I thought about my twin, I flinch at the scoff she answers with.

"And so I never assumed you'd only have one lover, but why disappear from my life? Did we not have fun? Did we not become close? I'm fine with sharing, even if I didn't expect a man in the picture."

"Well, I'm in love with this man," I say, meeting her gaze as chills trail down my spine. This is the first time I've said that. The first time I thought of it so consciously, and all of a sudden I want to ride back to Luke and tell him too.

She scowls at me. "When did that happen? Two months ago you told me in dramatic fashion how your heart cannot be tied down by love, and now all of a sudden you have feelings for this human? Feelings that pulled you out of every bed you frequented other than mine as well? Explain it to me, Kyranis, or I will begin to worry you have been charmed!"

I take a gulp of air, and it fills the empty space where my brain used to be. I'm not used to being confronted like this, and I'm not sure how to handle it. Should I just dismiss her and show my authority as prince? It doesn't feel right. It also doesn't feel like something Kyranis would have done, or she wouldn't have spoken to me the way she does. Then again, I'm not Kyranis.

"I don't know what to tell you. Maybe it's because he's human?"

She shakes her head, increasingly desperate. "So all we've had means nothing? Above all, I was sure we shared a friendship."

I hang my head, feeling guilty even though I'm not the one she clearly had feelings for. My brother didn't deserve this kind of affection. "I truly am sorry. Maybe after the wedding, I will be able to rebuild our friendship," I say as my shadow reaches out for Luke, seeking comfort in his closeness.

But he is *not* close, and my head jerks up as I focus on the path. "He's too far," I mutter, nudging the horse with my heels.

"The stag?" The Marquise perks up without a smile, but doesn't look like she's about to throw a tantrum, which is mature of her in the position we're in.

"Luke? Tristan?" I call out, turning my horse around, confused by the faltering thread of connection between Luke and me. The only time it's felt this broken was when Vinia gave him a lantern filled with Sunlight.

Could the stag's proximity do the same?

I sigh a breath of relief when Tristan emerges from between the trees in his black and red glory. "Is everything all right, Sire?"

I stall, and the worry I've been feeling turns into a violent throb in my temples. "Where's Luke? I can feel he's far."

Tristan opens his mouth, and the need to punch him makes me grab my own wrist to prevent that from happening. "He's close. Sire, *you* are the one I've been guarding since the day he was born."

Hardly. Despite his skill and good heart, if Tristan was the only one trying to keep my late brother alive, Kyranis would have left us all much, much sooner. There are many eels on my skin to prove that.

"I can take care of myself. You were meant to watch my promised!" I roar and dash to where I last saw Luke.

While the Marquise's face still looks as if she's bitten into a rotten sardine, she turns her attention to the forest around us and joins in the search. "Luke?" she yells out into the darkness between the trees as my stomach turns into stone.

I don't even have the time to yell at Tristan, because all I can think of is golden antlers piercing Luke's heart.

CHAPTER 31

LUKE

Do I know that the forest is dangerous? Yes. Am I taking my chances in order to talk to Carol before the wedding? Also yes.

Not even two weeks are left until I'm forever bound to Kyran, and I can't forget that the clock is ticking. I need to be braver if I am to find out the truth, unobscured by Kyran's sweet words and kisses.

When he holds me close, all and any rational thinking fades away, I melt into him as if our shadows are already one. I've never had sex that felt so intimate, and I've never really had someone I could call a friend with it holding so much meaning.

If all of this is some elven trickery meant to enslave me, my heart would shatter into a million pieces. I *want* to believe him. But what I've been through at school, the kind of deception and mistrust sowed in me took root too deeply for me to accept people's words at face value. I wish I wasn't broken like some skittish puppy kicked one time too many, but it is what it is.

I didn't plan to run after Carol, but the clock is ticking, so when I caught a glimpse of the other party passing through the woods not far from us, I grasped the opportunity of Tristan drifting off to spy on Kyran and the Marquise.

I'm not a great rider, but good enough to traverse the expanse of grassy undergrowth separating me from Carol's red cape. Kyran made sure I got the most pliant horse, and we spent time together last week with him teaching me the basics.

My heart thrashes in my chest when my mount leaps over a fallen tree, but the moon is growing each night, and I feel time ticking away all too fast in Kyran's charming presence.

If Carol isn't welcome at court, I have to seize this opportunity, even if it means making my prince angry.

They're faster than me, and likely have no idea about my presence, but I refuse to give up and follow them along a broad path through the woods.

I haven't thought about an excuse I can give them for being alone. I'm too frantic, and too busy trying not to fall off. Just as I'm about to make my last attempt to speed up so I can reach Carol and her Lady, a voice from the side startles me.

"Luke? Are you lost? Is the prince all right?" Anatole asks, riding up to me. His long hair is in a tight braid falling down his back, and it appears white in the moonlight.

Fuck.

I can't just say '*I'm here to talk to Carol, byeeee!*' so I take a deep breath, staring ahead at the sliver of red lost between the trees. "The woods are so confusing. One moment I was with them, the next, we lost sight of each other."

Anatole scoffs. "If you were mine, I wouldn't have taken my eyes off you. It's dangerous out here. Especially for a human," he says, matching my pace.

His words flare up so many conflicting feelings. I'm not impressed by his blatant flirting, mad at his criticism of Kyran when I was the one to suggest he talks to Marquise Coralis in the first place, but also scared as I remember the touch of sentient thorns trying to rip me apart when I first stepped off the track in the Nightmare Realm. It feels like it's been years since.

"I'm sure Prince Kyranis will soon find me. The shadow bond we have isn't easily broken." Which only reminds me I don't have much time.

"Sometimes, that's a curse," Anatole says, his expression more serious. "We have been coercing humans into bonds with shadow-wielders for so long now, but there should be other ways to fight Heartbreak. It's a shame it's so difficult to get the prince's ear."

"What other ways?"

"Our alchemists, astronomers, masters of shadowcraft, and wisers have many suggestions we could put to the test instead of the blunt force of a sword dipped in your shadow. The beast ought to be slayed for good, not chased away only to come back like a storm. Until all its hearts beat no more, it will keep returning for more."

This feels way above my pay grade.

"I'm sure the prince will listen in the future, but with all the omens of Heartbreak's upcoming visit, this is not the right time for experimenting."

"Yes, and look what happened to James! It's been seven years since he's been stuck in the shadowild, and nobody even mentions him by name," Anatole says as we reach the party, but Carol and her Lady remain out of my reach. Goddamn it.

"I heard divers were sent..." I don't know what those divers might be. Did they dive into the shadowild? Under the sea? I'm pretty sure Kyran mentioned going into the shadowild is impossible when not on dry land.

"And no body was found," Anatole adds grimly. "Wouldn't it be better if there was a way to not endanger Dark Companions? To not endanger... you?" He meets my gaze, and I'm torn between feeling uncomfortable and flattered.

But before I can answer, someone yells up front, "The stag!", and Anatole grabs his bow.

Golden radiance streams through a thatch of thin, bamboo-like trees far ahead. Shadows move, then fade as the animal runs off. Ahead of us, Sylvan whistles at his horse and dashes past Carol and her Lady as if he's possessed by the urge to get his hands on the creature's heart, but his family doesn't stay far behind.

I should have worn my moonshard glasses, but I worried they'd fall off while I'm on horseback, and now I can barely see the other hunting party in the dark.

I nudge my mount with my heels, perhaps a bit too firmly, and she dashes forward, making me stiffen. I'm not used to riding so fast, especially not with low branches smacking my face, but I might get lost if I fail to catch up now. It's pathetic that I need to depend on the protection of others, but I'm not dying for the sake of being perceived as brave.

This chase is already more exhilarating than any rollercoaster I've been on. A primal part of me wants to chase the stag, even though I have no weapon to put it down with.

I need to see this creature. I need to look into its eyes, see its golden fur. I need to—

I lean down when another branch is about to slam into my head, but as I rise too soon, it catches my cape instead.

A powerful force tugs at my throat, then pulls at my head, and I collapse, hitting the ground so hard my lungs empty. The edges of my vision turn black as I cradle the sore flesh of my throat. For a moment, I fear the force with which the cape pulled me off horseback might have done permanent damage, but I can still breathe. The world is spinning when I hear a *thump* close by, and I shriek when someone approaches, but what looms over me are not bloodstained antlers. It's Anatole.

"You're not... after him?" I croak, rubbing my throat.

He slings the bow over his arm and kneels by my side, grabbing my leg. "I heard your scream. Does your ankle hurt?"

"I... um..." I'm startled at his touch, and still overwhelmed by the fall. It's only when Anatole mentions my leg that I become aware of the ache originating in my ankle.

His fingers are warm, and as they gently squeeze my calf, I get the sense that if I wasn't wearing boots with many buckles, I might be feeling his touch on bare skin by now. "I'm not sure. I think my cape got stuck and just plucked me off the horse," I mutter, so sore I almost expect the coppery tang of blood in my mouth.

I realize it wasn't the wisest thing to tell Anatole when he moves above me and slides his fingertips over my bare neck next. "And you're breathing all right?"

I look into his eyes from up close, and my breath hitches. Is he trying to... seduce me? My throat most definitely feels like there's a cold lump in it when his leg not-so-discreetly nudges my knee to the side.

A sense of panic freezes me in place. I might be imagining things. Or he might be about to murder me in this dark forest, but as he leans in, and his fragrant, golden braid falls close to my face, the thumping in my ears becomes almost too loud.

I'm about to gently push Anatole back, so his pride remains intact, when Kyran's voice cuts through the air like a shadow blade. "Step away from my promised!"

Anatole's head shoots up and he pulls away, but I swear he's flushed. "I'm checking if his leg isn't broken. Where were you when he fell off his horse?" he asks without even adding a passive-aggressive 'Sire'.

"It's okay! I'm fine... I think!" I say, scrambling to move away from Anatole as Kyran leaps off horseback and dashes toward us in a series of long steps. Two more figures emerge from the woods behind me, but all I can see is the twist to Kyran's lips, the fire in his dark gaze.

"How curious. Last time I checked, his legs were nowhere near his shoulders!"

Anatole squints at him. "Or were they?"

Kyran releases a choked grunt, and then he has his hands around *Anatole's* throat and pushes him at the nearest tree. "How dare you! I should pluck your eyes out so you can never lay them on my promised again, you vile snake!"

"You're the one... breaking protocol! How is he to... make an informed... choice during courting... if you're *fucking*?" Anatole chokes out, grabbing Kyran's wrists as I get up, dazed. Is this really happening? Are two beautiful elven royals fighting over *me*?

I don't know if I should intervene, but Kyran seems to have the upper hand, so maybe I don't need to?

"It's you who dishonors your prince's promised with your dirty hands and your blue cloak," Kyran roars before smashing his fist between Anatole's eyes, and then into the side of his face.

"Kyranis, stop," Tristan mutters, stepping closer yet keeping his hands off the prince, as if he worries about possible repercussions.

"Maybe you shouldn't have left him all alone in the woods! All of our lives might depend on him!" Anatole slides his hand over Kyran's face, but Kyran is quick to grab his wrist with a shadow tentacle.

I can't let Kyran take the blame for that. "He didn't leave me, I rode off!" I say and step closer, because enough is enough. It's all fun and games until one of them decides it's time to pull swords out.

Kyran throws Anatole to the ground and spins toward me, his mane wild as if it's made of black snakes. His hands are like claws when they reach for me, and I step back, breathless with fear as the others disappear and stark, black trees shoot up from the ground, forming a dome above. The moon is gone, so are the stars, and it's only when my back hits something cold and strangely dull to the touch do I realize that we're no longer in the woods.

At least not in the usual sense.

This is the shadowild, his personal kingdom, and I have never seen him so mad.

I'm paralyzed as Kyran stumbles closer, somehow taller, broader in the shoulders, with thicker biceps and fists that could crush my nose and knock out all my teeth. But it's his voice, dark and raspy as if he dragged it through gravel, that plants real terror in my heart.

"You '*rode off*'? What the fuck does that mean? Why was he touching you?" he roars, and I spin around, dashing into the darkness like a spooked cat.

CHAPTER 32

Luke

I know only terror. The black woods around me are endless, primal, and just as I seem to be reaching the edge of the forest, new trees sprout from the ground in an even grid surrounding me from all sides as if this is a very old video game. Sound is so muted I can't hear Kyran, but for all I know he might be right behind me, a second away from crushing my throat as punishment for whatever he blames me for.

I'm breathless, running as if this is my very own purgatory. I have no idea how long it's been, but as I lose strength and my limbs turn heavy, the trees gain more detail, and all of a sudden I'm running from my boarding school.

I hear dogs barking. The shouting of the gym teacher who humiliated me at every turn. They're so close. I can almost sense their hot breath on my skin. I don't know if I'm delirious, or if Kyran, Prince of the Nightmare Realm can bring *my* nightmares to life, but all of this feels too real.

I don't want to be that kid again. I don't want to be stuck in a place with no way out, no agency, and no future beyond my next breath.

I leave my cloak behind, because it keeps catching on bushes, and I only make sure my next step isn't into some bear trap. I couldn't predict that darkness would open in the ground in front of me. It's too late when I run straight into the hole, but instead of descending, my body is falling *up*.

My mind spins, and as soon as I manage to stand again, I find myself trapped in a black corridor with floors covered by a gray carpet. The walls seem to pulse with smoke, like Kyran's sword did when he saved me from the tooth moths.

I dart through the first door, too frantic to look back.

I just... I just want to be safe. But as I dash for the door across from me, it just.... disappears, and my hands hit the wall. Frantic, I spin around, ready to find a different way out, but Kyran's tall form fills the door, blocking my way.

"What did he promise you?" Kyran hisses, and unlike everything else around us, his form remains painfully sharp. "Did you forget you wear *my* crest? That you're *my* promised? That you moan *my* name every night?"

My cheeks are hot, and I'm panting, but he is the master of this domain. There is nowhere for me to run.

"It had nothing to do with Anatole!" I choke out when I find my voice. My first instinct is to run, but when cornered, I will show claws.

Kyran's eyes flash with a smoky glow as he steps closer, his chest pumping hard, as if he's fighting the urge to squash me like a bug. "Then why did you seek him out? You wanted me gone so you could run to him! And you didn't care that I'd be worried!"

I can't believe that *this* is what his intuition tells him about me. "I was trying to find Carol!" I yell back, because what do I have left? He could kill me here and let the shadows swallow the body. "I wanted to talk to a Companion on my own, so I know what I'm actually in for!" I spread my arms and stand taller even though he towers over me.

Kyran opens his mouth, and his shoulders hunch, relaxing. "Carol? What? Why? I told you everything you need to know."

"And how would I know if it's true?" It hurts to say that, but something inside me is twisting, ripping, and it has nothing to do with the dark walls pulsing as if they're alive.

Kyran stills, color gone from his features. His breaths shallow.

"You don't trust me? After everything we've been through?" Were he someone else, I would have sworn his voice broke. "I give you everything you want..."

I want to hate him for the way he frightens me, for dropping me into the shadowild where I have no way out, but when I see the hurt in his eyes I feel only guilt. He needs to understand where I'm coming from.

I hug myself, taking deep breaths. "I can't trust you because... because I can't trust anyone. Ever. That's just... gone for me, okay?" I sniff, fighting tears as I realize I never said that out loud. It's always sat dormant on my heart like a cancerous growth I felt I had under control. But I don't. It's rotting me from the inside, and I don't want to *be* anymore.

Kyran reaches out for me, and while I'm on the verge of pulling away, when he curls his hands around my forearms, all I feel is relief. I'm no longer afraid.

"Luke, what do you mean? Why would it be gone?"

I try to speak but fall apart instead. The tears I was holding back spill down my cheeks, and I feel raw as if Kyran had taken a grater to my feelings and used it until no skin is left.

"I... I've been really hurt before," I utter, sobbing like a crybaby when I should have long left all this shit behind me. "I was in... in a bad place." This is useless. But when he pulls me close, when his long hair hides me from the world, and his scent——salt, wax, and leather——fills my lungs, all I want is to hand myself into his care.

"What happened?" Kyran asks, and all of a sudden the wall behind me turns soft like a mattress, the world's gravity flips again with a gentle push from Kyran, and we're lying on a bed.

I lean into him, all my walls crumble, and I can't stop sobbing. He strokes my shoulder as I regain enough composure to speak. Where do I even start with this bullshit when my whole body balks against me spilling my secrets?

I guess the answer is that I need to take off my armor. Starting with the actual breastplates, since they clank against each other like two cans. Physical barriers are so much easier to crumble than the emotional ones, yet it still feels like opening a wound when Kyran helps me with the buckles.

I only speak when both our breastplates clatter softly to the shadowy floor.

"When... I was a kid, twelve or something, I started being, I dunno, my mom said 'rebellious', but I think she was just sick of me, and she sent me to this strict boarding school. I hated it with every fiber of my being. I hated having to do as I was told, I hated being alone, I hated the monotony of every day being the same, and I hated that they made befriending people impossible. Rewards and punishments depended on following the rules and snitching on anyone who didn't. I soon learned I couldn't trust anyone, including the teachers."

Kyran's chest is my safe space, and as I press my ear to it, listening to the strong rhythm of his elven heart, even the pain of the past is a bit more bearable.

"That sounds like a nightmare," Kyran whispers, stroking my back in soothing circles. "I'm so sorry."

I hug him, wishing I could melt into him. "I tried to keep my head down, do what I was forced to, just to get through it. But then puberty hit me, I met this boy, and I dared opening up. I didn't snitch on him, I wanted to be around him, I wanted to be friends. And even though we didn't have much education in these things, I was starting to understand I only liked boys. That was beyond unacceptable at this school. I thought I was smart by then, that I knew all the best hiding spots. But we still ended up busted. It was very innocent, we were just making out.

"They interrogated us about each other for fucking hours like it was some torture prison. I denied everything at first, but then the teacher got violent and I knew it wouldn't stop until I told him what he wanted to hear. I couldn't bear for them to hurt my friend, so I took all the blame. When they finally let me go with a promise of weeks of extra duties, all I could think of was finding him, to make sure he was okay.

"Turned out he was very much fine. Because he blamed the whole fucking thing on me, called me names, and didn't want to speak to me again. I was so heartbroken, so defeated, so betrayed. I just wanted to disappear, needed to be free of that place. I stole pills, bartered for a razor, and... that's when you found me."

Kyran whimpers and cradles my face. "Luke... My sweet boy. He never deserved you. I'm so sorry," he rasps, blinking as if his eyes are itching.

"I thought you were only a dream, but I took that new chance on life, and decided not to trust anyone again. How could I when everyone was out to get each other in that godforsaken place? Every day I'd hear how my mother gave up on me, how I deserved the shit I got. I was done trying to make friends. Instead, I decided to become the biggest fucking menace that school ever saw. I ran away several times, I took the punishments, the detentions, the shitty food, just to get that glimpse of freedom, and the feeling that I could do something of *my* choosing."

Kyran strokes my face, swallows, and his tight lips twitch. "I know you're only here because you did end up in the River of Souls, but I would have never known you if I reached for a different hand. It feels like a weight on my chest. And it makes me feel guilty that I didn't even ask you why you ended up there. That I didn't let you stay in my world right then and there. I'm sorry. I understand what it's like to be trapped."

I shrug, even though tears keep streaming down my face as if to make up for the years when I'd stopped crying altogether. "You saved my life. What I did with that life later was my own responsibility. Made me who I am now. No one can turn back time. Eventually, I managed to get myself kicked out of the damn place. I'm pretty proud of that, even if I did play dirty. I earned my freedom, and my mother had to deal with that."

"You don't need her anymore. You don't need any of them," Kyran says with a kiss to my forehead. It feels warm, like a blessing that actually works, and I slide my arms around his neck, seeking comfort in his beautiful promises.

"And until you, I thought I didn't need *anyone*. That it was safest to be alone, so I kept people at a distance. If they weren't close, they couldn't hurt me. Then you barged into my life, took me to your Realm, threatened my freedom, all while making me fall for you, and I'm a mess, always looking where the trick is, ready for betrayal, ready to be trapped again. You of all people know how terrible it is to lose your freedom, so please understand why I'm terrified. I *want* to trust you. I just don't know how to take that last step. So I thought that if I talked to Carol, she could tell me that being a Dark Companion isn't so bad."

There. I've bared my soul. Lost every asset I had in this game by revealing my feelings. The rest lies in his hands. And I hope he won't use them to crush my heart.

Kyran hums, then slides his thumb across my cheeks, wiping away tears. "And if you did talk to her, maybe you would have convinced yourself someone set her up to lie to you." He sounds defeated, but he doesn't pull away and instead presses his forehead to mine in a gesture that has my soul throbbing with happiness. "I want you to feel safe with me. I want to give you a life worth living, not keep you imprisoned."

I take deep breaths, trying to calm down as I slide my hands over his back. His body on mine is such a comfort. "It's just... hard, when you have all this power, this place in the shadowild, your position at court, and I'm just a human keeping one secret of yours."

"It isn't *just* a secret. You're holding my life in your hands, and I trust you with it."

I look into his smoky eyes, still rattled by what I've shared, as I slowly take in what he's saying. All this time, I've been unable to trust him fully, when he's already made that choice with me. And it *is* a choice. Because there is never certainty in giving your heart to another. You have to trust that they don't crush it. And that feels like the hardest choice I've ever had to make.

"Will you take care of me?" I whisper. "Do you promise?"

Kyran's eyes hide whole galaxies, and each star within them promises a safe haven. He takes my hands, kisses them both, and pulls them to his face, as if I'm the prince, and he—my humble servant. "For as long as I breathe."

I might be about to make the biggest mistake of my life but choose to shed all doubts and suspicions.

I *choose* to trust him with my whole being.

I lean in to kiss his soft lips. "I'm sorry it took me so long."

Kyran pulls himself up, straddling my body, and his soft hair tickles my cheek with a promise of more to come. "Don't apologize. I was patient for too many years, but I could wait some more, for you."

I run my hands up his thighs, pondering this newfound freedom. It's as if my heart was squeezed in a container far too small, and now it can finally expand. I'm allowing myself to *feel*, and it's taking my breath away.

This amazing man, an elven prince, wants me.

"You don't have to wait. I'm yours."

He shivers in my arms, and then lowers himself on top of me, kissing first my forehead, then my lips. And for the first time, I let myself believe that nothing about his loving care is an act. Maybe I don't have to do everything myself. Maybe I can let someone carry half of the weight.

Kyran's whisper teases my ear. "You're the one person who makes me feel real. As If I'm not just someone else's shadow but a man like any other. Blood, flesh, and bone."

My fingers drift to the buttons at the front of his elegant riding jacket. "Let me see all that flesh then," I whisper with a growing smile despite my cheeks being still wet from tears. I want to—no, I *need* to feel him close. The emotional barrier that separated us for so long is no longer there, and I can't wait to find out what it's like to be naked with him now that my heart is free.

His eyes glint with anticipation, and while I've seen the same expression on so many faces before, none of the men I've been with was ever so hungry for me, not *me* specifically. I might be Kyran's first, but his devotion, his absolute inability to stay away from me make me believe that he wouldn't have been like this with just anyone. That maybe he and I really have been brought together by fate. That maybe we do belong together in ways I could have never anticipated.

One thing is for certain—if this is a dream, I want it to keep going forever.

"See me," Kyran begs, taking my hand and sliding it between the folds of his shirt.

My breath hitches when my fingers reach his pec. I love how he towers over me, how he can turn me into a blabbering mess, and how I can't get enough of him.

And I do feel safe with him. Safe enough to let go of inhibitions, to be unafraid of his shadowy lair, and to trust him with my body, soul, and shadow.

"Very real…" I purr, sliding my fingers up his hard stomach. This man is made of pure fucking muscle. So strong he can easily carry me, pin me down, and protect me as well.

The shadow bed stirs under us, as if it's full of tiny bubbles, and Kyran's eyes darken, his irises spilling over and coloring the whites around them black. The strange effect is gone when he blinks before sliding his knee between my thighs and cradling my head with one arm. "I can already see you in the red moonlight, ready to be mine forever."

It's silly. I never imagined I'd want to get married, but with Kyran? As soon as he mentions it, I melt, dreaming of long, happy years together. Vowing in front of the whole Nocturne Court that I am Kyran's.

"Not long now," I whisper, looking into his strange eyes, already unbuckling his belt, because, fuck it, we're here alone, and I don't care what's going on at the hunt.

He inhales, but when he speaks my name next, his voice sounds as if he's whispering through a copper pipe. The metallic, otherworldly quality of his words makes me curl my toes, but as the bed stirs under me again, I blink and raise my head to see shadows attaching themselves to Kyran in wispy strings like elongated leeches.

I must have made a face, because he hushes me with a peck on the cheek. "Don't be afraid… things are different in the shadowild."

"But you're… fine? This doesn't hurt you?" I ask as shadows swell under my fingers where I was touching his skin, no less warm and pleasant to the touch.

Kyran shakes his head, and I can't miss that his hair no longer acts as it normally does, instead floating in the air and merging into thick, flat strands. "It's an effort to keep my elven form here, for me at least. I spent most of my life as a creature of shadow," he says, and the darkness is back in his eyes, covering them whole, as if he's no longer a man.

I can't contain the shock of seeing him like this but keep still when his long finger pulls down the front of my shirt, flinging buttons away as if that was his plan all along.

I gasp, and my heartbeat quickens. The shadows cover him and melt into each other, making his form grow. Am I scared or excited? *I'm* not sure, but my dick is.

"Is this… safe?" I mutter, running my fingertips over his swelling forearm, black, matte, and soft as velvet.

Kyran's features have sharpened too, and when he smiles, it's like being in the arms of an exceedingly handsome praying mantis. As my heartbeat speeds up in response, the confused arousal I experienced earlier becomes more insistent too, and I wrap my legs around him as he speaks.

"I won't hurt you. My soul is still the same," he tells me, sinking his long fingers into my hair as the shapes around us pulse, creating abstract forms I have no interest in anyway. All I can see, smell, and hear is Kyran, and when he dives in to nip my neck, my moan gets lost in the darkness surrounding us.

I'm not sure if he's got undressed, or if the shadows clinging to him gave him a second skin, but he's definitely not wearing anything. Only the golden sun tattoo in the middle of his chest stands out. When he moves, his obsidian limbs leave behind wisps of smoke that don't smell of anything. But if this is his most natural form in the shadowild, I'm not afraid. There's nowhere safer than in Kyran's arms, and the way he kisses me is just as filled with need as always.

I run my hands up his massive arms, and all the way to the monstrous shoulders. I don't know what's wrong with me that I find this hot, but I do.

His clawed hands are the size of my head, and he pulls my shirt and jacket off with ease, leaving me exposed to his greedy lips and hands. The shadows are like flames in constant movement, but his face remains an island of pale flesh. He even has a pink flush on those perfect cheekbones and lips. When his tongue slides down my torso, leaving a wet trail, our mutual desire makes me rock until my groin rubs Kyran's chin, provoking him into dragging my pants off too.

I face this unfamiliar creature naked and vulnerable, and I want it to take me however it wishes. Kyran doesn't make me wait either and slides his clawed hands down my thighs as I arch up to kiss him with my heart rattling like mad. I'm not afraid, not really, but I'm still getting to grips with what he is when the shadows embrace him. This is what I want though. Kyran in his most natural and most raw state. No secrets, no inhibitions, nothing between us.

As soon as I try to pull myself up, he playfully pushes my wrists down to the soft bed, pressing his weight on top of me, and—oh, I feel the size of *him* against my belly.

Unlike the velvet of his arms, his cock is slick like lubricated latex, hot, pulsing, and already leaving wetness on my skin.

We both gasp as he thrusts against me, massaging my stomach with the shaft, but despite the hiss coming from his mouth next, he doesn't unleash all his power on me yet. Instead, he pulls me close, digging fingers into my flesh and teeth into the crook of my neck. He has my wrists pinned, but I don't resist, open to whatever my beautiful monster might need.

"Luke," he mutters in that strange, gravelly voice.

The shadows throb around us as I arch against him, but when gravity shifts, the room seems to roll around us. I find myself straddling his hips, with his hard dick between my thighs, and my wrists still captured in his massive paws.

"What is it, darling?" I say with a smirk, loving how his gaze glides over my exposed body.

Am I horny out of my mind? Yes. But am I feeling mushy inside over how much I crave to connect with my Prince of Darkness? Also yes.

Circles spread over his smooth black eyes, like water around a pebble thrown into a lake, and he squeezes my waist, holding me in place as he thrusts up, spreading the slick shadows between my legs, over my taint, cock, balls, my buttocks...

"I want you to sink onto me. I want to be the darkness inside you," he says in a voice that's dull yet somehow sexy, and it awakens a new yearning.

My face is on fire, but I want it. I want him inside me, and I want him watching me with those adoring eyes. They're black as tar, but I still recognize Kyran's desire in their burn. His cock slides between my buttocks and I rub against him needily, but he's holding my wrists, preventing me from taking this any farther.

His cock throbs like he can't wait to leave me spent and sticky.

When Kyran's hands move down my arms, tickle my pits, then caress my sides, I think I'm free to grab his cock, but as soon as I try to move, I realize he's now holding them in place with shadow.

He chuckles at my whine, but then those giant monster hands reach my ass. One pulls on my flesh, the other presses his cockhead to my opening. I guess we won't need lube, because the slippery fluid he's been leaking is more than enough.

"I... I need it," I mumble, biting my lip and pressing my hips down so he's inside me already. I want to feel that heat, that connection, and when he breaches me, I let out a soft moan. It hurts at first, but Kyran's hands tighten on my hips, as if he wants to protect me from my own lust. His soothing whisper sounds almost like a hum, but when I manage to relax, there's no better feeling than his cock sinking into me inch after wonderful inch.

He lets go, so I rest my palms on his forearms, giving myself to him and the shadowild. The ecstasy of being filled is like a high, and I half expect to see things that don't exist, but when I open my eyes, Kyran's looking at me, huge and intimidating in this new form.

But not to me.

It's others who need to fear him.

Thick strands of his black hair swarm around his head like snakes, and only his bone-pale face isn't covered in shadows despite them pooling in his glossy eyes.

Kyran's cock is big, but the beast he now has between his legs is stretching me to my limit. I crave to take it though, so I move against him, half-lucid with desire.

"Oh fuck... oh fuck..." I moan, as my own dick rubs against his velvety shadow-body. This is absolute insanity and I couldn't feel more at home.

I drown in the way he grabs my thigh, my side, and fucks me with growing fervor. I love being spread open for him, a vessel for his love, and the person he wants to melt into. Every touch, every thrust, every kiss, promises me a forever and wordlessly calls me special. Someone who can't be replaced by just another warm body.

My thoughts are in an endless whir, tugging me away from reality and into a space where time doesn't exist, and where I can endlessly feel him fucking me, squeezing me, *loving* me.

Gravity once again twists the world around us, and I give a choked cry when I find myself folded under Kyran, his balls heavy against my entrance. I wiggle my toes in the air, trying to get a grasp on my new position.

He's overwhelming, so fucking big some primal part of me drools in pure lust.

In this position, I can reach his face, so I arch up for a greedy kiss, legs wrapped around him, ass stretched around that thick, throbbing tool. Love and mushy feelings fall to the wayside when he speeds up his thrusts and all I can think of is the dirty, physical need to rut against him.

He rasps against my lips in that strange voice, and all I can do is moan as I wrap my arm around his shoulders. For a second I'm shocked that his hair parts like smoke, but I just go with it.

"It's so big," I whine. "Fuck me just like that."

"Whatever you need, my darling," he says while he keeps pumping, until my insides are soft and pliable. I feel so completely his. And while my life would have been different if he'd kept me at his side after we made our promise years ago, I wouldn't take back time because I want him the way he is, and my scars make me who I am. The man he desires.

"Mark me... complete me..." I babble, because his thrusts push at my prostate and I'm losing it. He's both monstrous, and beautiful, and mine. I want a piece of him inside me to prove it.

Kyran's black eyes settle on me, and he shows me a wicked grin with strangely sharp teeth. Before I know what's happening, he slides out of my embrace with the ease of an eel. I moan in displeasure, but he grabs my arm and turns me around.

I land face first in a silky pillow, and this beast of an elf descends on me. I don't even know what's pulling my legs apart, but it's probably shadows. He gets on top of me, panting like a hungry monster, and fills me to the hilt.

I yelp as the stretch makes me still, but my body yields with ease. He slides the massive, clawed hand to my neck and squeezes just enough to show me he could crush my throat but won't.

"I'm yours. Always yours, only yours," I whine to my beastly prince, overcome with lust and feelings more romantic than any I've ever experienced.

"Yesss..." Kyran hisses into my ear, pushing his cock in again and again, but then my eyes go wide.

Something is swelling inside me, and it presses against my prostate so intensely, all my defenses shatter.

I come so hard I seem to be losing my mind. Shameless moans and yelps escape my lips as I rock against him like an animal in heat.

"Wh-what is that?" I pant out, helpless under Kyran.

"My shadow can't wait to be one with yours," he murmurs, and while it's not the answer to my question, I close my eyes and let myself feel as he presses down on my body, slamming in over and over.

The bed turns liquid under us, then into smoke that somehow carries our weight, and as I float, spent and utterly *enthralled*, Kyran hugs me to his chest and stops moving. I let out a broken sob as heat explodes inside me. It's like nothing I've ever felt, but my lover's touch keeps me from writhing in panic. I trust Kyran. He would never put me in danger.

"Only you see all of me. Only you understand," Kyran whispers as he pants into my ear, pressing sweet kisses to the side of my head and to my shoulder, but his cock is shrinking, and soon enough, I feel it retreating from my body with a wet slap.

I don't yet have the brain capacity to ponder my future with him, but I'm lying under him, pumped out and sweaty, and couldn't be happier. My hole aches a little, but even that only serves as a reminder of the fuck of the century.

And he's right. I do see him. Easily. Even if his whole face was covered in shadow, I would have recognized him.

"I do. And I won't let you go," I turn, and when we end up side by side, I cup his face and kiss him. Feeling possessive over someone is new to me, but I embrace it. I'm not here to just take his affection. I'd fight for him.

Kyran opens his mouth, as if he wants to tell me something, but he hugs me instead, resting his head on my chest and curling his large form at my side, as if he couldn't imagine a better place to be.

"Will you stay?" he asks.

I nod, surprised by how easy the decision is, and I tear up again. "Yes," I choke out. For the first time in my life, I have someone of my own. Someone who promises to take care of me, someone I can trust, and depend on.

Kyran lets out a gasp, like a dog striving to comfort its master, and when he cups my face with his clawed hands, there's nothing monstrous about his strange features. He wants me, cares about me, and I can trust him with my life.

We kiss, slotting together like two hands during prayer, but a soft thump makes my lover look up. Can something endanger us here?

The sense of peace and relaxation drains out of me when I spot golden tracks appearing to our left like burns in shadow.

"The stag," Kyran utters.

CHAPTER 33

KYRAN

If anyone else understood how easy it can be to find the Stag of Sunrise by sinking into the shadowild, the hunt would have been long over. The golden tracks don't stay visible forever, fading into nothingness after a few moments, so we follow their path through the black expanse, adjusting our clothes as we go.

Anticipation throbs around my teeth, as if I could kill the creature with a bite to the throat, not crossbow bolts and daggers, but as excited as I am to seize my prize, it can't compare to the joy of Luke's promise.

He will stay.

He wants me to take care of him.

He's to be mine forever.

Joy flows through my veins like pure moonlight, and as I prepare a silver bolt and load it into my crossbow, all I can think of is the need to prove my own devotion to this human who has changed my life in ways I couldn't have anticipated.

He's accepted me the way I am. A sunspawn. A beast surrounded by shadow. I can let go of all inhibitions when I make him mine.

"We will leave now, and he will be nearby. Stay ready," I whisper, even though the stag won't hear us until we leave the shadows.

Luke stares at the golden tracks. "No one got to him yet," he says with a smile and a healthy flush on his cheeks. I could watch his face all day and not get bored. But I stifle the desire to pull him against me and choke him with kisses and instead stroke his cheek with the back of my hand. He leans in, his eyelashes flutter, and I can't push away the realization that something's changed between us for the better.

I have a lifetime to prove he's made the right choice.

But the stag might end up taken down by someone else at any moment, so I nod at my promised, steady myself, and let the shadows part. Moonlight is blinding as we step back into the material world, but it can't rival the glow of the stag's sunrise coat.

We're in a clearing. The animal is drinking from a tiny brook cutting through the mossy ground, but it senses my human the moment he appears. Its antlers are like massive branches peppered with gold dust, and when the stag faces us, heat rushes to my face, as if the Sunlight emanating from the beast is burning me already. I don't have to check to know my shadowcraft would be useless against this beast.

I send a bolt at its neck and grab another one, preparing to shoot, but the scent of blood soaking the pale fur seems to enrage the stag, and it charges toward us with a roar that makes the ground shake.

I urge Luke to run while I go the other way, to take attention off my human. But as soon as we go in two different directions, instead of chasing me, the creature focuses on Luke. I assumed it would chase the person who attacked it. Wrong. Luke's presence has the Stag of Sunrise frantic as if my promised is the cure to the pain it's feeling.

The stag's eyes glow red, as if filled with molten iron, when it lowers its antlers. It catches up to Luke so fast I have no time to wonder about its majestic size, or the sparks of gold bouncing off its fur. All I can think of is Luke's safety. Even killing the stag comes second.

Luke screams when he realizes the stag is right behind him, but I was ready for this. This beast cannot be restrained or attacked with shadowcraft, but I use my powers to push Luke out of the way. He falls into a bush, and the sharp antlers miss him. The stag narrowly avoids falling over head-first but still digs the lower tines of its magnificent crown into the ground. My muscles feel as though they might snap as I dash at top speed, faster than each time I came to my brother's aid in the past, earning all the eels floating over my skin.

My heart leaps when the beast struggles to free itself, likely stuck on some root. I notice my Luke crawling away from the cloven hooves, and I know this is my chance. The shadow of my own feet pushes me up, and I jump toward the golden creature, prepared to bear the brunt of its scorn.

I drop the crossbow and reach for my silver dagger as my heart slows.

I've ridden many horses, kelpies, and once even a bull. But the way the stag bucks under me as soon as my boot slides off its side, holds fury only the heat of the blazing sun can bring. I straddle its back behind the neck as it rips its antlers out along with a tangled root. I grab the fur on its back, because I have barely seconds before the beast manages to kick me off, and I sink the blade into flesh.

The animal roars with pure wrath, but it's already lost. Hot blood sprays my face as I stab my silver dagger into the stag's neck, right next to where my bolt still protrudes.

Then again. And again.

The creature jerks its head, shakes its rear to throw me off, but as the woods fill with the scent of its death, it's a losing battle. I scramble off when the massive stag loses balance, and I roll away when it collapses, soaking the ground with its blood.

The coppery droplets cool my face and hands as the world stops spinning. The stag's struggling to breathe, its tongue lolling as it moves its legs, trying to get away. I consider ending the beast's misery, but there is no need for it, since it stills before I can make up my mind.

A sense of peace settles over me, and I seek Luke, who peeks out from a spot by a bush, panting. Once he realizes the stag is no longer moving, he gets up and joins me.

"Are you okay?" He asks as I rise, trying to keep my legs from giving up under me. In the moment, when I delivered those brutal killing blows, I felt so very confident, but my body seems to be catching up onto the danger we both were in moments ago.

The beast's fur is rapidly losing its golden sheen, as if Sunlight is seeping out of it, no longer powered by its heart, and I know we need to act fast.

"I'm all right. You?" I ask, kneeling next to the stag and going right in with my blade. I don't have much experience with butchering animals, but none of this is about artistry, so I peel away the skin and cut into still-warm flesh, in a hurry to reach the heart before it loses its power. The creature's dark blood shines in the moonlight when I hack through cartilage and meat. Once I get to hold the heart in my hand, it's as exciting as my first kiss.

My heart flutters, my stomach feels light, and my cheeks flush.

The darkness inside the organ calls to me, whispering promises of unforeseen powers, which might just make me mightier than all my forebearers.

Luke stands next to me, watching it all with wide eyes. "The blood is almost like tar," he says.

The golden Sunlight radiated by the stag was a protective shell for all the shadow powers hidden in its black heart, and the mystery it hides can be all mine.

The temptation is sweet as honey cakes, and it makes my mouth itch for a sip, but then my eyes settle on Luke, and I remember what I've been fighting for all along.

"It's yours," I say, even though my chest cramps in protest, as if my body can't bear giving up on the promise of this hunt.

Luke stares between me and the heart. "Wh... what?"

The dark power pulses in my sticky hand, but I've already made my decision. I wasn't lying when I promised Luke I would take care of him. I want him to have *everything*. "You said you wanted to be special. That you wish you had power like mine. This is the only way," I say, offering him my hand.

Understanding pools in his eyes, making it obvious that I'm making the right choice. He's hungry for this power. "You'd... give this to me?" he asks, sliding his fingers onto the warm organ.

Somewhere in the background, I hear the pounding of hoofs and yelling, but whichever hunting party that is, they're too late.

I slide my arm around his shoulders and pull him close. His eyes shine in the moonlight, as if they're made of silver, and I give his lips the gentlest kiss before moving the dripping heart to his mouth and giving it a squeeze.

Blood trails down Luke's fingers, but he doesn't pull away and hums, touching my hand with both of his, as if he's afraid I might take the prize from him at the last moment. But I would never do that. He is my joy, my crown, my beloved, and what is this sacrifice in the face of his happiness?

My greedy little monster bites into the heart just like he latched onto mine. He shivers under my arm, so I stroke his back, watching his Adam's apple bob with every gulp he takes.

"Until it stops beating," I instruct, but the pulsing in my hand is already so faint, it won't take long.

Our eyes meet over the heart, and in that moment I know I couldn't love him more. He wants to embrace everything I give him, and stay with me as my Dark Companion. He's perfect. With his flush, his hair in a tangle and lips smeared with black blood, Luke is the most beautiful creature I've ever seen.

When the heart makes its last beat, Luke's pupils expand as if he's breathed in too much fairy dust. He looks around, lifting his bloodstained mouth off the heart, but the blackness doesn't stop with swallowing his irises, and expands to the whites too as shadowcraft awakens within him.

I ignore the thumping of hooves, enthralled by my lover, who shivers as his world alters forever. Shadows stir around him and crawl out like drops of syrup falling up rather than down, and he captures a few with his fingers as amazement flickers in his eyes.

Luke reaches into the shadow on his arm and pulls out a single black thread. "I c-can see it. My shadow tied to yours. I can sense you." There's so much amazement in his voice I want to kiss him to share his joy.

His mouth still holds the tang of blood, but it's no longer potent, so I hug him and bring our foreheads together. "I will show you so much more."

When his black eyes gloss over with tears, a sense of dread rises deep inside. Is he scared? Confused? Regretful?

"I... I love you," he utters, fighting a sob.

It's like being granted an audience with the moon itself after a lifetime of waiting. My chest swells with warmth. My skin is licked by fire. And with so many emotions taking hold of me at once, I can't find the right words to describe what I'm feeling.

Horses stop right next to us, and I swear it's Tristan's voice I hear behind me, but he remains transparent in the face of Luke's declaration. He will be mine forever, and I shall cherish and protect him for the rest of my days. Our lips meet, and he presses into my arms, needy like a vampire after his first taste of blood.

I'm so spellbound by him I initially push away the hand trying to grab my arm.

"Not now."

"I understand, Sire," Tristan says, breathing hard from the exertion of his ride. "I just want to confirm no one was hurt?" His voice drifts off when he takes in Luke's bloodstained mouth, hands, and his void-black eyes.

Several more riders are approaching, most likely to confirm that the hunt is over. I straighten up with pride.

"My promised—"

I spot the arrow headed straight for my heart half a second too late.

CHAPTER 34

LUKE

My body stiffens when I spot something in the air, but then Kyran brings me closer to his wide chest and shields me from it. Tristan's red hair flashes on the edge of my vision, and then he falls into Kyran with a dull grunt, grabbing his shoulder.

I sense blood, but it's not the stag's.

No, that sharp scent belongs to an elf, and I cover my mouth when Tristan descends to his knees, clutching at his throat with a sharp wheeze. A bolt is sticking out of his exposed thigh, but the veins on his neck turn black, as if poison was spreading from where the projectile broke the skin.

The Marquise gives a choked cry and dashes to our side with her own crossbow ready, but as Tristan collapses from a bolt meant for my Kyran, I'm too shocked to acknowledge her presence.

The contrast between light and dark is sharper, because the shadows feel tangible now. I can't explain it, they just *do*. Across the clearing, I spot a shadow moving down an ancient tree and slithering into the bushes. It couldn't have been cast by anything within sight, and it disappears like a black widow that has just delivered its venom. Kyran's too preoccupied with helping Tristan to take note of it, but my body remains alert to the presence of this unknown predator.

Several horses dash into the clearing, with Sylvan heading the party despite being the most insignificant member of the Goldweed line. His father and Elodie are right behind him, but as they halt, his heels hit the ground first.

"It's poison!" Kyran grits through his teeth, holding Tristan in his arms. "This was not a bolt meant for the stag."

Tristan gasps for air, his face turning gray, throat swelling. "M-my duty—" he tries to speak, but it becomes impossible for him, and all I can think of is that this poison was meant for Kyran.

"We will track this assassin!" Gabriel Goldweed yells out, and gestures at his daughter.

Elodie takes in the scene with a somber expression, but she stalls when her gaze lands on me. She must understand what happened despite me standing here uselessly.

And I see it. Her shadow recoils under her cloak when our eyes meet. She can't be afraid of me, can she? I'm barely a baby taking his first steps in my understanding of shadowcraft.

She follows her father out of the clearing as Sylvan runs to us with his cheeks going pink.

"What can we do?" I ask Kyran.

The reality of maybe losing Tristan hovers over us like a guillotine. I've seen death since I arrived in the Nightmare Realm, even brushed against it myself, but this is too damn close.

Tristan has often been my companion, eager to learn about my world, happy to joke around or teach me things. I know he has a violent side, there are eels on his forearms to prove it, but he lives in a cruel, dangerous world, so that's to be expected.

He's been nothing but kind to me.

He's a bright flame and doesn't deserve to go out this way.

Kyran clenches his teeth. "We need to get him to the medics in the palace."

"No! Don't move him!" Sylvan yells and drops to his knees by Tristan's side. Some of his silvery blond strands escaped the neat, slicked-back hairdo, and hang in his face. He's tiny, dainty even, but commands Kyran's attention like a scalpel that doesn't need to be large to cut deeply.

"What do you know about this?" Kyran asks. "Where is your brother?" he adds in a low voice that promises death and destruction for the wrong answer.

Sylvan looks up at him with eyes like two bright sapphires frozen in ice, but he's dipping his delicate fingers in the... ground? No. In the shadow. "I don't know and I don't care. Last time I saw him, he was nursing his bruised face. You wouldn't know anything about *that*, would you?"

"Focus on Tristan!" Kyran snarls as the Marquise paces right behind us.

Sylvan's lips are a tight line, and I watch him lift a pale shadow out of the ground around him. With a grunt of effort, he moves it over Tristan. "I know this poison. We need to slow down his heart so the venom doesn't spread all over his body, *then* get a medic here. That's his only chance."

Thick strands of Kyran's hair lift, as if lightning was about to strike him. "And your shadow helps with that, *how*?"

Sylvan is panting with effort, and a sheen of sweat glints on his forehead. "It might be weak, but it's a container."

I see it now. The pale shadow Sylvan has created is like a coffin holding Tristan's prone body. The small elf pulls out a vial containing a lilac powder from the pocket of his jacket and sprinkles it onto the barrier.

I'm gaining a whole new appreciation for alchemy, because brute force would not have saved Tristan. This way, he has a chance. We just need—

"I'll go fetch a medic!" the Marquise says, heading for her horse.

Kyran gets up as well. "The assassin is somewhere out there," he warns through gritted teeth, fists clenched. His shadow trembles, releasing wisps of smoke that crawl up his arms.

She shakes her head, mounting her mare. "I'll be fine. I wasn't the target."

"I'll find the bastard who did this and rip his fucking spine out of his back," Kyran growls as we watch the Marquise disappear between the trees.

"Is there anything I can do?" I ask, all too aware of just how painfully useless I am despite my awakening to shadowcraft.

Sylvan shakes his head, squinting at me as if I'm a splinter under his nail. "Well, it's not like you can help me hold it," he says, pointing to the translucent shadow coffin around Tristan.

At least my friend isn't choking anymore, and instead seems to drift off into a peaceful slumber. He reminds me of Sleeping Beauty in her glass coffin. The lilac powder sparkles in the moonlight, giving his skin an otherworldly glow.

"He can," Kyran says, still scanning the forest, his back turned to us. I can sense his anger. He's like a feral wolf dreaming of a hunt but chained to us for Tristan's safety. And mine.

Sylvan scoffs. "You really gave him the stag's heart? He's not even your Dark Companion yet."

As if I'm not here and I'm not worth addressing.

"But he will be. If this is what he needed to feel like my equal, then this is what he got." Kyran's voice turns raspy, as if the side he showed me in the shadowild is once again about to crawl out.

"You should track down the assassin. He has to die for what he did to Tristan," I say, because it seems I need to be the one to let him off the leash. I *need* to know the bastard who attempted to kill the man I love is no longer a threat. I might not be able to do it myself, but Kyran sure is. I can't imagine that I could have lost him. The thought alone is so painful my heart tears in half under its invisible knife.

He looks back but doesn't say anything, so I continue.

"Prince Sylvan will instruct me how to help him." I can only hope I'm not overestimating my newfound powers when Sylvan's top lip curls with unwithheld contempt. He doesn't think I'm worthy of the power Kyran granted me.

Sylvan shakes his head. "I don't know if it's wise to—"

"But I do," Kyran cuts him off and grabs a dagger he had strapped to his boot. His shadow seems to swell, becoming darker, and the smoky swirls wind around his calves as if they can't wait to hug him again.

I'm not sure what he's about to do, but he cuts open his sleeve, revealing a shadowy eel sliding over his wrist.

"Will those not be needed more when Heartbreak—" Sylvan tries, but Kyran has made his decision.

He pinches the eel and picks it off his skin. His eyes fill with darkness like they had in the shadowild. He grabs Gloomdancer, unsheathes it, and approaches Sylvan in two steps.

Sylvan yelps when Kyran drives it into the ground between him and me.

"Stay. Guard," Kyran orders... the sword as if it were a dog, and shadows erupt from it to both sides like a wall. He then turns to look at Sylvan with unsettling black eyes. The darkness inside them overflows and spills down his cheeks like tears made of liquid obsidian. "Instruct him how to help you. Attempt to cross this boundary or hurt him in any way, and you will suffer before I kill you, in ways you cannot even fathom. Do you understand me, *Prince* Sylvan?"

As he speaks, the wall grows to become a small shadow dome.

"B-but your sword..." I utter, not wanting him to lose any advantage in the fight to come.

"I'll manage," Kyran says and leans in through the barrier to give me the sweetest kiss, which doesn't belong on the lips of a man about to commit murder. "Stay safe, my promised."

"Make him pay," I whisper when he backs away.

He takes a deep breath, and even Sylvan's eyes go wide when shadows embrace more of Kyran's form, making him grow in size. He disappears between the trees, on the hunt for prey who believed themselves to be predators.

It's strange to be alone with Sylvan, and the silence stretches between us until he huffs with discomfort, holding his palms up. He kneels on the other side of Tristan, right behind the semi-transparent wall of shadow. Kyran protects me even when he's gone, and that makes my heart a little calmer.

"Hold your palms up," Sylvan says with his eyes fixed on Tristan. "I will transfer some of the weight, but you need to be open to it."

"H-how?"

Sylvan's white brows gather into a frown. "Just mentally. You just have to *want* to accept it. You are not picking it up, but helping me hold it, so I'm transferring it to you. It will feel like physical weight, that's what a lot of shadowcraft is like. You learn to use the shadow as an additional source of strength, but you also need to be fit to carry it in some instances—like this one. It can feel counterintuitive at the start, and it will leave your muscles exhausted."

I nod, assessing the illusive box enveloping Tristan. A strange, but manageable weight lands in my hands. It feels like we're holding a table together.

"Then... is it best to be physically strong in order to use shadowcraft effectively? Is that why your skill at it is lower than your brother and sister's? Because you're small?"

I wasn't intending to offend him, just trying to make sense of new information and how it might affect my future. But Sylvan's gaze pierces me like a dagger made of ice.

"Shut up," he says, and when an invisible weight drops into my open palms I swear he's added more to spite me.

CHAPTER 35

KYRAN

Power tastes very much like rare meat, with a bit of char to keep the senses sharp, and a sweet glaze for indulgence. There's a hint of personality in it too, but I can no longer recognize who grew the energy running through my veins, even though I've been wearing it on my skin in the form of an eel for a while.

I have never lost a serious fight, but by choosing the wrong moment to let my guard down, I risked my own life as well as Luke's, and now Tristan lies dying like a testament to my failure. I like him. Trust him. But I did not think he'd be ready to throw his life on the line to save mine. And whether he survives or not, I will have vengeance.

The moon seems so much brighter as I let shadows creep up my body, covering it whole until I become one with every dark spot looming beneath the trees. It's a risk to do such things outside the shadowild, but fury burns deep in my heart, and I want to let it run wild. My eyes roll back as my form stretches, passing from shadow to shadow, on the hunt for the elusive presence ahead.

I can almost smell the venom infecting Tristan's flesh. There's a trace of it in the air, but it marks my way to the elf who came here to put me down, the elf who hurt my cousin and endangered my promised.

There can be no mercy.

So I don't hold back and send my shadows to explore every crevice of darkness in the woods around me.

That's when I see it—the hitman is not alone. The mossy ground pulses beneath his feet far ahead, stained with the bitter aroma of poison, but two others stand in my way, thickening the shadows and confusing me with their presence.

I need to get rid of them fast.

I'm barely sapient as I leap from branch to branch, a predator living on rage and vengeance. There's an element of greed as well, because I used an eel to power myself for this, and here are two shadow wielders. Enemies. Their shadowcraft ripe for plucking. My thoughts scatter in a moment of hesitation, but Luke told me to take their lives, and it's an imperative burning deep in my chest.

I almost miss the first assassin creeping in the shadows. He's one with the bark of a tree, but once spotted, he's a beacon pulsing in the dark. Gloomdancer is missing from its place at my hip, but I don't need it to carry out revenge on behalf of my promised. At Vinia's execution, I made myself clear—anyone endangering Luke is as good as dead.

I dash through shadow, down the trunk, and land my feet on a pair of slender shoulders. The first would-be killer attempts to flee, grabbing me with her shadow, but she is young, inexperienced. She doesn't even manage to scream before I twist her head off as if it were a cog inside a clock.

A small shadow eel joins the others on my flesh.

The rush of the kill propels me forward. I'm in my element, chasing the man who could have taken my life today. I might resent my upbringing, but it taught me how to be ruthless with my enemies.

The Goldweeds arrived right after the assassination attempt, like clockwork, and if *I* had been hit with the poisoned bolt, any of the other princes and princesses could reach their dirty hands out for Luke. They might have locked him up and given him a miserable existence, and if he resisted the one who claimed him? Death would have been the easiest solution.

When I chose to take my brother's place, all I thought about was my own survival, my own freedom and happiness, but within the weeks since, Luke has wormed his way into my soul, and I cannot stand the thought of leaving him to the vultures. He deserves better.

He deserves the peace and happiness I can provide. The freedom he fought for as a child.

I will keep him safe.

He and I will rule together as Lord and his Dark Companion, and the Goldweeds, or whoever else ordered the hit on me, will pay the price for their betrayal once I get the assassin to confess.

The forest pulses around me. The beasts retreat, the birds go quiet, and as I dash through the shadows, no longer just an elf, I'm overwhelmed by every breath, every creak for miles around me.

The second assassin freezes on the path ahead. When he spots me, the veil he created to protect the retreat of the one who smells of poison drops. He holds my gaze, sinking into the shadowild. His eyes grow wide when I accelerate. I see him from afar in one moment, only to grab his hair in the next. With the dagger in my free hand, I slash at the bastard's exposed throat, and blood erupts from it in a lush fountain.

His eyes roll back when I release his mane, letting him fall into the nothingness of the other side. One more killer is left, and I am *not* letting that bastard get away.

Without his two accomplices to shroud him from me, I can practically taste his sweat. I don't know if he's aware how close he is to death now, but it doesn't matter. I shall hunt him down and then drag him back to the palace, so he can cry out the name of the one who sent him.

The dark trees turn into a blur as my gaze focuses on the path ahead, and I skirt through the shadows, moving at the speed of a leviathan slinking through the dark waves of Grief Ocean. Ever closer to the pathetic creature who believed itself capable of flicking *me* off the chessboard.

Such cheap moves would have worked against my brother, but am I not *the other twin*? The Sunspawn? The abomination who should have never been born? A beast should never be hunted when its mate is around.

As I dart from between the trees and into a moonlit grassland, fatigue dulls my focus and turns my limbs heavy. I've almost burned through the eel, but it doesn't matter. The assassin is ahead, speeding for a stone shelter among stormy hills. It might be where he and his associates were to regroup, but the mistake of failing to kill me at the first try was one that will cost him his life.

I'm no longer able to travel within the shadows like before, too exhausted to maneuver between realms at such high speed. Despite the ache in my legs, I am hungry for my target's blood and focus on his back and the pale braid swinging left and right like a convulsing snake.

Even the shadows enveloping me are thinning now, but it's like a word on the tip of your tongue. Almost there. I pour my energy into the claws of one hand, grow them, ready to pin him to the ground.

I *feel* the arrow coming this time, but as it speeds past me, I realize it was not meant for me.

Instead, it pierces the assassin's neck, swiftly followed by another. The second arrow gets him in the head, killing any hope I might have to learn the name of his employer.

I cry in protest and catch up to the poisoner, who's collapsed into the grass, but when I roll him over in hope that maybe he could still survive this, he looks back at me with empty eyes.

I roar in helpless anger, and the shadows clinging to me pulse on my skin when I recognize the stomping of hooves.

"Are you alright, cousin?" shouts a smooth voice I want to choke out of the bastard forever.

My fingers twitch with the need to curl around a graceful neck, because I had the chance to keep this witness alive, and only someone who needed to keep them quiet would have shot those two arrows.

"I heard what happened from my father," Anatole says. "Do you recognize him?" he asks and dismounts as if he hasn't just taken this kill from me to cover his pale ass!

I rush to my feet and shove him back so hard he bumps into his horse. "I had him! Stop sticking your fingers where they don't belong," I roar, and his eyes widen when he takes me in. A shiver trails down my back when I see my face reflected in his eyes. I don't look quite like myself, and my gaze is black as if I've covered my eyes with coal.

"Wha—" Anatole frowns, and despite my rage, I realize the golden sun tattoo cannot be covered by shadows. When they become a part of me, it becomes visible too. I force them all to the ground with a push so quick, it leaves me exhausted, but I can only hope he didn't realize what he was seeing.

"I came to help," he says through gritted teeth, but he's alert, his eyes searching mine for fuck knows what.

A raspy growl escapes my throat, and I shake my head. "You only helped yourself by getting him out of the way, didn't you?" I ask, taking a step toward him. "My promised told me to kill the traitors for him, but I doubt they're all dead."

"I don't know what's gotten into you, Kyranis. It's like he bewitched you. You waited seven years to go get him despite my prodding, and now you treat him like a flower in a secret orangery and attack *me*? Why would I be after you?"

Fury boils over, and I grab the collar of his shirt where it sticks out above the breastplate and tug him closer. I want to bite off his nose and spit it back in his face. "Both your sisters plotted to murder him. And now I've been attacked right before you arrived. To take Luke?" I growl, out of my mind with rage at the very idea of this bastard hurting my promised in any way.

The sick imagery of Anatole forcing Luke into his bed erupts in my mind against my will and it makes me want to let shadows engulf me again and rip him apart.

"Elodie had no idea what Vinia was planning," he says, because of course he'll be sticking to that story.

"Nobody believes that," I roar, shoving him away, because his sheer presence is agitating. I wish I could banish him forever. "And I don't want you creeping around him! He's *mine*!"

Anatole scoffs but doesn't even try to fight me, stepping away instead. "He was the one to join our hunting party! Are you blaming me for trying to get to know my future Lord's promised? Don't keep him on a leash. It's unsightly."

"It's none of your business what I do with him! If you're so desperate to know him, you'll get to do that once he and I are married. If I see you hovering around him one. More. Time. I will forget we're related!"

"This is not behavior I would expect from someone of your station," he says with a sneer. I bet he could have put ointment on his bruised face but has refrained from it just to show everyone what I did. And I'm not sorry in the slightest.

"Go on, tell others what a rude fuck I am. You think they'll strip me of my title? Doubt my claim to it? What they want is safety, not my vibrant personality," I say sharply and poke at his chest. He doesn't back away, but sweat shines on his temples and above his lip. He is nervous.

Well, of course he is. I'm near certain he was the one to order the hit, because who else could have done it? I cannot be sure, though, not with all three of the assassins dead, so I push down my anger and sigh. "Look, I almost died, Tristan is gravely injured, and if that bolt hit me, not him, our land would have no protection from Heartbreak, so *excuse me* for losing my patience, cousin!"

Anatole is losing his composure too, because he actually pokes me back, like an angry child. He's nowhere near as small as his brother, but unlike me, he's on the slender side. I could crush him if I wanted to, and he knows it.

"If you cared so much about the Realm, you would have let us find Dark Companions instead of forcing us to wait around for years. Instead, you're making us stick to old rules made centuries ago!"

I ball my hands into fists and step so close our foreheads almost touch. "The rules are there for a reason. Or do you want another Night of the Bloodknife, *cousin*?"

His defiance falters, and he looks away, as if bringing up the coup against the first Lord Nightweed makes him uncomfortable.

Anatole takes a deep breath and pulls away with his arms crossed. "I await your marriage with bated breath. I am certain it will be a charming affair, and your wedding night, the first time you ever lay your hands on your *beloved*. I'm sure you cannot wait." Bastard has the audacity to roll his eyes.

I want to punch him in Luke's name, but why give him more bruises to whine about when Tristan remains on the edge of death and my promised is out there all alone with the damn Goldweeds?

"You have no idea," I tell him and rush right past him, because I will *not* ask him for a ride.

At least he keeps any snide comments he might have to himself, and I walk off feeling his eyes on my back. I can only hope that as soon as Luke is my Dark Companion, they will stop their petty bullshit and admit defeat.

CHAPTER 36

LUKE

The attempt on Kyran's life a week ago was a jarring reminder that, for all its beauty, the Nightmare Realm is no fairytale. Being the heir apparent's promised places a target on my back as well as his, since getting rid of me would mean Kyran cannot formally ascend the throne. I can imagine Baroness Olivia Goldweed and her husband would be perfectly happy to take their chances against Heartbreak without Dark Companions of their own, if that means any of their children get closer to wearing a crown.

I'm so grateful that Kyran, my dark prince with eyes like smoke and arms I don't want to ever leave, offered me the gift of shadowcraft so I can be that little bit safer.

It was a shock to everyone, I can see it in their eyes, but *my man* chose to give up on more power to uplift *me*. To fulfill *my* dreams and make us a bit more equal. I'm so proud that just moments after receiving the dark gift I was able to use it for good and help keep Tristan alive.

I don't need declarations of love when Kyran offered me *that*.

Though an I-love-you would have been very, very welcome.

"Careful," Kyran tells me, pushing the blade of his sword against a column of shadow I erected. "Now that you can manipulate it, it's become a part of you. You can get hurt," he says, and I flinch, sensing a pressure at the tips of my fingers.

My breath hitches, even though I've felt it before. I'm still not used to something outside my body being touchable. The other day, Kyran tickled my shadow when he taught me how to make it material, and it was the most disconcerting feeling. Maybe that's what the sensation in a phantom limb is like?

Then again, the shadow is most definitely *not* phantom.

I have a long way to go until I can gain anything close to proficiency, even if I'm making progress. At least the novelty of gaining such a power makes me want to practice all the time and explore what it can do.

We're in a room Kyran reserves for our practice. It's mostly empty, with high ceilings, dark walls and long heavy curtains. For now, massive windows let in the silver light of the moon. In just five days, it will rise red, and the Blood Moon will mark our wedding day.

To say I can't wait would be an understatement.

My life has spun off track within a month. I wouldn't dream of leaving him at the altar like last time. In fact, if someone tried to stop me from marrying Kyran, I'd fight them tooth and nail, because he's proven himself to be the man of my dreams. I can barely believe I will get to promise him a forever in front of everyone, and that I will get to live out my days in this magical realm, far away from my hateful mother, mocking sneers, and all the people who ever made me miserable.

I, Luke Moor, who thought he'd never grow to trust anyone, will have an actual happily ever after.

How crazy is that?

Maybe I did get hit on the head in the parking lot behind Best Burger Bonanza, and all this is an elaborate coma dream? But if that's the case, I want to keep on dreaming, because my reality has never felt this good.

"But Tristan said my shadow is impossible to shatter, even for Heartbreak. That it's why dipping Gloomdancer in it as we battle Heartbreak will make such a difference."

He nods. "But then it's *me* using your shadow. There's a lot more to it, as you will learn, but this is different. If I attacked the shadow you're manipulating, I could hurt you through it."

I frown, confused. "Would *I* bleed or my shadow? *Can* a shadow bleed?"

"No," Kyran says and makes a little slash with his sword. I whine, stepping away when my index finger stings. It's a tiny cut, but I stare at it, deafened by the thudding of my own heart.

He pulls my hand close and sucks the injured digit to stop the bleeding. "I'm sorry. You will learn to avoid this. I should have warned you. I don't want to hurt you, but you did say not to go easy on you."

A whiney part of me regrets that a little, but I know I'll remember this lesson better after experiencing the consequences.

And then he does make it better with a kiss. "We'll put some salve on it later," he adds.

I have to take a deep breath. "Thank you. I've never been particularly brave, but now I want to be. For you. Because I have to be ready to aid you when Heartbreak comes. Or whenever you need me."

Kyran stalls, his eyes, dark gray as if they're swirling with wisps of smoke, are focused on my face, and I offer him a smile.

I used to sometimes dress very much out of the norm when going to parties, or when I was feeling rebellious, but even then, I was stared at rather than *seen*. Kyran? He actually *sees* me for who I am and never seems bored of that person. He is not going to attempt to change me. He won't have his fun and leave. He wants me to share everything with him, and that is more than anyone has ever offered me.

I'm so stupidly in love with him.

Sometimes, it takes my breath away. Other times, I remember he is the very reason I'm still alive, and I'm so thankful that he chose me on the day when *I* gave up on myself. I have no idea how, but when I felt like a dirty, unwanted rag, he saw a diamond. And now, years later, I want him to feel like a precious gem too.

He might be a prince, but I'm the only person who knows about his struggles, his years in captivity, his feelings of inferiority toward a twin who sounds like a terrible person. He deserves to rule this whole damn world, and I am making it my life's mission that he understands it.

"Beginnings are always a steep learning curve, but you'll get there," Kyran tells me, only to send a shadow whip toward my face. Instead of risking pain, I use my newfound powers to pull myself out of harm's way, and when the dark tentacle slaps the floor, Kyran claps.

"Perfect. Minimize risk."

Despite Sylvan taking offense at my comment about his size, wielding shadow does require strength, and I feel that in my muscles. "Gimme a second," I say, raising my hand. I just moved my whole body weight, and we've been doing this for two hours. I'm pumped out. "One day, I'll have shadow wings like Tristan, but that day has not yet come."

Kyran grins, and I find myself lifted off my feet. Dark tendrils creeping from under his feet bring me closer, until I'm tucked to his chest. No one has ever held me the way he does, as if he needs the comfort of my presence just as much as he wants to provide it to me. It's perfection.

"He seems eager to join us as your second teacher as soon as he heals," Kyran says and hands me a glass of water, which appears in his hand out of nowhere. In reality, he used his shadow to fetch it from the side table.

"He was impressed when I told him I was holding Sylvan's shadow with him," I say and gulp down the water.

Kyran's smirk tells me that feat wasn't impressive at all, but he won't say it. I rest my cheek against the soft fabric of his top. We're both wearing the elven version of sportswear for our training, which consists of stretchy leather pants that don't restrain movement and don't make squeaky sounds, and a long-sleeved top that clings to the body but doesn't overheat it.

As much as I love dressing up in fancy lace and frills, it's useful to have these as an option. I just wish I didn't get so sweaty next to Kyran, who is the epitome of elegance. Even when he sweats, he doesn't stink. He happens to be naturally perfect. Infuriating.

I'm embarrassed when he buries his face in my neck and smells me after all the training. When I attempt to pull away, he not only keeps me close but even lifts me up, taking away any choice I have in the matter. Not that I mind.

"You're developing so fast. I'm proud of you."

I wrap my legs around his waist, and my arms around his neck. "Stop it! You're gonna make me cry." I hide my face in his hair. Maybe I have daddy issues, but no one's ever been proud of me, and I still find it hard to accept that someone might be saying such things and mean them. I have to constantly keep myself from saying shit like 'Oh, no, I'm so slow', or 'I'm useless, I'll never get it right'. I saw firsthand how upset it made Kyran, and the last thing I want is to see him hurt over my self-esteem issues.

Kyran knocks on the door with the side of his boot, and Reiner, who's still suffering the consequences of leaving me with Vinia, opens it for us. I offer him a smile as my prince carries me away from the training room, down a wide corridor with beautiful paintings depicting stories from this realm's history hung on both walls. Two servants are busy in one of the alcoves we pass, swapping a large hunting scene out for several smaller pieces in ornate silver frames. I still at the sight of a familiar picture.

"No! Kyranis!" I reluctantly say his twin's name for the benefit of the servants who might hear me. "This is nepotism. You can't just swap that amazing painting for my doodles of Count Flapula."

He stalls and turns, so I face the other alcove, where a still life painting I did of the midnight blue roses Kyran gifted me already takes up the space of a more deserving artwork. I'm cringing with shame, because everyone will know my art doesn't belong in this gallery of excellence, and that the only reason it's here is because I'm fucking the prince.

"I like them," Kyran protests and gives my butt a little squeeze.

"Of course you do. Because I made them. But just like with the shadowcraft, I have a long way to go." I give his pointy ear a kiss anyway. It never ceases to amaze me that he's strong enough to carry me around with such ease.

But then I look at the painting more thoughtfully, fighting my initial reaction, and I have to admit that my still life isn't too shabby. The paintings hung here over the years are in a variety of styles, so it's not like mine stands out as the odd one out. Most of all, it makes me feel tender inside that Kyran's so proud of my work. The still life depicts the flowers he gave me. Our bed is just a shape in the background, but it's suggestively unmade, and my lobster pin features on top of his folded wedding shirt. A simple picture, but it's filled with our secrets.

"It's my home. I want to enjoy art that makes me feel good," Kyran says and continues down the corridor, with Reiner trailing ten steps behind us, his head lowered.

"I'll allow it," I say smugly, as if I can command a prince. "In the bedroom, I have something that'll make you feel really good after the training session," I add, but when I spot Reiner's little frown, I realize how that must have sounded, and my face goes hot.

This is a private area in the palace, so we don't meet any courtiers, but I'm still mortified that I said that out loud. Kyran, however, doesn't seem to mind.

"Oh really, what do you have in mind?" he asks and stands in front of the bedroom door while Reiner runs up to us and presses on the handle, allowing Kyran to walk inside hands-free.

I hug him more tightly. "You'll see." At this point it would have been more embarrassing to try excusing myself to Reiner, because he wouldn't have believed me anyway.

"Is there anything you need, Sire?" Reiner asks, staying just outside the door.

Kyran shakes his head. "Prepare some food for us. We will dine in about an hour. And, please, bring the coralberries Flap likes so much. It is his last day here after all."

"Of course, Sire," Reiner says and closes the door.

I sigh when Kyran sets me down. "Do we *have* to let him go?"

My prince refrains from providing an immediate answer and only does so once we see the massive cage we keep him in. "He is a wild animal. With time, he will grow and become a danger to you and everyone else."

I open the cage and have to admit the bat has grown in the time I've been nursing him to health. His purple ears and paws are getting longer, his teeth sharper, and while I trimmed his claws twice, they could definitely do some damage.

But when I grab Flap under the armpits and pull him out, he squeaks happily, and his yellow eyes seem to light up. "But he's not an animal. He's just a little baaaby!" And more than happy to cuddle with me as soon as I pull him close.

I understand Kyran's worries though. He lost his mother to despairs, and from her notes, I gather she also considered them to be *"tameable"*.

"I'm sorry," he says in a voice so quiet I feel like I'm torturing him by asking to let Flap stay.

With a sigh, I put Flap on the bed and let him roam. "You clearly think that's the right thing to do, and you know your realm best. Come on, I have something for you." I grab his hand and pull him to the bathroom.

Kyran's looking back toward the bat, as if he expects it to leap across the room and tear our eyes out, but in the end he stops resisting, and we leave it be.

"All right," he says, settling in a chair close to the window to remove his boots.

"Have I mentioned how much I love this bathroom?" Only a million times.

I smile and turn on the water. From the fish bone chandelier to the sculpted bathtub and stained glass windows, this room is a dream come true. The kind of luxury I could have never dreamed of in my world. Even the towels are borderline magical with how well they soak up water. They're made of a thick black fabric that resembles fluffy fleece and is light as cotton candy.

Some days, I fear I don't deserve them, or the massive bed, or even Kyran's affection, but my presence always brings a smile to his face, so maybe I'm really selling myself short?

In any case, I want to give back, so I reach into a jar where I stashed my latest creation and pull out the fist-sized bath bomb in shades of green and purple. Kyran catches my eye, not yet aware what's about to happen, so I hold his gaze and drop the final result of my experiments into the water.

A low fizz echoes through the air, prompting Kyran to shoot up and peek into the tub, where the bath bomb spins, releasing colorful bubbles. "It smells... like cherin and... roses?"

"Your favorites." I beam at him. "It's a bath bomb. I used to make them in my world in a variety of smells and colors. It took me a while to work out how to make something similar here, but Sabine got me in touch with a young alchemist who was very keen to help. I made this one especially for you."

Kyran stares at me, as if he's not sure he's heard me correctly. "For *me*?" he asks, and before I can catch my breath to answer, he sits on the edge of the tub and pulls me close, resting his face in the folds of my sweaty top.

I wrap my arms around his head and kiss his hair. "Yeah. Look, at the center, it releases these black wisps. It reminds me of your shadows, and I mixed in specks of shiny blue pigment to imitate the tear stone, like in the engagement ring you got me." I also made *him* a ring, but he'll be finding that out on our wedding day.

My eyes shut when Kyran pulls up my top and stuffs his face under it, kissing my damp skin, as if there was nothing he loved more than the scent of my sweat. Which is embarrassing, but also kind of reassuring. "I never got a gift this thoughtful."

Which makes me both sad and happy at the same time. But also, I get it. I understand him so well, because I've also not been given much before he came along. It's as if we were created to lick each other's wounds.

"You shower me with gifts all the time. I want you to feel appreciated," I whisper and stroke his head through the fabric, feeling so tender toward him my heart might just break.

It's so weird.

I still remember telling Kurt that I wasn't the marrying type.

Then, laughing at Kyran. Then trying to flee him, and making a deal, which involved him letting me go. Now I despise the thought of being apart from him. And I went from point A to point B in under a month.

"You being here is enough. Not that I don't appreciate the other perks," Kyran tells me before sliding out from under my top with his face pink and messy hair.

You'd never imagine a Prince of Darkness could be adorable, but he is.

"Like my human sweat?" I roll my eyes and pull my top off.

Kyran grins at me and licks me from navel to nipple as I gasp. "Mmm... like sea salt. Delicious. But if you want to get clean..."

Before I know what's happening, he tips back with me in his arms, and we splash into the water, sending bubbles into the air.

))●((

The amazing blowjob and time spent floating in the fragrant tub did take my mind off needing to part from Count Flapula, but once the rush of excitement was gone, the melancholic mood came back. Flap clings to my arm like a little puppy as Kyran takes my hand and leads the way into the caves that almost took my life only a day into my stay here.

But Kyran was there for me, no matter how angry he must have been about my betrayal.

"It's okay, you will be fine, Flap. You'll get to meet your family again," I say and stroke his purple head. At this point, I'm not sure if I'm reassuring him or myself.

We walk through the darkness that smells of sea and salt, listening to the flapping of shark skins high above. Kyran is holding a green lantern, but since my awakening to shadowcraft, I've been seeing in the dark much better.

I can't help but wonder if Flap wouldn't be happier leaving his family behind though. After all, no bat stayed back to help him when his wing was broken. Would he miss being a part of a bat colony when he could be fed coralberries every day and fly out whenever he pleases?

I don't miss home even though sometimes I'm annoyed that I can't google whatever question is on my mind, or get a burger with fries. Those are silly little things in comparison to what I've gained.

I squeeze Kyran's hand, wondering how it will feel to accompany him to the altar made of moon rock. Everyone will be watching, and he will show me off as if I'm the prize of a lifetime even though I'm just human. And a man at that, but this doesn't seem to matter here at all, and my gender has never made anyone bat an eye.

It's refreshing, and I briefly fantasize about asking Kyran to abduct my mom, just so she can see me walk down the aisle with someone she would have labeled as far too good for me.

It makes me smile, but her opinion ultimately doesn't matter. I no longer care what she thinks of me or whether she thinks of me at all.

We reach the bottom of the cave, which was covered by water last time I was here, and I take note of a bright glow ahead. As we pass a boulder and see its source, I'm stunned to see a blonde woman in clothes that don't quite fit into the gothic aesthetics of the court.

It's Carol, the human I was so desperate to talk to.

I glance at Kyran, not even needing to ask to know it's his doing.

He takes Flap from my arms. "This is Carol, Lady Guinevere's Dark Companion. By law, she's not allowed to be here, but if you don't tell, I won't," he says and, after pressing a kiss to my lips, retreats to where we came from. "Take as much time as you need."

Stunned, I watch him walk off with Flap, then turn to take in the woman's very human face.

"You must be Luke," she says with a smile and waves at me.

CHAPTER 37

LUKE

It's been only a month, but interacting with another human is still a bit of a shock. At first glance, elves and us look very much alike, but after weeks in the Nightmare Realm, Carol seems like a goose among ducks. There's more texture to her skin, her fingers are on the shorter side, which makes me realize that every single elf I've interacted with has elongated hands, and her small, round ears are accentuated with a silver cuff that stands out against bright blonde hair.

She's also not dressed in the ever-popular black and is instead wearing a dress in an emerald hue, which reaches just below her knees and, tastefully, exposes her cleavage.

After we greet each other, she makes a gesture with a gloved hand, and as I follow it, my gaze settles on a picnic blanket spread over the stone floor of the cave. There's a bottle, crystal glasses, and even an actual picnic basket that looks like straight from an old cartoon.

"My, aren't you a dreamboat! Best-looking human I've seen in ages!" Carol has a Southern accent that feels weirdly out of place yet only makes her seem more human.

I push back some hair behind my ear. "Am I? Maybe it's been a while since you've seen one," I joke, trying to find my feet in this situation. "Did Prince Kyranis get you to come here?"

"Oh, he did invite me. Gave me quite a scare when that messenger arrived at the door. I'm technically not allowed on palace grounds until after y'all's wedding, but, gee, I was so very excited to meet someone like me again," she says and opens the basket, placing real plates and cutlery on the blanket, before following that up with containers full of food.

A bit shell shocked, I sit down next to her to find that the blanket insulates us from the cold and hardness of the rock despite appearing thin.

I think to myself that we are nothing alike, but that won't really matter.

"It's my pleasure," I say, accepting a dainty plate of... apple pie? "I didn't expect this. I was trying to meet you before, but it's forbidden, and I didn't manage. I... worried it might not be allowed because you'd tell me to run away."

She stills with a spoon filled with black whipped cream, then erupts with a giggle. "Golly, I didn't think I looked terrified! Now, why would I have told you to run when you're the future Lord's promised? I did hear rumors that he's fast, and likes his partners easy, but to me he seemed perfectly gallant."

She speaks as if she was brought up by her granny. If that's the case, then her granny taught her to make a very nice pie, and the black whipped cream doesn't spoil the flavor one bit.

"I just..." I stuff my face with more food to give myself a second. "I need to know about this bond. I don't want to be anyone's slave, but if I marry him, I have to give up some power."

She winks at me over her own plate. "Well, I heard he already gave some up for *you*."

And he did so without the certainty of our bond. Something could always happen to stop our wedding, but he's already offered me a gift no one can take away. Maybe this means I don't need to talk to Carol anymore. But curiosity gets the best of me.

"Is it a dangerous life?"

"Not what the other Dark Companions would have told you, since, you know, they're no longer with us," Carol says, lowering her gaze to the slice of pie on her plate. "But my wife is careful and precise in her shadowcraft. She never put me at risk before herself. In the past... sixty—or was it seventy years—" she mumbles absent-mindedly, swallowing some of the pie, "The one time my wife almost lost control, she had me run away, and won the fight on her own. It's all about trust."

I stare at her, because my mind can't compute that my intuition wasn't wrong. This explains why she seems so... odd. I couldn't put my finger on it, but she looks twenty-three at most, and yet she must have been here seven years ago, during the last battle with Heartbreak.

"Wait. Are you saying Lady Guinevere found a way to stop you from aging?"

Carol's eyes settle on mine, and she chuckles. "Gee, no, she is excellent with her sword, but my youthful looks are not due to her efforts. It's just this place. Humans stop aging once they reach maturity, just like the elves. Unless something kills you, you will not die. It's quite a blast. All the girls I knew before are likely wrinkled and gray, but look at me: almost eighty and still kicking!"

I laugh incredulously. What I couldn't put my finger on now makes sense. "You're from... the fifties." It's more of a statement than a question as I think of her language and mannerisms. She's like those people who go to live abroad and still use the slang they grew up with, because they're detached from their homeland.

My heart beats faster when I realize what all of this means. I avoided thinking about me aging while Kyran always remained his perfect self because it was too frightening and gave me stomach cramps. I didn't want to ponder such a distant future at the point when even next month seemed so elusive.

Now I think of all the portraits of Dark Companions I've seen. It made sense to me that they would be made when the human first arrived, to avoid the sad reality of them withering away next to their elven partners. That might not have been the case.

I could stay forever young and share a long existence with the man of my dreams, who happens to be a literal prince.

How is *this* my reality?

Unaware of the tumultuous thoughts in my head, Carol goes on, "Yes, well, I do miss the food, and the colors, but it is a small price to pay, really. If I stayed, I'd have married my fiancé and maybe never even discovered that I don't like men *that* way. Here, people like us can be free to love. I saw the way you danced with the prince at the festival. It was quite beautiful."

I'm suddenly so moved, I have to squeeze her hand, and she lets me. "I'm so happy for you. Things are... much better now, but nothing like here, in the Nightmare Realm. Ironic name really, since I've not had a... good time in our world. I want to stay here, with the prince."

She smiles and leans in, pulling me into a quick hug. "If you two belong together, you will be so happy. I never knew a bond like this before I became my wife's Dark Companion. She's always aware of where I am, and I feel her care even now. Just the tiniest impulse through our bond." She laughs and waves it off. "Oh, look at me, swooning like I'm fifteen again!"

I shake my head, swallowing the last piece of delicious pie. It feels like the stars are aligning. I let her tell me more about Lady Guinevere, but then it's her turn to ask questions, and we spend some time with me explaining what the internet is (I still don't think she gets it), and that my green hair and black nail polish aren't 'the fashion' now.

I don't want Kyran waiting too long, and I will see Carol after the wedding anyway, so I help her pack up the picnic and snort when she happily says, "See you later, alligator!" when leaving through a narrow passage. I don't have the heart to tell her how old-fashioned that saying feels to me.

Once she's gone, I try to sneak up on Kyran and find him sitting on a rock, whispering something to Count Flapula.

"Boo!" I yell, pouncing him from the back and wrapping my arms around his neck.

Kyran shakes his head, unaffected. "I would have heard you from miles away. I will teach you how to muffle the sound of your steps with soft shadows."

I groan but only hug him tighter. "Thank you. I got more out of talking with Carol than I imagined I would."

"Yes? Did she convince you I will not chop off your limbs and keep you in a cage just for your shadow?"

I frown. "That was... surprisingly gruesome." Sometimes I forget I'm talking to an elf with a long history of violence painted on his skin with eels.

Kyran looks back and grins at me before bumping our foreheads together. "Is it hot though?"

I snort and kiss him. "A little. Maybe apart from the no arms and legs part. But the idea of being your prisoner is growing on me." Now that I don't consider myself one.

"Is it really?" he asks, rising to his feet, until he towers over me like a massive statue. "Should I put a little golden cuff on your wrist?"

I kinda like that I have to get to my toes to kiss him. "I wouldn't mind if you had it engraved with your crest." I may be a bit woozy with love, but I've evaded my feelings for so long I can hardly be blamed for being swept up in them now.

Kyran's eyes grow darker, and he pets Flap's head with a raspy grunt. "If we weren't here with this unruly baby—"

I sigh at this callback to reality. This is why we came down here. To let him go.

"I know, I know..." I pick Count Flapula out of Kyran's arms and give his fluffy purple forehead a kiss. "Time for you to spread your wings, my child." I laugh despite feeling like crying. I put him on the rock next to us, so he knows he's free, and wait for him to move. We won't leave until I'm sure he flies with ease.

"Did she tell you anything of interest?" Kyran asks as my fingers entwine with his.

I urge Flap a few inches farther when his golden eyes seek mine in confusion. "She did actually. She told me I won't age here. Which is... a bit of a revelation." I'd ask him why he didn't mention it so far, but it must have been so obvious to him it didn't warrant talking about.

"*That's* what convinced you? I should have advertised it right away," he says as Flap flicks its short, stubby almost-tail and spreads his leathery wings.

I try to avoid getting all emotional and look away from him, which Kyran takes as an invitation for a kiss.

"No, dumbass!" I laugh, stroking his arm. "I was already convinced. I made my decision and meant it. But I... kinda thought we'd have only some time before I grow old, gray, and get erectile dysfunction."

"You don't need to age for that last one," Kyran says, and I slap his stomach just as Flap sets off, rising toward the rock vault far above us with a happy yelp.

"What I mean is that I tried not to think about it. It's different to grow old *with* someone, but to grow old while your partner is a forever-beautiful elven Lord? That would have been difficult. I'm still processing this information. What will it be like to live in this body to a hundred? Then again, Reiner is what? Two hundred fifty? And he seems generally normal."

"He's still a fool, even at two hundred and fifty. I can't believe he left you alone with that Goldweed..." Kyran mumbles, still not over the scare of almost losing me at the very start of our relationship.

Flap's circling the cave. At this point I know him well enough to discern him from all the wild bats. Maybe Kyran is right, and this is where he belongs?

But my heart doesn't want to hear rational arguments, and I lean into my man, struggling to let go. At the end of the day, Flap isn't a domesticated animal, and it would have been cruel to isolate him from other members of his species.

"He was between a rock and a hard place. He learned his lesson," I say, avoiding the topic that breaks my heart right now, because Flap is making the same little squeaks as when he's searching for me. "Now that I know I could essentially live forever, I got to ask:

are you ready for an eternity with me? You're not getting rid of me easily. I *will* get pets, I like fancy clothes, and I'm addicted to art supplies."

Kyran weaves his fingers through my hair and makes me look up as we sit in the cave filled with the cries of bats and the flutter of drying shark skin. It feels as though we're the last two men to exist in this world, and in this moment, I think that no power could ever pull us apart.

"You're also pretty needy," Kyran tells me with a little smirk.

I elbow him gently. "Says the elf who complained yesterday that I took a bath without him."

But he doesn't flinch and scoops me right back into his arms. "We can just be needy together. How does that sound?"

My smile widens. "Pretty perfect."

A screech tears through the air, and Kyran turns to shield me from the animal flying at us, but then Flap lands on his shoulder.

I sigh and give Kyran my best puppy eyes while Flap licks Kyran's ear. "He doesn't want to go..."

Kyran opens his mouth, frozen in a position dangerously close to what a scared cartoon character might look like, but relaxes when Flap folds his wings and buries his muzzle in Kyran's hair, as if it's trying to groom him.

I swallow, and my heartbeat quickens because I think Kyran's defenses are crumbling. "I'll trim his claws, be careful as he matures, take safety precautions... Your mom wanted you to have one, Kyran, remember? What if this is a sign?"

His dark gaze meets mine, brows twitching as the facade of sensibility breaks. I hold my breath when Flap's long ear folds as he rubs his head against Kyran's. There's no denying it, my man is cracking like ice.

"I... well, he does seem unusually docile."

I smile and hug him so tightly I might be hurting his ribs. "He's gonna be our little baby. We'll arrange a bigger apartment for the two of us after the wedding," I say as if I have more than a few coins to my name. "And he will have room to fly."

"We could just... bring him here sometimes, so he has company," Kyran mumbles, and I laugh when Flap jumps to my shoulder and covers the back of my head with his wing before uttering a chuckle-like noise.

"Yes! Playdates!"

"It knows it's won," Kyran whispers, taking hold of both my hands. He's not super happy about this development, but he will not keep Flap away from me either. "But listen up, *Count*," he says, straightening his back and looking above me, presumably at Flap's cute little face. "You shall be a gentleman, steer clear of bad company, and keep those claws to yourself. Do we understand each other man to bat?"

The bat chitters, and Kyran reaches out, grabs the fragile claws attached to his wing, and gives them the gentlest shake.

I love Kyran so much right now I can't describe it. He's incredible and impressive as he wields his princely power, scorching hot when he lounges in my room with leather pants open in invitation, but he's also sweet and funny in moments like this one. I love all of him. I love him when he protects me, I love him when I see him reveal a soft spot for Flap, and I love him when he's vulnerable enough to show me his weaknesses.

I reach over to stroke his face. "Would you like to have a family with me one day?"

Kyran's breath wheezes when his gaze spears right through me, as if he's a man stuck in the desert and I—an oasis. "As in… children?" he asks, and I can distinctly sense his hands getting a bit damp around mine.

I nod. I never thought having children would be on the cards for me. Maybe I was just missing someone who I could trust with my future?

"You did say it's possible in the Nightmare Realm?"

Kyran nods, but he remains quiet, as if he doesn't trust himself to speak as he massages both my hands with his fingers. But there's a glow in his eyes, and when Flap coos with encouragement, I rest my cheek on his shoulder. "Yes, we just need a bit of alchemy, and a lady willing to bear our child."

"I've had… such a shitty family, Kyran. I want to make a good one. With you. I think you'd be a good dad. I see it in the way you are with Flap."

He blinks, flushing, as if my comment embarrassed him. "I didn't really do anything. You're the one who always takes care of The Count."

"You're tender with him when you think I'm not looking." I smirk, stroking his chest. "What will our child look like? Will it have shorter ears? Whose eyes will it have?" I ask, swept away by this idea. When I look up, I spot Kyran's eyes glossing over, but I won't tease him about it. He shouldn't be afraid to get emotional around me. I will always be his home, the safe space where he can be himself, not the Lord of the Nocturne Court.

"Our child will be an elf, like me," Kyran whispers, leaning in until our noses touch and I sense the warmth of his breath on my lips. "But I hope he'll be as bright and beautiful as you."

I kiss him, overcome by a tenderness I never imagined possible. I only ever envisioned falling in love as missing someone, being obsessive, wanting to fuck them all the time. But while that's true when it comes to Kyran, I've also awakened to something deeper. A care for him that isn't about how hot he is, or what he gives me. My love for him isn't selfish, about the way he makes *me* feel. I want what's best for him, I want him to feel good, and appreciate him for who he is.

"And we will take care of them. Even if they're twins," I laugh but also keep my voice down, because even saying that out loud feels dangerous.

A flurry of emotions passes over Kyran's face. Joy, gratitude, love, are all there, but so is a great sadness, as if he's questioning why his own parents never cared for him enough. But then he pulls me into his lap, to Flap's loud complaints, and I squeeze him back. Whatever happens, we will do everything in our power to make one another happy.

CHAPTER 38

LUKE

I have a strange sense of déjà vu when I walk down the corridor with Reiner following me. This time though, Kyran is at my side, because we're not hastily getting married. No, we're holding a grand ball before the ceremony.

Kyran wanted tonight to be a surprise, and while I had much more input on my wedding outfit choice this time, I don't know what else will happen. Kyran even ties a silk scarf over my eyes as he leads me by the hand.

Reiner trails behind us, adjusting my clothes every now and then, as if he didn't add the *"final touches"* an hour ago by presenting me with shimmering green pauldrons made of hundreds of beetle wings and pearls. I don't complain though, because he is a master of his craft when it comes to fashion. He looked both nervous and happy when sharing his ideas with me throughout the month. In a rare, unguarded moment, he admitted the wedding ensemble is always a crowning jewel when it comes to his creations, especially because it is always portrayed for posterity. He showed me his past designs with so much pride.

"It's such a shame the silver rib cage got lost in the sea," he huffs, but I know it's a dig at me.

Excuse me for almost drowning when I could have been diving to save a glorified anchor.

Just like last time, I was happy to go with what is apparently a traditional theme for a prince's Dark Companion—the moth. It's represented with a delicate cape attached at the nape and wrists. I've learned the ceremony starts in darkness, with only the prince or princess holding a candle in their hands. The symbolism is lost on me, but it's definitely like a moth to the flame, something, something.

Which, okay, maybe is a bit romantic, but also a little cringe when performed in front of so many people I don't know.

I've grown to like lace and semi-transparent fabrics for shirts. I love that my nipples distract Kyran when I wear them, so I couldn't deny myself the pleasure on our wedding day. The black lace top clings to my skin, and the embroidery depicts countless insect eyes. It doesn't end at the cuffs and instead seamlessly turns into gloves. Thanks to the fabric being so delicate, my black nail polish stands out underneath. Reiner did in fact learn to apply it.

All this finery is paired with leather breeches in the same iridescent colors as the beetle pauldrons, and my heart is so light I feel as though I could buzz and fly up to the ceiling like the fashionable insect I've turned into. Though the amount of jewelry I'm wearing would probably cause a crash-landing.

My fingers are adorned with beetle wing rings, a silver tiara with a play on moth antennae is attached to my soft waves, and even my elegant boots have silver buckles dripping with pearls.

I'm the world's most elegant moth, a prized gothic bird, and my prince's pet. I have never before been so proud, despite having no idea where I'm going. I trust Kyran to take care of me and take note of the gentle way he leads me across the floor, which taps under our feet as if it were made of crystal. He smells of darkness, sea salt, and that discreet flower undertone I've learned is lily of the abyss, a plant that only grows underground, fed not by moonlight but the illumination of phosphorus mushrooms. Each breath I take makes me feel safer, because this will be the first day of my new life, and I cannot wait to spend eternity with him.

My eyes tingle, and my throat aches with emotion, but Kyran's as confident as ever, and as the doors swing open ahead, sending a wave of cool air in my face, I squeeze his hand. The room is silent as we enter, but the presence of others is obvious in the scent of perfume and the whisper of breathing around us.

I'm baffled by the scent of a familiar food but don't question it and hold on to my fiancé's hand when two rocks strike together, and I can smell burning wax.

It is starting.

I will get married by the end of this ball.

It still feels unreal.

When gentle hands remove my blindfold, the room around us is too dark to see anything beyond the silhouettes of the courtiers bathed in the red glow coming through a skylight above. The sight of the Blood Moon takes my breath away, but when Kyran brings a candle closer to my face and our eyes meet, everything but him is forgotten.

"Let me lead you through the dark," he says, and I can't stop the shiver running down my body when his low, sexy voice curls in my ear.

I nod and blow out the candle as I've been instructed. At once, the ballroom reveals itself to us with hundreds of lights, and the gathered crowd claps, dazzling me with the sparkle reflecting off their outfits.

Servants rush to pull apart heavy velvet curtains and let in more blood-soaked moonlight. By the walls, large tables are piled to the brim with platters still hiding their contents under silver domes, and yet more staff starts coursing between the guests, serving them crystal chalices filled with a white liquid.

Kyran smiles at me, and he couldn't have been more handsome if he asked a witch to charm him. His skin is like pink alabaster. He is majesty, ethereal nobility, and my forever prince. From the high cheekbones and silky dark hair to the smoky gaze that pierces my soul, Kyran makes me lose all my snark, instead giving me ideas for sappy poems to describe his beauty. I could learn about metaphors and similes for eons and still remain unable to give him justice.

Caressed by the crimson illumination, he is carved from the night itself. His high-collared cloak absorbs the light on the outside, yet its satin lining shimmers with silver embroidery of thorns and roses. There is a simple elegance to his outfit. It has a double-breasted jacket shining with carved buttons, and the sword attached to his belt makes him look like a general. It's only fitting, since Kyran commands shadows as if they are his soldiers. But it's the crown adorning his head that reminds everyone he is their sovereign.

Woven of dark silver, its band resembles seaweed, and simple antlers grow out of it, bejeweled with blue and green stones. A symbolic reminder that he is master of both the forest and the sea.

But he is also the master of my heart.

On a balcony above, musicians play a soft background melody as we parade across the dining room I haven't before seen and finally stand in front of our seats as the courtiers follow our example and join us at the table. Tristan sits close by, alongside his parents, sister, and a handsome brunet I'm not familiar with. When he squeezes Sabine's hand and nods my way, it becomes clear that the elusive husband I've heard so much about has returned to the palace for the wedding. The Goldweeds sit right across from them, and farther away are other prominent guests, who all raise their drinks as I too am given a glass with the thick, white liquid.

The music reaches a sudden crescendo, only to die down as Kyran entwines our fingers. He takes his time to speak up, and for a moment I worry he might be too nervous, but when he opens his mouth, his voice is as confident as ever.

"Dear friends, thank you for joining us on this special day. After seven long years, we will once again welcome Dark Companions at court. My marriage to Luke Moor will also officially inaugurate my reign." He bows to me so elegantly I lose my breath. "Let us hope for an uninterrupted century, and for Heartbreak to never make it to our shores." When Kyran raises his glass, so does everyone else, and I take that as my cue.

"To my Dark Companion! To Luke Moor!"

"To Luke!" All the elves roar, and I catch myself saying it too, which is stupid, because I'm toasting myself, but I hope no one noticed and quickly sip from my cold chalice—

I frown at Kyran. "Is this...?" It tastes exactly like a malted vanilla milkshake from Best Burger Bonanza. When servants reach for the silver food domes and uncover platters of burgers and fries, I'm on the verge of sobbing. Not just because I have been missing familiar flavors, but because I mentioned it to Kyran, and once again he moved heaven and earth to make me happy. I don't deserve him, but I will take him anyway.

I get to my toes, kissing my prince while Reiner explains the food to excited courtiers. A cheeseburger lands on my plate, and I wish I could eat it off Kyran's bare chest.

The other servants serve fries in elegant bowls and instruct the guests about the choice of adding salt or ketchup, or both. One pronounces it *"ke-chip"* and I snort with laughter, so happy my heart is overflowing.

Sabine is so excited to taste the human food that she gets up despite her husband offering to help. They're all dressed in Bloodweed black and carmine which looks exquisite in the red light of the blood moon.

Tristan toasts to me with the milkshake, stuffing his mouth with fries and demanding more from a server already. I'm so glad to see him alive and kicking. For saving Kyran's life, he deserves burgers with extra pickles every day.

"How did you get all of this here?" I whisper to Kyran, chewing patty with a groan of satisfaction.

"It's my little secret," he tells me, biting a fry I put against his lips. "But I might show you after our wedding night."

We've had sex countless times already, yet the thrill of getting to go down on him when he's already my husband makes my balls throb with excitement. I want to be his, and no longer need to hide how close we are.

"Sabine wrote me so much about you," her husband says, watching me with the eyes of a doe. He seems too young to be a father, but he is an elf and therefore could easily be two hundred years old.

Sabine chuckles and gives him a peck on the cheek before meeting my gaze, clearly flustered. "Andros and I bonded over a treatise on what humans call religion. His mother spent a whole year in this place called Greece," she tells me as if it were a fantastical land of flying horses and gods, not a country like many others.

"That's where she met my father, actually," he adds with pride.

I lean closer, and when a drop of sauce is about to drip from my burger and onto my breeches, Reiner is there to catch it in a napkin. I'm a little embarrassed but pretend it didn't happen, only thanking Reiner in a whisper before turning back to the Bloodweeds.

"Are you saying your father is human?"

"Yes, he lives in the capital and would love to meet you one day. I love the names you helped us pick!" Andros says, all excited, and now that he said his father is Greek, I can kind of see it in his darker complexion and black hair. "Nathan or Natalie. Simply glorious."

Sabine told me he insisted on Braadley or Braadlina, so I'm glad I managed to save the poor child from that misery. Conversation flows easily, and even the Goldweeds attempt to take part, though they're more interested in discussing imperial politics than listening to my explanation of the difference between mythology and religion.

I rather enjoy Andros's company. He and Sabine seem like a good fit—both are nerdy, and excitable, and so damn *nice* it's almost hard to believe.

I might have had a glass of wine too much though, because by the time everyone gets up and heads next door, to the ballroom decorated with garlands of black leaves and pearls, I feel absolute confidence. Were it not for Kyran, I would make a fool of myself during our first dance, but he leads so well that it feels like floating over the marble floor.

Dozens of hands clap as the music speeds up, prompting Kyran to spin alongside me, with one arm secured around my waist. Each smiling face reminds me this is a celebration of my union with the man I love.

I'm not the deer in the headlights I was a month ago. I might not be an elf, but I'm already part of this realm. I've been gifted the opportunity to learn shadowcraft, and I resonate with the fashions of the court. My position will come with a degree of danger, but when was life ever safe for someone like me—poor, gay, and unwanted? I am happy to trade the misery of my former life for the risk that comes with being a Dark Companion if it means I get to stay here.

My head spins with good wine and joy, but I'm pumped out by dancing and consider going back to the table for seconds, since I don't know when I'll get to taste burgers again. Tristan wants to talk to Kyran, so I leave them be and venture out to grab more food and drink.

It's like trudging through bejeweled Jell-O, because courtiers are greedy for my ear and strive for my attention, offering everything from smiles to marriage advice. Even Marquise Coralis is suspiciously, sparing no well-wishes, which makes me wonder if she still plans to form a throuple with me and Kyran.

As impatient as I am, my behavior will now reflect on Kyran, so I remain generous with my time on the way back to the table. I'm close to reaching my throne (and burgers) when a familiar voice grabs my attention with a passionate tirade.

"We should invest more time and effort into discouraging Heartbreak rather than reacting only once he comes close to the shore. We do know he's repelled by pearls of mourning oysters. Why not try to use them on a bigger scale? Wouldn't you support such an idea if it meant less risk to the Nocturne Court? It's maddening and the Lord will hear about it from me every day until he chooses to listen."

I peek over my shoulder to spot Sylvan facing two guards, each of whom is at least a head and a hat taller than him. But while he might be small, he has a cutting tongue, like a pair of dainty scissors decorated with filigree, yet no less sharp than any other pair. His attire is elegant yet strikes me as armor rather than an outfit worn for the purpose of fashion and covers every bit of him with the exception of the face and fingers.

Sadly, even with his royal title he can't hold the attention of a dark-haired guard when a pretty servant girl walks by with a platter of French fries.

The other guard, one with a streak of silver in his red mane, is entertaining Sylvan's idea. He raises his eyebrows with a sigh. "I don't know, Prince Sylvan. It's not my place to ponder such things."

Sylvan raises his hands, exasperated. "But you should. Everyone should. If you visited me in my alchemy lab, I could show you—"

"Now? To your lab? I'm not sure if I should..." The guard's attention is piqued, but not in the way Sylvan was going for. He smiles and pushes back his hair, leaning that bit closer, as if he wants Sylvan to smell him.

Sylvan straightens but it barely gives him an extra half inch, which is negligible next to men with arms thick like the branches of an old tree. I bite my lips to keep in a giggle when Sylvan's ears go red, and he takes a step back, like an exasperated virgin.

"No, that's not—It was a form of speech," he rasps and clears his throat. "What I'm trying to suggest is that you should talk about this to your family and acquaintants. Maybe if pressure comes from many sides, the Lord will understand how important it is to study the beast."

The dark-haired guard shakes his head, and I note the servant he likes has gone to fetch more glasses. "With all due respect, Your Highness, why waste time reinventing the wheel? We used to sacrifice prisoners to appease Heartbreak—"

"Which would be a great alternative to overcrowding prisons and banishment," his friend adds.

"—Lord Larkin Nightweed was the first to find an alternative. Dark Companions and their powerful shadows are more than enough to chase the beast back into the ocean every time."

Sylvan rubs his face, as if he forgot he's wearing kohl around the eyes, and when he relaxes his arms, there are dark smudges on his cheekbones, which... actually make him look kind of mysterious. *If* I was into mini goth dudes pent-up with anger and self-righteousness. In my world, he'd probably be fighting fossil fuels or something, and be just as annoying about it.

"That is how we lost our former Lord and many knights seven years ago. Maybe it could have been prevented. So many creatures live in the same waters as Heartbreak yet survive. We should be actively looking for other solutions!"

The guard who watched the pretty girl shakes his head, and I'm shocked at the realization that he doesn't even bother to hide his incredulous smile. "Your Highness, do you truly believe you can stop a curse so old we don't even know its true origin? A curse countless others have fought over millennia? By putting some pearls on the beach? It's futile."

Despite the guards calling Sylvan Your Highness, the look they exchange would be crushing to anyone's ego.

Worse yet, I'm finally caught eavesdropping. One of the men meets my gaze over Sylvan's head. "I, for one, am very happy that our Lord is finally claiming a Dark Companion. Time for us all to also try our luck at the River of Souls. I'd drink to that if I weren't on the job..."

I think he's prompting me to butt in and allow it this one time, but I am not going to do that after witnessing the attempt on Kyran's life.

Called out, I step closer, because there's no use pretending I didn't overhear the conversation. Sylvan glares at me as if *I* was the dam holding him back from convincing everyone to research alternative ways to fight off Heartbreak. I guess he is not completely wrong, since the royals would *have* to come up with new ideas if I wasn't here.

I haven't seen much of him outside some official occasions, and the execution of his sister (which he likely blames me for too). It's unnerving that I'm not sure what kind of person he is. With his silver hair, he reminds me of a tiny, yet very sharp needle, which could slide under my nail and poison my blood.

He doesn't even bother to smile as his sapphire eyes settle on my face, and instead nods, as if I'm not worthy of listening to his voice.

I suppose entertaining hunky guards is more important than convincing the Lord's Dark Companion of anything. If he really wants to implement change, I'm the person to befriend.

But I need to make allies too, not scorn him, so I step closer and pick a glass of milkshake from a tray passing us by in the hands of a servant boy with a particularly pert butt. Seems that the guard who previously watched the girl is an equal opportunity ogler.

"You should talk to Kyranis next week. He's grateful for the way you helped Tristan at the hunt."

There. Me, the sly diplomat.

Learned all about restaurant politics at Best Burger Bonanza.

Sylvan's small yet plump mouth opens, as if my support was the last thing he expected. He looks almost like one of those modern artist's dolls, with perfect features and hair like silk, and I'm only slightly jealous.

"Next week? Prince Sylvan will probably be fishing for a pretty human, like the rest of us," the guard who tried to flirt with Sylvan says.

Sylvan's face reddens, but he purses his lips. "Why would I debase myself in such a way, risk my life at that, when there are other ways—" he stops talking when he notices his blunder. "Good day. Enjoy the celebration, Luke. After all, it has been organized at great cost to the Nocturne Court."

Meaning: *We spent money on importing your burgers when we could have funded* my *study*.

With that, he slinks away before anyone has a chance to answer, and his swishing cape hits me in the thigh.

I groan in exasperation, but I guess I did make an attempt at what will be a long road to peace with the Goldweeds. After exchanging a few more pleasantries with the guards, I walk away but still hear them whisper to each other as I walk away.

"Sylvan needs a dick in his mouth if he's to ever shut up about all that alchemy bullshit."

I have to bite my lip not to snort, but it does make me wonder. Maybe what I need to do is find out Sylvan's type, then find him a suitor. Who knows, maybe we could even become besties one day, because if he has ideas that would help us avoid endangering anyone, why not give them a try?

But as I'm reaching into a silver platter overflowing with crinkle cut fries, someone else does it too, and our fingers touch above the table, with a spark of electricity.

I pull my hand to my chest and look up to meet eyes as blue as Sylvan's.

Anatole has outdone himself tonight and is facing me clad in a suit bespeckled with tiny pearls and diamonds, which transform the midnight velvet into a skyspace crowded with whole galaxies. I'm taken aback when he pulls my hand close and bends to kiss my knuckles with the grace of a true fairytale prince.

"I'm assuming you might be busy in the next few days, so I wanted to congratulate you ahead of the ceremony."

"Oh. I... thank you," I say. I've been at the Nocturne Court for a month, but I'm still getting used to receiving gestures like this as a man. I've grown accustomed to them coming from Kyranis, but not other men. Especially not in public. It makes me feel like a pretty flower, and I can't help but be a little flattered, despite most definitely not being *a flower*.

Oh well. When in Rome, do as the Romans do.

Anatole's handsome face brightens in a smile. He clearly can grow a beard, but his skin is soft and smooth regardless. I'm so envious I can barely look away.

"Would you give me the pleasure of a dance?" he asks, glancing toward the ballroom where I left Kyran and Tristan not that long ago. While I am annoyed that I waded through the crowd to eat some fries only to not get any, I know this might be a good opportunity to learn what makes my enemies tick, and maybe make the first step to burying the hatchet?

After all, who knows why the animosity between the Goldweeds and Kyran first started? Maybe I could mediate? I did once talk a drunk neo-Nazi out of beating me up. That counts for experience in conflict-resolution, right?

So despite the beef patties calling my name, I follow Anatole's lead. "I heard your brother talking about strategy. Maybe we should hold a meeting for all the princes and princesses to discuss it?"

"I worry it will be too late after your bond is made," he says with a sigh and perfectly studied sad eyes, but still twirls me into a dance. "Lord Kyranis will want to use your shadow first and foremost. That's always the case. But if you survive, Heartbreak's next approach could be our chance."

Couples swirl around us in shimmering outfits that would give goth Etsy sellers a run for their money. I long to see where Kyran is and offer him a tantalizing wink that will keep him thinking all the dirty thoughts about me, but I can't spot him. Giving up, I focus on the man pulling my back against his chest and his hand on my collarbones in a gesture that's protective yet also sensual. I'm not quite sure how comfortable I am with this, but since everyone does it too, I stop overthinking it and turn my head to glance at Anatole.

"Kyranis wants the best for everyone in the Realm. I'm sure he will be open to it."

"I don't know about that. He's always seen me as his rival. He'd even risk *you* just to spite me."

I'm stuck for words, because that doesn't sound like Kyran at all. Then again, Anatole has known *Kyranis* all his life. But before I can form a sensible answer, Anatole pulls me much closer than the dance requires. And I know because I practiced it with Kyran many times.

His hand slides to my stomach instead of my chest and he licks—*licks*—my earlobe.

"You cannot fathom the things I could offer you, Luke, if you were mine."

What. The actual. Fuck? This is literally my pre-wedding party, and while the courtiers seem to have a lax attitude toward sex and romance, it's always been clear to everyone that Kyran's possessive of me. Who the fuck *licks* the groom at a wedding?

No-good people, that's who!

This isn't the first time someone has come onto me out of nowhere. I'm not hurt, or afraid, or traumatized, but I'm most definitely pissed off. Only shock keeps me from lashing out, as if my mind is still scrambling for an explanation that doesn't require me to elbow my future husband's cousin in the ribs.

Kyran appears in front of me out of nowhere, and I reach out for him as soon as I see the fury scorching his eyes.

He pulls me out of Anatole's embrace, but instead of leading me somewhere we could talk, he goes straight for his cousin and slams his fist into his pale face.

The music dies, replaced by surprised gasps and, all of a sudden, the party is over.

CHAPTER 39

KYRAN

Rage fills every inch of my body and cuts through my mind like a blade, severing rational thoughts and leaving me in a state of unguarded fury. I was annoyed when Anatole brought Luke onto the floor, but seeing him taste my mate's skin and watching Luke stiffen in response made me *go to war*.

How dare Anatole provoke me like this?

Pulling Luke away would have been a slight. I crossed the line with the punch, but how am I expected to control myself when this meddler, this man who's only alive because I could not prove his part in the assassination attempt, is infecting my beloved with his touch?

I'd rather walk all the way to the capital barefoot than let him be in the same room as Luke ever again.

Anatole stumbles away and falls into two dancing women, who yelp but manage to keep him upright as the music breaks off without warning, and all the guests retreat, as if they feared I might strike them next.

"You animal!" Anatole yells, his lip curling as he wipes blood from under his nose.

Luke takes a few steps my way as the whispers rise into a murmur, and I reach back, finding his hand. I'm not used to this kind of confrontation. Quiet kills? Yes. This? Why can't I cut off Anatole's nose, banish him, and be done with it?

"You should have kept your lips away from my promised!" I cut in, even louder, and the tone of the whispers alters as the figures around us blur, just shadows at the edge of my vision.

"We were merely dancing," Anatole scoffs, but it's for the public's benefit, because Luke shakes his head at me with a scowl.

"And that was too much already if you can't keep your hands and tongue where they ought to be."

Luke clears his throat and squeezes my hand, but the rage inside is like a winter storm, cold and savage. "It was extremely inappropriate."

I want Anatole to never as much as *look* at my lover again.

Tristan clears his throat, pushing through the crowd with a tense smile. I cannot avoid the looks of disgust thrown my way when my gaze seeks him out, but what was I expected to do? Stay courteous and explain *to my promised* why I'm not allowed to protect him from a pervert?

Kyranis would have, but I'm not him. I don't deliver blows with smug words but with my fists, and I need Luke to know that I will always stand by him and never sacrifice his wellbeing for manners.

"You're to stay away from him for the next *century*," I roar with my gaze pinned to Anatole. "If he enters a room, you leave it. If he is spoken about, you stay silent. If you hear he was eating stew, you don't have it for a week, so you don't even touch the same soup! Is that understood?"

Anatole pouts, eyeing me with reptile eyes. "Challenge accepted," he says and pats his rapier. "And if you lose, you will give him to me for a night."

I... *what?*

"Spit that out, you worm," I growl and take a step closer, but he pulls his blade halfway out, sending the courtiers farther away. I hear chuckles, excited whispers, as if no one at all is on my side in this conflict, when this man, this pathetic pervert doesn't deserve the honor of being cut down with the Gloomdancer.

It's like reliving the experience with my brother all over again. Anatole isn't interested in men either, yet he'd take Luke just to spite me.

"I'm not anyone's property, to be 'given'!" Luke says, shaking his head, and the silver antennae attached to his tiara tremble. He's so perfect today, and this *maggot* is spoiling his experience of the wedding ball.

Anatole shrugs. "Oh really? Prince Kyranis will own you after the bond is sealed. He can do with you as he pleases, and you will have no choice in the matter."

I can barely see straight, but I restrain my anger, for Luke. "I would never force my Dark Companion into anything he doesn't want. Don't measure me the same way you measure yourself!"

"Oh, please. We all know how your father treated his Companion after the Lordess's death." When Anatole focuses on Luke, I want to gouge his eyes out just so he never does that again. "That poor man had bruises for years."

Truths twisted to serve Anatole's purpose. Yes, my father argued with James often, but he didn't abuse him.

"Prince Kyranis is not his father," Luke says through gritted teeth. By this point we are a spectacle, but I don't even care. "I could even leave this Realm after the wedding if I wish to."

The gasps around us deafen me, and the questioning eyes turn to me, but Anatole gives a cruel chuckle.

"You think the Lord of the Nocturne Court would let you, a human, leave once you're bound?"

I hate that instead of answering, Luke gives me an uncertain glance. As if Anatole's words are sinking claws into him.

My legs weaken under me, and I pull Luke close, wrapping one arm around him. "What does it matter if I never intended to let Luke go? Why would he even want to leave?" I say and challenge the blond bastard with my gaze. Maybe he will strike? I could end his life and call it self-defense.

I know I said the wrong thing when Luke pulls out of my arms with an uncertain expression, but it's too late to take it back now.

"It's about it being my choice," he whispers, and I want to whisk him far away from here so we can talk about it instead of facing the gossiping crowd.

Anatole makes a point of assessing the state of his nails while his other hand rests on the rapier. He's a fucking master of ruining things, I have to give him that. "Are we having this duel or are you admitting defeat?" he asks impatiently, prompting another wave of chuckles from our audience, as if his disgusting proposition is a game, not real-life stakes. His sister Elodie even leans in to whisper something to him with a smile as they both eye me like two snakes.

Maybe for people for whom lovemaking is a pastime, this challenge is a trifle, a way to end a scandalous situation, but I would *never* willingly put Luke in this kind of situation.

Only already I have.

I left him alone and vulnerable, then swept in with violence instead of keeping my cool. It's pathetic.

Now Luke is watching me with a tense grimace. I might have stolen him from his home, but my intentions were never duplicitous. I want to keep him safe. Happy. In comfort. Is that really so wrong?

I almost wave Anatole off, just so I can have a moment alone with my promised, but my voice gets stuck in my throat when I realize this would have meant forfeiting the duel and defeat. The bastard put me in an impossible position, and he knows it.

"Not a chance. I only wish this was a real fight," I growl out, because none of us is allowed to make the other bleed during a duel at court. The use of shadowcraft is strictly forbidden, and we will attempt to cut off roses attached to our chests instead. Which plays into Anatole's hand, since I have seen him fence, and he might just be my superior when it comes to the sport.

Fucking bastard.

I hate him *so* much. I wish I could grab him with shadows and pulverize his skull, but no. All I can do is use my sword to cut the rose carefully attached to his chest by his sister. She even dares a mean smirk at me. The whole damn Goldweed family can get sucked into Heartbreak's innards for all I care. I'll let their hearts stew inside the beast forever, so they never know peace.

Sabine approaches me with a somber expression. I wish Luke was the one to attach my rose, but he doesn't know our customs. At least I hope it's just that, because he looks so distressed I want to hug and reassure him.

"Keep your head, Kyranis," Sabine whispers, resting her hands on her substantial bump as soon as she's done pinning a black flower to my chest. "Anatole will surely play dirty."

"He already has," I mumble and rub Sabine's arm, but I seek out Luke and swallow, itching to hear his voice.

"Please don't lose," he mumbles without lifting his eyes.

As if I'd let Anatole put his hands on him even if I lost. I'd sooner castrate the fucker and rot in the dungeons under the palace.

"Of course not," I say softly, but when even that doesn't earn me the grace of Luke's approval, my feet sink deeper into the marble floor. I raise my head, staring straight back at the bastard on the other side of the crowd. Familiar faces are masks of indifference, amusement, rage, or excitement. It's all a game to them, yet another performance on a big night, but my future with Luke is at stake, and I cannot fail him again.

Tristan orders the guards to stand watch around the impromptu battleground while my finely dressed guests crowd by the walls and climb onto the mezzanine on one side, eager for a great view of the spectacle to come.

They're still shuffling around, still not ready, but I'm not here to provide entertainment. I pull out Gloomdancer, leaping toward the menace who's spoiled this special day for me and my lover.

Anatole is ready and leans back while taking a swing at my chest.

Blood freezes in my veins when the tip of his rapier comes way too close to the flower, and I jump back so rapidly the heel of my shoe slips. The audience chuckles when I save myself by landing in an awkward scoot, with my left hand on the floor, but laughter is soon replaced by gasps when Anatole strikes.

Tension ignites every muscle, and I shoot up, slapping aside the blade of his rapier. His blue eyes widen, and he attempts to keep himself from falling farther toward me, but I grab his blade, pull on him, and slam my forehead against his.

The world spins in a rainbow of color as pain travels up my skull and all the way to the back, but when Anatole tries to twist his hands away, and pushes at the base of my fingers, I shove him back before he can break something.

Spilling his blood would also mean my loss, but if I play my cards right, I can give him a good battering without cuts. It's supposed to be an honorable duel, but he lost all honor when he licked Luke's ear.

Anatole looks back my way once there's sufficient distance between us, and my heart leaps with joy when I recognize the tiny groove between his brows as a sign of worry. I might not be as skilled at fencing as I am at shadowcraft, but I have also never measured my abilities against his. He and the real Kyranis, however, dueled many times—for training, fun, or to resolve conflict, and I am positive my twin didn't win a single time.

I am a *real* opponent, and Anatole is only now realizing he might have gotten himself into deep shit by provoking this fight. I should have demanded more than him keeping away from Luke, but maybe another opportunity will present itself in the future? I barely keep myself from grinning when my opponent falls back every time I attempt to close in on him. I am taller, stronger, and our clash earlier must have shown him that he needs to keep me at a distance if he is to have any chance of winning this.

Which he does not, because I am going to end him.

My perfect solution would have been to use my strength to overwhelm him, but with the stakes being so high, I'm tiptoeing around Anatole as we exchange jabs and cross swords while keeping our bodies so far apart neither of us can reach the other's rose. It's a game of time and focus, and while I imagine that some of my guests have already lost interest, I don't let that sway me.

This duel might be about Luke's safety, but I need to forget his existence for as long as I'm within Anatole's range. At this point, the duel is about waiting one another out and seizing the perfect opportunity, but after avoiding several of Anatole's traps, my sword hand is damp from the effort of needing to do this for so long.

I am exhausted, my throat is dry and going raw, and I want Luke in my arms—safe and reassured—but Anatole is equally tired. His next mistake makes my brain blare with dozens of bells, and when our swords cross and he comes one step too close, I seize the moment. I step on his foot to keep the bastard in place and dive in so fast my blade smoothly slides off his and shaves off the flower.

Anatole's eyes go wide, and the audience utters a collective gasp just as I feel a sting on my chest. A hot drop rolls down my skin and is immediately cooled by air where my cousin has split my shirt. I grin, ready to raise my blade in triumph, because not only has this pathetic villain lost the duel but also shown lack of skill by cutting into my flesh.

When Anatole's face brightens with a menacing grin, my own smile falters.

And as my friends, servants, and courtiers stare my way in horror, I realize there is nothing to celebrate.

My secret is out.

CHAPTER 40

Kyran

It's too late. The result of the duel doesn't matter.

The gasps around me tell me everyone can see the golden sun etched into my skin. And in this moment I know this duel was never about the rose, or even a night with Luke.

Anatole was after this very public opportunity to cut open my shirt in front of others. Maybe he saw a glimpse of gold when I caught up with the assassin. Maybe he was just suspicious of Kyranis's changed behavior. Maybe he had a spy notice something strange about me.

Whichever it was, it's doomed me.

Whatever happens now, I need to make sure Luke is safe.

I search for him, and he comes forward with parted lips and wide eyes. It's as if time has become a swamp and each passing heartbeat takes hours. I take in the shocked faces of courtiers, Tristan's mortified expression as he steps away from me. I am the tainted son, the mistake kept alive, and he flees as if my very existence could infect him.

But he has also seen Kyranis half-dressed many times. He's surely now calculating not only when I took his place but also thinks about the same accusation as everyone else.

"Murderer! Twin killer!" Anatole yells, but his voice is soaked with triumph rather than rage. This is what he wanted. He goaded me into this duel for this exact reason, and I fell into his trap.

I try to pull my shirt together even though it can't save me from all the fingers pointing my way, the enraged faces, the accusations already echoing in the ballroom. I have only been free for a month and found the truest of loves, but now the life I hoped for is ruined.

Blond hair flashes in the blur around me, and a figure hisses in Anatole's voice, "Die, Sunspawn!"

He dashes at me with the sharp rapier pointed straight at the golden sun tattooed over my heart. Maybe I should just let him end me, because the happiness I've been basking in is now over.

I'm limp like a balloon losing air, but then Luke emerges out of nowhere with a terrified gasp, and it dawns on me that if I die, he will be left to the vultures ready to pick at his shadow. I can only protect him as long as I live. And that means I have to stay alive, no matter how much hate and shame I'll need to endure.

But by the time I snap out of my self-pity, it's too late to deflect the weapon coming my way. Anatole changed the angle to go for my throat and—

It happens so fast I witness the events backwards.

Blood falls to the floor.

Luke screams.

A thick black shadow pushes Anatole's blade away.

Luke extends his hand.

He's saved me—despite everything—and hurt himself in the process, because he barely knows how to use his shadow. The smell of Luke's blood makes all my senses sharpen with one intention.

Kill. Kill. Kill.

No more trying to avoid cutting Anatole in a bid to strike his rose. I will rip the motherfucker to shreds, no matter who is here to witness it.

"You will pay for every drop of his blood!" I yell and make my offensive with fury pulsing in my veins.

I attack with the sole purpose of slicing open his stomach and making his insides spill out in a cascade of rot, so that everyone sees how vile Anatole Goldweed is inside.

This isn't the kind of fight he's used to, and I can already taste his sweet death on my tongue. He takes steps back so fast the crowd parts, screaming. Someone falls over, making room for him and to avoid my blade, but I'm in a trance, set on ending him. He isn't able to make a single attack, reduced to deflecting my sword.

Anatole tries to trap me in the entryway to the dining hall, but I'm way ahead of him. I slash off his cloak so he can't use it in the fight, and he stumbles back again. I sense shadow covering my eyes, the beast inside me desperate to come out.

The clang of metal sends the few stragglers in the dining room to their feet. Dishes clatter, someone yells, but I have tunnel vision. I'm in my element. This is what I was made for.

Anatole jumps on the table behind him, swift like a cat, but this is no playfight. I slam the pommel of my sword into his leg, excited to hear a crack of bone. Blood blooms on his pale stocking. I'm a wolf on the prowl, and his neck is next in line for breaking.

He loses balance, falls to the table, screaming, and lashes out with his rapier, well aware these are his last breaths. I grab the silver dome that's resting over a platter of food and use it as a shield to deflect his blows. I smack his wrist in the process, and his rapier falls.

"I wanted to duel Prince Kyranis! Not this imposter! This duel is void! Help! This monster is out of control!" Anatole yells as he rolls off the other side of the table and to the floor with no grace left in him.

He lands with a dull thud, in a pile of fries, and I realize I don't have to resort to just my sword anymore. Everything happened so fast I kept fighting according to previously established rules, but I can use my shadows in this unjust clash.

If he wants a monster, I can give him one. Everyone's seen the golden tattoo anyway. I let the shadows envelop me with a yell of pure rage, power, and satisfaction. I let my claws grow. Anatole has no idea who he picked a fight with—

Someone jumps on my back, and a collar snaps shut around my neck.

I scream out as my shadows are forced back and disperse like smoke.

It's agony. I'm *burning* on the inside.

I throw the person off me, and they fall to the marble floor with a yelp.

"Seize the imposter!" Anatole yells from behind the table, but there's a pained rasp in his voice.

I pull at the silver collar blocking my access to shadowcraft, half-lucid with rage.

"This Sunspawn doesn't deserve a Dark Companion!" Anatole continues, crawling under a bench with no dignity left. It's the right choice, because I don't need shadows to best him. I'll rip him apart with my bare hands. "His promised should be put down as a warning to others!"

The bastard is shredding my heart, but my need to protect Luke is stronger than the desire for revenge, and I dash toward my lover, reaching for his bleeding hand. "He didn't know! Luke Moor is innocent," I roar, pulling him close as my gaze settles on Tristan's pale, horrified features. He might hate me now, but at heart he's always been fair, so I drag Luke closer to him, prompting the guards to raise their pikes and point them at me. "Tristan, please. He's innocent."

Tristan's face is hard to read, but his mouth forms a tight line. "Hand him over then," he says, extending his arm.

Luke stares into my eyes with terror. "No. I'm not leaving your side." But if it's because his love is true or because he's frightened of what will happen to him away from me, I can't know. Not that it matters. I would protect him either way.

Behind a wall of guards, Anatole limps to his feet, his face red and bruised yet filled with satisfaction. "How did you murder the rightful crown prince, traitor? Where is his body?"

It's as though I've gone deaf, because the sudden silence feels unnatural. So many gazes slither over me with fear and disgust, and I feel so damn small, like a sick animal, its eyes crawling with maggots. Nobody wants to be seen close to me. Nobody wants me to exist. I'm everyone's shame. I'm the fall of the court and the end of the Nightweed bloodline. The secret that was to never come out.

"I... I didn't," I mumble, watching Luke rather than Anatole, because if my life is over, I want him at least to know that I didn't just go and murder my brother in cold blood, no matter how despicable he sometimes was.

"He should be executed on the spot!" Anatole yells, because of course this is his chance to begin the Goldweed reign.

Sabine steps to her brother's side, pale as bone. "No! That is not what our laws state," she says even though her voice trembles, and she won't look at me. "Decisions of such magnitude cannot be made so hastily. He may no longer be the crown prince, but he is *a* prince, and deserves to be considered for the right of succession."

Anatole spits on the floor, but since none of the guards move to put me down, he knows he's lost momentum.

His brother appears out of nowhere, but while he speaks up, he's keeping his distance from me. "And there is no need to kill his promised, as he might still make a fine Dark Companion to someone else, were Prince Ky—the prince's twin to die."

"Really? You're feasting on my corpse already?" I ask as hope drains from my body, leaving behind only the husk of the man Luke fell in love with.

I'm no one now.

The embodiment of tales we tell children to scare them. The jealous one. The brother killer.

Me.

I should have left Luke in peace and never tainted him with my hopes and desires. If I'd never gone to get him, no one would have known he was bound to me. No one would have reached out for him. He would be safe.

"Are you deaf, Princekiller?" someone hisses from the back of the room. "Where's the real prince?"

The mood shifts as fear seeps out of the elves, making room for suspicion and anger. I brace myself for anything, but I don't expect the burger flying through the air to hit the side of my head. It leaves behind a splash of ketchup as it falls apart and drops to the floor.

I shudder with humiliation as the word *murderer* echoes ever louder.

"Will you be quiet?" Sabine roars, and Tristan whistles, as if woken up from a bad dream.

That does the trick, and Sabine clears her throat, raising her soft voice as much as she possibly can. "Rules of succession are clear. Every prince and princess can now get a Dark Companion if they wish to risk it, and the next Lord or Lordess will emerge through a trial *tomorrow*. The council of Law Keepers will decide if Prince Kyranis's brother is eligible to take part."

"He shouldn't be eligible to *live* if you ask me. None of us knew of his existence," Anatole rasps.

"Come, Luke," Tristan says and urges my promised closer, eying me as though I'm a rabid wolf.

"D-don't do anything rash," Luke whispers, and seeing him pull away from me feels like opening a wound, but he will be as safe as he can be with Tristan.

I lift my hand, wondering if this isn't the last time I'm allowed to see him, but I keep all my desperate words in, because he deserves as much peace of mind as he can get.

I've only ever wanted to make him smile, but now here he is, with kohl streaking his face. The finery he was so excited to celebrate in is a mockery of our end. One of his sleeves is ripped, his tiara is askew, all because I wasn't smarter in handling the court wars I warned *him* about.

As Tristan leads my beautiful promised away, Luke keeps glancing back over his shoulder with eyes like two warm summer lakes. Does he resent me? Does he pity me? I cannot know.

I ignore the jeers flying my way, too worried about the threat radiating from all sides now that my powers have been taken away by the heavy collar. I try to remember Luke the way he was before the doomed duel, in case that is all I have left.

How he fed me fries, not caring about the rules of propriety and elegance. How he let me lead when we danced. How he whispered into my ear that he can't wait to promise me a forever.

CHAPTER 41

Kyran

The sudden storm is the Realm's answer to the melancholic song in my heart. Anger remains just under my skin, constant like the rain tapping on the stained glass window. But it's myself I'm blaming, not the court. Luke should have never been put in this position for my selfish reasons. Yet I chose myself, and as I watch the Blood Moon turn a dull brown behind the veil of cloud and water, the bright joy I simmered with this morning turns into self-pity.

I'm stuck far away from my beloved, a prisoner in my own bedroom. And that's only because I was lucky enough to have Tristan's support. He vowed on his life that I won't leave the palace grounds, and that is the only reason I have not been dragged to the dungeon by the same guards who served me hours ago. I'm grateful for his aid, but his kindness is yet another shackle trapping me. He has Luke, and if I were to defy the rules he's established and flee, his death would be on me.

I feel vulnerable without my shadowcraft. If the Goldweeds sent in an assassin now, I'd be dead before I could spot the danger, just a limp bag of bones and flesh, forgotten once again. My hope lies in them being too busy fetching Dark Companions of their own to pay any mind to the wretched Sunspawn they surely hope to humiliate in public.

I shudder when the itch to search the walls and windows for possible ways out overcomes my reason, but I can't betray the one man who's chosen to help me in the hour of my fall. I hate the way he watched me, as if I shed my elven disguise and revealed myself to be a wild, unpredictable beast, but how can I blame him when so many things I've done are monstrous?

With that choice made, all I have left is to wait for my sentence.

The moral judgment, passed by the court.

The decision whether I can even be considered a prince and compete for the title I intended to claim under false pretenses.

But most frightfully of all, I await the chance to see my Luke again. I was exposed as a liar, and a fraud. I might never become Lord. I might be banished, imprisoned, or executed. Why would Luke want to be bound to someone like me at all? He'd be forced to carry my shame like a brand.

On the other hand, my fear isn't just about losing the crown and a position promising freedom and power. If the Goldweeds win tomorrow's trial, I'm as good as dead, and then Luke will be at their mercy. They wouldn't let him go. He'd be either killed, so no one can have him, or forced to marry any of the other knights or royals as their Dark Companion, a fate that in some cases could be worse than death.

When I think of Luke abused, tortured, raped, or trapped in the shadowild, I want to sink claws into Anatole's throat. I grab a cup off my table and throw it at the wall so its pieces can join the rest of the porcelain I shattered so far.

The door next to the pile of broken crockery opens, and I duck, hiding behind the bed while I search for something I can use as a weapon. The collar feels ever heavier, a dead weight on my shoulders, and it might as well end up being the anchor to pull my body all the way to the depths of Grief Ocean, but as I wait, the familiar red mane puts me at ease.

Tristan steps inside, still dressed in wedding finery, yet every piece of clothing seems limp on him now, like feathers on a sickly bird. He closes the door behind him in silence. I don't think I've ever seen him this somber.

"We need to talk," he says and sits at the table, eying me from there without mercy.

The indignity of my actions hits home, and I shoot to my feet, approaching him without a moment's hesitation. "Is Luke fine?"

"Physically, yes. He's being detained in the Moon Tower, under shadow wards. But his situation is far from steady." Tristan taps his fingers against the table, not even looking at me. It reminds me of how excited he was in the morning to get his nails painted black with the human nail polish.

Maybe I should have never replaced my brother? Maybe I should have stayed hidden forever, or gone someplace far from the court, where no elf could recognize my face, living simply but enjoying my freedom.

"He doesn't deserve any of this," I say, settling in a chair across from Tristan.

"No, he does not. But I'm not here to talk about him. I need answers, Kyranis. Or whatever your name is. I took my knighthood vows at twenty. Just days after you—your brother—the two of you, were born. I dedicated my life to the cause of keeping him safe. I deserve the truth."

My back aches under the weight of his gaze, but I meet it all the same. "My name is Kyran, and my family kept me hidden in the shadowild."

He meets my gaze, as if he's finally ready to *see* me. "It's not... illegal to keep a sunspawn alive, but all of this feels so wrong. Not only a twin, but the twin of a crown prince?" Tristan shakes his head. "You don't seem feral. You've been brought up by your family."

I frown, unable to help the spike of hurt in my chest, because out of all the people at court, I have always seen Tristan as more of a friendly figure. "Of course I'm not feral. I am a man like any other. With needs for things that I have been denied since birth!"

When golden eyes settle on me, as if Tristan is surprised a monster like me is capable of forming complete sentences, the dam of pride and dignity crumbles. I know this might be my only chance to speak my truth, so I let words flow. I tell him how I envied Kyranis having actual playmates when I was forced to watch or play with toys, how I missed out on everything from family celebrations to first kisses. How I had to grieve my mother in solitude. How I was forced to remain unseen and live vicariously through a brother who grew to enjoy knowing I always watched.

How Kyranis seduced a boy I liked, how he'd have me replace him when it came to activities he didn't enjoy, and how I protected his life in secret, gathering countless eels on my skin. When I tell Tristan the specifics about a hunt I accompanied him on, because the real Kyranis was too hungover to participate, the golden eyes grow wide as dessert plates.

"All this time, I wasn't alone in protecting him." Tristan lets out the saddest chuckle, sliding his fingers into his hair. "And the duel with Swordmaster Fern from the capital. Was that you? He—you fought like I've never seen Kyranis fight before, and there was a crate of Nerunian wine at stake."

I give him a bitter smile. "I wasn't offered a single glass for that win. I was my brother's servant, paid in chances to have my existence acknowledged and to feel moonlight on my skin. I missed out on so much," I whisper, swallowing hard as Tristan meets my gaze. "He didn't even bother to choose his own Dark Companion and sent me to pick one instead, since we're twins and share the same blood."

Tristan's frown deepens and he hunches his shoulders. "I... served your brother the best I could, but I also recognized he was a very flawed prince. It seems that he was more rotten than I ever could have imagined. I thought he would get serious after your father's death, that he was just going through growing pains. I know all about the temptations of drinking and enjoying myself in beds that don't belong to me, but he had only grown meaner in the past years. Mistreated servants, toyed with hearts, and boasted about his place on the throne, for which he didn't seem to want to reach. When I got glimpses of him studying court documents, it felt like seeing a different person. Now I know why."

"I always liked talking with you," I say, relaxing when tension drains from Tristan's body. "You are a good friend. Thank you for taking care of Luke. I... I don't know what I'd do if anything happened to him," I admit, but while this is true, I hope that by making this point, I might ensure Tristan is even more protective of him.

"And I'm sorry about what happened to you, being kept in the shadowild... I don't envy what you've been put through. But you must understand I need to know how he died. You heard the accusations. To think that I spent my life as his guard and I didn't even know he perished? I'm struggling. Was he too sure of himself? He often dismissed me, giving me lots of free rein, but now I wonder if it's because he secretly had you watching over him. So I have to ask. Did you entrap him?"

"No," I say right away. "He went riding into the woods and found wolf pups in a den. He wanted to kill them, but the mother surprised him. She crushed his head in her jaws."

All true, even though I leave out some details. What is done is done.

"I might actually recall that day. I offered to go with him, but he brushed me off. And so, you decided to take his place?" Tristan asks, but it sounds more like a statement. There's nothing that suggests judgment in his voice, yet I still feel the need to defend my choice.

"I couldn't help him anymore. So why not seize my chance at a life worth living? Why not catch up on everything I've missed and become the Lord he could never otherwise be?" I ask, clutching onto the loose front of my damaged shirt. "For seven years he didn't bother with Luke. He never wanted the responsibility of a Lord, and we all knew Heartbreak was coming. I was ready to take it on. Not just for myself but for all of the Nocturne Court and the Nightmare Realm. And yes, maybe I also want the recognition after thirty-five years of being less than a shadow to my brother!"

Tristan watches me in silence, and a part of me regrets getting so heated, but it's the truth, damn it.

"I see. It pains me that I wasn't there to guard his life, but he made that choice. I made a vow to your bloodline, and I choose to trust you. In the last month, you've proven worthy of the crown. It's not my place to deny it to you. I will do all I can to help you become Lord of the Nocturne Court. But once you ascend, I request to be let go from my duty."

I'm struck by the formality of Tristan's words and utter, "Did you rehearse this speech?"

He grabs a spoon and throws it at me with a chuckle. "You absolute ratbag!"

I deflect it before it can strike my chest and grin at him, oddly at ease. "I'm just surprised. You don't usually talk like this. But why do you want to leave my side? Is it... me?" I ask, trying to not focus on the ache in my chest. "Or are you getting married to that milkmaid who pierced your nose and starting a farm of your own?"

Tristan sighs, resting his elbows on the table. I'm so glad to feel the atmosphere between us loosen. In the past month, I became entwined with Luke like a man and his shadow, but I've also befriended Tristan in a way I couldn't have predicted. We're so different. He's easygoing where I'm tense, and he's like a ray of moonlight where I thrive in darkness. Yet because of the bond with my brother, he treated me like an old friend, and that made me feel like a person, not just a tool for eviscerating enemies. I want to see him happy and help him pursue whatever he needs to.

"No, dumbass. But standing at the threshold of death shook me. I was never one to think much about the future, and I settled in well as the prince's guard. When that poison flowed through my veins, it reminded me that elves are as mortal as humans. We might not age the same way, but we can still perish within a heartbeat, and our realm is crawling with beasts, plants, and elves competing to kill you. But while I was frightened and didn't want to die, I also don't want to live like Reiner, limited to the comforts of the palace grounds for the sake of safety above all. I want to see the Realm. I want to see the *human* realm. Kyranis never wanted to go, so *I* never did. Now I want something for *myself*. I'm sure you understand that."

I lean forward as my heart throbs. "I do. And if I become the Lord, your wish will be granted. You out of all people deserve the right to follow your heart. You've given me and my brother enough."

Tristan grabs a tiny red cookie from a silver bowl in the middle of the table and eyes it with a thoughtful expression. "Sabine and her husband are trawling through tomes of laws to fight for your right to take part in the trial. Let's hope their years of fucking at the library help."

I freeze with my mouth open. "Sabine? Fucking at the library?"

"Where do you think that baby was made?" Tristan asks, biting into the pastry with a wicked grin.

I shake my head, but as the meaning behind his earlier words sinks in, I feel that the floor under my feet is about to form a sinkhole. "It's full moon tonight," I whisper, meeting his gaze. "I'll stand no chance if I don't have a Dark Companion."

"If you get to take part, they'll surely take off your collar."

I stand as frustration coils in my body, making it cramp. "It won't matter if Luke and I aren't married."

"How so? It's unlikely anyone else will have a Dark Companion so soon, so it will be anyone's game. Though I have heard Princess Elodie set out to the River of Souls," he adds with a twist of his lips.

I scowl, pacing in the middle of the room as I recall the horrified look crossing Luke's features when he realized everyone knew what I am. I can't stand it. Or the uncertainty of not being able to speak with him.

"Luke and I were to marry today. But why would he want me now? He must be so embarrassed. I spoiled everything for him, you, for everyone."

Tristan wraps his thick arms on his chest. "Anatole outdid himself, have to give him that. At least you broke his leg? He won't be healing from that so fast. But as for Luke... it's hard to say. I didn't have time to talk to him that much, but he was... crying."

It hurts like a big game arrow straight to the chest. "Oh Luke... no... what did he say?" I ask and return to the table, placing both my palms on the smooth wood. All pride I ever had is draining out of me in the face of my lover's distress. I want to cradle him in my arms and make all his worries disappear, but instead I'm trapped, so far away from him.

"He was asking about *you*, of course. Why would you question if he still wants to marry you? That boy is crazy about you. I had to restrain him in the corridor when he got the idea that he doesn't want to leave your side after all. His hand bled all over my jacket," Tristan points to the dark stains.

Words get stuck in my throat as I stare at the dark spots with dread and sadness crawling through my insides. "Because he didn't know I planned to keep him in the Nightmare Realm. He didn't understand that everyone would treat me as a pariah. Everything's changed now that he can finally see I'm not worthy of him." It flows out of me like an icy river, and I rub my face, trying to regain my composure. "I would give anything for a chance to see him."

Tristan gets up. "You are Crown Prince Kyran Nightweed. Of course you are worthy of him. And you *should* see him."

I look up, clutching the edge of the table. "But the tower's protected with shadow wards—"

Tristan grins. "I've got an idea."

CHAPTER 42

LUKE

The floor trembles under my feet, and as I slide down the wall, imagining what would happen if the tall and slender tower I've been locked in crumbles into the ocean, a sense of dread coils deep in my gut. The tremors finally stop, leaving me with a numbness wherever my flesh touches a surface. It's a reminder that Kyran and I were meant to serve as the weapon against the very thing causing the quakes, and our union just fell through for the second time.

But as the immediate fear for my life passes, I'm back to nursing the burning hole in the middle of my chest, and neither the scented candles peppered throughout the circular room, nor the fine furnishings can make me any less desperate.

I repeat the duel in my head over and over again, wondering if there was something I could have done. Every time I do that, Kyran's words jam the cogs in my brain.

What does it matter if I never intended to let Luke go?

I know his feelings for me are true, yet the seed of uncertainty is there, planted deep in the potent soil of my mistrust. I have to fight myself to chase off the voices suggesting everything about our love is fake.

At least I'm alone here so I can cry my heart out, uncaring about someone seeing what a mess I am. Yet as much as this potential betrayal of trust hurts, my mind is full of worries for Kyran. I, the guy who has no real friends and who doesn't care who he fucks as long as the sex is good, fell hard for a dude who might have been lying to me all along, and all I have on my mind is his safety.

I cannot begin to describe the distress of seeing him put in that collar like some wild animal in need of sedation. The powers he wields with the same ease a bird flies, gone in a flash. He's now defenseless in a palace filled with backstabbing Goldweeds and their associates, and all I can do is wait.

I rip off the rest of my cape in frustration, angry at how helpless I am. Maybe I should have fought to stay at his side. Then I could have... Could have *what*? The first time I used my new powers defensively, Anatole almost sliced my hand in half. I'm lucky for the healing salve Tristan gave me, because while it's not fixed the issue altogether, at least I feel no more pain, and he's assured me the wound will seal quickly.

I don't regret stepping in though. That blade was far too close to Kyran's neck.

Fucking Anatole.

A knock on the door startles me.

"Come in?" I say, surprised I, a prisoner, am given the courtesy of a knock. Though the door isn't even locked, because two guards are stationed close to it and would have dragged me right back in if I tried to sneak out.

The elegant handle dips, and I find myself speechless when a veiled woman enters the room, closing the door behind her. Layers of black tulle hide her features, but the design of her dress—clinging to the hips and featuring lush layers from the knees down tells me who it is.

I dart behind the desk to create distance between myself and Marquise Coralis, who never had any reason to like me. Now that she knows my promised might have had a hand in her lover's death, she might appreciate me less still.

"Kyran was just doing his best in a tough situation!" I say to get my words in first.

I watch her every move, but in this warded prison, even my miniscule shadowcraft skills are unavailable. This also means she cannot use hers to attack *me*, but that's a small consolation.

She exhales, making the front of her dark veil puff up. I only see a rough outline of her facial features when she steps into a ray of moonlight slipping in through a window, but they remain a blur, as if she doesn't want me to see her expression.

"So he's really gone? Kyranis?" she asks softly.

I deflate under the weight of all the stress I'm going through. "I'm sorry. Kyran couldn't tell you, you must understand that."

"I see it now. I actually think it was kind of him to not bed me under false pretenses, just to maintain the illusion of being the same man."

I keep it to myself that Kyran isn't interested in women, as that wouldn't be helpful to our case. "Kyran is a good man. And a good prince. And if only he gets the chance, he'll be a good Lord."

"I do hope that happens. Prince Anatole is… he doesn't grace me with favor. So while I mourn Prince Kyranis, I'm here to help you, as what my prince promised me can also be granted by yours. *If* he becomes Lord. But that lies in the hands of fate." She sighs, as if tonight has taken a toll on her too. "I will be frank. Prince Kyranis banished my sister from the Nocturne Court after she rejected his advances. The accusations against her were false, and I want her back. Don't forget my kindness when you speak to Prince Kyran." She pulls out a little key, confusing me further.

I glance at the door behind her, thinking of the guards who were nice enough to leave me a bottle of wine. "Are they… *dead*?" I whisper.

She stalls, then lifts her veil, revealing flushed features, which I see for the first time without makeup. She looks almost… human when compared to the porcelain-skinned goddess she's presented herself as every single time before.

"Of course not. It's for the balcony," she says, pointing at an iron door, which I couldn't open before.

"Oh. Okay. I… don't get it." I spread my arms. This is the tallest tower in the entire castle. I barely have enough upper body strength to do three pull-ups, let alone climb down a slippery rock wall during a storm.

She huffs and shakes her head, passing across the room. "The guards won't know you're gone, because you *will* be back. If we don't want an actual war with the Goldweeds, you have to be here in the morning but I'm giving you a chance to speak to Prince Kyran."

I still don't know how that's supposed to work, but then she opens the door into a wall of gray rain. As I'm about to step back, worried she intends to push me into the void below after all, a dark shape appears out of nowhere. I cross my hands over my lips to keep in a scream, but then two wings send water my way, and Tristan floats in the air just beyond the balcony with his hair hanging in wet streaks.

He waves at me, and I step toward him without a thought. He's the one who's saved my prince twice already, and if there's one other person I can trust in this den of snakes, it's him.

A whirl of icy rain hits me the moment I'm out of the room, but there's no time to hesitate, and I grab his hand, ready for anything.

I understand it all without words. Shadowcraft can't be used in the tower, but he's not *in* the tower.

Vertigo makes nausea rise in my throat when I take the leap of faith over the void under us and into Tristan's strong arms. I wrap my arms around his neck for good measure, but he's holding me so firmly, I feel safe despite hanging in the air, hundreds of feet above ground. Harsh wind covers my face with my own wet hair, saving me from the terrifying view.

Tristan's shadow wings are a solid black, and leathery, like those of a bat. Or a demon.

What matters is that he's here to take me to Kyran, which means he's alive and safe enough to have planned this. I scream into Tristan's shoulder when lightning cuts across the dark sky, contrasting with the moon that's now low in the sky and reached the shade of old blood.

But my savior fears nothing, and as I close my eyes, desperate not to look down. He carries me away from my prison with the ease of a seagull snatching someone's French fries.

My sense of balance spins, as if the laws of physics no longer matter in a storm such as this, but moments later, I dare to peek over my shoulder, and my stomach curls against my spine when I spot a large greenhouse perched at the very top of the palace.

It's hard for me to tell with the world twisting around me and rain smacking me in the face, but I'm pretty sure I'm being taken to the Ancestral Sanctuary Kyran pointed out to me on the way to the village. Which makes a lot of sense, as it's also high up, making it easier for Tristan to get there from my tower.

The glow of small, red lamps reveals the shapes of huge plants inside, but I don't get much chance to see them all in detail, because moments later, my feet meet a puddle, and Tristan steps away with a grin. "There."

I don't get to take a full breath of damp air before the glass door leading into the greenhouse swings open, revealing Kyran. He pulls apart a huge plush blanket, and I step right into his arms, out of the rain.

The misgivings he put in my head at the end of the ball no longer matter as I cling to him, seeking the comfort of his warmth, and of his soothing scent, which I can no longer live without. Tristan must have closed the glass door behind me, because I can't feel the wind on the back of my head any longer. I don't think about him anymore when Kyran's mouth opens mine. His tongue is pure bliss, and as I whimper, falling deeper into him, I lose my breath, trying to keep up with my lover.

We should talk about everything that's happened, about the wedding, our future, but I have to get my fill of him first. His tongue is so familiar by now, and yet it never fails to make my heart beat faster. A greedy part of me likes that I'm the only one who's ever tasted his soft lips.

My breath evens out in his presence. My body knows he can protect me from anything coming our way. But as my hands climb his shoulders and meet the collar made of silver and leather, I'm plucked out of our happy place and thrown into the dark reality.

I lean back, staring at the thick band with rows of symbols etched into it, but Kyran cups my face when he meets my gaze. "Are you all right?"

"Me? I... I'm fine," I dismiss it. "Tristan helped with my hand, and my prison even has wine, so can't say I'm complaining," I joke because I want to see him smile. Especially when he's in such a terrible position. He's a powerful man even without access to shadowcraft, but it must hurt him to have his skill taken away. "Are you allowed to be here?"

He exhales and steps back, grabbing a black robe with a long train and wide, lushly embroidered sleeves. "Change into this. I... don't want you to catch a cold because of me on top of everything else," he says, holding the garment open.

I have to turn around so he can open the buttons at the back of my wedding shirt, and I can't help the sadness filling my chest. He was supposed to be doing this on our wedding night. We were supposed to be happy.

"Thank you for bringing it," I whisper when I put my boots and breeches on a bench. I inconspicuously take the ring I made for him out of my pocket and slide it on my thumb, because my dreams of marrying him are still fresh and I can't risk losing it.

I don't know how much time we have and don't want to talk about what should have beens.

I still remember the sting I felt when Kyran told everyone he never planned to let me go, and while at this point I intend to stay at his side, it hurts to know this man I've fallen for so fast might not see me as his equal. Pretty words mean nothing in the face of his power, both political and tangible, but it's so difficult to think straight when he closes the robe around me and hugs me from behind.

"I was so worried. I'd rather die than let anything happen to you," Kyran whispers, nuzzling my ear with a fondness no lover has ever showed me.

"It's all fucking Anatole's fault. He asked me for a dance just to bait you."

I take the chance to take in our surroundings, and for a moment, the Sanctuary takes my breath away. The greenhouse is massive, with a glass ceiling high above us and a whole mixture of dark plants. So many of them are black, but a dark blue or burgundy peeks out here and there, with midnight blue roses featuring in a large number. Among all the lush greenery are paths leading past plinths adorned with carvings of fantastical creatures and seashells. They're topped with crystal domes under which skulls glisten in the glow of the red lights dotting the airy interior.

Some of the skulls occupy their spot alone, others in the company of one or more others, but all are laid out on decorative cushions, and some even bejeweled with gold, silver, and precious stones.

This garden of beauty and macabre is the gothiest thing I've ever seen. It reminds me of a baroque church.

Kyran pulls me away from the balcony and down a path leading to a wide aisle laid out with dark marble.

Raindrops drum against the roof and all the walls, filling the space with insistent music, but how can I focus on their rhythm when Kyran's chest is right next to me, drumming too?

"And I was foolish to fall for each one of his tricks. I'm so sorry," Kyran mumbles, and avoids my eyes when I try to meet his gaze. "You must be so embarrassed."

"No, I'm just glad he didn't hurt you." I turn around abruptly when I notice a melancholic melody reminiscent of a pipe organ. "What is that? Anyone there?" I call out in panic. The last thing we need is Kyran getting in even more trouble for stealing me away from the tower.

He kisses the side of my head. "It's just a music automaton. It's powered by rainwater."

I have to hold on to him when my knees feel a little unsteady with relief, but his presence can't erase the doubts in my heart, so I meet his eyes and ask, "Kyran, did you take me for granted? Did you assume you'd do with me whatever you like, whether I fell for you or not?"

He squeezes my hands and leans in to have my absolute attention. "No. Of course not. I mean... I assumed I'd convince you eventually, because... why would you run when I can give you everything? But if you hated it here, hated *me*, then... we would have worked something out," he finishes, dropping his voice.

I hate myself a little for accepting his answer, but at this point, I do love him. I *want* to trust him. "I want to stay with all my heart. I just want to know the choice is mine. It's important to me."

Kyran's lips twitch, as if he's fighting the urge to say something he doesn't want to. His face reflects absolute agony as he descends to one knee and rests his forehead against my stomach. "I would have used every trick under the sun to convince you. From the start, having you at my side meant I'd have the right to claim my title, that I'd have the power to stand against Heartbreak and any other dangers that might befall the Realm. I need this, Luke. It's been thirty-five years, and I need to permanently get rid of my shackles. The title of Lord was my only shot at true freedom. Believe me, the irony of needing to entrap you for that purpose is not lost on me."

I wrap my arms around his head and bend over to kiss it. He might be a prince, but he's the one on his knees in front of me. I sense the pain of his vulnerability. "I understand. Extreme situations make us do extreme things." I swallow, unsure if I should tell him about this, because I never told anyone, but he is the one person from whom I don't want to keep any secrets. "To get out of that terrible school where they hurt me, I seduced one of the teachers, then blackmailed him, threatening that I'll make sure everyone knows, unless he gets me kicked out of that place permanently. I would have killed someone if that's what it took."

Kyran kisses the middle of my injured palm, then nuzzles it, leaning against me as if he, the Crown Prince of the Nocturne Court and Lord of Shadows needs *my* protection. "I wish I could spill the blood of every person who ever hurt you. But if you'd rather go back to your world, if you cannot stand this one, then maybe that's what we could do? Together?" he asks softly. "I do want the crown, and my legacy. I fear that without them I will always live in fear of being hounded down, but I will give them up if that's what it takes for me to have you."

My heart melts when I look into his warm dark eyes. I stroke his silky hair with a sigh. I don't want him to live in fear. I don't want him to have to give up what he dreamed of when the alternative doesn't guarantee us safety. But knowing he'd give up his realm for me? I have never heard anything more romantic.

"You deserve the crown. You deserve to take your position at court after your brother wasted his chance. But I appreciate the gesture."

He's oddly quiet, as if I hurt him with something I said, but before I can ask, he kisses my hip and slides his arms around my waist, longing for my touch. "I always saved him. Sometimes, from legitimate danger, other times because he got himself into a mess. And he never thanked me. He took me for granted, almost as if he were doing me a favor just by acknowledging my existence in private. I warned him. I pleaded that he should be careful, but he wouldn't listen. The one in need of nursing wounds after his escapades? Always me."

I stroke his beautiful pointy ear with all the tenderness in my heart. "I'm so sorry. You tried. Maybe it's for the better that he ran out of luck."

The silence following my words feels heavy with meaning, and by the time he speaks, I know there's more to this story.

"It wasn't his luck that ran out but my patience. That day, he went hunting with just me to back him up. He wanted to seem like an accomplished hunter, for everyone to think that he slayed whatever beast he planned to come back with on his own. We argued when I didn't want to go deeper into the woods, and he told me he didn't need a sunspawn to help him. Then he found a den with wolf pups and started teasing them. I saw their mother creep closer but didn't warn him. He cried out for my help when she attacked but I let him handle the wolf himself. I chose not to save him this time. He always said his life would have been better without me, so I just gave him what he wanted. Does that make me a prince-killer?" he asks, meeting my gaze.

My stomach drops, and I know he wouldn't have told this story to anyone else in the world. I ache for him. "Oh, Kyran... You were put in an impossible situation. It was either him or an existence in his shadow, which you despised. After all I've heard about your brother? Good riddance." More importantly, I hope my words can ease Kyran's guilt.

"Now you know every dark corner of my heart." Warmth fills my heart when Kyran smiles before rising to his feet and making a broad gesture toward the display of skulls. "I told you about them, remember? The skulls of my ancestors and their Dark Companions, together, for all eternity. I wish—" He swallows, sliding his warm fingers through the hair at the back of my head. "I would often come here, alone, and dream of having a mate of my own, a Dark Companion whom I could share everything with. And now you're here with me."

I stroke the crystal dome as the rain and the automaton music create a melody in the background, interrupted only by thunder. "That is the most morbidly beautiful thing I've ever heard," I whisper and rise to kiss his lips.

The Blood Moon peeks from behind a thick cloud, and my heart sinks when I think that we missed our opportunity to marry tonight.

But is it really... missed?

I glance at my hand and the ring I put on my thumb. The ring I wanted to surprise him with. The night isn't over, and we're not apart.

I pull it off as my heart beats faster. If this works, Kyran will have better odds during the royal challenge, and... I just want him to be mine, and for me to be his.

I go down to one knee, naked under my fluffy robe, and hold up the ring. "You will never be alone again. Marry me?"

CHAPTER 43

LUKE

I have no doubt whatsoever that Kyran will say yes, but seeing his eyes go all glossy with emotion still gives me a thrill.

"Of course I will. I would love to," he adds with more vigor, and as I slide the ring onto his finger, he eyes it with his mouth open. "How unusual! Where did you get it?"

It fits perfectly. Of course. Because Reiner knows the size of Kyran's every finger. I get up and hug him with a smile. "I made it with Reiner's help. I wanted to give you something special, and in my world, we don't just give engagement rings, but exchange them at the marriage ceremony too. It's made out of the antler of the Stag of Sunrise. I wanted you to look at it and remember how grateful I am for what you gave me that day." After the stag's death, the vibrant golden sheen of its antlers turned into a matted dark gold, but that doesn't make it any less beautiful.

The midnight blue roses used in the ceremony we're about to perform grow so close I don't need to move to pick one off the bush. I manage to hold it between the thorns, and it breaks off easily. Kyran leads me to the end of the aisle where, under the dome of glass and violet leaves stands a stone altar with dark green moss growing all over the surface at the top. There's vials and bottles on a cupboard nearby, along with silver chalices, bowls, and other paraphernalia, but for now it stands empty, waiting for our ceremony to begin. I remember Kyran telling me something about feeding a spider our hair, and I really hope we don't have to.

"I know it's just symbolic, but I want to do it right," I say when I see the question in his eyes. "What do we need to do now? Just say my vow?"

His smile is joyful, as if the spectacular catastrophe at the ball thrown to celebrate our union is forgotten. But darkness seeps back into his eyes, and he grabs the collar on his neck, yanking on it so hard I fear he might do some damage to his upper spine.

"No. No, no, no...this cursed thing! For the ceremony to work I need to envelop us both in shadow, and I can't, I—" He breaks off, just as distraught as he was when a single slash through his shirt revealed the truth about him.

I'd do anything to ease his pain. After a lifetime on a leash, this must be excruciating to him. But then I remember I'm not in the warded tower anymore. I grab his hand. "You gave me the stag's heart and the gift of shadowcraft, remember? Can I... envelop us in *my* shadow?"

The absolute grief of his expression eases, turning into hope as he squeezes my hand and nods. Oh, how I love being the sun to his darkness.

"I love you, Luke Moor. I won't ever stop," he breathes, plucking the flower from my hand. The rain has eased, and the red glow of the Blood Moon seeps through the glass roof, as if it wants to bless us.

My heart is pounding so fast when I look into his handsome face and cover us in the thin veil of shadow. It's immaterial yet somehow makes this moment feel more intimate as it hides us from the world.

Kyran squeezes the rose, and it pains me to see blood drip from his clenched fist, but I don't stop him. I know this is what he wants to do. "My flesh will be your shield. My blood is yours to drink if you are thirsty. I shall perish before I let anything harm you. This I vow under the Blood Moon. I am yours for as long as our hearts beat."

I put my hand over his, feeling strangely small yet oh so safe. "I love you, Kyran Nightweed, Crown Prince of the Nocturne Court, Ruler of the Shadowild, Protector of the Nightmare Realm, and Knight of Grief Ocean." Yes, I've learned all his titles by heart, and I can't wait to add Lord to that list. "I am yours. Body, soul, and shadow. You will never be alone again, and you will always have my support. Whatever you choose, I will follow."

Kyran nods, swallowing as he leans down and kisses me. His blood smells borderline sweet, and as we connect, embracing in the petals of my shadow, warmth rushes under my skin, and then further, until I can almost sense Kyran's flesh without the need to touch it.

It's so beautiful.

I gasp when I sense the thread of connection between us grow thicker. I don't just hear his heartbeat, I *feel* it—in the touch of our lips, in our entwining fingers. My toes curl from the tickle when a wisp of shadow slides over them like a happy snake. My shadow isn't sentient, but like a moth that knows it needs to fly toward light. It knows it now belongs to both me and Kyran.

And I'm not afraid of the trust I granted him. I've never been this at peace with another person.

"Do you sense it? Despite the collar?" I whisper, breathless, and hug him when he shakes his head.

"I want it gone. I need to *feel* you." Kyran squeezes me so hard I briefly lose my breath, but then he lifts me, and my ass meets the dense cushion of moss. I look around, realizing he's sat me on the altar.

I swallow and let the robe fall from my shoulders, hoping it's not blasphemy to invite him between my legs in this sanctuary. "I'm all yours," I say, meeting his gaze. "Shadow, soul, and *body*, after all."

His jaw twitches in response, and he pulls up his shirt, dropping it to the floor as if it weren't made from expensive silk. I unwind the sash tying my outfit at the waist, and as I remove the remaining fabric, my nakedness makes Kyran's eyes burn like two coals.

He reaches out, as if wanting to touch me already, but then instead kicks off his boots as if they're piranhas biting his feet. He slides off his pants, facing me naked, with his cock already growing. Only then does he step closer and pushes apart my thighs in a gesture so breathtaking I end up grabbing his arms to keep myself upright.

"My Dark Companion. My consort. You're the only one I need," he whispers, squeezing me tightly as if he can't stand there being a sliver of empty space between our bodies.

I wrap my arms around his powerful chest, now all mine, mine, mine. My gums tingle with the need to kiss him, but I also want him inside me already, so I can forget how much trouble we're in the world beyond the walls of the sanctuary.

"Don't hold back," I urge him and kiss his warm shoulder. "I want you to *feel* me the way I feel your shadow. Inside, out, all over."

He growls—like a dog over a bowl of delicious meat—and I am honored to be the meal he's claiming.

"I wouldn't dream of holding back. This altar never knew an offering this fine," he rasps, taking hold of my cock as he nips my neck.

I groan against his skin, my dick stiffening as soon as he caresses it with those long, skillful fingers. Our bond pulses faster, and I struggle to comprehend how magical that is while also feeling like the most natural thing in the world.

I stroke every inch of his muscular back, relearning each ridge and valley of his body. Even with the collar on, he is a beast of a prince.

"I will make sure you never have enough of me. Of this," he whispers as I rest both of my heels on the edge of the altar top and grind against him, because as much as I enjoy making love slowly and sweetly, right now I desire something else. Something fast and intense enough to stifle my fears and reassure us both.

Kyran clasps his hands on my hips and thrusts back, his eyes so black I almost believe his shadow escaped the control of the magical collar, but then he reaches for the cupboard and shows me a dark blue vial. "Get me nice and slick, *husband*."

I shiver and don't care to ask what's in it. I trust that he knows it's safe to use. Or I'm just too brainless with lust. Either way, I extend my hand and he pours the oily liquid into my palm. I'm kissing him again when I reach for his cock.

There hasn't been a day when we haven't fucked in one way or another, but I'm still just as thirsty for his dick as I was the first time. Thick and veiny, it pulses in my hand as I stroke it, and I can't wait to feel it pumping into my body.

"I want you to come inside me. I want you to fuck me so hard I can still feel it when I'm back in that tower," I whisper and nip on his bottom lip.

His fingers squeeze my sides, as if he wants to pull me apart and crawl inside, but then we're kissing, and my hands are around his neck, and—oh—his hot prick nudges my entrance. I coil under him, raising my hips as the void inside me grows in need of filling.

I make incoherent sounds into his mouth as we squeeze and stroke each other, but then he pushes inside, and I'm losing my sense of direction, gravity, and space. Yes, it feels *that* good, and I let every damn plant in this sanctuary know it as I raise my voice.

"Yes!" I wrap my arms around his neck, pulling him close. Is this really my life? *He* is my husband? A fucking *prince*? Who knows how to give it to me at that?

I clench my ass around his dick. I want him to feel as much pleasure as he can. I want to hear him moan against my neck, bite me, squeeze me, come inside me so I feel we're one. I use his strong body as leverage when I pull him lower and wrap my legs around him, feet on his gorgeous ass.

His gaze cuts into me like a knife into butter as he slides in, until his pubes hit my buttocks. He's braced above me, panting through his teeth as if he can't handle the pleasure of being inside me. The red lamps color his skin, the trees planted around us, even the rain rolling over the glass roof as he stiffens, stretches, and then flexes, making a sharp jab with his hips.

"I was always meant to have you like this. You were mine from the moment I pulled you from that river," Kyran rasps, wrapping me in his arms as his stomach works to rock that thick tool inside me.

He's right. I've lived my life dealing with mediocre men, when all this time I was meant for Kyran.

He fucks me almost too hard, but I love that edge of pain and moan out my desire. My own dick is stiff and leaking pre-cum, as he makes me his plaything. My legs are spread wide for him, and I just can't get enough of it.

"Yours. Always yours," I mumble incoherently, as he fucks my hole as if he wants to mark it as his.

I don't know. Maybe it's working.

All I can think of is the need to be his pliant Dark Companion. To give him my body the same way I offer him my shadow whenever he wishes to use it. He wants me before breakfast? Middle of the night? In the bath? In the damn throne room, on my knees? He can have me.

I'm obsessed with him. And the whole world can get lost as long as I have him between my legs. In my arms. In my mouth.

I dream of his hot cum drying on my skin and his beautiful hands squeezing my flesh. I want him to see only me and want only me. Forever.

"Oh, yes, darling... You feel amazing," he whispers, and that alone pushes me to the edge.

Kyran's features twitch, and he speeds up, fucking me as if he's trying to rival the pace of a machine gun. I arch off the mossy altar, tugging on my cock as my insides radiate hot sweetness. And then, under the Blood Moon, Kyran lets out a roar of triumph and comes inside me.

I moan with every thrust he still makes, creaming my needy hole. "That's it, I want every drop inside me," I utter breathlessly as I jerk off with his thick, throbbing dick buried deep inside me.

"I will give you as much as you want. I won't ever let you go," Kyran whispers, holding my gaze as he trembles, filling me with the heat of his desire. "These are mine to play with too."

When he pinches my nipple and pulls on it, I come so hard I don't care if my moans bring the guards in here. I'm pumped out, leaving jets of cum all over his stomach, and my mind could as well be the moss I'm sitting on, because I can't think. My husband looks like a dream come to life with his long black hair hanging to the sides of his flushed face.

I'm so completely in love with him.

We're married, we're shadowbound, and no one can take that away from us.

Our breaths grow more languid, our skin cools, but I'm not ready to let him go yet and play with his hair as he rests his weight on top of me, happy and sated, the collar keeping him from using his full potential forgotten.

I don't know what tomorrow has in store for us, but as I kiss Kyran's cheek, so very thankful that he saved me from myself all those years ago, I know we will survive if we face the unknown together.

CHAPTER 44

KYRAN

The tremor traveling from the floor all the way to my hip is yet another reminder of the impending danger, which my good-for-nothing brother ignored for far too long. But my personal safety and Luke's rests on even shakier foundations than the coast's current defenses against Heartbreak. Sabine is heavily pregnant and in no shape to fight, and Tristan has long given up his rights to the throne, which leaves me in a perilous position.

If I'm not allowed to compete for the title and it goes to one of the Goldweeds, we're both as good as dead. And while I wish I could be certain of victory in the event of fair combat, my fight against Vinia proved that deception and cunning are in Goldweed nature. I learned my lesson and will never be sure of anything until fate makes its judgment.

One thing I do know—extinguishing the Nightweed line has long been a wish of the Goldweeds, and they would not miss an opportunity like this. Which leaves me in pieces after a sleepless night. The joy of bonding with Luke kept my heart warm for many hours, but as he left and I grew cold, the weight of the responsibility resting on my shoulders crept in.

I kiss the antler ring Luke so lovingly slid on my finger last night and drop into a chair, staring at the moon rising above the ocean. Back when I was hidden away, freedom and a life of normal experiences seemed like an unachievable dream, but while I could envision material goods, privilege, and the attention of handsome men, I never let my imagination drift off to a fantasy where someone saw me as worthy of true affection.

When I claimed Luke a month ago, it didn't occur to me our bond could go beyond physical attraction, but he's become my world. I want to give him all the riches I have and the most tender affection. Everything I have is his, and last night, when he held me in the sanctuary, I knew that our feelings for one another would never falter. He is so sweet in the way he surprises me with little things and forgives me for my blunders. His heart is much kinder than he lets on, and I love that I'm the one who got to pry its shell open and feel its softness.

I need to stand triumphant today, if not for myself then for him.

A knock on the door startles me, and I get to my feet.

Sabine looks as though she hasn't slept all night, and that could actually be the case, for which I am eternally grateful. She is so far into her pregnancy and should be resting, not spending time navigating legal texts and arguing my case.

She gets straight to the point. "Because the prejudice against a twin is not law, and no one can actually prove fratricide was committed, you are allowed to participate in the tournament." She has to take a deep breath and holds her belly as her eyes close. I help her sit in the chair I've just vacated. She's pale, and her hair is more out of order than usual, but a smile tugs on her lips.

"You're really not Kyranis, are you?"

I flinch, stepping away. "I'm sorry. I didn't want to be deceitful. It just seemed like the only way to... join life," I utter.

She waves me off, and when I offer her a glass of coralberry juice, she drinks it all as she takes me in. "You don't have to explain it, little cousin. What's done is done, but I'm looking forward to getting to know you once all this is over."

I'm struck by a tightness in my throat, but when she smiles and strokes my forearm, I understand that she wants me to win this, and I kiss her cheek. "Thank you. May your child have all the blessings."

She chuckles. "Don't get so sentimental on me, Kyran. They're waiting for you at the arena." I exhale, nod, and rise to my feet, heading for the marble console by the entrance, where I left Gloomdancer. I'm dressed for the challenge, in my riding clothes, but it's only as I pick up the blade that reality sinks in.

I shall win the title. For myself *and* Luke.

"My promised as well?" I ask, anxious to see him.

Sabine smirks when I help her to stand. "You mean your *Dark Companion*?"

My heart beats faster when I remember I can call him that now. "And husband," I add with pride.

She shakes her head and walks with me to the carriage that will take her to the arena. "Congratulations. I heard from Tristan, and I can't wait to see the faces of the Goldweeds when the two of you announce the news. Elodie might also have a Dark Companion, but I've not heard from her yet."

I'm surprised she has no similar news on Anatole, but it's irrelevant, so I thank her once more and step outside, where two guards who arrested me yesterday wait for me with severe expressions. They were just doing their job, of course, but I let them roast in uncertainty and lead the way down the hallway, then across a reception space, and through the empty palace.

On days like this, even those lowest in rank are offered unconditional leave, so almost all the servants are at the arena, awaiting the spectacle.

I'm ready to give them one, and as I take Crab's reins from Drustan's hand, the slivers of doubt I've been plagued with all night start growing thin.

"Good luck, Your Highness," Drustan says before whistling for a mount of his own, and I embark on the royal trail, with the two guards as my entourage.

Sabine apologizes for keeping me collared, but apparently her husband, who is one of the Law Keepers, awaits me by the arena with a key. I can't wait to get the damn thing off. It's because of it that I almost didn't bond with Luke last night, so its existence grates on me even more. I was on the verge of tears, but Luke thought on his feet as usual and embraced me with his own shadow. I can't think of a more perfect way for him to use his new powers.

We begin our descent into the bay, but I can already see the arena built out of black rock in the shape of an amphitheater facing the sea. At least it's no longer raining, but the wind remains strong, and brings high waves onto the sunken stage. The moon is bright and silver when it slips out from behind the clouds to wish me luck. It was a witness to my marriage after all.

Spectators hold flags with the colors of all the royal houses, even the Bloodweeds, despite none of them participating in the challenge. The noise made by countless elves reminds me that my life and Luke's aren't the only ones at stake today. I am the superior choice for the new Lord—the most skilled warrior, and unlike Anatole or Elodie, I shall never prioritize my dynastic interests over the good of my people.

I know what it means to be left wanting.

I know how it hurts to be ignored.

I will not only be a champion in the hour of blood and sword, but also a fair Lord in peace time.

I need to win today.

And I shall.

As I ride through the open gates and onto the parade track climbing along the edge of the arena, the noise of the audience briefly dies, just to erupt in a mixture of cheering and jeers. It seems the entire principality has come to watch the freak of nature who replaced the heir apparent in secret. But I keep my head high and seek the familiar figure in the royal box.

Luke smiles at me, and the sight of him brightens my heart in ways I can't describe. He's a ray of moonlight in any darkness that might encroach on me. I want to keep him hidden from danger, but as my Dark Companion he's ready to be at my side, and he'd resent me if I didn't accept his help.

When I reach the box from which we will descend into the water, watched by all the spectators, I'm surprised to see not Elodie but Sylvan at Anatole's side. His expression is grim and he's also in his riding leathers, but strapped to them are dozens of vials and pouches. I have no idea what they might be for. Is he intending to poison the leviathan?

The crescent-shaped arena, huge enough to accommodate a sea monster, booms with noise, but when I step closer to Luke and spot my crest on the cape slung over his arm, I want to ravage him in the backrooms, after throwing out the servants. As I step closer, Anatole blocks my way in his fine black leathers, and spits between us with an expression colored by unadulterated loathing.

"You're a fraud and everyone here knows it, regardless of what the letter of the law says."

My fingers twitch with the desire to knock his jaw out of alignment, but I keep the fury in and meet his gaze as if he doesn't have the capacity to slight me. I'm satisfied enough to see that he's limping a little. Guess even the best potions can't heal a broken bone overnight.

"Is Elodie not participating after all?"

Sylvan takes a deep breath and avoids my gaze. Taking into account that he barely reaches my shoulder, he'd have to arch his head a lot to do that. He usually wears at least an inch of heel, but for the competition, he's opted for flats, and it shows.

"She drowned. The River of Souls took her."

I never had much love for Elodie, but it must hurt to lose two family members in such a short time, so I nod and say my condolences. It is only then that I notice the ribbon in faded hues on both the Goldweed brothers' shoulders, a symbol of mourning.

The one close person I ever lost was my mother, so I can't know how they feel. It is a shame that they're choosing to put their lives on the line too, in a fight that won't be even. Especially Sylvan, who's never had much talent for shadowcraft.

When Anatole refuses to move, I step around him instead of creating a scene and finally, *finally* reach out for Luke. Andros, who's been waiting alongside him, shows me a coal-black key and approaches me from behind with an apologetic expression.

I look into my beloved's deep green eyes when Andros unlocks the collar and pulls it off me.

Not that we've completed the marriage ritual, I was expecting to sense the warm embrace of his shadow, but instead lust spills into my heart, then drains down my body. It's like a hit of fairy dust, and I can't fight its intensity. My breath quickens, my heart beats faster, and my shadow seems to have gotten a mind of its own, because it pulls Luke closer before I can consider it myself. I've never experienced anything like it. My shadows are as voracious to lick and consume him as I am.

Luke chuckles and doesn't put up a fight when my dark appendages grab his ass. "Hello to you too, *husband* dearest."

I barely pay attention to the sudden silence around us, because when Luke's lips touch mine, I'm his completely.

It's impossible to miss Anatole hissing though, "You. Did. Not."

A wicked chuckle crawls up my throat, and I hug Luke, turning to take in both the Goldweeds and Tristan, who waves at me with a silly smile.

"Oh, I did."

Sylvan's pale as he clutches the utility belt armed with all the potions in the world. He's not too proud to ignore the fact that his already small chances of winning the contest have just become miniscule.

"But…. that's an unfair advantage," he says, frowning at Andros, who clears his throat and offers both my opponents a tight smile.

"Unfortunately, there is nothing in the rules of succession about treating a situation like this as anything special. You were both well within your rights to join your sister and procure Dark Companions of your own."

"They were separated!" Anatole yells, pointing to us as if his tantrum can undo our bond. "Both had guards at their doors. How did this happen?"

Andros spreads his arms. "I do not know. They were both in their respective quarters in the morning."

Luke bites back a smile. Unable to keep his hands to himself either, he wraps his arm around my waist.

"Well, then you can perish together." Anatole glares at us, no longer bothering to keep up the mask of politeness. I don't know if this is worse than his prostrating and groveling, or if I prefer to see his true face.

I glance at Sylvan's tense features. "You can still back out of this."

He flushes like an untouched bride on her wedding night. "No. I've made up my mind. You're underestimating me, like everyone else, but when I'm crowned, I will change how things are done." There's a surprising amount of conviction in his voice. He really thinks he can win this.

Anatole squints at his brother. "A crown might make you a little taller, but not bigger where it counts," he says and, in a gesture so vulgar I didn't expect it in this setting, even from him, he glances at Sylvan's crotch.

I might not like Sylvan, but I pity him now. These are the exact bully tactics my brother used over the years to make me feel like living in his shadow was my only choice. That if I ever showed my true self to anyone, they would despise me without exception. That I didn't deserve respect or love just because of the order of our birth.

I can't keep quiet.

"He's the only sibling you have left," I say, but before either of the brothers can respond, the crowd above and around us roars at the horn announcing the arrival of the leviathan.

I look back in time to see the pearly white hump glimmer above the surface as beaters chase him into the mouth of the arena, and the huge doors completing its circle rise above the water.

This is it. Sink or swim in its purest form, because if I don't win, I don't trust any of the brothers to keep me and Luke alive. If I lose, I'll attempt to flee with my husband while there's still commotion. Otherwise, we're as good as dead.

Andros raises his arm, and I spot Sabine joining Tristan with flushed cheeks.

"There are three contenders for the throne!" Andros tells the excited crowd, amplifying his voice with a big Ostar shell. "Prince Kyra....n Nightweed, Prince Anatole Goldweed, and his brother, Prince Sylvan Goldweed. They will descend into the water on kelpies to prove their skill in facing a beast of the sea and attempt to remove a pearl from under the leviathan's tongue. Whoever manages it first, and brings it to the chalice," he makes an elegant gesture toward a large silver goblet in the middle of the royal box, "will become our new Lord. Until the pearl is in place, any means of winning are allowed."

The last part sends a murmur through the crowd, and I'm all too aware of what this means. I might get the pearl but still have to watch out for Anatole stabbing me in the back to pry it out of my hands.

I mount Crab, who is so eager to get in the water he paces in place. Soon his back legs will turn into a fishtail, and his front hooves will grow shiny black webbing, so he can carry me in the waves with ease. At least in the arena, the sea is only as violent as the leviathan's movements make it. But when Luke approaches to squeeze my hand, and we both watch the beast coil in the vast pool of water, the horn blows again. And then, again. It's a frantic cry that has our audience get to their feet.

"What is that?" Luke asks in a dull voice, and when I stand in the stirrups, narrowing my eyes to see what brought on the shrieks I'm starting to hear, a new island emerges from the waters beyond the arena, on the far-off horizon.

But it's no island, and every single person gathered for the event realizes it at the same time.

"Run, Heartbreak is coming!"

CHAPTER 45

Kyran

The audience descends into chaos, and I only snap out of the shock when a man is knocked out of his row by a group of running youngsters and drops into the seats below. It's every elf for themself now, but I will stand strong. It is my duty to protect my people at all cost, even those who called me Sunspawn out of their seats in the auditorium.

Still, while I am an experienced fighter, with many eels on my skin to prove it, I have never taken on a beast like the mountain rising ever higher above the surface and sending giant waves toward the arena.

Fearful for its life, the leviathan thrashes, but he wouldn't be any safer in the strip of sea between the shore and the approaching monster, so I ignore the way it sprays water out of the hole on its back and glance at Tristan.

"We need Lady Guinevere and Carol. Fetch them!"

Sabine stares out into the sea, grabbing her stomach with a pained moan.

No. Not now.

But, of course, it just *had to* happen now.

Her husband is at her side, but Tristan looks up at me wide-eyed. I understand his question without words.

"Make sure she's safe," I tell him. "Get Lady Guinevere! Alert the knights at the palace. If... If we fail to stop the beast, you will be the only prince left."

He nods, already taking Sabine into his arms. "I will send reinforcements. You just need to keep it away for long enough."

He wants to reassure me, but we both know it's a gamble at this point. So many great shadow wielders died seven years ago, our force is much depleted, *and* we only have two Dark Companions on our side.

"What do I do?" Luke asks, tugging on my arm. Despite his paleness, he's ready to take on the responsibility. I chose so well with him. If I could remember the exact date I pulled him out of the River of Souls, I'd make it a holiday at the Nocturne Court.

Anatole mounts his kelpie with a focused expression but Sylvan stares at the approaching mountain of flesh as if he's become a statue. We can't see all of Heartbreak well. It's far away, and some of its shape is obscured by shadows, but in the far distance, what we know to be arms, legs, guts and faces move without reason, twitching and stirring as if Heartbreak is covered in maggots.

Some elves' hearts can stop at just the sight of it, before the beast even reaches them. But most also know this and don't stick around to stare at the gore-filled spectacle making its way to the shore.

I slide off my kelpie and pull Luke into my arms, smelling his hair and attempting to remember the warmth and texture of his skin. I wish I could be sure this fight will end in victory, but there aren't many of us, and if my father and so many of his knights fell in the last battle against Heartbreak, how am I to predict the outcome of this day?

This might be mine and Luke's last hug, last kiss, but even if we both perish, I don't regret a single thing.

"I... I don't think I can do it," says a voice so quiet I barely pick up the words in the noise around us.

My nose slides across Luke's cheekbone when I glance at Sylvan, who's clutching at his damn potions. They might have been enough to outwit two elves, but most definitely not go against a monster capable of swallowing hundreds of lives in one attempt. His lips quiver, his hands shake, and I find myself pitying him, because retreat is the sensible thing in his situation. Why throw away one's life in an unwinnable fight?

"Help alert anyone who might not know what's happening. Someone has to do it," I say harshly and kiss Luke's forehead.

Anatole scoffs. "You just want all the glory," he says and doesn't even bother to look back at his brother as he slides on a mask meant for breathing underwater and urges his kelpie to dive right in.

Sylvan nods at me and turns away, but I notice him wiping away tears. Of fear or shame? I don't have time to work it out. Someone this afraid of the monster would only be a hindrance in a fight with Heartbreak.

I focus on Luke and cup his cheeks. I hate that I can already hear some of the screeches coming from the open mouths on Heartbreak's monumental body, because it means the beast is too close, and I don't have much more time.

"I'm sending you to my shadowild, so you can be with me and stay safe. You remember how to get out if you need to? You will have to reach the shore. You won't be able to cross the veil while out at sea."

He nods but the twist of his lips breaks my heart. He's so brave. And he doesn't try to convince me that we should flee, though I have no doubt he's terrified for both our safety.

"I love you. Please stay as safe as you can," he says, rubbing one eye.

My whole being aches with the need to protect him, even at the cost of many lives, but this is the day I was born for, and by tying his life to mine, Luke agreed to share this burden with me.

This is our destiny.

"I love you too, Dark Companion." And with that, I let my shadow cover him whole, until he's merely a dark shape. His material form is safe in the shadowild. I won't let him be harmed, and now that he too has the gift of shadowcraft, he should be able to free himself if I am no longer there to help him. Just thinking about this being our last goodbye hurts like getting stabbed, but if I am to be the Lord of the Nocturne Court, I need to be worthy of it.

Crab's salivating and nervously stomping at our side, and I pet his neck as the mountain of mangled flesh comes ever closer. Like the embodiment of death, it obscures even the moon. I mount my kelpie, turn it around, and storm toward the gate of the arena, with Luke's weightless presence behind me.

While I sense his arms around my waist, a shadow cannot speak, so the touch will have to suffice for reassurance.

I pull on the mask made of the same squid leather as my outfit. It has artificial gills at the cheeks to help me breathe underwater if Crab needs to dive. The glass lenses obscure some of my vision, but it's better than salt stinging my eyes.

There's no time to lose. When we reach the edge of the arena, I slap my mount on the side, and the kelpie dives straight into the sea, unafraid of the beast ready to devour our hearts. Or maybe he just doesn't yet comprehend the threat.

Anatole is ahead of me, and while no one has spoken about it, it seems obvious that if either of us manages to stop Heartbreak, the title of Lord will be theirs. I have no doubt that is what propels my ratbag of a cousin toward the terror in front of us against all reason.

Crab twitches under me as his hindquarters shift into their true form, but while he attempts to dash to the side at first, almost as if he's trying to flee from the monster, I pull on the reins and click my tongue to direct him back toward the mass of twitching flesh. The moonlight reveals only so much from afar, but my stomach sinks, and my thighs stiffen as it rolls my way. Every instinct in my body tells me to run as far as I can and leave others to be devoured, but I am better than that, and it doesn't matter that what I can observe of the creature is as big as a third of my castle. We're in deep waters, and for all I know, I am only seeing a fraction of its corpulent form on the surface.

We don't know how many hearts we need to find and stab to make the beast retreat, as a number has never been determined. It will be my job to eviscerate as many as needed, and if I'm lucky, Anatole will help, not hinder my efforts. At this point, I'd even be willing to do the leviathan challenge with him again, if we both survive. It seems like child's play in comparison to the task ahead.

Luke presses my cheek, making me look to the side in time to notice a massive wave. I urge Crab to duck under it, and my steed couldn't be happier, as it's in the water that he is most in his element.

As soon as I can see under the waves, I'm struck that the ball of flesh, bone, and blubber reaches so deep I can't see the end of it. It's so enormous the farthest parts of it disappear in the darkness beneath us.

We emerge much closer to the creature, and my heart beats unnaturally fast. As if it can sense that if I die here, it will be forever entombed in Heartbreak's monstrous body.

The despairs now seem like barely dandruff shed by the beast, specks of dust in comparison to the size of this behemoth.

"Cold feet?" Anatole yells, even though he's surely on the verge of losing his mind as well.

The flesh mountain pulses, as if the countless souls it's swallowed over millennia are attempting to get out, but I know that the arms, legs, and grotesque tentacles growing out of the misshapen creature wiggle about looking for their next victim, not freedom.

Purple like bruised flesh, it's so close the proximity is making my head spin, as if I'm standing on the edge of a cliff, but then Crab whinnies, losing balance, and I spot an intestine-like tendril wrapped around my mount's front leg. Terror crawls up my spine, but Luke's shadow holds me closer, and I snap out of my stupor, reaching for my sword. I let my own darkness cover the blade, unwilling to waste Luke's shadow for anything but the beast's hearts. I hold on to Crab's mane as I lean down and sever the tentacle, freeing him.

I don't bother to acknowledge Anatole's childish question, too startled by the screech of dozens of mouths opening all over Heartbreak's flank, and as I pull on Crab's reins to slow him, eyes open to stare at me. Some are human, some in colors only elves can have, some dilated with fear, others squint at me, full of anger.

When Crab bucks under me and whinnies, I ignore the fear burning in the pit of my stomach, slide my feet out of the stirrups and stand on my steed's back. Crab's trembling under me, unsteady as he recoils from the reach of a long arm with skin peeling off to reveal bone. It's shaped like an elf's but vastly longer, as if it belonged to an ancestor outgrowing me by half.

I don't *want* to see more of the beast, but I need unobstructed vision to succeed so I pull my mask off. I regret it when I get a whiff of the pungent stench of Heartbreak's flesh.

But before Crab can shake me off, I leap up, using my shadow to give myself momentum. Luke's touch is constant, as if his weightless presence is a long-lost limb, not a ghost at my side. I wish us both a good judgment day as I descend onto the huge predator and stab a bloated mound of flesh pulsing in an all-too familiar rhythm.

When pus seeps out of the open wound revealing a tar-black heart, I can no longer push away the inevitable. I need Luke's potent shadow.

I stare up at him, worried he might back out, too afraid now that he's seeing the madness up close, but his expressionless face remains turned toward me. He steps closer, knowing exactly what I have to do.

My Dark Companion spreads his arms in invitation, and I press the tip of my blade to his chest. I dip the Gloomdancer into his shadow, unreasonably worried. I *know* what I'm doing, just smothering the sword without hurting my mate in any way, but it still messes with my head to see a blade embedded in his chest.

I rip it out, filled with fresh rage at Heartbreak and stab my sword into the black, pulsing organ. I don't know who this heart once belonged to, but they are no longer with us.

The beast stirs, making everything around me shake, and my blade cuts into the twisted mass making up most of the monster as gravity pulls me back toward the water. I bite the inside of my cheek when I need to kick away a wretched, rotten arm. When my sword catches on a bone, I stop sliding down and grab at a misshapen appendage to steady myself before glancing to the side, at the gray figure standing next to me as if gravity didn't work on it at all. Luke nods at me, as if to signify he's fine.

The monster beneath my feet growls, sending a tremor up my limbs. I solidify my shadow to give myself more support as I start my climb, trying not to think too much about the soft mass under my feet being the flesh of elves Heartbreak has accumulated over centuries. Countless lives lost. And for what? To feed its insatiable hunger?

Three shadow tendrils grow out of my back, assisting the ascent, and while the monster is monitoring me with fields of mismatched eyes, I ignore them, on my way to the top.

Luke is right by my side, crawling up on all fours without trouble, because his immaterial fingers easily slide into Heartbreak, and he weighs nothing. Most importantly, he cannot be killed by a physical force when he's like this, so I don't have to worry about him.

Anatole's cursing my whole bloodline, the Realm, and the Sea of Sorrows, but when I spot him at last, he's almost unrecognizable, with dark blood coloring his skin and hair. Heartbreak growls and shifts to the side, like a ball turning in the water, and momentum sends me toward Anatole.

He squeezes a fatty mound with his thighs and slashes at a whole cluster of black, pulsing hearts, shrieking like a madman. Without a Dark Companion, he had to infuse his blade with his own shadow and it flickers, fading with every heart he manages to pierce.

I fight gravity as the beast keeps turning in an effort to shake us off, but just as I'm about to lose my footing, Luke solidifies next to me, keeping me from tumbling off, and I seize the opportunity to slash at a big, red blob. Rancid blood explodes all over me, and I press my tongue against my palate in a desperate attempt not to smell it. But the beast thrashes and shakes, so I continue, getting ever closer to Anatole as Heartbreak shifts, forcing me to move.

Beyond my cousin's back are the green lights of the arena, and I roar, stabbing another heart while Luke assists me, unaffected by the shaking.

Anatole falls over, frantically grabbing at a white rock oddly reminiscent of a chair-sized tooth, and when his eyes peek at me, two white ovals embedded in blood-red features, he sneers, gasping for air.

"You cheated all of us. You never deserved a Dark Companion to begin with, Sunspawn!" He spits the insult out as though he might resent *me* more than the beast we're both fighting.

He jabs the flesh nearby to stabilize his position, the flesh mountain stirs, and I lean back when the surface under my feet parts. Rows of pearly whites—smooth, flat, or extremely sharp—peek at me from inside the gash opening in the monster, wide as if it was struck by a castle-sized axe. They're not arranged in any sensible way, yet form a mouth, which makes the sight even more of a horror.

I stumble away from it just as the beast's toxic exhale reaches my senses, only to meet a hard body. I look back to see a flash of blond hair soaked with dark red blood, but before I can decide what's happening, a shove sends me toward the huge mouth with a throbbing sphincter at the very bottom of its red throat.

Terror flashes through my body, but as my Dark Companion slows my descent, I twist my body and yank at Anatole's arm. The beast chooses this moment to shake in a spasm of muscles, and my cousin rolls past me with a shriek. His shadow tentacles grab the first rows of teeth, but the intestines twitching inside the monstrous mouth have already captured him, twisting around his limbs and midsection.

Anatole's eyes are wide when his hand slips, and he hits his chin on a large tooth, but when his gaze meets mine, he reaches for me, as if he didn't attempt to toss me into that very same hell moments ago.

I see his shadow wrestle the creature's appendages, but he's weakening and utters something through his teeth. I can't understand the words, but I know what he's asking for.

Mercy. For me to help him, when *he* wouldn't piss on me if I were on fire. When instead of fighting alongside me, he tried to push me to my death.

For a split second, I consider that maybe he could be useful in the future, but the truth is that he'd stab me in the back at his earliest convenience.

So I slice apart another heart instead of moving any closer.

His eyes fill with tears that soon spill, washing away some of the blood on his cheeks, but the sound he makes is pure fury. At least until it turns into a scream of agony when the fleshy tentacles wrapped around his body coil. Anatole's face pales, and his eyes bulge while his hips get twisted sideways with a terrifying snap of bone. Then again. And again. Blood gushes out of his mouth when the beast pulls his bottom half off, dragging it down its mouth pit. As death claims Anatole, his hold on the teeth loosens, his shadows disperse, and his torso rolls down lifelessly.

My head's burning with pure terror as I lean forward, watching the sphincter unclench to reveal concentric rows of fangs leading deeper into the massive beast. Anatole's head pops like a blood-filled balloon as soon as the muscles holding the sharp teeth tighten around it. I need to fight off a wave of nausea when some of it sprays up, and I sense the tiniest bit of new wetness on my skin.

I seek Luke's support as the lipless mouth narrows, and the monster rolls to the other side, so the farther edge of the open cavern looms above my head. I'm about to recoil and get out of reach of those damn teeth when a familiar moan makes me look up, to where flesh bulges, pushing teeth apart. It's like watching a wart grow at an alarming speed, and my stomach drops when I realize it's gaining the shape of a face. A familiar one at that. When Anatole, whose face I've just seen crushed, stares at me with terror-stricken eyes and utters a scream so sharp it could make me bleed, I sense madness knocking at my door.

His tongue rolls out, unnaturally long, and his eyes bulge, each looking in opposite directions. I can't move. Or think. Or even yell in fear, but as I fight through the stupor, knowing I can either fight or die, something cuts my legs from under me, and I tumble down the funnel of flesh and teeth.

A creak resonates in my ear, and a part of me knows it's Luke shouting my name in a realm beyond a thin veil of shadows, but there's no stopping my descent toward the loosening mouth pit.

All I can hope for is that when my body becomes one with so many others, my spirit will not stay alongside it.

Because I'm about to die, crushed and ripped apart like my cousin.

Full of regret, I cling to memories of the one thing that was good about my life.

TAKEN BY THE LORD OF THE NOCTURNE COURT

My Luke.

CHAPTER 46

KYRAN

There's that moment when I almost want to let Heartbreak have me, because when memories play through my head like a theater of madmen, I struggle to see much of worth in my past. So many lonely days, shame, humiliation over not being my brother. My life only started when I let him perish, and as I think of Luke watching me last night when we shared promises on the mossy altar in the Ancestral Sanctuary, my blood heats up again.

I still have so much to do, so many kisses to give. I refuse to forsake the future. When my thoughts sharpen, shredding uncertainty and fear, I try to slow my descent toward the monster's throat. I swallow a grunt when my forearm clashes with one of the massive teeth, but pain can't stop me, and as I tumble, both my hands rip at the sleeve of my leather top.

One of the eels I keep on my skin would be enough.

Just one.

I don't have time to coax it closer and rip it off despite the abrupt gesture feeling like opening a wound. The eel squirms in my hand, but I manage to inhale it while pushing the fingers of my other hand into the beast's flesh. If I'm lucky, I'll be able to slow my fall for just enough time—

Luke grabs my wrist, giving me additional stability. His shadowy face has no features, but his brows seem to furrow in exertion while he holds me up.

The power from the eel hits me, coursing through me like fairy dust, and my mouth stretches into a smile as heat throbs in my veins.

I try not to think of the monster's muscles clenching right under my feet in a desperate bid to crush me too. He can't have me. Four black tentacles shoot up to grab the teeth high above, then I stab my sword into flesh for leverage. I'm already sweating, exhausted, and I prioritize my safety over looking for more of the black hearts. I can't chase Heartbreak away from our shores if I'm dead.

I will not end up like Anatole. Not with Luke watching. But as that thought passes through my head, I wonder what would happen to him if I got out, and *he* ended up as the beast's meal. He cannot be harmed by the material world while he's in the shadowild, but if the beast swallowed him and carried him away, neither of us would have a way to free him. He can't leave the shadow realm in the sea. He'd be stuck forever, like my father's poor Dark Companion, and die of thirst and starvation, all alone in the dark.

I cannot let that happen. I need to fight, if not for myself, then for him.

But as I'm about to leap and get out of the monster's throat, something wraps around my neck and squeezes hard. The world darkens, my limbs weaken, and it takes all my focus and strength to not drop Gloomdancer.

Luke's shadow figure reaches toward me as the tentacle drags me down the funnel of flesh and teeth. I reach back, but my brain is shutting off from the pressure just below my jaw.

It's a goodbye after all.

He hesitates, only to dash my way, on a suicide mission that might end up with him stuck alongside my corpse forever. I grab at the veiny noose dragging me to my death and try to shout, but I cannot produce sound anymore. From the corner of my eye, I see the edges of the toothy sphincter widen to swallow me whole, but as I fall in, to my inevitable death, Luke disintegrates into a splash of gray reminiscent of quicksilver and hits me with his warmth.

His shadow covers me from my feet to the tip of my head. The tentacles around my neck snap as if his form is a guillotine. The monster's teeth try to crush my legs when I fall, but Luke's shadow is steel. He's utilizing the skills I taught him, and the exertion is costing him everything. I can already feel it through our bond. He's half-lucid but keeps holding on to me as my shield.

I drop into something soft and wet, finally catching my breath as blood rushes back to my brain, offering clarity of mind.

I'm inside Heartbreak, the beast my people fear more than anything, yet Luke's shadow is hugging me from every side, and I've never felt safer. He's there for me the same way I want to stand by him, and this material proof of his love makes my heart soar even as I face muscular walls.

I'm grateful that I cannot smell the rot around me, because some of the flesh is bloated and discolored as if it's about to burst and cover me with pus. But I can still see, and when I face a collection of bones and muscle still covered in ripped leather, I need to compose myself to avoid leaving the contents of my stomach inside the beast.

Anatole's form is already being incorporated into the creature, his ribcage wide open. His heart is frantically pulsing with the energy of a fresh kill. I resented this man, and he felt the same about me, but no one deserves a fate like this, so I stab his blackening heart, and as it bleeds out, I can almost sense Anatole's spirit leaving in peace. He deserves this much mercy.

I look around, because there's no time to lose. Luke's shadow is paling, and I worry that he'll overexert himself. But when I ask him to rest, the flat imprint of his form darkens. Such a stubborn man. But he is doing this for us, so I ignore the worry caused by his quickening heartbeat and focus, because he'll only be able to keep this up for so long.

That's when I spot them.

Right above me, huge clusters of black hearts are attached to the roof of this... stomach like leeches, all beating in one rhythm. I sense their beating under my feet and all around me.

I grab my sword, tasting victory on my tongue. In the attempt to kill me, the beast let me into its treasure trove.

I *will* make this ravenous giant retreat, and then cut my way out of its innards, back into the moonlight. Excitement reverberates in my bones as I reach into the rip on my chest and coax an eel to the surface. I can sense its trepidation as I pluck it off my flesh, but then its smoky form dissolves into my lungs, and I leap, grabbing at a vein as thick as my bicep to hold myself up as I stab and slash.

The muscular walls throb with a shuddery moan, but what other encouragement do I need? I want this beast gone, and I shall stop at nothing.

Tendrils like fingers with endless knuckles attempt to grab me, stall me, but Luke's protection keeps me invulnerable to their grasp, and as I cut through the hearts of the behemoth's many victims, it becomes clear we have been fighting him wrong this whole time.

Heartbreak does not have many weak points in its outer shell, but now that I'm inside him, protected by my Dark Companion, hearts of all shapes and sizes are like fruit in a gory orchard.

Ripe and ready to be plucked with my sword made razor-sharp by Luke's human shadow. I spare none I can see. I might not be able to topple Heartbreak's mountainous form today, but if I can do enough damage to keep it away for a hundred years or more, it will be a service to the Realm, and to myself. Maybe one day we can hunt this beast down, bring the fight to its lair when we're ready, and end it once and for all.

I'm smiling when I slash through several hearts in one go, unbothered by the rain of thick black blood spilling on me. But then Luke's hold on me weakens, and I feel our bond falter as his shadow form slides off my shoulders.

Panic takes hold, and I gather all my power to keep him close. My shadow forms a cradle for his form, enclosing him against my back, but as his protection withdraws, I'm hit by the stench of death. It's excruciating, like having rotten mice carcasses rubbed into my nose and tongue, but fetor won't kill me. Losing Luke would.

Our situation dawns on me in a flash when the muscular walls around me flex, and I reach to my chest, ripping out two eels at a time, and then a third, once the two pass down my trachea.

I have never felt such immense power. As red tints the edges of my vision, I leap up to find the sphincter gone, as if the monster has altered its form since swallowing me. Confusion only lasts a moment, and I slash through a heart, then deeper into distended flesh.

A part of me hopes Luke would soon recover and come to, but he remains immobile, the spark of life inside him flickering so weakly it's putting me in a state of despair.

Not him. Please, anyone but him.

I'm in a frenzy, and as my form changes, overflowing with shadow, I sheathe my sword and unleash the beast within. I let my claws grow and rip at the flesh in the beast's side. Even if the wall of Heartbreak's body is thicker than the outer walls of my palace, they're not endless and I *will* get through them.

The monster trembles, but I keep clawing through flesh, blubber, and tendons, so it takes me a while to realize I'm sensing Heartbreak's descent.

It's retreating. Going back into the ocean and deeper underwater.

And it's taking us with it.

I can't dig this gore-filled tunnel any faster, but I still try. Covered in my own shadows, I am able to swallow the eels off my body without using my hands. I'm like a maggot, but instead of burrowing into Heartbreak's flesh, I'm set on fighting my way out. My only solace is that Luke's still alive, and I need to get to him, the real him.

My body is covered in blood and other secretions, but I'm not terrified anymore. I consume eels every time I grow weaker, but as I take Luke's shadow deep into my own, each second starts with new determination.

I slash, hit, drill, just to be farther from the center of the beast and closer to the surface, but when my claws cut through a thick membrane and hit water, I'm so elated that for a moment the purpose of all this suffering is forgotten. It's only when I listen to Luke's pulse again that I gather my remaining strength and rip myself out into the moonlit waters.

The empty depths would have been frightening any other time. Now they feel like salvation, and I flap my monstrous arms about, beckoned by the shimmering surface above.

Heartbreak is such a massive presence in the sea, its movement creates currents and whirls that keep sucking me in. But I won't surrender. I'd give my last breath to get Luke out of here, but when I spot a familiar figure in the water, it's a relief to know that won't be necessary. Crab swims our way with the agility only a creature born in the sea can have. He comes close enough for me to grab his mane and then we go up, up, up, faster than if he were a balloon of air.

Exhaustion hits me with new force, and I shed my shadow form on the way to the surface, holding on to Luke. My muscles are on fire, my lungs ache from burning through all the eels, and I want to collapse into a bed.

As soon as my head is above water, I gasp for air and pull Luke close.

Heartbreak is now only a dark shape looming far below. For how long have I managed to chase him away? One day we will find out.

"Luke! Luke, wake up," I beg, nudging Crab with my heels so he swims faster. The shore's getting closer, but I cannot dive into the shadowild before we reach it, and the uncertainty of it is killing me.

I'm pretty sure he's starting to loll his head on my shoulder, and as soon as Crab hits the beach, just off the arena, I jump off his back and sink into my shadowild. Someone's yelling my name, but I ignore them, focused on Luke. I've heard of Dark Companions falling into month-long comas or even dying after the power of their shadows was abused, and while Luke was the one who chose to prioritize me over his own wellbeing, I cannot allow such a tragic end to our story.

Entering the other realm is second nature, and I can do so even in the state of fatigue I'm in. When I spot Luke, spread out on a pedestal of shadows and pale as if death has claimed him already, I let out a frantic whine.

"My love," I utter, joining him, full of trepidation, but when his eyes open at my touch, a massive weight lifts off my chest. His plump lips part, and I kiss them, hoping to pass him some of my own life force.

Luke's face is stained with blackened tears, and when he speaks, his voice is raspy as if he's been screaming for hours. "Y-you're okay?" He utters and tries to sit up, but his arms feel so weak around me I hold him up instead.

"Yes. You saved me. And through that *you* saved us all," I whisper, brushing my lips against his forehead as we hug in the black expanse of the shadowild, safe from monsters and prying eyes.

He rubs his cheek against mine. "Teamwork."

I'm not sure what that means exactly, but I nod. "Teamwork."

Luke has the funniest little expression, which reminds me of the pleased face Flap makes when he's fed coralberries.

"Has Heartbreak really retreated? Is it over?" Luke asks with a whisper as his hug becomes a little firmer.

I nod, then kiss him, then nod again as we squeeze one another, riding the waves of relief. "We were born for this day," I tell him, resting my forehead against his.

Luke glances at me with tears in his eyes. "Is it normal that I feel like... there's a hole in my stomach?"

For a moment, I look down between us, terrified, but then reality dawns on me. He's starving. I have to laugh. "Yes. We'll eat as soon as possible."

I say we, but until I get the smell of Heartbreak's insides out of my throat, I won't be eating *anything*.

Luke smiles back at me. "I love you. I was so scared."

TAKEN BY THE LORD OF THE NOCTURNE COURT

I'm stuck with my mouth open as the echo of fear comes over me, flashing our lucky escape through my head. "Me too. You fainted. I worried you might not wake up. When I said I'd never take your power for as long as I have my own, I was not just reciting a phrase. But you risked everything for me. Thank you," I whisper, because as good as it would feel to ask that he never takes such risks again, I am eternally grateful for his aid.

"You did something even better. You gave *me* power, so I could choose to protect you. I saw what… happened to Anatole. I would do anything to prevent you from meeting the same fate. You're my beloved prince." He strokes my cheeks with a smile, and the bond I was so desperate to feel yesterday throbs between us.

With him as my Dark Companion, I'm ready to face the world.

We kiss as I pull us out of the shadowild, and once again, there's a breeze on my skin and black sand under us. It's so quiet without Heartbreak's reverberating roars I could wrap myself around him like a she-wolf around her pups and fall asleep right here, on the shore. But we are no longer alone, and as I look up to take in the guards, Tristan, Lady Guinevere, Carol, and many others who chose to stay and fight, in case I failed, a sense of contentment settles in my chest.

"Heartbreak will be gone for a while," I say before settling my gaze on Sylvan, who stands meekly in the back. "I am sorry about your brother. He fought bravely," I lie, because there is no point in describing his shameful actions.

Only now I realize that I ripped apart my top for easy access to the eels. I've burnt through them all over the course of the battle, and only the golden sun is left to mark my skin. I am no longer ashamed of it, and silently challenge the onlookers to accuse me of crimes against my brother now, after I saved them all.

No one dares.

Baroness Olivia Goldweed clenches her fist by her mouth and throws her remaining son a hateful glare, but she says nothing.

Sylvan is bone-pale and dirty as he steps forward in the silence interrupted only by the sound of waves hitting the shore. He goes down to one knee in the black sand. "All hail, Lord of the Nocturne Court, Kyran Nightweed. Ruler of the Shadowild, Protector of the Nightmare Realm, and Knight of Grief Ocean."

There will be no more fighting for the title. The gathered knights kneel one by one, and Luke raises my hand to his lips, kissing the wedding ring he made for me.

They all know what I am, that I am a sunspawn, and they accept me as their Lord.

The nobles brave enough not to hide in the palace start clapping and cheering.

Not for my brother.

For me.

EPILOGUE

Luke

Over the years, I had so many dreams about moving out of Mom's home. They always involved showing her that I could make something out of myself, that I'm proud of who I am, as an artist and gay man.

I just never thought I'd be doing it in style.

Kyran insisted we come prepared, so now there are two massive kelpie-drawn wagons parked behind our uber-goth carriage, and elven servants course between my old room and the vehicles, fetching my clothes, books, and everything else I've accumulated over the years. Neighbors watch on from their porches and windows, and if they have any comments about me or the tall, dark, and handsome gentleman holding me under his arm, they're keeping them to themselves.

My mother will no doubt hear all about it tomorrow. But that won't be my problem anymore. I can't wait to be out of here. The plan is to spend months decorating our new apartments within the palace and fill them with all the lovely things I've squirreled away over the years. I even have a few gifts for Sabine's baby boy, Nathan. She will surely be over the moon to get some human toys.

Mother's standing by the door, watching every box. She warned me that I better make sure I'm only taking *my* possessions. She seems smaller, and so much less imposing now that she holds no power over me. She's just a lady in her forties in a canary-yellow cardigan, with short blonde hair, and a golden cross around her neck.

I try to ignore her altogether, because she yelled at me when I appeared. Both over being gone for over a month, and for arriving without warning with the intention to move.

Though she later mumbled something about it being appropriate that I lurk at night, since I'm the spawn of Satan.

When one of the servants passes us with a box of books, I grab *Dracula* from the top and show it to Kyran.

"Look! The book I told you about. I can't wait for you to read it."

He strokes the gold-embossed letters of the title and leans in to kiss my head. "We should give it a better cover," he says, which likely means that he wants the paperback rebound in leather. He is the Lord of the Nocturne Court after all, so why not?

"Could you at least have the decency to refrain from lewd behavior in public?" Mom says in the loudest of whispers.

Kyran frowns at me. "She must be exceedingly bored to care about trivial things like other people's romantic habits."

"I can hear you!" Mom raises her voice. I think she's frustrated that something is going right for me for once. She wants me to be as miserable as she has always been.

I spread my arms. "Good!"

"Where shall I put these, my Lord?" One of the servants asks, presenting him with a box of old soap and shampoo bottles which I don't have the heart to admit are pretty much worthless.

"You can put them in the main wagon, just make sure they don't spill over the other items," Kyran says as if all of my belongings were precious. I love him so much.

"*Lord*," Mom scoffs, shaking her head.

I square my shoulders. "Now you have a problem with my *husband's* title?"

She wags her finger at me. "The only Lord you need is our Lord and Savior Jesus Christ!"

At my side, Kyran stands straighter. "Who is he?"

I swear, this entire trip is worth the expression of utter bewilderment on my mom's face.

"Ha. Ha. Very funny. Be a darling and practice your atheism off my property," she says with a disgusted sneer.

Kyran lifts his chin, pulling me a little closer, and his protectiveness makes my heart melt. "I don't know what that means, but I could easily take on this lord of yours in a duel."

I snort and turn my face into Kyran's shoulder, because I might disintegrate from sheer amusement.

"You can't duel Jesus Christ!" My mother raises her voice, all serious, which makes the exchange even more surreal. "I am done here! I don't care if you ever come back," she yells and walks into the house, slamming the door.

Which is extra awkward because one of the elven servants is still inside, and looks at us through the window, unsure what to do.

Moments later, Mom opens the door for him, but in a way that allows her to remain unseen, and slams it right behind him.

Kyran hums and wraps me in his arms, affectionate as ever. "She's certainly... a character. But she was the one to mention the local lord. I did not start it."

I stroke his chest with a grin. "You did not." I give him a kiss in front of the spying neighbors and turn to the carriage.

Flap is inside, in a large cage, and I want to reassure him that we're almost done, but Kyran pulls on my arm.

"I have something special for you."

I love being showered with his thoughtful gifts, so I grin with excitement.

He leads me to the large trunk at the back of our carriage with a satisfied smile, as if he's particularly proud of himself. He lifts the lid, revealing... a chained and gagged man.

My instinct is to step back, but as I stare at the bruised face, recognition seeps into my bones, and now I realize why Kyran was asking about my old teacher last week. The teacher who I seduced, yet who shouldn't have gone for it with a vulnerable sixteen-year-old. He should have helped me instead of abusing his power.

I swallow in disbelief, but a little satisfaction still curls inside my stomach. It's not like the cops can trace an abduction into the Nightmare Realm.

"I... um..." No appropriate words come to me, and I'm not sure what kind of reaction he expects.

"Do you like it, husband?" Kyran asks as Mr. Trevisse flinches, attempting to free himself despite the chains holding him in place. When he peers up at me with bloodshot eyes, Kyran smacks the bastard's thigh with the elegant cane he's holding. "I wasn't sure how to present him to you, so I asked Sabine for her opinion, and we decided that I shouldn't kill him without you."

"K-kill him?" I ask wide-eyed, and my heart speeds up. Mr. Trevisse makes even more muffled noises. Maybe it's the morbidity of the Nocturne Court rubbing off on me, but I kinda enjoy seeing him suffer. He deserves it for what he put me through. But does he deserve to *die*?

"Well... yes. He hurt you." Kyran strokes my shoulder, so gallant in his black outfit and cape. He's like a cat bringing me a half-dead mouse and asking for approval.

It's so sweet of him that he thinks I deserve to be avenged.

But as I meet my ex-teacher's eyes and see the pathetic piece of trash that he is, the desire for murder just isn't there. But he does deserve punishment.

I turn to look up into Kyran's dark eyes. "Can we not? I'd like to keep him in our dungeon. For four years. So he can find out how I felt."

I am disappointing my husband, who slowly lowers the cane and tightens his lips before exhaling. "Of course, my love. We shall administer whatever torture you desire," he ends up saying and slams the trunk shut before Mr. Trevisse can sneak in another whine.

I do like seeing him cry.

I squeeze Kyran's hand. "It's very thoughtful of you though."

He relaxes with a loud exhale. "Oh, good. I was worried it wasn't to your taste. You humans can be pretty lax when it comes to revenge sometimes."

I wrap my arms around his waist as the first wagon drives away. "Do we have time for one more stop? To celebrate the move?"

Kyran raises those perfect black eyebrows. "What do you have in mind?"

I pull him down for a kiss. "I know just the place."

☽ ☽ ● ☾ ☾

There's such familiarity in sitting in the booth at the very back of Best Burger Bonanza. This was where I used to go on dates, to make the most of the staff discount, and where

I liked to spend my breaks. And despite working in this place for years, I never stopped enjoying their food which, while trashy by nature, never disappoints.

I might just miss this in the long term, but there's no time like the present, and as I push a fry into Kyran's mouth and hear him groan with pleasure, my grandest desires revolve around blowing him in the carriage on the way back home.

It's not slutty if I do it with my husband.

Kurt still works here, and was so relieved to see me, but when he heard I'd gotten married, he let me know how disappointed he was that I didn't make him my best man. He only relented when I said we eloped, and let him pet Flap. Kurt is now feeding my pet bat carrot sticks, and they seem like best friends already.

But the crowning jewel of this visit is headed our way.

Sylvan looks pretty fetching in the mint green stripes of BBB. *Not*. This uniform is flattering on no one. His pointy ears are tucked under the baseball cap, so now he appears deceptively human, even though his face is still freakishly symmetrical, and his eyes glisten like two sapphires.

In the modern clothes he could be mistaken for a teen with a very careful skin care regime, not a banished elven prince.

He's carrying a tray with our burgers, and I made sure Kurt supervised the cooking process, so Sylvan didn't spit on them. All the servants who helped us move are already eating theirs in other booths, but they're sneaking glances at Prince Sylvan Goldweed, who is now serving *them*, and I'm sure he's aware of it.

He's been banished for a period of fifty years for the crime of not disclosing a plot to murder Kyran. Because yes, the Goldweeds have been behind it, as the castle guards found out thanks to Elodie's hidden diary. Heads would have rolled if all of Sylvan's siblings weren't already dead. His father fled the court and has not been seen since. His mother publicly renounced both her husband's and progeny's actions in order to stay, but I don't suppose her relations with them featured much familial warmth anyway.

And Sylvan? He was spared an execution as a reward for saving Tristan's life, though I suspect Kyran sees a bit of himself in the Goldweed princeling. Two underdogs from different branches of the same noble bloodline. Scorned, belittled, and yet stubborn enough to fight for the crown.

Still, not brave enough to fight off Heartbreak, and it must pain him that we all know it. Maybe that shame is even part of his punishment.

I get a glimpse of the silver collar around Sylvan's neck, and I can't help my satisfaction. The smug bastard was happy to see it on Kyran. Now he is getting a taste of his own medicine. It blocks his access to shadowcraft and will teach him all about humility.

"Anything else, my lord?" he says through gritted teeth as he puts the tray on our table a little too abruptly.

He's lucky that we found him a job here and he's not forced to figure it all out on his own. Though he does have to live with my mom, so that's punishment I wouldn't wish on my worst enemy. I suppose Kyran couldn't stop himself from subjecting his cousin to a bit of everyday torture.

"Thank you, cousin. That is all."

"You two look nothing alike," Kurt says, rubbing Flap between the long ears and making them tilt to the sides like two antennae. "The Prince of Darkness," he says and points at Kyran before moving his gaze to Sylvan. "A dolled-up version of an ice prince."

Sylvan squints at him as I snort. I can only hope he's not giving Kurt a hard time, but Kurt knows how to befriend anyone, so I doubt he's struggling.

"Dolled-up?" Sylvan asks coolly, but I can sense he's seething.

Kurt shrugs. "I mean it as a compliment. You've got that..." he gestures around Sylvan's face. "That whole pretty boy thing going on."

"How dare you disrespect me!" Sylvan grabs a handful of ketchup packets and throws them at Kurt, but they just bounce off him as he laughs.

"Not in front of the baby!" Kurt yells back, shielding Flap with his body.

I smile at Kyran as they bicker. "I told you it's the perfect punishment."

He smirks and pulls me close, settling both his warm hands around my waist as I curl against him, drunk on the sense of safety his love offers. "You have many good ideas, my love. What was the one you mentioned before we embarked? The one you wanted to *show* rather than tell me?"

"So I was thinking... We could get matching tattoos? They don't have to be the same thing. Just something connected to each other. I want to get a shadowy eel on my chest. I did *conquer* a shadow wielder after all." I wiggle my eyebrows at him and feed him another fry. "Would you like to do that with me?"

Kyran nods, but his gaze drifts off as he plays with my fingers, contemplating the idea. "You definitely deserve an eel over the heart for taming someone like myself. As for me... I think what makes us most similar is our fight for freedom. Remember when you told me about the key you stole to escape your school? Maybe I should get that?"

He pulls on my sleeve to reveal my wrist and the ink on it. The symbol I never want to forget. I swallow, feeling all tender inside, because he sees all of me, and knows me so well. We might not have spent that much time together, but we've been tested and stood beside each other in circumstances regular people never have to deal with.

What I saw inside of Heartbreak still haunts my dreams, but whenever I wake up, Kyran is there for me, protecting me, so with each passing night I feel safer. I became stronger that day, and even though I dread the time the beast comes back, I know I'll stand alongside Kyran, ready to aid him in any way he needs.

"It also stands for being the master of my own destiny." I whisper and give him a kiss on the cheek. "It's only fitting that you have it too. Whenever we're apart, you will be able to look down on it and remember I'm yours."

Kyran smirks and brings my hand to his lips. "Darling, I never want to be apart from you. Not for more than a few hours."

I laugh and grab a burger. "How are you both so sweet and so deadly?"

"Practice?" He winks at me and leans closer. "Better tell me if that key also opens your legs."

I almost choke on my food laughing, but then give a serious glance down his body. "You already have the tool for that."

The End

Would you like to find out what Reiner's reward for all his efforts is? Read the bonus scene here: http://kamerikan.com/freebies
Thank you for reading our book! If you enjoyed it and want to find out what happens to Sylvan, Tristan, and the others next, follow us on Amazon and join our Facebook group, the K.A. Merikan Playroom
For more extra content, swag, Q&As, ARCs, and exclusive fiction, join us on Patreon: http://patreon.com/kamerikan
Please, remember to review the book on your favorite platform, as it helps us out a lot :)

Kyran and Luke by Zel Carboni

KINGS OF HELL MC

Laurent AND THE BEAST

K.A. MERIKAN

Laurent and the Beast

K.A. Merikan

--- **Nothing can stop true love. Not time. Not even the devil himself.** ---

1805. Laurent. Indentured servant. Desperate to escape a life that is falling apart.
2017. Beast. Kings of Hell Motorcycle Club vice president. His fists do the talking.

Beast has been disfigured in a fire, but he's covered his skin with tattoos to make sure no one mistakes his scars for weakness. The accident not only hurt his body, but damaged his soul and self-esteem, so he's wrapped himself in a tight cocoon of violence and mayhem where no one can reach him. Until one night, when he finds a young man covered in blood in their clubhouse.

Sweet, innocent, and as beautiful as an angel fallen from heaven, Laurent pulls on all of Beast's heartstrings. Laurent is so lost in the world around him, and is such a tangled mystery, that Beast can't help but let the man claw his way into the stone that is Beast's heart. In 1805, Laurent has no family, no means, and his eyesight is failing. To escape a life of poverty, he uses his beauty, but that only backfires and leads him to a catastrophe that changes his life forever. He takes one step into the abyss and is transported to the future, ready to fight for a life worth living.

What he doesn't expect in his way is a brutal, gruff wall of tattooed muscle with a tender side that only Laurent is allowed to touch. And yet, if Laurent ever wants to earn his freedom, he might have to tear out the heart of the very man who took care of him when it mattered most.

☽ ☽ ● ☾ ☾

Themes: time travel, servitude, serial killer, cruelty, motorcycle club, alternative lifestyles, disability, demons, tattoos, impossible choices, deception, crime, self-discovery, healing, virginity, black magic, gothic

Genre: Dark, paranormal romance

Length: ~135,000 words (Book 1 in the series, can be read as a standalone)WARNING: This story contains scenes of violence, offensive language, and morally ambiguous characters.

Available on AMAZON

THE BLACK SHEEP AND THE ROTTEN APPLE

K.A. MERIKAN

THE BLACK SHEEP AND THE ROTTEN APPLE

K.A. MERIKAN

"How does one start a relationship with another man when it is forbidden?" "One needs to decide that the other man is worth dying for."

Cornwall, 1785
Sir Evan Penhart. Baronet. Highwayman. Scoundrel.
Julian Reece. Writer. Wastrel. Penniless.

No one forces Julian Reece to marry. Not his father, not his brother. No one. When he is thrust into a carriage heading for London to meet his future bride, his way out comes in the form of an imposing highwayman, riding a horse as black as night. Julian makes a deal with the criminal, but what he doesn't expect is that despite the title of baronet, the robber turns out to be no gentleman.

Sir Evan Penhart is pushed into crime out of desperation, but the pact with a pretty, young merchant's son turns out to have disastrous consequences. Not only is Evan left broke, but worse yet, Julian opens up a Pandora's box of passions that are dark, needy, and too wild to tame. With no way to lock them back in, rash decisions and greedy desire lead to a tide that wrecks everything in its way.

But Julian might actually like all the sinful, carnal passion unleashed on him. How can he admit this though, even to himself, when a taste of the forbidden fruit could have him end up with a noose around his neck? And with highway robbery being a hanging offense and the local constable on their back, Julian could lose Evan before he can decide anything about the nature of his desires.

☽ ☽ ● ☾ ☾

Themes: highwayman, abduction, ransom, forbidden love, self-discovery, danger, crime, Cornwal, Britain, England, Georgian

Genre: Dark romance, historical

Length: ~140,000 words (standalone novel)

WARNING: Steamy content. Contains violence, distressing scenes, abuse, offensive language, and morally ambiguous protagonists.

Available on AMAZON

About the Author

K.A. Merikan is a duo of queer writers who don't believe in following the well-trodden path. In their books you can dip your toe into dangerous romance with mafiosi, outlaw bikers and bad boys, all from the safety of your sofa. They love the weird and wonderful, stepping out of the box, and bending stereotypes both in life and in fiction. Their stories don't shy away from exploring the darker side of M/M romance, and feature a variety of anti-heroes, rebels, misfits, and underdogs who go against the grain.

Be prepared for shocking twists, dark humor, raw emotions, and sizzling hot scenes.

e-mail: **kamerikan@gmail.com**
http://kamerikan.com
Merch and more: http://shop.kamerikan.com

More information about works in progress and publishing at:
Facebook: https://www.facebook.com/groups/1817541075240882
Patreon: https://www.patreon.com/kamerikan

Printed in Great Britain
by Amazon